100
Greatest Stories for Young Children

First published in hardcover in India in 2020 by Hachette India

(Registered name: Hachette Book Publishing India Pvt. Ltd)
An Hachette UK company
www.hachetteindia.com

This paperback edition published in 2025

1

A few words and phrases considered archaic, and those considered offensive now, have been changed in a few stories in this volume. Archaic punctuation has also been modified in places to make the text more accessible to young readers. The stories in this book are a reflection of their time and may contain certain cultural, racial and gender prejudices and stereotypes. The stories are being presented as they were originally created, because to do otherwise would be to claim these prejudices never existed. These can be used as discussion points with young readers to prevent perpetuating such prejudices and stereotypes. Some stories may contain depictions of conflict or violence. Hachette India does not endorse or support those depictions or stereotypes.

Hardback ISBN 978-93-89253-70-2
Paperback ISBN 978-93-5731-524-1

Hachette Book Publishing India Pvt. Ltd
4th & 5th Floors, Corporate Centre,
Plot No. 94, Sector 44, Gurugram 122003, India

Typeset in Garamond 13.5/16.5pt
by Manipal Technologies Limited, Manipal

Contents

1

THE CROW AND THE PITCHER

AN AESOP'S FABLE; RETOLD BY J.H. STICKNEY

A thirsty Crow once spied a pitcher, and flew to it to see if by chance there was any water in it.

When she looked in, she saw that there was water, but that it was so far from the top that she could not reach it, though she stretched her neck as far as she could.

She stopped, and thought to herself, 'How shall I get that water? I am perishing with thirst, and there must be some way for me to get some of it.' Some pebbles were lying on the ground; and, picking them up in her beak, she dropped them one by one into the pitcher.

They sank to the bottom; and at last the water was pushed up by them to the top, so that the Crow could easily drink it.

'Where there's a will, there's a way,' said the Crow. ❋

2

CHICKEN-LICKEN

A FAIRY TALE; RETOLD BY MABIE, HALE AND FORBUSH

As Chicken-licken was going one day to the wood, *whack!* an acorn fell from a tree on to his head.

'Gracious goodness me!' said Chicken-licken, 'the sky must have fallen; I must go and tell the King.'

So Chicken-licken turned back, and met Hen-len.

'Well, Hen-len, where are you going?' said he.

'I'm going to the wood,' said she.

'Oh, Hen-len, don't go!' said he, 'for as I was going the sky fell on to my head, and I'm going to tell the King.'

So Hen-len turned back with Chicken-licken, and met Cock-lock.

'I'm going to the wood,' said he.

Then Hen-len said, 'Oh Cock-lock, don't go, for I was going, and I met Chicken-licken, and Chicken-licken had been at the wood, and the sky had fallen on to his head, and we are going to tell the King.'

So Cock-lock turned back, and they met Duck-luck.

'Well, Duck-luck, where are you going?'

And Duck-luck said, 'I'm going to the wood.'

Then Cock-lock said, 'Oh! Duck-luck, don't go, for I was going, and I met Hen-len, and Hen-len met Chicken-licken, and Chicken-licken had been at the wood, and the sky had fallen on to his head, and we are going to tell the King.'

So Duck-luck turned back, and met Drake-lake.

'Well, Drake-lake, where are you going?'

And Drake-lake said, 'I'm going to the wood.'

Then Duck-luck said, 'Oh! Drake-lake, don't go, for I was going, and I met Cock-lock, and Cock-lock met Hen-len, and Hen-len met Chicken-licken, and Chicken-licken had been at the wood, and the sky had fallen on to his head, and we are going to tell the King.'

So Drake-lake turned back, and met Goose-loose.

'Well, Goose-loose, where are you going?'

And Goose-loose said, 'I'm going to the wood.'

Then Drake-lake said, 'Oh, Goose-loose, don't go, for I was going, and I met Duck-luck, and Duck-luck met Cock-lock, and Cock-lock met Hen-len, and Hen-len met Chicken-licken, and Chicken-licken had been at the wood, and the sky had fallen on to his head, and we are going to tell the King.'

So Goose-loose turned back, and met Gander-lander.

'Well, Gander-lander, where are you going?'

And Gander-lander said, 'I'm going to the wood.'

Then Goose-loose said, 'Oh! Gander-lander, don't go, for I was going, and I met Drake-lake, and Drake-lake met Duck-luck, and Duck-luck met Cock-lock, and Cock-lock met Hen-len, and Hen-len met Chicken-licken, and Chicken-licken had been at the wood, and the sky had fallen on to his head, and we are going to tell the King.'

So Gander-lander turned back, and met Turkey-lurkey.

'Well, Turkey-lurkey, where are you going?'

And Turkey-lurkey said, 'I'm going to the wood.'

Then Gander-lander said, 'Oh! Turkey-lurkey, don't go, for I was going, and I met Goose-loose, and Goose-loose met Drake-lake, and Drake-lake met Duck-luck, and Duck-luck met Cock-lock, and Cock-lock met Hen-len, and Hen-len met Chicken-licken, and Chicken-licken had been at the wood, and the sky had fallen on to his head, and we are going to tell the King.'

So Turkey-lurkey turned back, and walked with Gander-lander, Goose-loose, Drake-lake, Duck-luck, Cock-lock, Hen-len and Chicken-licken.

And as they were going along, they met Fox-lox. And Fox-lox said, 'Where are you going?'

And they said, 'Chicken-licken went to the wood, and the sky fell on to his head, and we are going to tell the King.'

And Fox-lox said, 'Come along with me, and I will show you the way.'

But Fox-lox took them into the fox's hole, and he and his young ones soon ate up poor Chicken-licken, Hen-len, Cock-lock, Duck-luck, Drake-lake, Goose-loose, Gander-lander and Turkey-lurkey; and they never saw the King to tell him that the sky had fallen. ❋

3

THE DOG AND HIS REFLECTION

AN AESOP'S FABLE; RETOLD BY J.H. STICKNEY

A dog once had a nice piece of meat for his dinner. Some say that it was stolen, but others, that it had been given to him by a butcher, which we hope was the case.

Dogs like best to eat at home, and he went trotting along with the meat in his mouth, as happy as a king.

On the dog's way there was a stream with a plank across it. As the water was still and clear, he stopped to take a look at it. What should he see, as he gazed into its bright depths, but a dog as big as himself, looking up at him, and lo! the dog had meat in his mouth.

'I'll try to get that,' said he. 'Then with both mine and his what a feast I shall have!' As quick as thought he snapped at the meat, but in doing so he had to open his mouth, and his own piece fell to the bottom of the stream.

Then he saw that the other dog had lost his piece, too. He went sadly home.

It is very foolish to be greedy.

4

THE TALE OF PETER RABBIT

BEATRIX POTTER

Once upon a time there were four little Rabbits, and their names were – Flopsy, Mopsy, Cotton-tail and Peter.

They lived with their Mother in a sandbank, underneath the root of a very big fir tree.

'Now, my dears,' said old Mrs Rabbit one morning, 'you may go into the fields or down the lane, but don't go into Mr McGregor's garden: your Father had an accident there; he was put in a pie by Mrs McGregor. Now run along, and don't get into mischief. I am going out.'

Then old Mrs Rabbit took a basket and her umbrella, and went through the wood to the baker's. She bought a loaf of brown bread and five currant buns.

Flopsy, Mopsy and Cotton-tail who were good little bunnies, went down the lane to gather blackberries. But Peter, who was very naughty, ran straight away to Mr McGregor's garden and squeezed under the gate!

First he ate some lettuces and some French beans; and then he ate some radishes; And then, feeling rather sick, he went to look for some parsley.

But round the end of a cucumber frame, whom should he meet but Mr McGregor!

Mr McGregor was on his hands and knees planting out young cabbages, but he jumped up and ran after Peter, waving a rake and calling out, 'Stop thief!'

Peter was most dreadfully frightened; he rushed all over the garden, for he had forgotten the way back to the gate. He lost one of his shoes among the cabbages, and the other shoe amongst the potatoes.

After losing them, he ran on four legs and went faster, so that I think he might have got away altogether if he had not unfortunately run into a gooseberry net, and got caught by the large buttons on his jacket. It was a blue jacket with brass buttons, quite new.

Peter gave himself up for lost and shed big tears; but his sobs were overheard by some friendly sparrows, who flew to him in great excitement and implored him to exert himself.

Mr McGregor came up with a sieve, which he intended to pop upon the top of Peter, but Peter wriggled out just in time, leaving his jacket behind him. And rushed into the tool-shed, and jumped into a can. It would have been a beautiful thing to hide in, if it had not had so much water in it.

Mr McGregor was quite sure that Peter was somewhere in the tool-shed, perhaps hidden underneath a flowerpot. He began to turn them over carefully, looking under each.

Presently Peter sneezed – '*Kertyschoo!*' Mr McGregor was after him in no time. And tried to put his foot upon Peter, who jumped out of a window, upsetting three plants. The window was too small for Mr McGregor, and he was tired of running after Peter. He went back to his work.

Peter sat down to rest; he was out of breath and trembling with fright, and he had not the least idea which way to go. Also he was very damp with sitting in that can.

After a time he began to wander about, going *lippity – lippity* – not very fast, and looking all round.

He found a door in a wall; but it was locked, and there was no room for a fat little rabbit to squeeze underneath.

An old mouse was running in and out over the stone doorstep, carrying peas and beans to her family in the wood. Peter asked her the way to the gate, but she had such a large pea in her mouth that she could not answer. She only shook her head at him. Peter began to cry.

Then he tried to find his way straight across the garden, but he became more and more puzzled. Presently, he came to a pond where Mr McGregor filled his water-cans. A white cat was staring at some goldfish, she sat very, very still, but now and then the tip of her tail twitched as if it were alive. Peter thought it best to go away without speaking to her; he had heard about cats from his cousin, little Benjamin Bunny.

He went back towards the tool-shed, but suddenly, quite close to him, he heard the noise of a hoe – *scr-r-ritch*, *scratch*, *scratch*, *scritch*. Peter scuttered underneath the bushes. But presently, as nothing happened, he came out, and climbed upon a wheelbarrow and peeped over. The first thing he saw was Mr McGregor hoeing onions. His back was turned towards Peter, and beyond him was the gate!

Peter got down very quietly off the wheelbarrow and started running as fast as he could go, along a straight walk behind some blackcurrant bushes.

Mr McGregor caught sight of him at the corner, but Peter did not care. He slipped underneath the gate and was safe at last in the wood outside the garden.

Mr McGregor hung up the little jacket and the shoes for a scarecrow to frighten the blackbirds.

Peter never stopped running or looked behind him till he got home to the big fir tree.

He was so tired that he flopped down upon the nice soft sand on the floor of the rabbit-hole and shut his eyes. His mother was busy cooking; she wondered what he had done with his clothes. It was the second little jacket and pair of shoes that Peter had lost in a fortnight!

I am sorry to say that Peter was not very well during the evening.

His mother put him to bed and made some camomile tea; and she gave a dose of it to Peter! 'One tablespoonful to be taken at bedtime.'

But Flopsy, Mopsy and Cotton-tail had bread and milk and blackberries for supper. ❋

5

THE TALE OF SQUIRREL NUTKIN

BEATRIX POTTER

This is a tale about a tail – a tail that belonged to a little red squirrel, and his name was Nutkin. He had a brother called Twinkleberry, and a great many cousins; they lived in a wood at the edge of a lake.

In the middle of the lake there is an island covered with trees and nut bushes; and amongst those trees stands a hollow oak tree, which is the house of an owl who is called Old Brown.

One autumn when the nuts were ripe, and the leaves on the hazel bushes were golden and green – Nutkin and Twinkleberry and all the other little squirrels came out of the wood, and down to the edge of the lake.

They made little rafts out of twigs, and they paddled away over the water to Owl Island to gather nuts.

Each squirrel had a little sack and a large oar, and spread out his tail for a sail.

They also took with them an offering of three fat mice as a present for Old Brown and put them down upon his doorstep.

Then Twinkleberry and the other little squirrels each made a low bow, and said politely – 'Old Mr Brown, will you favour us with permission to gather nuts upon your island?'

But Nutkin was excessively impertinent in his manners. He bobbed up and down like a little red cherry, singing –

'Riddle me, riddle me, rot-tot-tote!
A little wee man, in a red red coat!
A staff in his hand and a stone in his throat;
If you'll tell me this riddle, I'll give you a groat.'

Now this riddle is as old as the hills; Mr Brown paid no attention whatever to Nutkin. He shut his eyes obstinately and went to sleep.

The squirrels filled their little sacks with nuts and sailed away home in the evening.

But next morning they all came back again to Owl Island; and Twinkleberry and the others brought a fine fat mole, and laid it on the stone in front of Old Brown's doorway, and said – 'Mr Brown, will you favour us with your gracious permission to gather some more nuts?'

But Nutkin, who had no respect, began to dance up and down, tickling old Mr Brown with a *nettle* and singing –

'Old Mr B! Riddle-me-ree!
Hitty Pitty within the wall,
Hitty Pitty without the wall;
If you touch Hitty Pitty,
Hitty Pitty will bite you!'

Mr Brown woke up suddenly and carried the mole into his house.

He shut the door in Nutkin's face. Presently a little thread of blue smoke from a wood fire came up from the top of the tree, and Nutkin peeped through the keyhole and sang –

'A house full, a hole full!
And you cannot gather a bowl-full!'

The squirrels searched for nuts all over the island and filled their little sacks.

But Nutkin gathered oak-apples – yellow and scarlet – and sat upon a beech-stump playing marbles, and watching the door of old Mr Brown.

On the third day the squirrels got up very early and went fishing; they caught seven fat minnows as a present for Old Brown.

They paddled over the lake and landed under a crooked chestnut tree on Owl Island.

Twinkleberry and six other little squirrels each carried a fat minnow; but Nutkin, who had no nice manners, brought no present at all.

He ran in front, singing –

'The man in the wilderness said to me,
"How many strawberries grow in the sea?"
I answered him as I thought good –
'As many red herrings as grow in the wood.'

But old Mr Brown took no interest in riddles – not even when the answer was provided for him. Which was ridiculous of Nutkin, because he had not got anything to give to Old Brown.

The other squirrels hunted up and down the nut bushes, but Nutkin gathered robin's pincushions off a briar bush and stuck them full of pine-needle pins.

On the fourth day the squirrels brought a present of six fat beetles, which were as good as plums in plum-pudding for Old Brown. Each beetle was wrapped up carefully in a dock-leaf, fastened with a pine-needle pin.

But Nutkin sang as rudely as ever –

'Old Mr B! Riddle-me-ree!
Flour of England, fruit of Spain,
Met together in a shower of rain;
Put in a bag tied round with a string,
If you'll tell me this riddle, I'll give you a ring!'

On the fifth day the squirrels brought a present of wild honey; it was so sweet and sticky that they licked their fingers as they put it down upon the stone. They had stolen it out of a bumblebees' nest on the tippitty top of the hill.

But Nutkin skipped up and down, singing –

'Hum-a-bum! buzz! buzz! Hum-a-bum buzz!
As I went over Tipple-tine
I met a flock of bonny swine;
Some yellow-nacked, some yellow backed!
They were the very bonniest swine
That e'er went over Tipple-tine.'

Old Mr Brown turned up his eyes in disgust at the impertinence of Nutkin. But he ate up the honey!

The squirrels filled their little sacks with nuts. But Nutkin sat upon a big flat rock, and played ninepins with a crab apple and green fir-cones.

❋

On the sixth day, which was Saturday, the squirrels came again for the last time; they brought a new-laid egg in a little rush basket as a last parting present for Old Brown.

But Nutkin ran in front laughing, and shouting –

'Humpty Dumpty lies in the beck,
With a white counterpane round his neck,
Forty doctors and forty wrights,
Cannot put Humpty Dumpty to rights!'

Now old Mr Brown took an interest in eggs; he opened one eye and shut it again. But still he did not speak.

Nutkin became more and more impertinent –

'Old Mr B! Old Mr B!
Hickamore, Hackamore, on
the King's kitchen door;
All the King's horses,
and all the King's men,
Couldn't drive Hickamore, Hackamore,
Off the King's kitchen door.'

Nutkin danced up and down like a *sunbeam*; but still Old Brown said nothing at all. Nutkin began again –

'Arthur O' Bower has broken his band,
He comes roaring up the land!
The King of Scots with all his power,
Cannot turn Arthur of the Bower!'

Nutkin made a whirring noise to sound like the wind, and he took a running jump right on to the head of Old Brown!

Then all at once there was a flutterment and a scufflement and a loud 'Squeak!' The other squirrels scuttered away into the bushes.

When they came back very cautiously, peeping round the tree – there was Old Brown sitting on his doorstep, quite still, with his eyes closed, as if nothing had happened.

But Nutkin was in his waistcoat pocket!

This looks like the end of the story; but it isn't.

Old Brown carried Nutkin into his house and held him up by the tail; but Nutkin pulled so very hard that his tail broke in two, and he dashed up the staircase and escaped out of the attic window.

And to this day, if you meet Nutkin up a tree and ask him a riddle, he will throw sticks at you, and stamp his feet and scold, and shout – '*Cuck-cuck-cuck-cur-r-r-cuck-k-k!*' ❋

6

THE MOON'S MESSENGER

SOMADEVA; RETOLD BY JAYASHREE BHAT

There was once a lovely, cool lake called Chandrasaras that was always full of water, even in summer. It was surrounded by fruit-bearing trees and near it grew crisp, sweet carrots. And so, it was home to a small drove of hares and their king, Silimukha.

One summer, all the lakes nearby dried up except for Chandrasaras. Silimukha was unperturbed because his hares had plenty to eat and drink. He was just about to take an afternoon nap when he heard a thud.

'What was that?' asked Vijaya, a friend of Silimukha's.

'I don't know, but let's go see what it could have been,' said Silimukha, his nose twitching. They ran ahead, towards the lake, and soon the thuds became louder. Suddenly, they saw a huge, grey creature in front of them.

'What is that?' asked Vijaya curiously. 'Is it an animal?'

'I don't know, but it does have two tails, one in the front and one at the back!' exclaimed Silimukha.

Of course it was an elephant, and the hares had never seen one before. As they watched, the elephant took a long drink of water from the lake. Then, he filled his trunk and threw some of the water on his back to cool himself off.

'Harrrrrrrumph!' said the elephant.

'Ooooh, it talks!' said Vijaya.

'Shhhh!' said Silimukha.

'This is just great!' said the elephant loudly, 'I am going to bring my entire herd to this place – all one hundred of them!' Harrumphing happily and swinging his tiny tail, he left.

Vijaya and Silimukha looked at each other in horror. 'There are more of him?' groaned Vijaya.

'A hundred, he said!'

The hares looked thoughtfully at each other. 'I have a plan...' said Silimukha.

A few minutes later, Silimukha began running towards the elephant. Soon, he had caught up with the huge creature, who was ambling along slowly. Climbing on to a boulder, he said in his loudest voice, 'Stop!'

The elephant looked around in confusion.

'Here!' yelled Silimukha.

'Oh, you little thing, what do you want?' asked the elephant kindly.

Drawing himself to his fullest height and puffing out his furry chest, Silimukha said, 'I am a messenger from the Moon, so listen to me carefully.'

'A messenger from the Moon?' snorted the elephant.

'Yes. The Moon lives in the lake you just drank from, and he is very, very angry. If you return here, you and your entire herd will be punished.'

'What utter nonsense! The Moon doesn't live in a lake.'

'If you don't believe me, come back here at midnight.'

The elephant agreed and Silimukha returned to Chandrasaras, hoping his plan would work. At midnight, the elephant returned and called, 'Little hare, I am here.'

'Follow me,' said Silimukha and led the elephant to the lake. 'There!' he said, pointing to the reflection of the Moon in the lake.

Hidden behind a bush, Vijaya cried out as loudly as he could, 'You drank from my home! And you used it to have a bath!'

'I-I am sorry, sir,' stuttered the elephant, 'I did not know you lived here.'

'Very well,' said Vijaya grandly, 'I forgive you. Go away and never come back.'

'Y-yes, yes,' said the elephant, swinging his trunk in worry. 'I won't return.' He quickly retraced his steps and ran away while the hares cheered.

'You did it!' whooped Vijaya.

'No, we did it,' said Silimukha as he nibbled on a juicy carrot. ❋

– *Read more such enchanting stories in* A Treasury of Tales from the Kathasaritasagara, *retold by Jayashree Bhat and published by Hachette India.*

7

THE LITTLE GINGERBREAD MAN

A FAIRY TALE; RETOLD BY G.H.P.

One day, the cook went into the kitchen to make some gingerbread. She took some flour and water, and treacle and ginger, and mixed them all well together, and she put in some more water to make it thin, and then some more flour to make it thick, and a little salt and some spice, and then she rolled it out into a beautiful, smooth, dark-yellow dough.

Then she took the square tins and cut out some square cakes, and with some round tins she cut out some round cakes, and then she said, 'I'm going to make a little gingerbread man for little Bobby.'

So she took a nice round lump of dough for his body, and a smaller lump for his head, which she pulled out a little for the neck. Two other lumps were stuck on beneath for the legs and were pulled out into proper shape, with feet and toes all complete, and two still smaller pieces were made into arms, with dear little hands and fingers.

But the nicest work was done on the head, for the top was frizzed up into a pretty sugary hat; on either side was made a dear little ear, and in front, after the nose had been carefully moulded, a beautiful mouth was made out of a big raisin, and two bright little eyes with burnt almonds and caraway seeds.

Then the gingerbread man was ready for baking, and a very jolly little man he was. In fact, he looked so sly that the cook was afraid he was plotting some mischief, and when the batter was ready for the oven, she put in the square cakes and she put in the round cakes; and then she put in the little gingerbread man in a far back corner, where he couldn't get away in a hurry.

Then she went up to sweep the parlour, and she swept and she swept till the clock struck twelve, when she dropped her broom in a hurry, and exclaiming, 'Lawks! the gingerbread will be all baked to a cinder,' she ran down into the kitchen, and threw open the oven door. And the square cakes were all done, nice and hard and brown, and the round cakes were all done, nice and hard and brown, and the gingerbread man was all done, too, nice and hard and brown; and he was standing up in his corner, with his little caraway-seed eyes sparkling, and his raisin mouth bubbling over with mischief, while he waited for the oven door to be opened.

The instant the door was opened, with a hop, skip, and a jump, he went right over the square cakes and the round cakes, and over the cook's arm, and before she could say 'Jack Robinson' he was running across the kitchen floor, as fast as his little legs would carry him, towards the back door, which was standing wide open, and through which he could see the garden path.

The old cook turned round as fast as she could, which wasn't very fast, for she was rather a heavy woman and she had been quite taken by surprise, and she saw lying right across the doorway, fast asleep in the sun, old Mouser, the cat.

'Mouser, Mouser,' she cried, 'stop the gingerbread man! I want him for little Bobby.' When the cook first called, Mouser thought it was only someone calling in her dreams, and simply rolled over lazily; and the cook called again, 'Mouser, Mouser!'

The old cat sprang up with a jump, but just as she turned round to ask the cook what all the noise was about, the little gingerbread man cleverly jumped under her tail, and in an instant was trotting down the garden walk. Mouser turned in a hurry and ran after, although she was still rather too sleepy to know what it was she was trying to catch, and after the cat came the cook, lumbering along rather heavily, but also making pretty good speed.

Now at the bottom of the walk, lying fast asleep in the sun against the warm stones of the garden wall, was Towser, the dog.

And the cook called out, 'Towser, Towser, stop the gingerbread man! I want him for little Bobby.'

And when Towser first heard her calling he thought it was someone speaking in his dreams, and he only turned over on his side, with another snore, and then the cook called again, 'Towser, Towser, stop him, stop him!'

Then the dog woke up in good earnest and jumped up on his feet to see what it was that he should stop. But just as the dog jumped up, the little gingerbread man, who had been watching for the chance, quietly slipped between his legs, and climbed up on the top of the stone wall, so that Towser saw nothing but the cat running towards him down the walk, and behind the cat the cook, now quite out of breath.

He thought at once that the cat must have stolen something, and that it was the cat the cook wanted him to stop. Now, if there was anything that Towser liked, it was going after the cat, and he jumped up the walk so fiercely that the poor cat did not have time to stop herself or to get out of his way, and they came together with a great fizzing, and barking, and

meowing, and howling, and scratching, and biting, as if a couple of Catherine wheels had gone off in the wrong way and had got mixed up with one another.

But the old cook had been running so hard that she was not able to stop herself any better than the cat had done, and she fell right on top of the mixed up dog and cat, so that all three rolled over on the walk in a heap together.

And the cat scratched whichever came nearest, whether it was a piece of the dog or of the cook, and the dog bit at whatever came nearest, whether it was a piece of the cat or of the cook, so that the poor cook was badly pummelled on both sides.

Meanwhile, the gingerbread man had climbed up on the garden wall, and stood on the top with his hands in his pockets, looking at the scrimmage, and laughing till the tears ran down from his little caraway-seed eyes and his raisin mouth was bubbling all over with fun.

After a little while, the cat managed to pull herself out from under the cook and the dog, and a very cast-down and crumpled-up-looking cat she was. She had had enough of hunting gingerbread men, and she crept back to the kitchen to repair damages.

The dog, who was very cross because his face had been badly scratched, let go of the cook, and at last, catching sight of the gingerbread man, made a bolt for the garden wall. The cook picked herself up, and although her face was also badly scratched and her dress was torn, she was determined to see the end of the chase, and she followed after the dog, though this time more slowly.

When the gingerbread man saw the dog coming, he jumped down on the farther side of the wall, and began running across the field. Now in the middle of the field was a tree, and at the foot of the tree was lying Jocko, the monkey. He wasn't asleep – monkeys never are – and when he saw the little man running across the field and heard the cook calling, 'Jocko, Jocko, stop the gingerbread man,' he at once gave one big jump. But he jumped so fast and so far that he went right over the gingerbread man, and as luck would have it, he came down on the back of Towser, the dog, who had just scrambled over the wall, and whom he had not before noticed. Towser was naturally taken by surprise, but he turned his head around and promptly bit off the end of the monkey's tail, and Jocko quickly jumped off again, chattering his indignation.

Meanwhile, the gingerbread man had got to the bottom of the tree, and was saying to himself, 'Now, I know the dog can't climb a tree, and I don't believe the old cook can climb a tree; and as for the monkey I'm not sure, for I've never seen a monkey before, but I am going up.'

So he pulled himself up hand over hand until he had got to the topmost branch.

But the monkey had jumped with one spring onto the lowest branch, and in an instant he also was at the top of the tree.

The gingerbread man crawled out to the furthermost end of the branch, and hung by one hand, but the monkey swung himself under the branch, and stretching out his long arm, he pulled the gingerbread man in. Then he held him up and looked at him so hungrily that the little raisin mouth began to pucker down at the corners and the caraway-seed eyes filled with tears.

And then what do you think happened? Why, little Bobby himself came running up. He had been taking his noon-day nap upstairs and in his dreams it seemed as if he kept hearing people call 'Little Bobby, little Bobby!' until finally he jumped up with a start and was so sure that someone was calling him that he ran downstairs, without even waiting to put on his shoes.

As he came down, he could see through the window in the field beyond the garden the cook, and the dog, and the monkey, and could even hear the barking of Towser and the chattering of Jocko. He scampered down the walk, with his little bare feet pattering against the warm gravel, climbed over the wall, and in a few seconds arrived under the tree, just as Jocko was holding up the poor little gingerbread man.

'Drop it, Jocko!' cried Bobby, and drop it Jocko did, for he always had to mind Bobby. He dropped it so straight that the gingerbread man fell right into Bobby's uplifted pinafore.

Then Bobby held him up and looked at him, and the little raisin mouth puckered down lower than ever, and the tears ran right out of the caraway-seed eyes.

But Bobby was too hungry to mind gingerbread tears, and he gave one big bite, and swallowed down both legs and a piece of the body.

'OH!' said the gingerbread man, 'I'M ONE-THIRD GONE!'

Bobby gave a second bite, and swallowed the rest of the body and the arms.

'Oh!' said the gingerbread man, 'I'm two-thirds gone!'

Bobby gave a third bite and gulped down the head.

'*Oh!*' said the gingerbread man, '*I'm all gone!*'

And so he was – and that is the end of the story. ❀

8

THE HARE AND THE TORTOISE

AN AESOP'S FABLE; RETOLD BY J.H. STICKNEY

'What a dull, heavy creature,' says the Hare, 'is this Tortoise!'

'And yet,' says the Tortoise, 'I'll run with you for a challenge.'

'Done,' says the Hare, and then they asked the Fox to be the judge.

They started together, and the Tortoise kept jogging on still, till he came to the end of the course. The Hare laid himself down midway and took a nap – 'for,' says he, 'I can catch up with the Tortoise when I please.' But it seems he overslept, for when he came to wake, though he scudded away as fast as possible, the Tortoise had got to the post before him and won the challenge.

Slow and steady wins the race.

9

MONKEY AND CROCODILE

A PANCHATANTRA TALE; RETOLD BY NARINDAR UBEROI KELLY

There was a great big rose-apple tree that grew close to the bank of an enormous river. It bore delicious fruit that ripened every day and was enjoyed immensely by a red-faced monkey named Ruddy.

One day a crocodile named Oily crawled out of the river on to the bank and burrowed into the soft sand. Ruddy saw him and welcomed his guest. 'No one is more important than a guest to me, no matter how unexpected,' he said. 'Please accept these scrumptious rose-apples that I throw down to you as my offering.'

Oily enjoyed them very much, spent time in easy conversation with Ruddy and took some rose-apples home to his wife.

'Where did you find these?' she asked, 'They are like ambrosia.'

'I have made a new friend, Ruddy, and he gets them from the tree and gives them to me,' replied Oily.

Then the wife reasoned that if the monkey ate such heavenly fruit every day, he must have a heart with extraordinary powers. So she said to Oily, 'If you value me at all, please bring me the monkey's heart so that after I eat it, I will never grow old or sick but will be your loving wife forever.'

Oily objected strongly. 'Ruddy is like a brother to me now. Remember, brothers by friendship are even more precious than brothers by birth. He gives me this wonderful fruit every day. I cannot kill him!'

But the wife was adamant. 'You have never said no to me before. Monkeys and crocodiles are natural enemies. Bring me his heart or I will die of starvation for I will eat nothing else.'

Completely dejected, Oily returned to the rose-apple tree, thinking, 'How can I possibly kill my friend?'

Ruddy had missed his friend and upon seeing him return, said cheerfully, 'What shall we discuss today as we eat the rose-apples?'

'My wife is very upset that I have not invited you home,' replied Oily. 'She has prepared a great welcome for you. So come with me.'

Ruddy was delighted and replied, 'I hold the six aspects of friendship very dear: to receive, to give, to listen, to talk, to dine and to entertain. But we monkeys live in trees and you live in water. How can I come to your house? Please bring your wife here.'

'Our house is on a sandbank,' said Oily, 'and you will be quite comfortable there. No need to worry. Just climb on my back and I will take you there.'

So Ruddy climbed upon the crocodile's back, but when Oily took off at considerable speed, Ruddy was frightened and asked Oily to slow down. But Oily knew that Ruddy was out of his depth in the fast-moving water and now completely in his power. He could not stop himself from bragging, 'My wife wants to eat your heart. Better say your last prayers!'

Ruddy was, however, very quick-witted and said immediately, 'Why didn't you tell me on the shore? I have a second heart that I keep in my hole in the rose-apple tree. That one is my sweet heart. The heart I carry around is very ordinary and will not do your wife any good.'

Oily was delighted. Now he could give his wife the monkey's sweet heart and still have a friend. So he turned back to the shore and helped Ruddy climb high up the rose-apple tree.

Ruddy, meanwhile, was thinking, '*One should never be too trusting.* I have escaped death and thus am reborn today.'

After waiting a while, Oily shouted up to Ruddy, 'Give me the heart then, so I can make my wife happy, and be back at the regular time and talk about interesting things.'

'You are not only a traitor but a fool!' said Ruddy. 'How can anyone have two hearts? Don't ever come back here. ❋

10

THE MAN, THE BOY AND THE DONKEY

AN AESOP'S FABLE; RETOLD BY JOSEPH JACOBS

A man and his son were once going with their donkey to market. As they were walking along by his side a countryman passed them and said, 'You fools, what is a donkey for but to ride upon?' So the man put the boy on the donkey, and they went on their way.

But soon they passed a group of men, one of whom said, 'See that lazy youngster, he lets his father walk while he rides.'

So the man ordered his boy to get off, and got on himself. But they hadn't gone far when they passed two women, one of whom said to the other, 'Shame on that lazy lout to let his poor little son trudge along.'

Well, the man didn't know what to do, but at last he took his boy up before him on the donkey. By this time they had come to the town, and the passers-by began to jeer and point at them. The man stopped and asked what they were scoffing at.

The men said, 'Aren't you ashamed of yourself for overloading that poor donkey of yours – you and your hulking son?'

The man and boy got off and tried to think what to do. They thought and they thought, until at last they cut down a pole, tied the donkey's feet to it, and raised the pole and the donkey to their shoulders. They went along amid the laughter of all who met them until they came to a bridge, when the donkey, getting one of his feet loose, kicked out and caused the boy to drop his end of the pole. In the struggle the donkey fell over the bridge, and his forefeet being tied together, he was drowned.

Try to please everyone, and you will please no one. ❀

11

WINNIE-THE-POOH

'IN WHICH WE ARE INTRODUCED TO WINNIE-THE-POOH AND SOME BEES, AND THE STORIES BEGIN'

A.A. MILNE

Here is Edward Bear, coming downstairs now, bump, bump, bump, on the back of his head, behind Christopher Robin. It is, as far as he knows, the only way of coming downstairs, but sometimes he feels that there really is another way, if only he could stop bumping for a moment and think of it. And then he feels that perhaps there isn't. Anyhow, here he is at the bottom, and ready to be introduced to you. Winnie-the-Pooh.

When I first heard his name, I said, just as you are going to say, 'But I thought he was a boy?'

'So did I,' said Christopher Robin.

'Then you can't call him Winnie?'

'I don't.'

'But you said –'

'He's Winnie-ther-Pooh. Don't you know what "ther" means?'

'Ah, yes, now I do,' I said quickly; and I hope you do, too, because it is all the explanation you are going to get.

Sometimes Winnie-the-Pooh likes a game of some sort when he comes downstairs, and sometimes he likes to sit quietly in front of the fire and listen to a story. This evening—

'What about a story?' said Christopher Robin.

'What about a story?' I said.

'Could you very sweetly tell Winnie-the-Pooh one?

'I suppose I could,' I said. 'What sort of stories does he like?'

'About himself. Because he's *that* sort of Bear.

'Oh, I see.'

'So could you very sweetly?'

'I'll try,' I said.

So I tried.

Once upon a time, a very long time ago now, about last Friday, Winnie-the-Pooh lived in a forest all by himself under the name of Sanders.

('What does "under the name" mean?' asked Christopher Robin.

'It means he had the name over the door in gold letters, and lived under it.'

'Winnie-the-Pooh wasn't quite sure,' said Christopher Robin.

'Now I am,' said a growly voice.

'Then I will go on,' said I.)

One day when he was out walking, he came to an open place in the middle of the forest, and in the middle of this place was a large oak tree, and, from the top of the tree, there came a loud buzzing-noise.

Winnie-the-Pooh sat down at the foot of the tree, put his head between his paws and began to think.

First of all he said to himself, 'That buzzing-noise means something. You don't get a buzzing-noise like that, just buzzing and buzzing, without its meaning something. If there's a buzzing-noise, somebody's making a buzzing-noise, and the only reason for making a buzzing-noise that I know of is because you're a bee.'

Then he thought another long time and said, 'And the only reason for being a bee that I know of is making honey.'

And then he got up and said, 'And the only reason for making honey is so as *I* can eat it.' So he began to climb the tree.

He climbed and he climbed and he climbed, and as he climbed he sang a little song to himself.

It went like this:

Isn't it funny
How a bear likes honey?
Buzz! Buzz! Buzz!
I wonder why he does?

Then he climbed a little further...and a little further... and then just a little further. By that time he had thought of another song.

It's a very funny thought that, if Bears were Bees,
They'd build their nests at the bottom of trees.
And that being so (if the Bees were Bears),
We shouldn't have to climb up all these stairs.

He was getting rather tired by this time, so that is why he sang a Complaining Song. He was nearly there now, and if he just stood on that branch...

Crack!

'Oh, help!' said Pooh, as he dropped ten feet on the branch below him.

'If only I hadn't –' he said, as he bounced twenty feet on to the next branch.

'You see, what I *meant* to do,' he explained, as he turned head-over-heels, and crashed on to another branch thirty feet below, 'what I meant to do –'

'Of course, it was rather –' he admitted, as he slithered very quickly through the next six branches.

'It all comes, I suppose,' he decided, as he said goodbye to the last branch, spun round three times, and flew gracefully into a gorse-bush, 'it all comes of *liking* honey so much. Oh, help!'

He crawled out of the gorse-bush, brushed the prickles from his nose, and began to think again. And the first person he thought of was Christopher Robin.

('Was that me?' said Christopher Robin in an awed voice, hardly daring to believe it.

'That was you.'

Christopher Robin said nothing, but his eyes got larger and larger, and his face got pinker and pinker.)

So Winnie-the-Pooh went round to his friend Christopher Robin, who lived behind a green door in another part of the forest.

'Good morning, Christopher Robin,' he said.

'Good morning, Winnie-*ther*-Pooh,' said you.

'I wonder if you've got such a thing as a balloon about you?'

'A balloon?'

'Yes, I just said to myself coming along: "I wonder if Christopher Robin has such a thing as a balloon about him?" I just said it to myself, thinking of balloons, and wondering.'

'What do you want a balloon for?' you said.

Winnie-the-Pooh looked round to see that nobody was listening, put his paw to his mouth and said in a deep whisper, '*Honey!*'

'But you don't get honey with balloons!'

'*I* do,' said Pooh.

Well, it just happened that you had been to a party the day before at the house of your friend Piglet, and you had balloons at the party. You had had a big green balloon; and one of Rabbit's relations had had a big blue one and had left it behind, being really too young to go to a party at all; and so you had brought the green one and the blue one home with you.

'Which one would you like?' you asked Pooh.

He put his head between his paws and thought very carefully.

'It's like this,' he said. 'When you go after honey with a balloon, the great thing is not to let the bees know you're coming. Now, if you have a green balloon, they might think you were only part of the tree, and not notice you, and if you have a blue balloon, they might think you were only part of the sky, and not notice you, and the question is: Which is most likely?'

'Wouldn't they notice you underneath the balloon?' you asked.

'They might or they might not,' said Winnie-the-Pooh. 'You never can tell with bees.' He thought for a moment and said, 'I shall try to look like a small black cloud. That will deceive them.'

'Then you had better have the blue balloon,' you said; and so it was decided.

❋

Well, you both went out with the blue balloon, and you took your gun with you, just in case, as you always did, and Winnie-the-Pooh went to a very muddy place that he knew of, and rolled and rolled until he was black all over; and then, when the balloon was blown up as big as big, and you and Pooh were both holding on to the string, you let go suddenly, and Pooh Bear floated gracefully up into the sky, and stayed there – level with the top of the tree and about twenty feet away from it.

'Hooray!' you shouted.

'Isn't that fine?' shouted Winnie-the-Pooh down to you. 'What do I look like?'

'You look like a Bear holding on to a balloon,' you said.

'Not –' said Pooh anxiously, '– not like a small black cloud in a blue sky?'

'Not very much.'

'Ah, well, perhaps from up here it looks *different*. And, as I say, you never can tell with bees.'

There was no wind to blow him nearer to the tree, so there he stayed. He could see the honey, he could smell the honey, but he couldn't quite reach the honey.

After a little while he called down to you.

'Christopher Robin!' he said in a loud whisper.

'Hallo!'

'I think the bees *suspect* something!'

'What sort of thing?'

'I don't know. But something tells me that they're *suspicious*!'

'Perhaps they think that you're after their honey.'

'It may be that. You never can tell with bees.'

There was another little silence, and then he called down to you again.

'Christopher Robin!'

'Yes?'

'Have you an umbrella in your house?'

'I think so.'

'I wish you would bring it out here, and walk up and down with it, and look up at me every now and then, and say 'Tut-tut, it looks like rain.' I think, if you did that, it would help the deception which we are practising on these bees.'

Well, you laughed to yourself, 'Silly old Bear!' but you didn't say it aloud because you were so fond of him, and you went home for your umbrella.

'Oh, there you are!' called down Winnie-the-Pooh, as soon as you got back to the tree. 'I was beginning to get anxious. I have discovered that the bees are now definitely Suspicious.'

'Shall I put my umbrella up?' you said.

'Yes, but wait a moment. We must be practical. The important bee to deceive is the Queen Bee. Can you see which is the Queen Bee from down there?'

'No.'

'A pity. Well, now, if you walk up and down with your umbrella, saying, 'Tut-tut, it looks like rain,'

I shall do what I can by singing a little Cloud Song, such as a cloud might sing... Go!'

So, while you walked up and down and wondered if it would rain, Winnie-the-Pooh sang this song:

'How sweet to be a Cloud
Floating in the Blue!
Every little cloud
Always sings aloud.

'How sweet to be a Cloud
Floating in the Blue!
It makes him very proud
To be a little cloud.'

The bees were still buzzing as suspiciously as ever. Some of them, indeed, left their nest and flew all round the cloud as it began the second verse of this song, and one bee sat down on the nose of the cloud for a moment, and then got up again.

'Christopher – *ow!* – Robin,' called out the cloud.

'Yes?'

'I have just been thinking, and I have come to a very important decision. *These are the wrong sort of bees.*'

'Are they?'

'Quite the wrong sort. So I should think they would make the wrong sort of honey, shouldn't you?'

'Would they?'

'Yes. So I think I shall come down.'

'How?' asked you.

Winnie-the-Pooh hadn't thought about this. If he let go of the string, he would fall – *bump* – and he didn't like the idea of that. So he thought for a long time, and then he said, 'Christopher Robin, you must shoot the balloon with your gun. Have you got your gun?'

'Of course I have,' you said. 'Rut if I do that, it will spoil the balloon,' you said.

'But if you *don't*,' said Pooh, 'I shall have to let go, and that would spoil *me*.'

When he put it like this, you saw how it was, and you aimed very carefully at the balloon, and fired.

'*Ow!*' said Pooh.

'Did I miss?' you asked.

'You didn't exactly *miss*,' said Pooh, 'but you missed the *balloon*.'

'I'm *so* sorry,' you said, and you fired again, and this time you hit the balloon, and the air came slowly out, and Winnie-the-Pooh floated down to the ground.

But his arms were so stiff from holding on to the string of the balloon all that time that they stayed up straight in the air for more than a week, and whenever a fly came and settled on his nose he had to blow it off. And I think – but I am not sure – that that is why he was always called Pooh.

'Is that the end of the story?' asked Christopher Robin.

'That's the end of that one. There are others.'

'About Pooh and Me?'

'And Piglet and Rabbit and all of you. Don't you remember?'

'I do remember, and then when I try to remember, I forget.'

'That day when Pooh and Piglet tried to catch the Heffalump –'

'They didn't catch it, did they?'

'No.'

'Pooh couldn't, because he hasn't any brain. Did *I* catch it?'

'Well, that comes into the story.'

Christopher Robin nodded.

'I do remember,' he said, 'only Pooh doesn't very well, so that's why he likes having it told to him again. Because then it's a real story and not just a remembering.'

'That's just how *I* feel,' I said.

Christopher Robin gave a deep sigh, picked his Bear up by the leg, and walked off to the door, trailing Pooh behind him. At the door he turned and said, 'Coming to see me have my bath?'

'I might,' I said.

'I didn't hurt him when I shot him, did I?'

'Not a bit.'

He nodded and went out, and in a moment I heard Winnie-the-Pooh – *bump* – *bump* – *bump* – going up the stairs behind him. ❋

12

WINNIE-THE-POOH

'IN WHICH EEYORE LOSES A TAIL AND POOH FINDS ONE'

A.A. MILNE

The Old Grey Donkey, Eeyore, stood by himself in a thistly corner of the Forest, his front feet well apart, his head on one side, and thought about things. Sometimes he thought sadly to himself, 'Why?' and sometimes he thought, 'Wherefore?' and sometimes he thought, 'Inasmuch as which?' – and sometimes he didn't quite know what he *was* thinking about. So when Winnie-the-Pooh came stumping along, Eeyore was very glad to be able to stop thinking for a little, in order to say 'How do you do?' in a gloomy manner to him.

'And how are you?' said Winnie-the-Pooh.

Eeyore shook his head from side to side.

'Not very how,' he said. 'I don't seem to have felt at all how for a long time.'

'Dear, dear,' said Pooh, 'I'm sorry about that. Let's have a look at you.'

So Eeyore stood there, gazing sadly at the ground, and Winnie-the-Pooh walked all round him once.

'Why, what's happened to your tail?' he said in surprise.

'What *has* happened to it?' said Eeyore.

'It isn't there!'

'Are you sure?'

'Well, either a tail *is* there or it isn't there. You can't make a mistake about it. And yours *isn't* there!'

'Then what is?'

'Nothing.'

'Let's have a look,' said Eeyore, and he turned slowly round to the place where his tail had been a little while ago, and then, finding that he couldn't catch it up, he turned round the other way, until he came back to where he was at first, and then he put his head down and looked between his front legs, and at last he said, with a long, sad sigh, 'I believe you're right.'

'Of course I'm right,' said Pooh.

'That Accounts for a Good Deal,' said Eeyore gloomily. 'It Explains Everything. No Wonder.'

'You must have left it somewhere,' said Winnie-the-Pooh.

'Somebody must have taken it,' said Eeyore. 'How Like Them,' he added, after a long silence.

Pooh felt that he ought to say something helpful about it, but didn't quite know what. So he decided to do something helpful instead.

'Eeyore,' he said solemnly, 'I, Winnie-the-Pooh, will find your tail for you.'

'Thank you. Pooh,' answered Eeyore. 'You're a real friend,' said he. 'Not Like Some,' he said.

So Winnie-the-Pooh went off to find Eeyore's tail.

It was a fine spring morning in the Forest as he started out. Little soft clouds played happily in a blue sky, skipping from time to time in front of the sun as if they had come to put it out, and then sliding away suddenly so that the next might have his turn. Through them and between them the sun shone bravely; and a copse which had worn its firs all the year round seemed old and dowdy now beside the new green lace which the beeches had put on so prettily. Through copse and spinney* marched Bear; down open slopes of gorse and heather, over rocky beds of streams, up steep banks of sandstone into the heather again; and so at last, tired and hungry, to the Hundred Acre Wood. For it was in the Hundred Acre Wood that Owl lived.

'And if anyone knows anything about anything,' said Bear to himself, 'it's Owl who knows something about something,' he said, 'or my name's not Winnie-

* *A small area covered with trees*

the-Pooh,' he said. 'Which it is,' he added. 'So there you are.'

Owl lived at The Chestnuts, an old-world residence of great charm, which was grander than anybody else's, or seemed so to Bear, because it had both a knocker *and* a bell-pull. Underneath the knocker there was a notice which said:

PLES RING IF AN RNSER IS REQIRD.

Underneath the bell-pull there was a notice which said:

PLEZ CNOKE IF AN ANSR IS NOT REQID.

These notices had been written by Christopher Robin, who was the only one in the forest who could spell; for Owl, wise though he was in many ways, able to read and write and spell his own name WOL, yet somehow went all to pieces over delicate words like MEASLES and BUTTERED TOAST.

Winnie-the-Pooh read the two notices very carefully, first from left to right, and afterwards, in case he had missed some of it, from right to left. Then, to make quite sure, he knocked and pulled the knocker, and he pulled and knocked the bell-rope, and he called out in a very loud voice, 'Owl! I require an answer! It's Bear speaking.' And the door opened, and Owl looked out.

'Hallo, Pooh,' he said. 'How's things?'

'Terrible and Sad,' said Pooh, 'because Eeyore, who is a friend of mine, has lost his tail. And he's Moping about it. So could you very kindly tell me how to find it for him?'

'Well,' said Owl, 'the customary procedure in such cases is as follows.'

'What does Crustimoney Proseedcake mean?' said Pooh. 'For I am a Bear of Very Little Brain, and long words Bother me.'

'It means the Thing to Do.'

'As long as it means that, I don't mind,' said Pooh humbly.

'The thing to do is as follows. First, Issue a Reward. Then –'

'Just a moment,' said Pooh, holding up his paw. '*What* do we do to this – what you were saying? You sneezed just as you were going to tell me.'

'I *didn't* sneeze.'

'Yes, you did, Owl.'

'Excuse me, Pooh, I didn't. You can't sneeze without knowing it.'

'Well, you can't know it without something having been sneezed.'

'What I said was, 'First *Issue* a Reward.'

'You're doing it again,' said Pooh sadly.

'A Reward!' said Owl very loudly. 'We write a notice to say that we will give a large something to anybody who finds Eeyore's tail.'

'I see, I see,' said Pooh, nodding his head. 'Talking about large somethings,' he went on dreamily, 'I generally have a small something about now – about this time in the morning,' and he looked wistfully at the cupboard in the corner of Owl's parlour; 'just a mouthful of condensed milk or what not, with perhaps a lick of honey –'

'Well, then,' said Owl, 'we write out this notice, and we put it up all over the forest.'

'A lick of honey,' murmured Bear to himself, 'or – or not, as the case may be.' And he gave a deep sigh, and tried very hard to listen to what Owl was saying.

But Owl went on and on, using longer and longer words, until at last he came back to where he started, and he explained that the person to write out this notice was Christopher Robin.

'It was he who wrote the ones on my front door for me. Did you see them, Pooh?'

For some time now Pooh had been saying 'Yes' and 'No' in turn, with his eyes shut, to all that Owl was saying, and having said, 'Yes, yes,' last time, he said 'No, not at all,' now, without really knowing what Owl was talking about.

'Didn't you see them?' said Owl, a little surprised. 'Come and look at them now.'

So they went outside. And Pooh looked at the knocker and the notice below it, and he looked at the bell-rope and the notice below it, and the more he looked at the bell-rope, the more he felt that be had seen something like it, somewhere else, sometime before.

'Handsome bell-rope, isn't it?' said Owl.

Pooh nodded.

'It reminds me of something,' he said, 'but I can't think what. Where did you get it?'

'I just came across it in the Forest. It was hanging over a bush, and I thought at first somebody lived there, so I rang it, and nothing happened, and then I rang it again very loudly, and it came off in my hand, and as nobody seemed to want it, I took it home, and –'

'Owl,' said Pooh solemnly, 'you made a mistake. Somebody did want it.'

'Who?'

'Eeyore. My dear friend Eeyore. He was – he was fond of it.'

'Fond of it?'

'Attached to it,' said Winnie-the-Pooh sadly.

So with these words he unhooked it and carried it back to Eeyore; and when Christopher Robin had nailed it on in its right place again, Eeyore frisked about the forest, waving his tail so happily that Winnie-the-Pooh came over all funny, and had to hurry home for a little snack of something to sustain him. And, wiping his mouth half an hour afterwards, he sang to himself proudly:

Who found the Tail?
'I,' said Pooh,
'At a quarter to two
(Only it was quarter to eleven really),
I found the Tail!' ❋

13

THE ANT AND THE GRASSHOPPER

AN AESOP'S FABLE; RETOLD BY JOSEPH JACOBS

In a field one summer's day a Grasshopper was hopping about, chirping and singing to its heart's content. An Ant passed by, bearing along with great toil an ear of corn he was taking to the nest.

'Why not come and chat with me,' said the Grasshopper, 'instead of toiling and moiling in that way?'

'I am helping to lay up food for the winter,' said the Ant, 'and suggest that you do the same.'

'Why bother about winter?' said the Grasshopper. 'We have got plenty of food at present.'

But the Ant went on its way and continued its toil.

When the winter came the Grasshopper had no food and found itself dying of hunger, while it saw the ants distributing every day corn and grain from the stores they had collected in the summer.

Then the Grasshopper knew: *It is best to prepare for the days of need.* ❋

14

THE BIG JUICY CARROT

ENID BLYTON

One fine morning, Bobtail, the rabbit, met Long-ears, the hare, and they set off together, talking about this and that.

They stopped by a hedge and lay quiet, for they could hear a cart passing. Bobtail peeped through and saw that it was a farm cart, laden with carrots and turnips. How his mouth watered!

And then, just as the cart passed where the two animals were crouching, a wheel ran over a great stone, and the jerk made a big, juicy, red carrot fall from the cart to the ground. The hare and the rabbit looked at it in great delight.

When the cart had gone out of sight, the two of them hurried into the lane. Bobtail picked up the carrot. Long-ears spoke eagerly. 'We both saw it at once. We must share it.'

'Certainly,' said Bobtail. 'I will break it in half.'

So he broke the carrot in half – but although each piece measured the same, one bit was the thick top part of the carrot, and the other was the thin bottom part. Bobtail picked up the top part – but Long-ears stopped him.

'One piece is bigger than the other,' he said. 'There is no reason why *you* should have the bigger piece, cousin.'

'And no reason why *you* should, either!' said the rabbit crossly.

'Give it to me!' squealed the hare.

'Certainly *not*!' said the rabbit. They each glared at the other, but neither dared to do any more.

'We had better ask someone to judge between us,' said the hare, at last. 'Whom shall we ask?'

Bobtail looked around, but he could see no one but Neddy the donkey, peering over the hedge at them.

'There isn't anyone in sight except silly old Neddy,' he said. 'It's not much good asking *him*. He has no brain to speak of!'

'That's true,' said Long-ears. 'He is an old stupid, everyone knows that. But who else is there to ask.'

'No one,' said Bobtail. 'Well, come on, let's take the carrot to the donkey and ask him to choose which one of us shall have the larger piece.'

So they ran through the hole in the hedge and went up to Neddy. He had heard every word they said and was not at all pleased to be thought so foolish.

The two creatures told him what they wanted.

'If I am so silly as you think, I wonder you want me to judge,' said Neddy, blinking at them.

'Well, you will have to do,' said the rabbit. 'Now tell us – how are we to know which of us shall have the bigger piece?'

'I can soon put that right for you, even with *my* poor brain!' said Neddy. He took the larger piece in his mouth and bit off the end.

'Perhaps that will have made them the same size!' he said, crunching up the juicy bit of carrot he had bitten off.

But no – he had bitten off such a big piece that now the piece that *had* been the larger one was smaller than the other!

'Soon put *that* right!' said Neddy, and he picked up the second piece. He bit a large piece off that one and then dropped it. But now it was much smaller than the first piece!

The hare and the rabbit watched in alarm. This was dreadful!

'Stop, Neddy!' said Long-ears. 'Give us what is left. You have no right to crunch up our carrot!'

'Well, I am only trying to help you!' said Neddy indignantly. 'Wait a moment. Perhaps *this* time I'll make the pieces equal.'

He took another bite at a piece of carrot – oh dear, such a big bite this time! The two animals were in despair.

'Give us the rest!' they begged. 'Do not eat any more!'

'Well,' said Neddy, looking at the last two juicy pieces, and keeping his foot on them so that the two animals could not get them, 'what about my payment for troubling to settle your quarrel. What will you give me for that?'

'Nothing at all!' cried Long-ears.

'What! Nothing at all?' said Neddy in anger. 'Very well, then – I shall take my own payment!'

And with that he put his head down and took up the rest of the carrot. Chomp-chomp-chomp! He crunched it all up with great enjoyment.

'Thanks!' he said to Long-ears and Bobtail. 'That was very nice. I am obliged to you.'

He cantered away to the other side of the field, and as he went, he brayed loudly with laughter. The two big-eyed creatures looked at one another.

'Bobtail,' said Long-ears, 'do you think that donkey was as foolish as we thought he was?'

'No, I don't,' groaned Bobtail. 'He was much cleverer than we were – and you know, Long-ears, if one of us had been sensible, we would *both* now be nibbling carrots instead of seeing that stupid donkey chewing it all up!'

They ran off – Bobtail to his hole and Long-ears to the field where he had his home. As for Neddy, he put his head over the wall and told his friend, the brown horse, all about that big juicy carrot.

You *should* have heard them laugh! ❋

– Liked the story? Read many more exciting tales in the Enid Blyton's Springtime Stories.

15

GOLDILOCKS AND THE THREE BEARS

A FAIRY TALE; RETOLD BY KATHERINE PYLE

There was once a little girl whose hair was so bright and yellow that it glittered in the sun like spun gold. For this reason she was called Goldilocks.

One day Goldilocks went out into the meadows to gather flowers. She wandered on and on, and after a while she came to a forest, where she had never been before. She went on into the forest, and it was very cool and shady.

Presently she came to a little house, standing all alone in the forest, and as she was tired and thirsty she knocked at the door. She hoped the good people inside would give her a drink and let her rest a little while.

Now, though Goldilocks did not know it, this house belonged to three bears. There was a GREAT BIG FATHER BEAR, AND A MIDDLING-SIZED MOTHER BEAR, and a *dear little baby bear*, no bigger than Goldilocks herself. But the three bears had gone out to take a walk in the forest while their supper was cooling, so when Goldilocks knocked at the door no one answered her.

She waited awhile and then she knocked again, and as still nobody answered her she pushed the door open and stepped inside. There in a row stood three chairs. One was a GREAT BIG CHAIR, and it belonged to the father bear. And one was a MIDDLING-SIZED CHAIR, and it belonged to the mother bear, and one was a *dear little chair*, and it belonged to the baby bear. And on the table stood three bowls of smoking hot porridge. 'And so,' thought Goldilocks, 'the people must be coming back soon to eat it.'

She thought she would sit down and rest until they came, so first she sat down in the GREAT BIG CHAIR, but the cushion was too soft. It seemed as though it would swallow her up. Then she sat down in the MIDDLE-SIZED CHAIR, and the cushion was too hard, and it was not comfortable. Then she sat down in the *dear little chair*, and it was just right, and fitted her as though it had been made for her. So there she sat, and she rocked and she rocked, and she sat and she sat, until with her rocking and her sitting she sat the bottom right out of it.

And still nobody had come, and there stood the bowls of porridge on the table. 'They can't be very hungry people,' thought Goldilocks to herself, 'or they would come home to eat their suppers.' And she went over to the table just to see whether the bowls were full.

The first bowl was a GREAT BIG BOWL with a GREAT BIG WOODEN SPOON in it, and that was the father bear's bowl. The second bowl was a MIDDLE-SIZED BOWL, with a MIDDLE-SIZED WOODEN SPOON in it, and that was the mother bear's bowl. And the third bowl was a *dear little bowl*, with a *dear little silver spoon* in it, and that was the baby bear's bowl.

The porridge that was in the bowls smelled so very good that Goldilocks thought she would just taste it.

She took up the GREAT BIG SPOON, and tasted the porridge in the GREAT BIG BOWL, but it was too hot. Then she took up the MIDDLE-SIZED SPOON and tasted the porridge in the MIDDLE-SIZED BOWL, and it was too cold. Then she took up the *little silver spoon* and tasted the porridge in the *dear little bowl*, and it was just right, and it tasted so good that she tasted and tasted, and tasted and tasted until she tasted it all up.

After that she felt very sleepy, so she went upstairs and looked about her, and there were three beds all in a row. The first bed was the GREAT BIG BED that belonged to the father bear. And the second bed was a MIDDLING-SIZED BED that belonged to the mother bear, and the third bed was a *dear little bed* that belonged to the dear little baby bear.

Goldilocks lay down on the GREAT BIG BED to try it, but the pillow was too high, and she wasn't comfortable at all.

Then she lay down on the MIDDLE-SIZED BED, and the pillow was too low, and that wasn't comfortable either.

Then she lay down on the *little baby bear's bed* and it was exactly right, and so very comfortable that she lay there and lay there until she fell fast asleep.

Now while Goldilocks was still asleep in the little bed the three bears came home again, and as soon as they stepped inside the door and looked about them they knew that somebody had been there.

'SOMEBODY'S BEEN SITTING IN MY CHAIR,' growled the father bear in his great big voice, 'AND LEFT THE CUSHION CROOKED.'

'AND SOMEBODY'S BEEN SITTING IN MY CHAIR,' said the mother bear, 'AND LEFT IT STANDING CROOKED.'

'*And somebody's been sitting in my chair,*' squeaked the baby bear, in his shrill little voice, '*and they've sat and sat till they've sat the bottom out*'; and he felt very sad about it.

Then the three bears went over to the table to get their porridge.

'WHAT'S THIS!' growled the father bear, in his great big voice, 'SOMEBODY'S BEEN TASTING MY PORRIDGE, AND LEFT THE SPOON ON THE TABLE.'

'AND SOMEBODY'S BEEN TASTING MY PORRIDGE,' said the mother bear in her middle-sized voice, 'AND THEY'VE SPLASHED IT OVER THE SIDE.'

'*And somebody's been tasting my porridge*,' squealed the baby bear, '*and they've tasted and tasted until they've tasted it all up*.' And when he said so the baby bear looked as if he were about to cry.

'IF SOMEBODY'S BEEN HERE THEY MUST BE HERE STILL,' said the mother bear; so the three bears went upstairs to look.

First the father bear looked at his bed. 'SOMEBODY'S BEEN LYING ON MY BED AND PULLED THE COVERS DOWN,' he growled in his great big voice.

Then the mother bear looked at her bed. 'SOMEBODY'S BEEN LYING ON MY BED AND PULLED THE PILLOW OFF,' said she in her middle-sized voice.

Then the baby bear looked at his bed, and there lay little Goldilocks with her cheeks as pink as roses, and her golden hair all spread over the pillow.

'*Somebody's been lying in my bed*,' squeaked the baby bear joyfully, '*and here she is still!*'

Now when Goldilocks in her dreams heard the great big father bear's voice she dreamed it was the thunder rolling through the heavens.

And when she heard the mother bear's middle-sized voice she dreamed it was the wind blowing through the trees.

But when she heard the baby bear's voice it was so shrill and sharp that it woke her right up. She sat up in bed and there were the three bears standing around and looking at her.

'Oh, my goodness me!' cried Goldilocks. She tumbled out of bed and ran to the window. It was open, and out she jumped before the bears could stop her. Then home she ran as fast as she could, and she never went near the forest again. But the little baby bear cried and cried because he had wanted the pretty little girl to play with. ❋

16

TALKING CAVE

A PANCHATANTRA TALE; RETOLD BY NARINDAR UBEROI KELLY

There was a deep cave in a mountainside where a jackal named Planner lived. He was a very cautious jackal and always checked to see whether the cave was safe to enter.

One day, as the sun was about to set, a lion named Crusher was passing by the same cave. He thought to himself that some wild animal was bound to come into the cave for shelter at night, so he hid inside and waited.

When the Jackal returned, he called out, 'O Cave, O Cave, How goes it?'

He waited awhile and then called out again: 'O Cave, why won't you speak to me? We had a deal that when I come to you and call out, you would answer me promptly.'

Again he waited for some time and said, 'OK, I will go to the other cave, which will probably be more polite than you.'

Upon hearing the Jackal, the Lion thought to himself that the Cave was not answering because he sensed that the Lion was there and was afraid to do so. 'I will answer the Jackal's greeting myself,' the Lion thought, 'and when he enters, I'll make a meal of him.'

So the Lion roared a greeting that echoed deeply in the cave and terrified all the creatures who heard it. The Jackal, of course, fled, thinking it is always wise to know what to fear, and plan ahead. ❋

– *Read more such ancient Indian stories in* The Panchatantra: Teaching Tales of Old India *by Narindar Uberoi Kelly, published by Hachette India.*

17

THE MAGIC PORRIDGE POT

THE BROTHERS GRIMM; RETOLD BY KATHERINE PYLE

There was once a poor widow who had only one daughter, a child who was so good and gentle that everyone who knew her, loved her.

One day the child went into the forest to gather firewood, and she was very sad because there was nothing left in the house to eat, and because she and her mother so often had to go hungry.

She had already gathered a bundle of sticks, and was about to go home, when she saw a poor old woman who had also come to the forest for wood. The woman was so bent and stiff that it was pitiful to see her. The child felt sorry for her and wished to help her.

'Good mother,' said she, 'let me gather the wood for you; it must be hard for you to stoop.'

She put down her own load and gathered for the old woman as much as she was able to carry. 'I would take it home for you,' said the little girl, 'but my mother is waiting for me, and I must make haste, for I am already late.'

'Child,' said the old woman, 'you have a good heart, and you deserve to be rewarded.' She then drew out from under her cloak a little iron pot. 'Take this,' she said. 'It is a magic pot. Whenever you are hungry you have only to say –

"Boil, little pot,
Till the porridge is hot,"

and it will begin to boil and fill up with sweet porridge. When you have had enough say –

"Cease, little pot,
The porridge is hot,"

and it will stop boiling.'

She made the child repeat the words after her several times, and she then gave her the pot and hobbled away through the forest.

The child was filled with joy at the thought that now she and her mother need never be hungry again. She ran home as fast as she could, carrying the pot with both hands.

When she came in her mother asked her where the wood was.

'I have brought home something better than wood,' cried the child. 'The wood only warms us, but here is something that will feed us as well.' She set the pot upon the table and said –

'Boil, little pot,
Till the porridge is hot.'

The pot at once began to bubble and boil, and soon it was full and brimming over with sweet porridge. The mother caught up a spoon and dipped some of the porridge out into a bowl, but the more she dipped out the more there was in it. When all the bowls in the house were full, the child said –

'Cease, little pot,
The porridge is hot,'

and at once the pot stopped boiling.

The mother was overjoyed at the treasure the little girl had brought home. 'Come,' cried she, 'let us sit down and eat.'

'Yes, dear mother,' said the child, 'but first I will carry some of the porridge to the neighbours who were so kind to us when we had nothing.'

She filled a large kettle with porridge and started out with it, but no sooner had she gone than the mother began to wonder whether they had kept enough for themselves. She did not feel satisfied, so she said to the pot –

'Boil, little pot,
Till the porridge is hot.'

Immediately the pot began to bubble and boil. Soon it was full and the porridge began to run over. The mother wished to stop it, but she had forgotten what to say.

'Enough!' she cried. 'Stop! Stop!' but the porridge still boiled up and over the edge of the pot. The mother caught up the spoon and again began dipping out the porridge; she dipped as fast as she could. Soon all the pots and pans in the house were full and still the pot continued to boil out porridge. In despair the mother seized the pot and threw it outside the door, but the porridge flowed out from it in a stream and ran down the road.

The little girl was coming home when she met the stream of porridge, and at once she guessed what had happened. She ran as fast as she could and when she came to the place where the pot lay she cried –

> 'Cease, little pot,
> The porridge is hot.'

At once the pot stopped boiling, but already enough porridge had been wasted to have fed the whole countryside.

After that the mother never again dared to tell the pot to boil. When they wished for porridge it was the child who spoke to it. But from then on she and her mother never lacked for anything, for the porridge was so delicious that people came from far and near to buy it from them. ❋

18

THE WISHING TREE

SOMADEVA; RETOLD BY JAYASHREE BHAT

There once lived a king called Malayaprabha, who ruled over the kingdom of Kurukshetra. The land in the kingdom was fertile, the treasury was full and everyone lived happily.

One year, there was a terrible famine, so the people went to their king and begged, 'Your Majesty, help us! The crops have failed, and our children are starving.'

The king was about to open the doors of the treasury when his scheming chief minister stopped him. 'Your Majesty, there are just too many poor people. If you begin to give all of them money, the treasury will soon be empty. Let the people fend for themselves.'

When the king's son Induprabha heard this, he said, 'Father, these people are in need. How can you turn them away?'

'If I give away everything I have, how will I run the kingdom?' said the king, remembering the minister's words.

'B–but, Father, you are the king!' cried Induprabha. 'It is your duty to help your people!'

'If you think you have all the answers, why don't *you* find a source of unlimited wealth?' said the king furiously.

Determined to bring justice to the people of the kingdom, Induprabha decided he would seek help from the only ones who could actually help him – the gods. He retreated deep into a dark forest and performed penances so severe that even the birds fell silent. At long last, pleased with his devotion, Indra appeared before him.

'Rise, my son, and tell me what you seek,' said Indra.

With folded hands, Induprabha bowed and said, 'My lord, turn me into a wishing tree so that I can fulfil every man's need, and no one goes hungry ever again.'

'So be it!' said Indra. No sooner had the words left his mouth than Induprabha began to turn into a tree. First, his feet became rooted to the ground. Next, his arms turned into wide boughs and lush, green leaves shot out of them. His hair turned into yellow flowers that nodded in the wind. Birds twittered as they sat on the wide branches while butterflies danced around him. Induprabha was now a wishing tree!

News about the wishing tree travelled fast, and people came from far and wide to have their wishes granted. Illnesses were cured, hungry stomachs were fed, families were united, rivalries were forgotten – no wish was too hard for the wishing tree and soon, Kurukshetra turned into paradise for its people.

Many years passed in peace and prosperity. One day, Indra came to the wishing tree and said, 'Induprabha, you have led a good life here on Earth, helping thousands in need. You have earned your place in heaven. Come with me.'

The wishing tree's branches shook in the breeze.

As the wind blew, it seemed like the leaves were whispering. 'How can my job ever be done, my lord? Even an ordinary tree gives fruits and flowers and helps people. How can I then, a wishing tree, go to heaven and leave those who need me the most behind?'

Pleased with his reply, Indra said, 'Well, then let us take all the people of Kurukshetra to heaven. Surely you will come with me then?'

The wind whooshed gently through the tree as it answered, 'My lord, if you are pleased with me, please take my people to heaven. I will remain here so that anyone else in need may get their wishes fulfilled.'

Delighted, Indra said, 'You, Induprabha, are a gem amongst men. You will forever be praised among mankind, and people will always think of you when they are in need.' And as he had promised, Indra gathered the people of Kurukshetra and left for heaven.

If you pass by a tree with yellow flowers, birds on its boughs and butterflies around it, you *will* make a wish, won't you? ❋

– *Read more such classic stories in* A Treasury of Tales from the Kathasaritasagara, *retold by Jayashree Bhat and published by Hachette India.*

19

THE BUNDLE OF STICKS

AN AESOP'S FABLE; RETOLD BY J.H. STICKNEY

An Old Man had many Sons, who were often quarrelling. He tried to make them good friends, but could not. As the end of his life drew near, the Old Man called them all to him and showed them a bundle of sticks tied tightly together. 'Now,' said the Father, 'see if you can break this bundle of sticks.'

Each of the Sons in turn took the bundle and tried with all his might to break it, but could not. When all had tried and given it up, the Father said, 'Untie the bundle, and each of you take a stick and see if you can break that.' This they could do very easily.

Then said the Father, 'Now, if you will stop quarrelling and stand by each other, you will be like the bundle of sticks – no one can do you any harm; but if you do not keep together, you will be as weak as is one of the little sticks by itself, which anyone can break.' ❋

20

BRUCE AND THE SPIDER

A SCOTTISH LEGEND; RETOLD BY JAMES BALDWIN

There was once a king of Scotland whose name was Robert Bruce. He needed to be both brave and wise, for the times in which he lived were wild and rough. The King of England was at war with him and had led a great army into Scotland to drive him out of the land.

Battle after battle had been fought. Six times had Bruce led his brave little army against his foes; and six times had his men been beaten and driven into flight. At last his army was scattered, and he was forced to hide himself in the woods and in lonely places among the mountains.

One rainy day, Bruce lay on the ground under a rude shed, listening to the patter of the drops on the roof above him. He was tired and sick at heart, and ready to give up all hope. It seemed to him that there was no use for him to try to do anything more.

As he lay thinking, he saw a spider over his head, making ready to weave her web. He watched her as she toiled slowly and with great care. Six times she tried to throw her frail thread from one beam to another, and six times it fell short.

'Poor thing!' said Bruce. 'You, too, know what it is to fail.'

But the spider did not lose hope with the sixth failure. With still more care, she made ready to try for the seventh time. Bruce almost forgot his own troubles as he watched her swing herself out upon the slender line. Would she fail again? No! The thread was carried safely to the beam and fastened there.

'I, too, will try a seventh time!' cried Bruce.

He arose and called his men together. He told them of his plans and sent them out with messages of cheer to his disheartened people. Soon there was an army of brave Scotchmen around him. Another battle was fought and the King of England was glad to go back into his own country.

I have heard it said that, after that day, no one by the name of Bruce would ever hurt a spider. The lesson which the little creature had taught the king was never forgotten. ❋

21

THE FOX AND THE GRAPES

AN AESOP'S FABLE; RETOLD BY J.H. STICKNEY

It was a sultry day, and a Fox was almost famished with hunger and thirst. He was just saying to himself that anything would be acceptable to him, when, looking up, he spied some great clusters of ripe, black grapes hanging from a trellised vine.

'What luck!' he said; 'if only they weren't quite so high, I should be sure of a fine feast. I wonder if I can get them. I can think of nothing that would so refresh me.' He gave a great spring and nearly reached the lowest clusters. 'I'll do better next time,' he said.

He tried again and again, but did not succeed so well as at first. Finding that he was losing his strength and that he had little chance of getting the grapes, he walked slowly off, grumbling as he did so: 'The grapes are sour, and not at all fit for my eating. I'll leave them to the greedy birds. They eat anything.' ❋

22

MR PINK-WHISTLE COMES ALONG

ENID BLYTON

'Sooty!' called Mr Pink-Whistle to his big black cat. 'I'm going for a walk. It's a lovely sunny winter's day. I'll be back in time for lunch.'

Sooty went to the door to see him off. He went briskly down the garden path and out of the gate. The frost crunched under his feet as he went, and the pale December sun shone down on him. What a lovely day!

I think I'll go down to the pond to see if there are any children sliding on the ice, he thought. So off he went, down the lane, up the hill, down the hill, and across a meadow where frost whitened the long grass in the ditches.

Mr Pink-Whistle was just putting his leg over the stile to go to the pond when his sharp ears heard a sound. He had pointed brownie ears and could hear like a hare!

Now, what's that? he thought, a leg half over the stile. *Is it an animal? Or a child? Or just a noise?*

It seemed to come from a little tumble-down shed by the hedge. Mr Pink-Whistle listened. Yes, there certainly was a noise – a sniffy sort of noise: sniff-sniff-gulp, sniff-sniff!

'I'd better go and find out,' said Pink-Whistle, and he got down from the stile and went to the little shed. He poked his head inside. It was rather dark and he couldn't see anything at first. Then he saw something white. 'Dear me!' said Pink-Whistle. 'Is that a face I see? Does it belong to someone? Who are you?'

The face was peeping out of a pile of hay in the corner of the shed.

'Yes, but please go away. This is my shed. It's private.'

Pink-Whistle didn't go away. He was sure that he could see the face was very miserable. He came right into the shed.

Somebody scrambled out of the hay crossly. It was a boy of about ten. 'I told you this was *my* shed,' he said. 'It's on my father's land and he said I could have it for my own. You're trespassing!'

'Was it you I heard sniff-sniff-sniffing?' asked Pink-Whistle. 'What's the matter?'

'Nothing,' said the boy. 'Nothing to do with you anyway. Don't you know when people want to be alone? I wish you'd get out of my shed.'

'I'm going,' said Pink-Whistle. 'But it's a pity you haven't even a dog to keep you company. If you're unhappy, it's nice to have a dog's nose on the knee.'

He walked back to the door. 'Come back,' said the boy suddenly, sitting down on the hay and rubbing a very dirty hand over his face. 'I like what you said just now. You might understand if I tell you something. You wouldn't have said that if you hadn't understood what friends dogs are, would you?'

'No,' said Pink-Whistle, turning back. 'So it's something to do with a dog, is it? Your own dog, I suppose.'

'Yes,' said the boy in a shaky sort of voice. 'You see, I've got no brothers or sisters, so my daddy gave me a dog for my own. My very own, you understand – not one that's shared by the whole family. Buddy was my own, every whisker of him, every hair.'

'That's a splendid thing,' said Pink-Whistle. 'I expect you belonged to him as much as he belonged to you. You were his friend as much as he was yours.'

'I'm glad you understand,' said the boy. 'It's nice to tell somebody. Well, Buddy's gone. Somebody's stolen him. He was a black spaniel with big, loving eyes, and he cost my father a lot of money. That's why he's been stolen, because he's valuable.'

Sniff-sniff-sniff! The boy rubbed his hand over his eyes again. 'I'm ten,' he said, ashamed, 'and too old to make a fuss like this, like a four-year-old. I know all that, so you needn't tell me. But a dog sort of gets right into your heart if he's your own.'

'I shall begin to sniff, too, in a minute,' said Pink-Whistle. 'I know exactly what you feel. You're thinking how miserable your dog will be without you, and you're hoping that nobody is being cruel to him, and you're wondering if he's cowering down in some corner, puzzled and frightened. Well, that's enough to make anyone feel miserable.'

'He disappeared yesterday,' said the boy. 'Two men came to the farm to ask if they could buy chickens – and I'm sure they took Buddy away. They may have given him some meat with a sleeping powder in it and got him like that. The police say they can't trace the men and they haven't had any report of a black spaniel anywhere.'

'I see,' said Pink-Whistle. 'Er – do you happen to know me by any chance, young lad?'

'My name's Robin,' said the boy. 'No, I don't know you. I've never ever seen you before, have I?'

He peered closely at Pink-Whistle. The sun shone in at the little shed window just then and he suddenly saw Pink-Whistle clearly. He saw his green eyes and pointed ears and he gave a little cry.

'Wait! Wait! Yes, I've seen your picture somewhere in a magazine or a book. Yes, I remember now. Why – surely you're not Mr Pink-Whistle?'

'I am,' said Pink-Whistle, beaming all over his face, pleased that the boy knew him. 'And I like to go about the world putting wrong things right.'

'Get back Buddy for me then, please, please, please!' said Robin, clutching hold of Mr Pink-Whistle's arm. 'I never thought you were real, but you are. Can you get back Buddy?'

'I'll do my best,' said Pink-Whistle. 'I'll go now. Cheer up, get out of this dark shed and go home and find some work to do. Perhaps I can put things right for you.'

He walked out of the shed. Robin ran after him, suddenly very cheerful indeed. He was amazed. To think that Mr Pink-Whistle should come along just then – what a wonderful thing!

Pink-Whistle went back home. He called Sooty, his cat, and told her about Robin. 'Go to the farm and speak to the farm cats,' he said. 'They will have noticed these two men and have seen if Buddy was taken away by them. Find out all you can.'

Sooty ran off, tail in the air. She soon came back with the news. 'Yes, master! The farm cats say that the men came back that evening, threw down meat for Buddy and then went away. Buddy ate it and fell asleep. Then the men came back and put him into a sack. The cats heard them saying they were going to Ringdown Market on Thursday. You will find them there.'

'Thank you, Sooty!' said Pink-Whistle. 'That's all I want to know.'

The next Thursday, Pink-Whistle set off to Ringdown Market. It was a long way away, but he got there at last. What a babble of sound there was! Horses whinnying, sheep baaing, hens clucking, ducks quacking, turkeys gobbling, geese hissing and cackling!

Pink-Whistle looked for a black spaniel. There were three for sale at the market. Which was Robin's? Mr Pink-Whistle decided to make himself invisible. This was a gift he sometimes used, and he used it now!

One moment there was a kindly old man walking about – the next moment he wasn't there at all! An old woman selling eggs was most astonished. She blinked her eyes in wonder and then forgot about it. Pink-Whistle went up to a black spaniel. 'Buddy!' he whispered. 'Buddy!'

The dog took no notice. So that one wasn't Robin's dog. Pink-Whistle went up to the second spaniel and whispered. But he wasn't Robin's dog either.

'Buddy!' whispered Pink-Whistle to the third spaniel, who was lying miserably on some sacks behind two men selling hens. 'Buddy!'

The dog sprang up at once, his tail wagging. He looked all around. Who had called him by his name?

One of the men turned round sharply.

'Lie down, you!' he shouted. Pink-Whistle felt very angry indeed. Aha! These fellows wanted punishing.

They wanted frightening. Well, he would have a grand game and give them a wonderful punishment.

He began to bark like a dog and Buddy pricked up his ears at once. Then Pink-Whistle pretended that Buddy was speaking.

'Hens, peck these men!' he cried. And then it seemed to the men as if a whole flock of invisible hens were all around them, pecking hard – but really, of course, it was Mr Pink-Whistle jabbing at them with his hard little forefinger – peck-peck-peck!

The men cowered back, squealing. Everyone came to see what the matter was. Pink-Whistle called out again in a barking sort of voice, so that it seemed as if Buddy was talking. 'Geese, attack these men!'

And dear me, what a cackling there was from old Pink-Whistle then, what a hissing – and what a jab-jab-jabbing from top to bottom of the scared men. Everyone stared, amazed. What was happening? Where did the cackling and hissing come from? Who was jabbing the men?

'Serves them right,' said somebody. 'I never did like those two.'

And then Pink-Whistle decided to be a butting goat! What fun he was having – and what a wonderful punishment he was giving the two men!

'Goat, butt them!' he cried. The men looked everywhere, scared, wondering if an invisible goat was coming at them.

Biff! Pink-Whistle ran first at one man and then the other. Biff! Bang! Biff! The men felt exactly as though a big, rather solid goat was butting them back and front. Pink-Whistle butted one man right over and he rolled on top of Buddy. Buddy promptly snapped at him and growled.

Pink-Whistle immediately growled, too, and talking in his growling voice, said, 'Bull, toss these men!'

The men gave a loud howl. Hens had pecked them geese had jabbed them, a goat had butted them! Surely, surely they were not going to be tossed by a bull, and an invisible one, too, coming at them from any side!

'Run for it!' yelled one man, and he ran for his life. The other followed. Pink-Whistle galloped after them, making his feet sound like a bull's hooves – clippitty-clippitty-clop. How the men howled!

Pink-Whistle couldn't follow them very far because he was laughing so much. How he laughed! People were really puzzled to hear loud chuckles and not to see anyone there.

'Well, I don't know what's upset those two fellows,' said a burly farmer, 'but I'm glad to see the back of them. Rascals, both of them!'

Pink-Whistle went back to where the dog Buddy lay on the sacks, puzzled and frightened. Buddy suddenly heard a quiet, kindly voice talking to him, and invisible fingers undid the knot of rope that tied him to a rail.

'Come with me, Buddy,' said the voice, and Buddy went obediently. He sniffed at Mr Pink-Whistle's invisible legs. How very peculiar to smell legs that didn't seem to be there! Buddy couldn't understand it – but then, he didn't really understand anything that had happened since he had left Robin. His world seemed quite upside down and not at all a nice place.

It was a long way to the farm where Robin lived – but as they got nearer to it Buddy became very excited indeed. His nose twitched. He pulled against the hand on his collar.

'Not so fast, Buddy,' said Mr Pink-Whistle. 'I want to come with you.'

Buddy took another sniff at the invisible legs. Well, they smelt all right, so the person with them ought to be all right, too. He trotted along obediently, getting more and more excited.

It was dark when at last they came to the farm. Buddy pulled and pulled at Pink-Whistle's hand. The little man led him to his kennel. 'Get in there and wait!' he ordered. 'And bark. Bark loudly!'

Buddy crept in and then he barked. How loudly he barked. 'Wuff-wuff-wuff, WUFF-WUFF. Robin, I'm back, where are you? WUFF-WUFF!'

And Robin heard of course. He would know Buddy's bark anywhere! He sprang up at once, his face shining. 'Mother! That's Buddy's bark! He's back!'

he cried and raced out of the house to the yard. He came to the kennel, calling joyfully, 'Buddy! Buddy! I'm here!'

And, before Buddy could squeeze past the invisible Mr Pink-Whistle, there was Robin, squeezing into the kennel! He got right in, and then you really couldn't tell which was boy and which was dog, they hugged and licked and rolled and patted, and yelped and shouted so joyfully together!

At last, tired out, they sat peacefully together in the kennel, Buddy's nose on Robin's knee and Robin's arm round Buddy's neck. Only Buddy's tongue was busy, lick-lick-licking at Robin's hand.

'Buddy, I do wish I could say a big thank you to Mr Pink-Whistle!' said Robin. 'I don't even know where he lives, though. I'd say, Mr Pink-Whistle, I'm your friend for ever and ever!'

Pink-Whistle heard it all. He was peering in at the kennel, as happy as could be. He had put a lot of things right in his life, but surely this was one of the very best! He stole away in the darkness, a very happy little man indeed. ❋

– *Read many more exciting stories by Enid Blyton in* Winter Stories.

23

BELLING THE CAT

AN AESOP'S FABLE; RETOLD BY J.H. STICKNEY

Once upon a time the mice sat in council and talked of how they might outwit their enemy, the Cat. But good advice was scarce, and in vain the president called upon all the most experienced mice present to find a way.

At last a very young mouse held up two fingers and asked to be allowed to speak, and as soon as he could get permission he said: 'I've been thinking for a long time why the Cat is such a dangerous enemy. Now, it's not so much because of her quickness, though people make so much fuss about that. If we could only *notice* her in time, I've no doubt we're nimble enough to jump into our holes before she could do us any harm. It's in her velvet paws, there's where she hides her cruel claws till she gets us in her clutches –

that's where her power lies. With those paws she can tread so lightly that we can't hear her coming. And so, while *we* are still dancing heedlessly about the place, she creeps close up, and before we know where we are she pounces down on us and has us in her clutches. Well, then, it's my opinion we ought to hang a bell round her neck to warn us of her coming while there's yet time.'

Everyone applauded this proposal, and the council decided that it should be carried out.

Now the question to be settled was, who should undertake to fasten the bell round the Cat's neck?

The president declared that no one could be better fitted for the task than he who had given such excellent advice.

But at that the young mouse became quite confused and stammered an excuse. He was too young for the deed, he said. He didn't know the Cat well enough. His grandfather, who knew her better, would be more suited to the job.

But the grandfather declared that just because he knew the Cat very well he would take good care not to attempt such a task.

And the long and the short of it was that no other mouse would undertake the duty; and so this clever proposal was never carried out, and the Cat remained mistress of the situation.

It is one thing to say that something should be done, but quite a different matter to do it. ❋

24

THE MICE THAT ATE IRON

SOMADEVA; RETOLD BY JAYASHREE BHAT

Long ago, there was a merchant's son who spent all of his father's money after the old man's death. Finally, the only thing he had left was an iron weighing scale. Now, the weighing scale was made of a thousand *pala*s* of iron and was really very valuable.

One day, the merchant's son had to travel to another city, and so he left his only possession in the care of his friend, whom he trusted with all his heart.

'Don't you worry,' his friend said, his eyes gleaming with greed. 'I'll take good care of this and oil it every day.'

After a month, when the merchant's son went to collect his scale, his friend said, 'I'm very sorry but

**An ancient unit of weight. 1* pala *is said to be equal to about 50 grams.*

your scale is gone! It was eaten up by the mice in my warehouse!'

'By mice! Whatever do you mean? How can mice eat *iron*?' exclaimed the merchant's son.

'I think the iron that was used to make the scale was quite sweet, and so the mice took a liking to it,' said his friend solemnly.

Realizing that he had been cheated, the merchant's son did not argue further. He only said, 'Oh well, what can we do? What's gone is gone. Anyway, I have had a long journey. Can you please give me some food? I am afraid I have no money – the scale was my only possession. And I have been living on only these *amalaka* fruits for so long.'

His friend, delighted at having made a fool out of the merchant's son, said, 'Of course, of course.' He went into the kitchen to get the food.

Meanwhile, his young son entered the room. 'May I have an *amalaka*?' he said shyly.

'Of course, but these are a bit dried up. Come with me, I'll take you to a tree full of juicy *amalaka*s!'

Saying this, the merchant's son held the child's hand and led him to another friend's house.

'Look after this child for me, will you? I will be back soon,' he said to his puzzled friend.

He then returned to the house of the first friend, who was pacing up and down the courtyard, looking really anxious.

'You!' he shouted when he saw the merchant's son. 'Where is my son? I know he was with you.'

'I am very sorry, but your son is gone,' said the merchant's son solemnly. 'A hawk swooped down and picked him up, and before I could do anything, it flew away with him.'

His friend turned purple with anger, clenched his fists and said, 'Where have you taken my son!'

'I just told you – a hawk took him!'

'I-I am taking you to the king!' blustered his friend.

'As you wish, let us go,' the merchant's son said calmly.

In the king's court, the merchant's friend wailed, 'Your Majesty, this man claims a hawk took my son and flew away with him! He thinks I'm a fool! I want my son back!'

Turning to the merchant's son, the king asked, 'What is this nonsense? How is this possible?'

'Your Majesty, if a mouse can eat iron, a hawk can definitely carry off a boy,' the merchant's son replied.

He then narrated the day's events to the king who roared with laughter and made sure the weighing scale was restored to its rightful owner. And the boy was soon returned to his rather shamefaced father. ❋

– *Read more such delightful stories in* A Treasury of Tales from the Kathasaritasagara, *retold by Jayashree Bhat and published by Hachette India.*

25

THE BOGEY-BEAST

FLORA ANNIE STEEL

There was once a woman who was very, very cheerful, though she had little to make her so; for she was old, and poor, and lonely. She lived in a little bit of a cottage and earned a scant living by running errands for her neighbours, getting a bite here, a sup there, as reward for her services. So she made the best of everything, and always looked as spry and cheery as if she had not a want in the world.

Now one summer evening, as she was trotting, full of smiles as ever, along the high road to her hovel, what should she see but a big black pot lying in the ditch! 'Goodness me!' she cried. 'That would be just the very thing for me if I only had something to put in it! But I haven't! Now who could have left it in the ditch?'

And she looked about her expecting the owner would not be far off, but she could see nobody.

'Maybe there is a hole in it,' she went on, 'and that's why it has been cast away. But it would do fine to put a flower in for my window; so I'll just take it home with me.' And with that she lifted the lid and looked inside. 'Mercy me!' she cried, fair amazed. 'If it isn't full of gold pieces. Here's luck!'

And so it was, brimful of great gold coins. Well, at first she simply stood stock-still, wondering if she was standing on her head or her heels. Then she began saying: 'Lawks! But I do feel rich. I feel awful rich!'

After she had said this many times, she began to wonder how she was to get her treasure home. It was too heavy for her to carry, and she could see no better way than to tie the end of her shawl to it and drag it behind her like a go-cart.

'It will soon be dark,' she said to herself as she trotted along. 'So much the better! The neighbours will not see what I'm bringing home, and I shall have all the night to myself, and be able to think what I'll do! Perhaps I'll buy a grand house and just sit by the fire with a cup o' tea and do no work at all like a queen. Or maybe I'll bury it at the garden foot and just keep a bit in the old china teapot on the chimney-piece. Or maybe – Goody! Goody! I feel that grand I don't know myself.'

By this time she was a bit tired of dragging such a heavy weight, and, stopping to rest a while, turned to look at her treasure.

And lo! It wasn't a pot of gold at all! It was nothing but a lump of silver.

She stared at it, and rubbed her eyes, and stared at it again. 'Well! I never!' she said at last. 'And me thinking it was a pot of gold! I must have been dreaming. But this is luck! Silver is far less trouble – easier to mind, and not so easy stolen. Them gold pieces would have been the death o' me, and with this great lump of silver –'

So she went off again planning what she would do, and feeling as rich as rich, until becoming a bit tired again she stopped to rest and gave a look round to see if her treasure was safe; and she saw nothing but a great lump of iron!

'Well! I never!' says she again. 'And I mistaking it for silver! I must have been dreaming. But this is luck! It's real convenient. I can get penny pieces for old iron, and penny pieces are a deal handier for me than your gold and silver. Why! I should never have slept a wink for fear of being robbed. But a penny piece comes in useful, and I shall sell that iron for a lot and be real rich – rolling rich.'

So on she trotted full of plans as to how she would spend her penny pieces, till once more she stopped to rest and looked round to see her treasure was safe. And this time she saw nothing but a big stone.

'Well! I never!' she cried, full of smiles. 'And to think I mistook it for iron. I must have been dreaming. But here's luck indeed, and me wanting a stone terrible bad to stick open the gate. Eh my! But it's a change for the better! It's a fine thing to have good luck.'

So, all in a hurry to see how the stone would keep the gate open, she trotted off down the hill till she came to her own cottage. She unlatched the gate and then turned to unfasten her shawl from the stone which lay on the path behind her. Aye! It was a stone sure enough. There was plenty light to see it lying there, sober and peaceable as a stone should.

So she bent over it to unfasten the shawl end, when – 'Oh my!' All of a sudden it gave a jump, a squeal, and in one moment was as big as a haystack. Then it let down four great lanky legs and threw out two long ears, nourished a great long tail and romped off, kicking and squealing and whinnying and laughing like a naughty, mischievous boy!

The old woman stared after it till it was fairly out of sight, then she burst out laughing, too.

'Well!' she chuckled, 'I am in luck! Quite the luckiest body hereabouts. Fancy my seeing the Bogey-Beast all to myself; and making myself so free with it, too! My goodness! I do feel that uplifted – that *GRAND*!'–

So she went into her cottage and spent the evening chuckling over her good luck. ❋

26

THE CAMEL AND THE PIG

AN INDIAN FABLE; RETOLD BY P.V. RAMASWAMI RAJU

A camel said, 'Nothing like being tall! See how tall I am.' A pig who heard these words said, 'Nothing like being short; see how short I am!'

The camel said, 'Well, if I fail to prove the truth of what I said, I will give you my hump.'

The pig said, 'If I fail to prove the truth of what I have said, I will give up my snout.'

'Agreed!' said the camel.

'Just so!' said the pig.

They came to a garden enclosed by a low wall without any opening. The camel stood on this side of the wall, and, reaching the plants within by means of his long neck, made a breakfast of them.

Then he turned jeeringly to the pig, who had been standing at the bottom of the wall, without even having a look at the good things in the garden, and said, 'Now, would you be tall or short?'

Next they came to a garden enclosed by a high wall, with a wicket gate at one end. The pig entered by the gate, and, after having eaten his fill of the vegetables within, came out, laughing at the poor camel, who had had to stay outside, because he was too tall to enter the garden by the gate, and said, 'Now, would you be tall or short?'

Then they thought the matter over, and came to the conclusion that the camel should keep his hump and the pig his snout, observing:

'Tall is good, where tall would do;
Of short, again, it is also true!'

27

THE DOLLS' FEAST

SUKUMAR RAY; TRANSLATED BY SREEJATA GUHA

The dolls' mother, Khuki, was very busy indeed. You see, it was Little Doll's birthday today, and so there was a big feast planned. Upon a tiny table, miniature plates were laid out and the food was neatly arranged on them. All around the table, there were real chairs, tiny ones, placed for the other dolls to sit on when they came for the feast.

The youngest of Khuki's older brothers, Chhoto Dada, was all of four and a half years old. He piped up, 'Dolls cannot eat; why on earth do you celebrate their birthday?'

But Khuki was not one to be cowed down. 'Dolls can do *everything*,' she argued. 'Who said they can't? Who said they can't talk or eat?'

When Doll-boy fell ill, didn't he cry 'Ma, Ma'? Of course he did! How else did Khuki come to know that he was unwell? Khuki's dada didn't know the answers to these questions. So he just shouted, 'Silly girl! Stupid girl!' and made faces at her as he ran away.

Khuki went to her mother to lodge a formal complaint against her brother. Ma heard her out and finally said, 'Dolls are not always alive to everyone. The day you see them being alive and eating food, call your dada and show him.'

'It would be such fun if they could do that today!' said Khuki. 'I believe when we sleep at night, their day begins. Or else we would have been able to see them!

'Remember how the tin soldier had fallen off the bed one night? They must have been squabbling that night. Why else would he fall off the bed? Starting today, I shall keep my eyes and ears peeled when I go to bed!'

The feast for Little Doll's birthday was truly awesome. There were dough sweets, dough cookies, tiny coconut laddus and minuscule patties made of treacle – such were the wonders on the table that day. That night, before going to bed, Khuki wiped down and cleaned all her dolls, and put them to bed after reminding them, 'Look here, the food is all laid out on the table. Do wake up and finish all of it...'

After explaining in detail who would sit where, what they would eat after what, the kind of punishments that would be doled out for the types of naughtiness that could be displayed, and after scolding Naughty Doll roundly and cuddling Little Doll fondly, Khuki finally hit the bed. The minute she did, she was off to dreamland.

The pitter-patter of feet began as soon as Khuki went to sleep. One of them was roaming at the foot of the dolls' bed and near Khukumoni's shoes in a corner of the room, where the picture books were kept. It was sniffing around and biting things. It bit off a corner of the alphabet book, chewed it, but did not like the taste too much; it sucked on a shoelace and found no juice in it. It bit into the tin doll – oh boy, that was hard!

Suddenly, in the dark, it spotted something: what were all those things laid out on the table?

Rushing in, it overturned the chair, leapt up on the table and sniffed around urgently before it let out a soft yelp of joy. '*Keech keech keee—ch*!' This meant, 'Darling, hurry up and come see what I have found!'

Immediately, another one of the same kind arrived with more pitter-patter, splitter-splatter of feet. They both looked exactly the same – furry and grey, with the same thin, long tail and the same sharp nose and beady black eyes. The two were excited beyond words. *Tuptap-top* they were gobbling up all that they saw, as they screeched away in their language, 'Eat this! Try some of that! This one is delicious. That one is soooo tasty!' And in this manner, all the food on the table was polished off in no time at all.

Khuki woke up in the morning and found – lo and behold – all the food had been eaten up! She had no idea when the dolls had woken up, eaten all the food and gone back to sleep. 'Eaten! Eaten! They have eaten all the food!' Khuki's elated screams fetched Ma, Baba, Chhoto Dada, Boro Dada, everyone right there.

When they saw what had happened and they heard what Khuki had to say, they all said, 'Very true! This is a miracle indeed!'

Only Chhoto Dada said, 'Sure, she has just eaten all the food herself, and now she says that the dolls have eaten it!' How unfair.

Actually, the truth of the matter was known only to Mother and Father, because they had spotted the marks from the rats' feet in the corner of Khuki's room. But if any of you try telling this to Khuki, she will never believe a word of what you say. ❋

– *Read more stories by Sukumar Ray in* The Mad and Magical World of Sukumar Ray, *translated by Sreejata Guha and published by Hachette India.*

28

THE LION AND THE MOUSE

AN AESOP'S FABLE; RETOLD BY JOSEPH JACOBS

Once when a Lion was asleep a little Mouse began running up and down on him; this soon wakened the Lion, who placed his huge paw upon him, and opened his big jaws to swallow him.

'Pardon, O King,' cried the little Mouse, 'forgive me this time. I shall never forget it. Who knows, but I may be able to do you a good turn one of these days?'

The Lion was so tickled at the idea of the Mouse being able to help him, that he lifted his paw and let him go.

Some time later, the Lion was caught in a trap, and the hunters who desired to carry him alive to the King, tied him to a tree while they went in search of a wagon to carry him on.

Just then the little Mouse happened to pass by, and seeing the sad plight in which the Lion was, went up to him and soon gnawed away the ropes that bound the King of the Beasts.

'Was I not right?' said the little Mouse.

A kindness is never wasted. ❋

29

THE PRINCESS AND THE PEA

HANS CHRISTIAN ANDERSEN

Once upon a time there was a prince who wanted to marry a princess; but she would have to be a real princess. He travelled all over the world to find one, but nowhere could he get what he wanted. There were princesses enough, but it was difficult to find out whether they were real ones. There was always something about them that was not as it should be. So he came home again and was sad, for he would have liked very much to have a real princess.

One evening a terrible storm came on; there was thunder and lightning, and the rain poured down in torrents. Suddenly a knocking was heard at the city gate, and the old king went to open it.

It was a princess standing out there in front of the gate. But, good gracious! what a sight the rain and the wind had made her look. The water ran down from her hair and clothes; it ran down into the toes of her shoes and out again at the heels. And yet she said that she was a real princess.

'Well, we'll soon find that out,' thought the old queen. But she said nothing, went into the bedroom, took all the bedding off the bedstead, and laid a pea on the bottom; then she took twenty mattresses and laid them on the pea, and then twenty eider-down beds on top of the mattresses.

On this the princess had to lie all night. In the morning she was asked how she had slept.

'Oh, very badly!' said she. 'I have scarcely closed my eyes all night. Heaven only knows what was in the bed, but I was lying on something hard, so that I am black and blue all over my body. It's horrible!'

Now they knew that she was a real princess because she had felt the pea right through the twenty mattresses and the twenty eider-down beds.

Nobody but a real princess could be as sensitive as that.

So the prince took her for his wife, for now he knew that he had a real princess; and the pea was put in the museum, where it may still be seen, if no one has stolen it.

There, that is a true story. ❃

30

THE THREE LITTLE PIGS

AN ENGLISH FAIRY TALE; RETOLD BY MABIE, HALE AND FORBUSH

Once upon a time, when pigs could talk and no one had ever heard of bacon, there lived an old piggy mother with her three little sons.

They had a very pleasant home in the middle of an oak forest, and were all just as happy as the day was long, until one sad year the acorn crop failed; then, indeed, poor Mrs Piggy-wiggy often had hard work to make both ends meet.

One day she called her sons to her, and, with tears in her eyes, told them that she must send them out into the wide world to seek their fortune.

She kissed them all round, and the three little pigs set out upon their travels, each taking a different road, and carrying a bundle slung on a stick across his shoulder.

The first little pig had not gone far before he met a man carrying a bundle of straw, so he said to him, 'Please, man, give me that straw to build me a house?' The man was very good-natured, so he gave him the bundle of straw, and the little pig built a pretty little house with it.

No sooner was it finished, and the little pig thinking of going to bed, than a wolf came along, knocked at the door, and said, 'Little pig, little pig, let me come in.'

But the little pig laughed softly, and answered, 'No, no, by the hair of my chinny-chin-chin.'

Then said the wolf sternly, 'I will *make* you let me in; for I'll huff, and I'll puff, and I'll blow your house in!' So he huffed and he puffed, and he blew

his house in, because, you see, it was only of straw and too light; and when he had blown the house in, he ate up the little pig, and did not leave so much as the tip of his tail.

The second little pig also met a man, and *he* was carrying a bundle of furze*; so piggy said politely,

* *Gorse; a spiny shrub*

'Please, kind man, will you give me that furze to build me a house?'

The man agreed, and piggy set to work to build himself a snug little house before the night came on. It was scarcely finished when the wolf came along and said, 'Little pig, little pig, let me come in.'

'No, no, by the hair of my chinny-chin-chin,' answered the second little pig.

'Then I'll huff, and I'll puff, and I'll blow your house in!' said the wolf. So he huffed and he puffed, and he puffed, and he huffed, and at last he blew the house in, and gobbled the little pig up in a trice.

❋

Now, the third little pig met a man with a load of bricks and mortar, and he said, 'Please, man, will you give me those bricks to build a house with?'

So the man gave him the bricks and mortar, and a little trowel as well, and the little pig built himself a nice strong little house. As soon as it was finished the wolf came to call, just as he had done to the other little pigs, and said, 'Little pig, little pig, let me in!'

But the little pig answered, 'No, no, by the hair of my chinny-chin-chin.'

'Then,' said the wolf, 'I'll huff, and I'll puff, and I'll blow your house in.'

Well, he huffed, and he puffed, and he puffed, and he huffed, and he huffed, and he puffed, but he could *not* get the house down. At last he had no breath left to huff and puff with, so he sat down outside the little pig's house and thought for a while.

Presently he called out, 'Little pig, I know where there is a nice field of turnips.'

'Where?' said the little pig.

'Behind the farmer's house, three fields away, and if you will be ready tomorrow morning I will call for you, and we will go together and get some breakfast.'

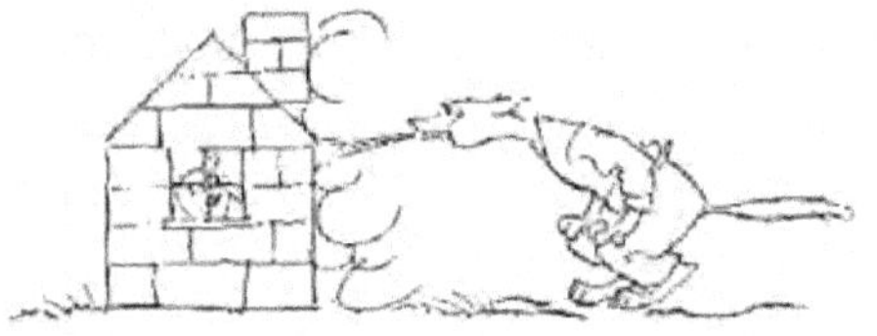

'Very well,' said the little pig; 'I will be sure to be ready. What time do you mean to start?'

'At six o'clock,' replied the wolf.

Well, the wise little pig got up at five, scampered away to the field, and brought home a fine load of turnips before the wolf came. At six o'clock the wolf came to the little pig's house and said, 'Little pig, are you ready?'

'Ready!' cried the little pig. 'Why, I have been to the field and come back long ago, and now I am busy boiling a potful of turnips for breakfast.'

The wolf was very angry indeed, but he made up his mind to catch the little pig somehow or other; so he told him that he knew where there was a nice apple tree.

'Where?' said the little pig.

'Round the hill in the squire's orchard,' the wolf said. 'So if you will promise to play me no tricks, I will come for you tomorrow morning at five o'clock, and we will go there together and get some rosy-cheeked apples.'

The next morning piggy got up at four o'clock and was off and away long before the wolf came. But the orchard was a long way off, and besides, he had the tree to climb, which is a difficult matter for a little pig, so that before the sack he had brought with him was quite filled he saw the wolf coming towards him.

He was dreadfully frightened, but he thought it better to put a good face on the matter, so when the wolf said, 'Little pig, why are you here before me? Are they nice apples?' he replied at once: 'Yes, very; I will throw down one for you to taste.' So he picked an apple and threw it so far that whilst the wolf was running to fetch it he had time to jump down and scamper away home.

The next day the wolf came again and told the little pig that there was going to be a fair in the town that afternoon, and asked him if he would go with him.

'Oh! Yes,' said the pig. 'I will go with pleasure. What time will you be ready to start?'

'At half-past three,' said the wolf.

Of course, the little pig started long before the time, went to the fair and bought a fine large butter-churn, and was trotting away with it on his back when he saw the wolf coming.

He did not know what to do, so he crept into the churn to hide, and by so doing started it rolling.

Down the hill it went, rolling over and over, with the little pig squeaking inside.

The wolf could not think what the strange thing rolling down the hill could be, so he turned tail and ran away home in a fright without ever going to the fair at all. He went to the little pig's house to tell him how frightened he had been by a large round thing which came rolling past him down the hill.

'Ha! Ha!' laughed the little pig. 'So I frightened you, eh? I had been to the fair and bought a butter-churn; when I saw you I got inside it and rolled down the hill.'

This made the wolf so angry that he declared that he *would* eat up the little pig, and that nothing should save him, for he would jump down the chimney.

But the clever little pig hung a pot full of water over the hearth and then made a blazing fire, and just as the wolf was coming down the chimney he took off the cover and in fell the wolf.

He was never troubled by a wolf again. ❋

31

CLEVER OLD GANDER

A PANCHATANTRA TALE; RETOLD BY NARINDAR UBEROI KELLY

There was a big fig tree that stood in the middle of the forest and had many broad branches. In this tree lived a flock of wild geese. In time, there grew a vicious creeping vine underneath it. Noticing it, the Old Gander said, 'This vine that is beginning its climb up our fig tree bodes ill. Someone could easily climb up it one day and kill us. We should cut it down while it is still thin and easily cut.' But the geese disliked his advice and decided to do nothing. The vine eventually wound around and all the way up the trunk of the fig tree.

One day, when the geese were away searching for food, a hunter came by, easily climbed up with the help of the vine, laid a trap and went home for the night.

When the geese returned, they all got caught in the net.

'Oh dear,' the Old Gander thought, 'the very disaster I predicted has come true and we are all caught and in danger of dying.'

The geese, realizing their mistake, begged him to let bygones be bygones. 'Please, Sir, help us,' they begged him. 'What should we do now?'

The Old Gander replied, 'If you are really ready to take my advice, play dead when the villainous hunter returns. Thinking us dead, he will simply throw each of us to the ground and not bind us. When the last one is on the ground, and he is still up in the tree, we must all rise up together and fly away as fast as we can.'

Early the next morning the hunter arrived and saw the 'dead' flock of geese and threw them down one by one. The geese followed the advice of the clever Old Gander, waited for the last goose to hit the ground, and then flew away together. ❋

– Read more such ancient Indian stories in The Panchatantra: Teaching Tales of Old India *by Narindar Uberoi Kelly, published by Hachette India.*

32

THE MILKMAID AND HER PAIL OF MILK

AN AESOP'S FABLE; RETOLD BY J.H. STICKNEY

Dolly the Milkmaid was a good girl and careful in her work, so her mistress gave her a pail of new milk for herself.

With the pail upon her head, Dolly tripped gaily along on her way to the town, where she was going to sell her milk.

'For this milk,' said Dolly, 'I shall get a shilling, and with it I will buy twenty of the eggs laid by our neighbour's fine fowls. The mistress will surely lend me a hen, and, allowing for all mishaps, I shall raise a good dozen of chicks. They will be well grown before the next fair-time comes around, and it is then that chickens bring the highest price. I shall be able to sell mine for a guinea.

'Then I shall buy that jacket that I saw in the village the other day, and a hat and ribbons, too. And when I go to the fair, how smart I shall be!

'Robin will be there, and will come up and offer to be friends again. But I won't make up too easily; and when he wants me for a partner in the dance, I shall just toss up my head and –'

Here Dolly gave her head the least bit of a toss, when down came the pail, and all the milk was spilled upon the ground.

Poor Dolly! It was her goodbye to eggs, chickens, jacket, hat, ribbons and all.

Don't count your chickens before they are hatched! ❋

33

THE COSY LION

FRANCES HODGSON BURNETT

When I got to the Cave, the Lion was sitting outside his door and he was crying. He was one of these nasty-tempered, discontented Lions who are always thinking themselves injured; large round tears were rolling down his nose and he was sniffling. But I must say he was handsome. He was big and smooth and had the most splendid mane and tail I ever saw.

He would have been like a King if he had had a nicer expression. But there he sat sniffling.

'I'm so lonely,' he said. 'Nobody calls. Nobody pays me any attention. And I came here for the Society. No one is fonder of Society than I am.'

I sat down on a flowering branch near him and shouted at him, 'What's the use of Society when you eat it up?' I said.

He jumped up and lashed his tail and growled, but at first he could not see me.

'What's it for *but* to be eaten up?' he roared. 'First I want it to entertain me and then I want it for dessert. Where are you? Who are you?'

'I'm Queen Crosspatch – Queen Silverbell as was,' I said. 'I suppose you have heard of *me*?'

'I've heard nothing good,' he growled. 'A good chewing is what *you* want!'

He *had* heard something about me, but not enough. The truth was he didn't really believe in Fairies – which was what brought him into trouble.

By this time he had seen me and he was ignorant enough to think that he could catch me, so he laid down flat in the thick, green grass and stretched his big paws out and rested his nose on them, thinking I would be taken in and imagine he was going to sleep. I burst out laughing at him, and swung to and fro on my flowery branch.

'Do you want to eat me?' I said. 'You'd need two or three quarts of me with sugar and cream – like strawberries.'

That made him so angry that he sprang roaring at my tree and snapped and shook it and tore it with his claws. But I flew up into the air and buzzed all about him and he got furious – just furious. He jumped up in the air and lashed his tail and *thrashed* his tail and CRASHED his tail, and he turned round and round and tore up the grass.

'Don't be a silly,' I said. 'It's a nice big tufty sort of tail and you will only wear it out.'

So then he opened his mouth and roared and roared. And what do you suppose *I* did? I flew right into his mouth. First I flew into his throat and buzzed about like a bee and made him cough and cough and cough – but he couldn't cough me up. He coughed and he houghed and he woughed. He tried to catch me with his tongue and he tried to catch me with his teeth, but I simply made myself tinier and tinier and got between two big fierce white double ones, and took one of my Fairy Workers' hammers out of my pocket and hammered and hammered and hammered until he began to have such a jumping toothache that he ran leaping and roaring down the Huge Green Hill and leaping and roaring down the village street to the dentist's to get some toothache drops.

You can just imagine how all the people rushed into their houses, and how the mothers screamed and clutched their children and hid under beds and tables and in coalbins, and how the fathers fumbled about for guns. As for the dentist, he locked his door and bolted it and barred it, and when he found *his* gun he poked it out of the window and fired it off as fast as ever he could until he had fired fifty times, only he was too frightened to hit anything. But the village street was so full of flashes and smoke and bullets that Mr Lion turned with ten big roars and galloped down the street, with guns fired out of every window where the family could afford to keep a gun.

When he got to his home in the Huge Green Hill, he just laid down and cried aloud and screamed and kicked his hind legs until he scratched a hole in the floor of his cave.

'Just because I'm a Lion,' he sobbed, 'just because I'm a poor, sensitive, helpless, orphan Lion nobody has one particle of manners. They won't even sell me a bottle of toothache drops. And I wasn't going to touch that dentist – until he had cured me and wrapped up the bottle nicely in paper. Not a touch was I going to touch him until he had done that.'

He opened his mouth so wide to roar with grief that I flew out of it. I had meant to give him a lesson and I'd given him one. When I flew out of his mouth, of course his beautiful double teeth stopped aching. It was such a relief to him that it made quite a change in his nature and he sat up and began to smile. It was a slow smile which spread into a grin even while the teardrops hung on his whiskers. ❋

– Excerpted from *The Cosy Lion: As Told by Queen Crosspatch.*

34

THE PARADISE OF CHILDREN

NATHANIEL HAWTHORNE

Long, long ago, there was a child named Epimetheus, and another child was sent by the gods to be his playfellow. Her name was Pandora.

The first thing that Pandora saw when she entered the cottage where Epimetheus lived was a great box. And the first question she put to him was this, 'Epimetheus, what have you in that box?'

'My dear little Pandora,' answered Epimetheus, 'I do not myself know what it contains.'

The world nowadays is a very different sort of place from what it was then. There was no danger or trouble of any kind, and no clothes to be mended, and there was plenty to eat and drink. No labour had to be done, no tasks studied, all was sport and dancing, or talking, or carolling like birds, or laughing merrily all day long.

But Pandora was not altogether happy about the box. 'Where can it have come from?' she continually asked herself, 'and what on earth can be inside it?' At last she spoke to Epimetheus. 'At least,' she said, 'you can tell me how it came here.'

'It was left at the door,' Epimetheus replied, 'by a person who was dressed in an odd cloak and had on a cap that seemed to be made partly of feathers so that it looked as if it had wings.'

'What sort of a staff had he?' asked Pandora.

'Oh,' cried Epimetheus, 'It was like two serpents twisting around a stick.'

'I know him,' said Pandora thoughtfully. 'It was Mercury, and he brought me here as well. Most probably it contains pretty dresses for me to wear, or toys for us both, or something nice for us to eat.'

'Perhaps so,' answered Epimetheus, turning away, 'but we have neither of us any right to lift the lid.'

One day not long after that Epimetheus went to gather figs and grapes. He was tired of hearing about the box. And as soon as he was gone, Pandora kneeled on the floor and looked intently at the box. Her curiosity grew so great that at last she touched the box.

First, she tried to lift it. It was heavy, much too heavy. She raised one end of the box and then let it fall with a pretty loud thump. A moment afterward she thought that she heard something stir inside the box. Suddenly her eyes fell on a curious knot of gold that tied it.

It was a very intricate knot, but Pandora gave the cord a kind of twist and it unwound itself, as if by magic. And then the thought came into her naughty little heart that, since she would be suspected of looking into the box, she might as well do so.

As Pandora raised the lid of the box the cottage was suddenly darkened, for a black cloud had swept quite over the sun and seemed to have buried it alive. There had, for a little while past, been a low growling and grumbling, which all at once broke into a heavy peal of thunder. But Pandora lifted the lid and looked inside. It seemed as if a sudden swarm of winged creatures brushed past her, taking flight out of the box while, at the same time, she heard the voice of Epimetheus in the doorway exclaiming in pain, 'Oh, I am stung! I am stung! Naughty Pandora, why have you opened this wicked box?'

Pandora let the lid fall and looked up. The thundercloud had so darkened the room that she could not clearly see what was in it. But she heard a disagreeable buzzing, as if a great many huge flies or giant bees were darting about. And then she saw a crowd of ugly little shapes, looking very spiteful, and having bats' wings and terribly long stings in their tails. It was one of these that had stung Epimetheus. Pandora herself began to cry. An odious little monster had settled on her forehead and would have stung her if Epimetheus had not brushed it away.

Now, if you wish to know what these ugly things were, I must tell you that they were the whole family of earthly Troubles. There were a great many species of Cares. There were more than a hundred and fifty Sorrows. There were Diseases in a vast number of strange and painful shapes. There were more kinds of Naughtiness than it would be of any use to talk about. In short, everything that has since afflicted the souls and bodies of mankind had been shut up in the mysterious box in order that the happy children of the world might never be harmed by them.

Pandora flung open the windows and doors to try and get rid of them and, sure enough, away flew the winged Troubles and so pestered and tormented the people everywhere about that none of them so much as smiled for many days afterward.

Meanwhile, Epimetheus sat down sullenly in a corner with his back to Pandora. She was crying as if her heart would break.

Suddenly there was a gentle little tap on the inside of the lid.

'What can that be?' cried Pandora.

Again the tap! It sounded like the tiny knuckles of a fairy's hand.

'Who are you,' asked Pandora, 'inside of this dreadful box?'

A sweet little voice said, 'Lift the lid and you shall see.'

'No, no,' answered Pandora, 'I have had enough of lifting the lid.'

'Ah,' said the sweet little voice again, 'you had much better let me out.'

Indeed, there was a kind of cheerful witchery in the tone that made it almost impossible to refuse anything that this little voice asked. Pandora's heart had grown lighter at every word that came from the box. Epimetheus, too, had left his corner and seemed to be in better spirits.

So the two children lifted the lid. Out flew a sunny and smiling little personage and hovered about the room, throwing light wherever she went. Have you ever made the sunshine dance into dark corners by reflecting it from a bit of looking glass? Well, so appeared the winged cheerfulness of this fairylike stranger amid the gloom of the cottage. She flew to Epimetheus and laid the least touch of her finger on the inflamed spot where the Trouble had stung him and the pain was gone. Then she kissed Pandora on the forehead and her hurt was cured likewise.

'Who are you, beautiful creature?' asked Pandora.

'I am to be called Hope,' explained the sunshiny figure, 'and I was packed by the gods into the box to make amends for the swarm of ugly Troubles. Never fear! We shall do pretty well in spite of them.'

So Pandora and Epimetheus found Hope, and so has everybody else who has trusted her since that day. The Troubles are still flying around the world, but we have that lovely and lightsome fairy, Hope, to cure their stings and make the world new for us. ❋

– *Abridged from the original story.*

35

THE THREE BILLY GOATS GRUFF

A NORWEGIAN FAIRY TALE; RETOLD BY GUDRUN THORNE-THOMSEN

Once on a time there were three Billy Goats, who were to go up to the hillside to make themselves fat, and the family name of the goats was 'Gruff.'

On the way up was a bridge, over a river which they had to cross, and under the bridge lived a great ugly Troll with eyes as big as saucers and a nose as long as a poker.

First of all came the youngest Billy Goat Gruff to cross the bridge. 'Trip, trap; trip, trap!' went the bridge.

'*Who's that tripping over my bridge?*' roared the Troll.

'Oh, it is only I, the tiniest Billy Goat Gruff, and I'm going up to the hillside to make myself fat,' said the Billy Goat, with such a small voice.

'Now, I'm coming to gobble you up,' said the Troll.

'Oh, no! Pray do not take me – I'm too little, that I am,' said the Billy Goat. 'Wait a bit till the second Billy Goat Gruff comes, he's much bigger.'

'Well! Be off with you,' said the Troll.

A little while after came the second Billy Goat Gruff across the bridge.

'Trip, trap! trip, trap! trip, trap!' went the bridge.

'*Who is that tripping over my bridge?*' roared the Troll.

'Oh, it's the second Billy Goat Gruff, and I'm going up to the hillside to make myself fat,' said the Billy Goat. Nor had he such a small voice, either.

'Now, I'm coming to gobble you up!' said the Troll.

'Oh, no! Don't take me, wait a little till the big Billy Goat comes – he's much bigger.'

'Very well! Be off with you,' said the Troll.

But just then up came the big Billy Goat Gruff.

'Trip, trap! trip, trap! trip, trap!' went the bridge, for the Billy Goat was so heavy that the bridge creaked and groaned under him.

'*Who's that tramping on my bridge?*' roared the Troll.

'It's I – the big Billy Goat Gruff,' said the Billy Goat, and he had a big hoarse voice.

'Now, I'm coming to gobble you up!' roared the Troll.

'Welcome! I have two spears so stout,
With them I'll thrust your eyeballs out;
I have besides two great big stones,
With them I'll crush you body and bones!'

That was what the big Billy Goat said; so he flew at the Troll, and thrust him with his horns, and crushed him to bits, body and bones, and tossed him out into the river, and after that he went up to the hillside.

There the Billy Goats got so fat that they were scarcely able to walk home again, and if they haven't grown thinner, why, they're still fat; and so –

'Snip, snap, stout.
This tale's told out.'

36

LITTLE RED RIDING HOOD

A EUROPEAN FAIRY TALE; RETOLD BY WATTY PIPER

There was once a sweet little maid who lived with her father and mother in a pretty little cottage at the edge of the village. At the further end of the wood was another pretty cottage and in it lived her grandmother.

Everybody loved this little girl. Her grandmother perhaps loved her most of all and gave her a great many pretty things. Once she gave her a red cloak with a hood which she always wore, so people called her Little Red Riding Hood.

One morning Little Red Riding Hood's mother said, 'Put on your things and go to see your grandmother. She has been ill; take along this basket for her. I have put in it eggs, butter and cake, and other dainties.'

It was a bright and sunny morning. Red Riding Hood was so happy that at first she wanted to dance through the wood. All around her grew pretty wildflowers which she loved so well and she stopped to pick a bunch for her grandmother.

Little Red Riding Hood wandered from her path and was stooping to pick a flower when from behind her a gruff voice said, 'Good morning, Little Red Riding Hood.' Little Red Riding Hood turned around and saw a great big wolf, but Little Red Riding Hood did not know what a wicked beast the wolf was, so she was not afraid.

'What have you in that basket, Little Red Riding Hood?'

'Eggs and butter and cake, Mr Wolf.'

'Where are you going with them, Little Red Riding Hood?'

'I am going to my grandmother, who is ill, Mr Wolf.'

'Where does your grandmother live, Little Red Riding Hood?'

'Along that path, past the wild rose bushes, then through the gate at the end of the wood, Mr Wolf.'

Then Mr Wolf again said 'Good morning' and set off, and Little Red Riding Hood again went in search of wild flowers.

At last the wolf reached the porch covered with flowers and knocked at the door of the cottage.

'Who is there?' called the grandmother.

'Little Red Riding Hood,' said the wicked wolf.

'Press the latch, open the door and walk in,' said the grandmother.

The wolf pressed the latch and walked in where the grandmother lay in bed. He made one jump at her, but she jumped out of bed into a closet. Then the wolf put on the cap which she had dropped and crept under the bedclothes.

In a short while Little Red Riding Hood knocked at the door, and walked in, saying, 'Good morning, Grandmother, I have brought you eggs, butter and cake, and here is a bunch of flowers I gathered in the wood.' As she came nearer the bed she said, 'What big ears you have, Grandmother.'

'All the better to hear you with, my dear.'

'What big eyes you have, Grandmother.'

'All the better to see you with, my dear.'

'But, Grandmother, what a big nose you have.'

'All the better to smell with, my dear.'

'But, Grandmother, what a big mouth you have.'

'All the better to eat you up with, my dear,' he said as he sprang at Little Red Riding Hood.

Just at that moment Little Red Riding Hood's father was passing the cottage and heard her scream. He rushed in and with his axe chopped off Mr Wolf's head.

Everybody was happy that Little Red Riding Hood had escaped the wolf. Then Little Red Riding Hood's father carried her home and they lived happily ever after.

37

THE THREE WISHES

A SWEDISH FOLKTALE; RETOLD BY ELEANOR L. SKINNER & ADA M. SKINNER

Once upon a time in the heart of a forest lived a woodcutter and his wife. They were very poor indeed. Their little cabin, built of rough-hewn logs, had only one room, which was very scantily and poorly furnished. One day the woodcutter said to his wife, 'How miserable we are! We work all day, and we have barely enough food to keep life in our bodies! Surely there are few who work as hard as we do and have so little!'

The housewife replied, 'Yes, indeed, we are very miserable.'

'Well, I'm off for another day's work,' sighed the husband. 'My lot is too hard.'

He picked up his axe and made his way to the place in the forest where he was to perform his task. Suddenly, a dear little fairy whose face was wreathed in smiles danced into the path and stood before him.

'I am the wishing fairy,' she began. 'I heard what you said about your work and your life, and my heart aches for you. Now, because I am a fairy, it is in my power to grant you three wishes. Ask for any three things you desire and your wishes shall be granted.'

The fairy disappeared in the twinkling of an eye, and the woodcutter was left standing alone in the forest. Was he dreaming? He couldn't believe his own senses! He thought of a thousand wishes all in an instant. He would go home and talk the matter over with his wife. He turned in his path and retraced his steps to the cabin.

'Are you ill?' demanded his wife, who came to the door.

'Oh, no, indeed, I am not ill; I am very, very happy!' he burst forth. 'I met a fairy in the forest. She told me that she was very, very sorry for me, and that she would help me by granting three wishes. Think of it! Any three wishes in the world will be granted by the charming fairy.'

'Wonderful!' said the housewife.

'Oh, how happy the very thought of it makes me! Come, let us sit down and talk the matter over; for I assure you it is not easy to come to a decision. I am indeed, very, very happy.'

They drew up their chairs to the little table and sat down.

'I am *so* hungry,' began the woodcutter. 'Let us have dinner, and then, while we are eating, we can talk about our wishes and see which three are nearest our hearts' desires.'

They began their humble meal immediately, and the husband continued, 'Of course one of our wishes must be great riches. What do you say?'

'Oh, yes, indeed,' said his wife. 'I should love a beautiful house to live in, also carriages and fine clothes, and servants and –'

'Oh, for that matter,' said the husband, 'we could wish for an empire.'

'Or rich jewels, such as great numbers of pearls and diamonds! What a wish that would be,' said the wife, whose face was all aglow.

'I have it,' burst forth the woodman, 'let us wish for a fine large family, five sons and five daughters, what say you to that?'

'Oh!' returned his wife, 'I think I prefer six sons and four daughters.'

So they continued weighing one wish with another until they seemed almost in despair about coming to a decision regarding which three wishes would be the wisest and best. They finally stopped talking and ate their simple food in silence. The woodcutter did not seem to relish his soup and dry bread.

'Oh,' he cried out suddenly, 'how I wish I had some nice savoury sausage for dinner!' No sooner had the words fallen from his lips than a large dish of fine sausages appeared on the table. What a surprise! The two were so astonished that for a few moments they could not speak.

Then the wife said impatiently, 'What do you mean by making such a foolish wish? Do you not see that this dish of sausage means that one wish has been granted and that there are but two left? How could you make such a stupid, stupid wish?'

'Well,' replied the husband, 'to be sure I have been foolish. I really did not think what I was saying. However, we may still wish for great riches and an empire.'

'Humph!' grumbled the wife. 'We may wish for riches and an empire, but what about a fine large family? You have certainly been foolish in wishing for that horrid sausage. I suppose, however, you prefer sausage to a fine family;' and she burst out into tears of lamentation, crying, 'How could you? How could you be so foolish? Oh, dear! Oh, dear! How very foolish and stupid you have been.'

Finally her husband lost all patience and cried out, 'I'm tired of your grumbling! I wish the sausage were on the end of your nose!'

In an instant the sausage was fastened to the end of the poor woman's nose. How comical she did look! The husband and wife were so astonished that they could not speak. The poor woman again burst into tears.

'Oh!' she cried. 'How could you? How could you? First, you wished for sausage, and second, you wished that the sausage were fastened to my poor nose. It is terrible. It is cruel. Two wishes have been granted. There remains but one! Oh, dear, dear!'

The husband, who now saw what a dreadful mistake he had made, said meekly,

'We may still wish for great riches.'

'Riches indeed!' snapped his wife. 'Here I am with this great sausage fastened to the end of my nose. What good would riches do me? How ridiculous I am. It is all your fault. I was so happy at the thought of great riches, beautiful jewels, and a fine family, and now I am sad and miserable.' She continued to weep so pitifully that her husband's heart was touched.

'I wish with all my heart that the sausage were not on your nose,' he said. In an instant the sausage disappeared. There the two sat lamenting; but as the three wishes had been granted there is nothing further to be said. ❋

38

HOW BHEEMA GOT STRONG – AND STRONGER!

UPENDRAKISHORE RAY CHOWDHURY; TRANSLATED BY SWAPNA DUTTA

Long, long ago there was a city named Hastinapur close to the place we now know as Delhi. Vichitraveerya, the king of Hastinapur, had two sons named Dhritarashtra and Pandu. Dhritarashtra was the elder son, but he was blind.

As the kingdom could not be ruled by a blind king, Pandu, the younger brother, was crowned instead. Dhritarashtra was greatly upset, but perhaps he might have borne it better had his son been the eldest among the next generation of princes and in that case, his son would inherit the throne after Pandu. But unfortunately for him, Pandu was the first to have a son.

When the sons of Dhritarashtra were old enough to realize that the kingdom could never be rightfully theirs, they grew to hate the Pandavas, as the sons of Pandu were called. Dhritarashtra's sons were called the Kauravas, descendants of the Kuru clan.

Duryodhana was the eldest son of Dhritarashtra, followed by Dushasana and ninety-eight others. Dhritarashtra also had a daughter named Dushala. Pandu had five sons. The eldest was Yudhishthira, followed by Bhima and Arjuna. They were the sons of his first queen, Kunti. The twins — Nakula and Sahadeva — were the sons of Madri, his second queen.

The brothers were devoted to each other although they had different mothers. The Pandavas had been born with the special blessings of different gods. The patron-god of Yudhishthira was Dharma; Bhima's was Pavana and Arjuna's was Indra. Nakula and Sahadeva had the twin-gods, the Ashwini Kumars, as their patrons. The patron gods were believed to take special care of the boys.

Alas! The Pandavas were not fated to remain happy for long. They were very young when Pandu died and Madri, unable to bear the sorrow, also died with him. The five little brothers had no one save Kunti to care for them. They continued to remain in the palace with Dhritarashtra's sons and grew up together, studying from the same teachers and playing the same games.

However, the sons of Dhritarashtra were no match for Bhima. Whenever they tried to play he would knock their heads together. The Kauravas were a team of hundred brothers while the Pandavas were just five. But they failed miserably when it came to tackling Bhima. If they played in the water, Bhima grabbed ten of them and dived so deep that they were left gasping. If they climbed a tree to get fruits, he kicked the tree so hard that both the fruits and the Kauravas fell down together.

So they hated Bhima, especially Duryodhana, who felt that he would be a great danger to them if allowed to grow up, and was determined to kill him at the first opportunity. With Bhima out of the way, they could simply imprison the others. So wicked Duryodhana made a plan and said, 'Let us all go for a dip in the Ganga.'

The Pandavas, not knowing his secret plan, thought it would be great fun and agreed enthusiastically.

The venue selected was Pramankoti, a house by the river. The boys were thrilled to see the elaborate meal awaiting them. They grabbed the sweets and shared them delightedly. It was exactly the chance Duryodhana had been waiting for. Adding poison to a handful of sweets, he fed them to Bhima who ate them without suspecting anything.

Everyone jumped into the river, swimming and splashing until they were exhausted and got out to change. But Bhima, severely poisoned, lay unconscious on the riverbank. Duryodhana tied up his hands and feet with creepers and threw him into the river.

Bhima sank deep. But when God decides to protect someone not even a thousand enemies can kill him! Had Bhima fallen anywhere else, he would have certainly died. But the spot where Duryodhana had pushed him led directly to Patala, the kingdom of Vasuki, the king of snakes.

Bhima fell plump on a heap of snakes, squashing many to death. The rest fell on Bhima and bit him everywhere. But their bite acted as an antidote to the poison and Bhima sat up. Tearing off the creepers, he swept off the snakes, killing many of them. The others rushed to Vasuki crying, 'Please come, Maharaj, and save us from this dangerous human being.'

An astonished Vasuki came to check what was wrong and cried, 'Why, it's Bhima! You are related to me, my dear.' Vasuki embraced him and gave him many precious gems as gifts.

Vasuki's kingdom had a huge store of nectar — the elixir of life. The snakes, realizing that he was an honoured guest, took him there, saying, 'Drink as much as you like.'

Bhima soon gulped down a tubful and then did not stop until he had finished eight huge tubs. After that, he slept for eight full days.

When Yudhishthira did not see Bhima on his way back he thought that Bhima must have returned home earlier. After reaching home, he asked Kunti, 'Mother, Bhima left long before we did, but he isn't here. Have you sent him on an errand?'

'No, dear, I haven't seen him after you left,' cried Kunti in alarm. 'That's worrying! Please look for him.'

Yudhishthira fetched his uncle Vidura, a wise and saintly man, and Kunti told him what had happened. 'What if Duryodhana has killed my Bhima?' she cried, 'He detests him so much!'

'Hush!' said Vidura, 'You'll make matters worse if Duryodhana hears you. Don't panic about Bhima. Wise Vyasadeva told me that all your sons will live long and his words always come to pass. I am sure Bhima will return home safe.' But despite his words, Kunti and the four brothers remained worried.

Bhima, waking up after his long sleep, felt stronger than ten thousand elephants. The snakes dressed him up in white, put a white garland round his neck, fed him sweet *payasam* and left him on the riverbank. When he returned home, everyone was overjoyed to see him. On hearing about his adventures, Yudhishthira warned him not to mention them to anyone else. From then on, the Pandavas tried to be more careful, fully convinced that Dhritarashtra, Duryodhana and his uncle Shakuni hated them bitterly. ❋

– *Read the rest of the story in the* Mahabharata for Young Readers *by Upendrakishore Ray Chowdhury, translated by Swapna Dutta.*

39

ANDROCLES AND THE LION

AN AESOP'S FABLE; RETOLD BY JOSEPH JACOBS

A slave named Androcles once escaped from his master and fled to the forest. As he was wandering about there he came upon a Lion lying down, moaning and groaning.

At first he turned to flee, but finding that the Lion did not chase him, he turned back and went up to him.

As he came near, the Lion put out his paw, which was all swollen and bleeding, and Androcles found that a huge thorn had got into it, and was causing all the pain. He pulled out the thorn and bound up the paw of the Lion, who was soon able to rise and lick the hand of Androcles like a dog.

Then the Lion took Androcles to his cave, and every day used to bring him meat to eat. But shortly afterwards both Androcles and the Lion were captured, and the slave was sentenced to be thrown to the Lion, after the latter had been kept without food for several days.

The Emperor and all his Court came to see the spectacle, and Androcles was led out into the middle of the arena. Soon the Lion was let loose from his den, and rushed bounding and roaring towards his victim. But as soon as he came near Androcles he recognized his friend, and fawned upon him, and licked his hands like a friendly dog.

The Emperor, surprised at this, summoned Androcles to him, who told him the whole story. Whereupon the slave was pardoned and freed, and the Lion let loose in his forest. ❋

40

MR TWIDDLE'S COLD

ENID BLYTON

'Don't you feel well, Twiddle?' asked Mrs Twiddle one morning. 'You didn't want your breakfast, and you keep sniffing.'

'Well – perhaps I don't feel very well,' said Twiddle, frowning. 'My throat's a bit sore. I'd better not go out and chop all the wood, had I?'

'Well, I don't know about that,' said Mrs Twiddle. 'It's a nice sunny day and it might do you good to get out and chop the wood. You might have an appetite for your lunch then.'

Twiddle immediately felt sure that his throat was very bad, and he gave a little cough. 'I believe I'm going to have a cough, too,' he said. 'I really do not feel well. I can't chop wood this morning.'

"Well, you can turn out all the drawers in that big cupboard over there, then,' said Mrs Twiddle. 'You've been saying for months that you never have time to – now you've got all the morning, if you don't go out and chop the wood.'

'I don't think I feel well enough to turn out drawers either,' said Twiddle, and gave another loud sniff. 'Dear me – where's my hanky? I'm afraid I've got a heavy cold coming on. I'd better go and keep warm by the fire, my love.'

He gave such a deep, hollow cough that Mrs Twiddle was quite startled. She looked at him. Now – was he pretending, or was he not? He did look a little pale. Perhaps he was sickening for something.

'I'll just call in at the doctor's when I'm out and ask him to come along and see you,' she said. 'Now, if he comes, please be polite, and offer him a cup of tea and a piece of my cake on this cold day.'

'The doctor's away,' said Twiddle, settling himself into his chair. 'Oh, get off my knee, cat! Why does this cat always jump on my knee when I sit down?'

'Let the cat be,' said Mrs Twiddle. 'It's lazy like you and likes a warm sit-down when it can get it. I know the doctor's away, but there's another one come to take his place till he comes back. And very, very clever he is, too, so I've heard tell. Very up-to-date, with plenty of new ideas and new ways. Now, don't you fall fast asleep, Twiddle – you keep awake and let him in when he knocks.'

'All right, all right,' said Twiddle, opening his newspaper. 'Bless me, here's that cat again. Can't you take her out with you, dear?'

'Don't be silly, Twiddle,' said Mrs Twiddle, bustling about. 'Now, I'll leave the kettle on for you to make tea when the doctor comes – and the biscuits on a plate – and the cake's there in its tin. Now, don't forget.'

'Anyone would think I was giving a tea-party,' grumbled Twiddle, and began to read the paper. Soon he heard Mrs Twiddle calling goodbye, and then the front door slammed. Good. Now he would have a bit of peace! He shut his eyes and in half a minute he was sleeping soundly. The cat got back on his knee and purred contentedly.

At about eleven o'clock there came a knock at the front door – *rat-tat-tat*! Twiddle woke up and the cat leaped off his knee in fright. *Rat-tat-tat*! The knocking came again.

'It's the doctor,' said Twiddle, and got up in a hurry. 'Now, I mustn't forget to offer him something to eat and drink.'

He went to the front door and opened it, wondering what sort of fellow the new doctor was. A very tall man stood there, with a thick beard, carrying a small black bag in his hand.

'Come in, come in,' said Twiddle. 'I'm sorry to call you out on a day like this – so cold and miserable. But I've got the kettle on for a cup of tea! Come along in.'

The man looked pleased. He followed Twiddle in and watched him turn up the gas under the kettle in the kitchen. Then he looked at the biscuits with pleasure.

'Sit down,' said Twiddle. 'I won't be long making the tea. You do like tea, don't you?'

'Well, it'll be nice to have a warm drink,' said his visitor, and went to sit down by the fire. Twiddle made some tea and then brought in the big pot. He cut some of Mrs Twiddle's cherry cake and put that on a plate too.

The visitor ate a large slice and took some biscuits, too. 'A very good cake,' he said. 'Well now – I suppose we'd better get to work. Would you stand up please?'

Twiddle stood up. The man undid his bag and Twiddle looked inside. There were scissors of all sizes there, and a knife, besides several other things.

'Would you stretch out your arms, Mr Twiddle?' said the man, and took a tape measure from his bag. 'First the right – thank you. Now the left. Thank you.'

'Aha – new ways and methods!' said Twiddle, jokingly. 'Measuring instead of medicine, I suppose? I quite thought you'd want to see my throat!'

'Well – I'll have to measure that, too,' said the man, looking rather puzzled. 'And now will you please bend your elbow, sir? I must just run my measure from shoulder to elbow and elbow to wrist.'

Mr Twiddle began to fumble for his handkerchief, for he felt a sneeze coming. It came – and it was a most enormous one: '*A-whoooosh-ooo*!'

'Sorry,' said Twiddle. 'I really have got a nasty cold.'

'So your wife told me when she asked me to call this morning,' said his visitor, writing something down in a notebook. 'I was sorry to hear it.'

'Don't you take the temperatures of the people you call on?' asked Twiddle, who loved his being taken.

The man looked at him in surprise, decided it was a joke, and laughed loudly.

'Ha, ha! Not usually, sir. It would be rather a waste of time, wouldn't it?'

Twiddle began to feel that there was something rather peculiar about this doctor. Why should taking a temperature be a waste of time? Usually it was the first thing a doctor did when he came to see a patient.

'Well, I should have thought it was a waste of time measuring my arms,' he said. 'But still I suppose it's something new and up-to-date.'

'Er – well – no, not exactly,' said the man, who was now beginning to look a little alarmed himself. He did a little more measuring, and Twiddle began to feel tired of it. He sat down in the chair.

'Don't you think I ought to go to bed?' he asked. 'And aren't you going to look at my tongue?' He stuck it out and the man backed away at once.

'Er – well – it looks quite a good tongue,' he said. 'Quite. But I don't usually look at tongues – unless you want me to measure yours, do you? Ha, ha, ha!'

Twiddle began to feel that he didn't like this doctor at all. He might be very modern and up-to-date with a lot of new ways – but he was silly, really silly. Didn't he know that doctors always looked at tongues?

'Er – I suppose it wouldn't be at all good for me to go out and chop wood the morning, would it?' He asked, hoping that the man would say no, certainly he must not go out and chop wood.

'Well, sir - I should ask your wife about that,' said the man, shutting the bag with a snap and turning to go. 'She'd know. If I may say so, you certainly don't seem well to me. You seem – well – a bit peculiar. Strange, you know. Not at all yourself!'

Twiddle gave such a loud snort that the man fled into the hall in fright and shot out of the front door. *Slam*! He was gone!

'Well, give me my old doctor any day, said Twiddle in disgust. 'That one's an idiot. *A-whoooosh-oo*!'

He sat down, and the cat jumped on his knee. He was just snoozing when he heard the front door open and shut. Ah, that was Mrs Twiddle. She came bustling into the room.

'Well, dear, how do you feel? You look better.'

'I don't,' said Twiddle, gloomily. 'That doctor came. He wouldn't even look at my tongue.'

'You've been dreaming,' said M, Twiddle. 'You know the doctor hasn't been. He's not coming till half past twelve.'

'He has been – black bag and all,' said Twiddle, crossly. 'He drank some tea, and ate some of your cake and said it was good too.'

Mrs Twiddle looked at the empty teacups and the cut cake in surprise. '*Did* he come?' she said. 'Well, well – he said he couldn't arrive till last thing this morning. What did he say about your cold?'

'Nothing. I told you, he wouldn't even look at my tongue,' said Twiddle gloomily. 'He didn't look at my throat either – he just measured it very carefully and wrote down something about it in his notebook, but he didn't tell me what it was. And he didn't prescribe me any medicine either. What a doctor! He kept on measuring me – that's about all he did. Huh! New-fangled, up-to-date ways indeed. Give me old Doctor Brown. At least he knows about throats and tongues and medicines.'

'Measuring you!' said Mrs Twiddle, puzzled. 'Twiddle, you've been asleep. Oh, yes you have, so don't deny it. Asleep and dreaming! Though why you want to go and dirty two cups and saucers when you got your tea, I don't know.'

"I was not asleep and dreaming,' said Twiddle, offended. 'I tell you that doctor took a tape measure and measured me from head to foot. He must have been quite mad.'

Mrs Twiddle sat down in a chair very suddenly and she began to laugh. She laughed till she almost fell off her chair and the tears ran down her cheeks. Twiddle stared at her in astonishment and frowned.

"What's so funny about this?' he cried, rapping the table so hard that the cat leaped out of the window.

'Sending me a doctor like that! I won't see him again, I tell you that!'

'Twiddle! Oh, Twiddle – you really will be the death of me,' gasped Mr Twiddle. 'Have you forgotten that you ordered a new suit?'

'No, of course not. That's nothing to do with it,' growled Twiddle.

'But it is,' said Mrs Twiddle, wiping away the tears of laughter. 'I went to the tailor's this morning, and asked him to send a man to measure you for your new suit as you weren't very well and couldn't come to the shop. They said they'd send a man as soon as they could.'

'Good gracious! Was that man who came the tailor's man?' said Twiddle. 'I thought he was the doctor. Yes – he had scissors and things in his bag and he kept on and on measuring me. And I kept asking him to look at my tongue and take my temperature! Oh, my dear – he must have thought *I* was mad!'

'He probably did,' said Mrs Twiddle and she began to laugh again, quite helplessly. Twiddle got up in disgust. He didn't like being laughed at. 'If you don't stop laughing I'll go out and leave you here alone,' he said. But Mrs Twiddle didn't hear him, she was laughing too much. So, when the real doctor came at half past twelve, Twiddle was nowhere to be seen.

'Oh, Doctor – do come in,' said Mrs Twiddle. 'Now where has Twiddle disappeared to? Twiddle, Twiddle?'

'I heard someone chopping wood in your woodshed, and whistling loudly,' said the doctor. 'Would that be your husband? It didn't sound as if there was much the matter with him, Mrs Twiddle.'

'Er – well, no – I don't think there is, really,' said Mrs Twiddle. 'He's just suffered from an attack of muddle-headedness, but I've cured that now, Doctor. I think he must have forgotten that he thought he had a cold!"

Twiddle had forgotten! He had been so angry that he had gone out to chop wood, and now he was feeling happy and good-tempered again. Mrs Twiddle laughed to herself.

'Funny old Twiddle!' she said. 'I'll make him his favourite stew for lunch – he'll be so very hungry!'

She was quite right. He was! ❋

– *To enjoy many more amusing stories of the muddle-headed Mr Twiddle, read* Mr Twiddle Fetches Polly and Other Stories *(Star Reads Series 3), published by Hachette India.*

41

HOW THE MONKEY SAVED HIS TROOP

A JATAKA TALE; RETOLD BY ELLEN C. BABBITT

A mango tree grew on the bank of a great river. The fruit fell from some of the branches of this tree into the river, and from other branches it fell on the ground.

Every night a troop of Monkeys gathered the fruit that lay on the ground and climbed up into the tree to get the mangoes, which were like large, juicy peaches.

One day the king of the country stood on the bank of this same river, but many miles below where the mango tree grew. The king was watching the fishermen with their nets.

As they drew in their nets, the fishermen found not only fishes but a strange fruit. They went to the king with the strange fruit. 'What is this?' asked the king.

'We do not know, O King,' they said.

'Call the foresters,' said the king, 'They will know what it is.'

So they called the foresters and they said that it was a mango.

'Is it good to eat?' asked the king.

The foresters said it was very good. So the king cut the mango and giving some to the princes, he ate some of it himself. He liked it very much, and they all liked it.

Then the king said to the foresters, 'Where does the mango tree grow?'

The foresters told him that it grew on the river bank many miles farther up the river.

'Let us go and see the tree and get some mangoes,' said the king.

So he had many rafts joined together, and they went up the river until they came to the place where the mango tree grew.

The foresters said, 'O King, this is the mango tree.'

'We will land here,' said the king, and they did so. The king and all the men with him gathered the mangoes that lay on the ground under the tree. They all liked them so well that the king said, 'Let us stay here tonight, and gather more fruit in the morning.' So they had their supper under the trees, and then lay down to sleep.

When all was quiet, the Chief of the Monkeys came with his troop. All the mangoes on the ground had been eaten, so the monkeys jumped from branch to branch, picking and eating mangoes, and chattering to one another. They made so much noise that they woke up the king. He called his archers saying: 'Stand under the mango tree and shoot the Monkeys as they come down to the ground to get away. Then in the morning we shall have Monkey's flesh as well as mangoes to eat.'

The Monkeys saw the archers standing around with their arrows ready to shoot. Fearing death, the Monkeys ran to their Chief, saying: 'O Chief, the archers stand around the tree ready to shoot us! What shall we do?' They shook with fear.

The Chief said: 'Do not fear – I will save you. Stay where you are until I call you.'

The Monkeys were comforted, for he had always helped them whenever they had needed help.

Then the Chief of the Monkeys ran out on the branch of the mango tree that hung out over the river. The long branches of the tree across the river did not quite meet the branch he stood on. The Chief said to himself: 'If the Monkeys try to jump across from this tree to that, some of them will fall into the water and drown. I must save them, but how am I to do it? I know what I shall do. I shall make a bridge of my back.'

So the Chief reached across and took hold of the longest branch of the tree across the river. He called, 'Come, Monkeys; run out on this branch, step on my back and then run along the branch of the other tree.'

The Monkeys did as the Chief told them to do. They ran along the branch, stepped on his back, then ran along the branch of the other tree. They swung themselves down to the ground, and away they went back to their home.

The king saw all that was done by the Chief and his troop. 'That big Monkey,' said the king to the archers, 'saved the whole troop. I will see to it that he is taken care of for the rest of his life.'

And the king kept his promise. ❋

42

THE GOOSE AND THE GOLDEN EGG

AN AESOP'S FABLE; RETOLD BY JOSEPH JACOBS

There was once a Countryman who possessed the most wonderful Goose you can imagine, for every day when he visited the nest, the Goose had laid a beautiful, glittering, golden egg.

The Countryman took the eggs to market and soon began to get rich. But it was not long before he grew impatient with the Goose because she gave him only a single golden egg a day. He was not getting rich fast enough.

Then one day, after he had finished counting his money, the idea came to him that he could get all the golden eggs at once by killing the Goose and cutting it open. But when the deed was done, not a single golden egg did he find, and his precious Goose was dead.

Those who have plenty want more and so lose all they have.

43

THE FOOLISH FARMER AND THE KING

RETOLD BY W.H.D. ROUSE

Once there was a foolish Farmer, who had a son at court, serving the King. This Farmer was a very poor man, and all he had to plough his fields with was one pair of oxen. Two oxen was all he had, and one of them died.

The poor Farmer was in despair. One ox was not enough to draw the plough over the heavy land, and he had no money to buy another. So he sent a message to his son, that he was wanted at home.

When the son came, his father told him that one of his oxen was dead, and he had no money to buy another. So he begged his son to ask the King to give him an ox.

'No, no,' said his son, 'I am always asking the King for something. If you want an ox, you must ask him yourself.'

'I can't do it!' said the poor Farmer. 'You know what a muddlehead I am. If I go to ask the King for another ox, I shall end by giving him this one!'

'Well, what must be, must be,' said his son. 'Anyhow, I cannot ask the King, but I'll train you to do it.'

So he led his father to a place which was dotted all over with clumps of grass. The young courtier tied up a number of bundles of this grass, and arranged them in rows. 'Now, look here, father,' said he, 'this is the King, that is the Prime Minister, that is the General, here are the other grandees,' pointing to each bundle as he said the name. 'When you come into the King's presence, you must begin by saying: "Long live the King!" and then ask your boon.' To help him to remember, the son made up a little verse for his father to say, and this is the verse:

'I had two oxen to my plough, with which my work was done.
Now one is dead: O, mighty king, please give me another one!'

'Well,' said the Farmer, 'I think I can say that.' And he repeated it over and over, bowing and scraping to the bunch of grass that he called the King.

Every day for a whole year the Farmer practised; and how the ploughing got on meanwhile I do not know. Perhaps he lived on the seed-corn, and did not plough at all.

At the end of the year he said to his son, 'Now I know that little verse of yours! Now I can say it before any man! Take me to the King!'

So together father and son trudged away to the King's palace. There on a throne he sat, in gorgeous robes, with his courtiers all around him, the Prime Minister, the General, and all, just as the young man had told his father. But the poor Farmer! His head was beginning to swim already.

'Who is this?' said the King to the Farmer's son, who, as you know, was a courtier, so the King knew him.

'It is my father, Sire,' he answered.

'What does he want?' the King asked.

All eyes were turned on the Farmer, who by this time was as red as a turkey-cock, and hardly knew whether he stood on head or heels. However, he plucked up courage, and out came the verse, as pat as a pancake:

'I had two oxen to my plough, with which my work was done.
Now one is dead: O, mighty king, please take the other one!'

The King couldn't help laughing; and he saw there must be a mistake somewhere. 'Plenty of oxen at home, eh!' said he, keeping up the joke.

'If so, Sire,' said the Farmer's son with a bow, 'you must have given them.'

The King thought that rather neat. 'If I have not given you any so far,' said he, smiling, 'I will do it now.'

And when the pair got home, the Farmer in despair at his blunder, lo and behold! – in his cow-house were half a dozen of the finest oxen he had ever seen! So the poor old Farmer got his oxen, though he did make a muddle of the verse. ❋

44

THE JACKAL AND THE DRUM

SOMADEVA; RETOLD BY JAYASHREE BHAT

Long ago, there lived a jackal in a forest deep within the Vindhyas. He was a good hunter, and every day he would eat a hearty meal before he went to sleep.

One day, he wandered all over the forest, but could not find anything to eat. Exhausted and hungry, he kept wandering until he reached the edge of the forest. Now, the jackal did not know this but a battle had just taken place on that spot, and the field was now abandoned. '*Boom boom boom boom*!'

The jackal almost jumped out of his skin when he heard this sound. 'What is that terrifying noise?' he whimpered, his tail between his legs. 'What on earth can that be?'

'*Boom boom boom boom!*' came the sound again.

'Nooo!' he wailed. 'What is this strange, noisy animal? Or worse, is it a yaksha or a *vetala* out to kill me?'

'*BOOM BOOM BOOM BOOM!*' The sound was much louder this time.

I must kill it before it eats me, the jackal thought, shivering with fear. Bravely, he went closer and saw a circular object with a bit of leather stretched over it.

Do you know what that was? You guessed right – it was a battle drum! An arrow was hanging from a tree and every time the wind blew, the shaft of the arrow struck the drum hard, making the booming sound.

Slowly, the jackal sniffed the drum. *Hmm... it is not an animal,* he thought. Putting his fear aside, he gave it a small kick and then fiercely bit into it. Picking the drum up with his teeth, he shook his head violently until the drum broke. With quick bites, he then tore the leather of the drum into shreds.

There! It is dead now! he thought. Feeling better after his courageous move, he went back home, a song on his lips.

If you come across something scary, you would be brave like the jackal, too, wouldn't you? ❋

– *Read more such stories in* A Treasury of Tales from the Kathasaritasagara, *published by Hachette India.*

45

THE EMPEROR'S NEW CLOTHES

HANS CHRISTIAN ANDERSEN; RETOLD BY ANDREW LANG

Many years ago there lived an Emperor who was so fond of new clothes that he spent all his money on them in order to be beautifully dressed. He did not care about his soldiers, he did not care about the theatre; he only liked to go out walking to show off his new clothes. He had a coat for every hour of the day; and just as they say of a king, 'He is in the council-chamber,' they always said here, 'The Emperor is in the wardrobe.'

In the great city in which he lived there was always something going on; every day many strangers came there. One day two imposters arrived who gave themselves out as weavers, and said that they knew how to manufacture the most beautiful cloth imaginable. Not only were the texture and pattern uncommonly beautiful, but the clothes which were made of the stuff possessed this wonderful property that they were invisible to anyone who was not fit for his office, or who was unpardonably stupid.

'Those must indeed be splendid clothes,' thought the Emperor. 'If I had them on I could find out which men in my kingdom are unfit for the offices they hold; I could distinguish the wise from the stupid! Yes, this cloth must be woven for me at once.' And he gave both the imposters much money, so that they might begin their work.

They placed two weaving-looms, and began to do as if they were working, but they had not the least thing on the looms. They also demanded the finest silk and the best gold, which they put in their pockets, and worked at the empty looms till late into the night.

'I should like very much to know how far they have got on with the cloth,' thought the Emperor. But he remembered when he thought about it that whoever was stupid or not fit for his office would not be able to see it. Now he certainly believed that he had nothing to fear for himself, but he wanted first to send somebody else in order to see how he stood with regard to his office. Everybody in the whole town knew what a wonderful power the cloth had, and they were all curious to see how bad or how stupid their neighbour was.

'I will send my old and honoured minister to the weavers,' thought the Emperor. 'He can judge best what the cloth is like, for he has intellect, and no one understands his office better than he.'

Now the good old minister went into the hall where the two imposters sat working at the empty weaving-looms. 'Dear me!' thought the old minister, opening his eyes wide, 'I can see nothing!' But he did not say so.

Both the imposters begged him to be so kind as to step closer, and asked him if it were not a beautiful texture and lovely colours. They pointed to the empty loom, and the poor old minister went forward rubbing his eyes; but he could see nothing, for there was nothing there.

'Dear, dear!' thought he. 'Can I be stupid? I have never thought that, and nobody must know it! Can I be not fit for my office? No, I must certainly not say that I cannot see the cloth!'

'Have you nothing to say about it?' asked one of the men who was weaving.

'Oh, it is lovely, most lovely!' answered the old minister, looking through his spectacles. 'What a texture! What colours! Yes, I will tell the Emperor that it pleases me very much.'

'Now we are delighted at that,' said both the weavers, and thereupon they named the colours and explained the make of the texture.

The old minister paid great attention, so that he could tell the same to the Emperor when he came back to him, which he did.

The imposters now wanted more money, more silk, and more gold to use in their weaving. They put it all in their own pockets, and there came no threads on the loom, but they went on as they had done before, working at the empty loom. The Emperor soon sent another worthy statesman to see how the weaving was getting on, and whether the cloth would soon be finished. It was the same with him as the first one; he looked and looked, but because there was nothing on the empty loom he could see nothing.

'Is it not a beautiful piece of cloth?' asked the two imposters, and they pointed to and described the splendid material which was not there.

'Stupid I am not!' thought the man. 'So it must be my good office for which I am not fitted. It is strange, certainly, but no one must be allowed to notice it.' And so he praised the cloth which he did not see, and expressed to them his delight at the beautiful colours and the splendid texture. 'Yes, it is quite beautiful,' he said to the Emperor.

Everybody in the town was talking of the magnificent cloth.

Now the Emperor wanted to see it himself while it was still on the loom. With a great crowd of select followers, amongst whom were both the worthy statesmen who had already been there before, he went to the cunning imposters, who were now weaving with all their might, but without fibre or thread.

'Is it not splendid!' said both the old statesmen who had already been there. 'See, Your Majesty, what a texture! What colours!' And then they pointed to the empty loom, for they believed that the others could see the cloth quite well.

'What!' thought the Emperor, 'I can see nothing! This is indeed horrible! Am I stupid? Am I not fit to be Emperor? That were the most dreadful thing that could happen to me.'

'Oh, it is very beautiful,' he said. 'It has my gracious approval.' And then he nodded pleasantly, and examined the empty loom, for he would not say that he could see nothing.

His whole Court round him looked and looked, and saw no more than the others, but they said like the Emperor, 'Oh! It is beautiful!' And they advised him to wear these new and magnificent clothes for the first time at the great procession which was soon to take place. 'Splendid! Lovely! Most beautiful!' went from mouth to mouth; everyone seemed delighted over them, and the Emperor gave to the imposters the title of Court Weavers to the Emperor.

Throughout the whole of the night before the morning on which the procession was to take place, the imposters were up and were working by the light of over sixteen candles. The people could see that they were very busy making the Emperor's new clothes ready. They pretended they were taking the cloth from the loom, cut with huge scissors in the air, sewed with needles without thread, and then said at last, 'Now the clothes are finished!'

The Emperor came himself with his most distinguished knights, and each imposter held up his arm just as if he were holding something, and said, 'See! Here are the breeches! Here is the coat! Here the cloak!' and so on. 'Spun clothes are so comfortable that one would imagine one had nothing on at all, but that is the beauty of it!'

'Yes,' said all the knights, but they could see nothing, for there was nothing there.

'Will it please Your Majesty graciously to take off your clothes,' said the imposters, 'then we will put on the new clothes, here before the mirror.'

The Emperor took off all his clothes, and the imposters placed themselves before him as if they were putting on each part of his new clothes which was ready, and the Emperor turned and bent himself in front of the mirror.

'How beautifully they fit! How well they sit!' said everybody. 'What material! What colours! It is a gorgeous suit!'

'They are waiting outside with the canopy that they will hold over Your Majesty in the procession,' announced the Master of the Ceremonies.

'Look, I am ready,' said the Emperor. 'Doesn't it sit well!' And he turned himself again to the mirror to see if his finery was on all right.

The chamberlains who were used to carry the train put their hands near the floor as if they were lifting up the train; then they did as if they were holding something in the air. They would not have it noticed that they could see nothing.

So the Emperor went along in the procession under the splendid canopy, and all the people in the streets and at the windows said, 'How matchless are the Emperor's new clothes! That train fastened to his dress, how beautifully it hangs!'

No one wished it to be noticed that he could see nothing, for then he would have been unfit for his office, or else very stupid. None of the Emperor's clothes had met with such approval as these had.

'But he has nothing on!' said a little child at last.

'Just listen to the innocent child!' said the father, and each one whispered to his neighbour what the child had said.

'But he has nothing on!' the whole of the people called out at last.

This struck the Emperor, for it seemed to him as if they were right; but he thought to himself, 'I must go on with the procession now.' And the chamberlains walked along still more uprightly, holding up the train which was not there at all. ❋

46

GOPAL'S BOOKS

SUKUMAR RAY; TRANSLATED BY SREEJATA GUHA

As soon as lunch ended, Gopal picked up a few of his schoolbooks, and with the most innocent expression on his face, he headed up the stairs. His *mama** asked, 'Hey there, Gopal, where are you off in this midday heat?'

'I am going to the terrace to study,' replied Gopal.

'Why the terrace for studies? Why don't you sit here and study?'

'This is too noisy a space, too many people all around; Bhola makes a ruckus. It's difficult to concentrate,' said Gopal at once.

'All right. Go and study hard.'

Gopal went away, and Mama felt pleased. 'Thank god the boy is focussing on his studies.'

**Mother's brother; uncle*

At this moment, Bhola-babu made his entrance. He was all of three or four years old, and everyone doted on him. His first words were, 'Where is Dada?'

'Dada is studying on the terrace. Why don't you sit here and play?' asked Mama.

Bhola instantly plonked down on the floor and began to shower Mama with questions: *Why is Dada studying? What happens if you study? How does one study?* and many, many more. Mama was in the mood for some newspaper reading. He felt breathless with the spate of questions, and finally he exclaimed, 'Listen, Bhola-babu, why don't you go and play with Bhojiya? I shall buy you toffees in the evening.' Bhola walked away quickly.

Half an hour later, Bhola-babu re-entered the room and announced, 'Mama, I, too, would like to do studies.'

'Sure, why not?' laughed Mama. 'Wait till you are a little older. I shall buy you colourful picture books and you can study all you like.'

Bhola piped up, 'No, no, not that kind of studies. I want to do the studies that Dada is doing.'

'And what kind is that?' Mama queried.

'We–ell,' Bhola began, 'the kind where you have very colourful, very thin sheets of paper, thin sticks and glue... You cut up the paper and paste the sticks on to it with the glue... *that* kind of studying.'

This description of Gopal Dada's studying made Mama stop in his tracks. He tiptoed his way to the terrace on the third floor, peeped into the room stealthily and found his erudite nephew sitting on the windowsill, completely focused on the task of making kites. Two textbooks lay on the divan near the entrance of the room.

With great care, Mama picked up the two books and went back downstairs.

In a short while, Gopal was sent for. The minute he came and stood before him, Mama asked, 'How many days till school reopens?'

'Eighteen days,' said Gopal promptly.

'I hope you are studying hard? Or are you playing truant?'

'Not at all. I was studying all this while,' piped up Gopal.

'What were you studying?' Gopal mumbled, 'Sanskrit.'

'So... Don't you need your books to study Sanskrit? Do you really need to get creative with thin sheets of paper, thin sticks and glue?'

Gopal's eyes nearly popped out of their sockets. What on earth was Mama saying? He was stunned into silence as he stared at his uncle, utterly dumbfounded.

'Where are the books?' Mama asked.

'Up in the attic...'

Mama fished out the books from where he had hidden them and held them before Gopal. 'What are these?'

He grabbed Gopal by the ear and made him sit in one corner of the room.

Gopal's kites, thread, spool and all his other kitemaking accessories remained in Mama's custody for the next eighteen days. ❋

– *Read more stories by Sukumar Ray in* The Mad and Magical World of Sukumar Ray, *translated by Sreejata Guha and published by Hachette India.*

47

THE COLD SNOWMAN

ENID BLYTON

It happened once that some children built a great big snowman. You should have seen him! He was as tall as you, but much fatter, and he wore an old top hat, so he looked very grand. On his hands were woollen gloves, but they were rather holey. Down his front were large round pebbles for buttons and round his neck was an old woollen scarf. He really looked very grand indeed.

The children went indoors at teatime, and didn't come out again, because it was dark. So the snowman stood all alone in the backyard, and he was very lonely.

He began to sigh, and Foolish-One, the little elf who lived under the old apple tree, heard him and felt sorry. He ran out and spoke to the snowman.

'Are you lonely?' he asked.

'Very,' answered the snowman.

'Are you cold?' asked Foolish-One.

'Who wouldn't be in this frosty weather?' said the snowman.

'I'm sorry for you,' said Foolish-One. 'Shall I sing to you?'

'If you like,' said the snowman. So the elf began to sing a doleful little song about a star that fell from the sky and couldn't get back. It was so sad that the snowman cried a few tears, and they froze at once on his white, snowy cheeks.

'Stop singing that song,' he begged the elf. 'It makes me cry, and it is very painful to do that when your tears freeze on you. Ooooh! Isn't the wind cold?'

'Poor snowman!' said Foolish-One, tying the snowman's scarf so tightly that he nearly choked.

'Don't do that!' gasped the snowman. 'You're strangling me.'

'You have no coat,' said Foolish-One, looking sadly at the snowman. 'You will be frozen stiff before morning.'

'Oooh!' said the snowman, in alarm. 'Frozen stiff! That sounds dreadful! I wish I wasn't so cold.'

'Shall I get you a nice warm coat?' asked the elf. 'I have one that would keep you very cosy.'

'Well, seeing that you only come up to my knees, I'm afraid that your coat would only be big enough for a handkerchief for me,' said the snowman. 'Ooh! There's that cold wind again.'

Just then a smell of burning came over the air, and the elf sniffed it. He jumped to his feet in excitement. Just the thing!

'Snowman!' he cried. 'There's a bonfire. I can smell it. Let us go to it and warm ourselves.'

The snowman tried to move. He was *very* heavy, and little bits of snow broke off him. But at last he managed to shuffle along somehow, and he followed the dancing elf down the garden path to the corner of the garden where the bonfire was burning.

'Here we are!' said the elf, in delight. 'See what a fine blaze there is. Come, snowman, draw close, and I will tell you a story.'

The snowman came as close to the fire as he could. It was certainly very warm. He couldn't feel the cold wind at all now. It was much better.

'Once upon a time,' began the elf, 'there was a princess called Marigold. Are you nice and warm, snowman?'

'Very,' said the snowman, drowsily. The heat was making him sleepy. 'Go on, Foolish-One.'

'Now this princess lived in a high castle,' went on Foolish-One, leaning against the snowman as he talked. 'And one day – are you sure you're quire warm, snowman?'

'Very, very warm,' murmured the snowman, his hat slipping to one side of his head. Plonk! One of his stone buttons fell off. Plonk! Then another. How odd!

Foolish-One went on with his story. It wasn't a very exciting one, and the snowman hardly listened. He was so warm and sleepy. Foolish-One suddenly felt sleepy, too. He stopped in the middle of his tale and shut his eyes. Then very gently he began to snore.

He woke up with a dreadful jump, for he heard a most peculiar noise.

'Sizzle-sizzle-sizzle, ss-ss-sss-ss!'

Whatever could it be? He jumped up. The fire was almost out. The snowman had gone! Only his hat, scarf and gloves remained, and they were in a pile on the ground.

'Who has put the fire out?' cried Foolish-One in a rage.

'Snowman, where are you? Why have you gone off and left all your clothes? You will catch your death of cold!'

But the snowman didn't answer. He was certainly quite gone. Foolish-One began to cry. The fire was quite out now, and a pool of water lay all round it. Who had poured the water there? And where, oh where, was that nice snowman?

He called him up the garden and down. He hunted for him everywhere. Then he went home and found his thickest coat and warmest hat. He put them on, took his stick and went out.

'I will find that snowman if it takes me a thousand years to do it!' he cried. And off he went to begin his search. He hasn't found him yet! Poor Foolish-One, I don't somehow think he ever will!

– Now, YOU know what happened to that snowman, don't you? Read many more fun stories in Christmas Wishes *by Enid Blyton.*

48

BLACK BEAUTY
'MY EARLY HOME'

ANNA SEWELL

The first place that I can well remember was a large pleasant meadow with a pond of clear water in it. Some shady trees leaned over it, and rushes and water-lilies grew at the deep end. Over the hedge on one side we looked into a ploughed field, and on the other we looked over a gate at our master's house, which stood by the roadside. At the top of the meadow was a grove of fir trees, and at the bottom a running brook overhung by a steep bank.

While I was young I lived upon my mother's milk, as I could not eat grass. In the daytime I ran by her side, and at night I lay down close by her. When it was hot we used to stand by the pond in the shade of the trees, and when it was cold we had a nice warm shed near the grove.

As soon as I was old enough to eat grass my mother used to go out to work in the daytime and come back in the evening.

There were six young colts in the meadow besides me. They were older than I was; some were nearly as large as grown-up horses. I used to run with them, and had great fun; we used to gallop all together round and round the field as hard as we could go. Sometimes we had rather rough play, for they would frequently bite and kick as well as gallop.

One day, when there was a good deal of kicking, my mother whinnied to me to come to her, and then she said, 'I wish you to pay attention to what I am going to say to you. The colts who live here are very good colts, but they are cart-horse colts, and of course they have not learned manners. You have been well-bred and well-born; your father has a great name in these parts, and your grandfather won the cup two years at the Newmarket races; your grandmother had the sweetest temper of any horse I ever knew, and I think you have never seen me kick or bite. I hope you will grow up gentle and good, and never learn bad ways; do your work with a good will, lift your feet up well when you trot, and never bite or kick even in play.'

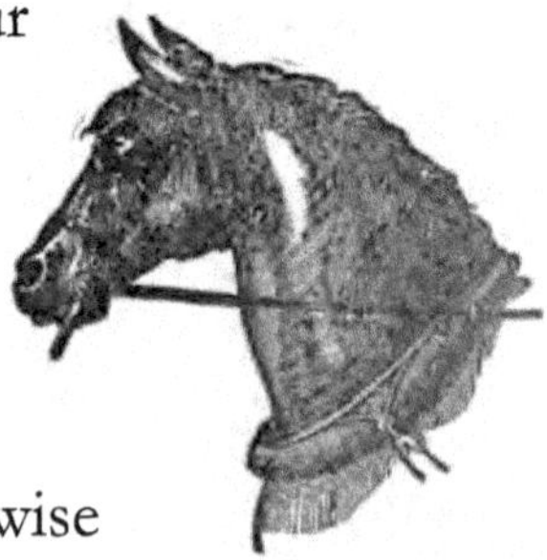

I have never forgotten my mother's advice. I knew she was a wise old horse, and our master thought a great deal of her. Her name was Duchess, but he often called her Pet.

Our master was a good, kind man. He gave us good food, good lodging and kind words; he spoke as kindly to us as he did to his little children. We were all fond of him, and my mother loved him very much. When she saw him at the gate she would neigh with joy and trot up to him. He would pat and stroke her and say, 'Well, old Pet, and how is your little Darkie?' I was a dull black, so he called me Darkie; then he would give me a piece of bread, which was very good, and sometimes he brought a carrot for my mother. All the horses would come to him, but I think we were his favourites. My mother always took him to the town on a market day in a light gig.

There was a ploughboy, Dick, who sometimes came into our field to pluck blackberries from the hedge. When he had eaten all he wanted he would have what he called fun with the colts, throwing stones and sticks at them to make them gallop. We did not much mind him, for we could gallop off; but sometimes a stone would hit and hurt us.

One day he was at this game and did not know that the master was in the next field; but he was there, watching what was going on. Over the hedge he jumped in a snap, and catching Dick by the arm, he gave him such a box on the ear as made him roar with the pain and surprise. As soon as we saw the master we trotted up nearer to see what went on.

'Bad boy!' he said. 'Bad boy! to chase the colts. This is not the first time, nor the second, but it shall be the last. There – take your money and go home; I shall not want you on my farm again.' So we never saw Dick any more. Old Daniel, the man who looked after the horses, was just as gentle as our master, so we were well-off. ❋

– *Excerpted from* Black Beauty *by Anna Sewell.*

49

THE BLIND MEN AND THE ELEPHANT

A JATAKA TALE; RETOLD BY JAMES BALDWIN

There were once six blind men who stood by the roadside every day and begged from the people who passed. They had often heard of elephants, but they had never seen one; for, being blind, how could they?

It so happened one morning that an elephant was driven down the road where they stood. When they were told that the great beast was before them, they asked the driver to let him stop so that they might see him.

Of course they could not see him with their eyes; but they thought that by touching him they could learn just what kind of animal he was.

The first one happened to put his hand on the elephant's side. 'Well, well!' he said, 'now I know all about this beast. He is exactly like a wall.'

The second felt only of the elephant's tusk. 'My brother,' he said, 'you are mistaken. He is not at all like a wall. He is round and smooth and sharp. He is more like a spear than anything else.'

The third happened to take hold of the elephant's trunk. 'Both of you are wrong,' he said. 'Anybody who knows anything can see that this elephant is like a snake.'

The fourth reached out his arms and grasped one of the elephant's legs. 'Oh, how blind you are!' he said. 'It is very plain to me that he is round and tall like a tree.'

The fifth was a very tall man, and he chanced to take hold of the elephant's ear. 'The blindest man ought to know that this beast is not like any of the things that you name,' he said. 'He is exactly like a huge fan.'

The sixth was very blind indeed, and it was some time before he could find the elephant at all. At last he seized the animal's tail. 'O foolish fellows!' he cried. 'You surely have lost your senses. This elephant is not like a wall, or a spear, or a snake, or a tree; neither is he like a fan. But any man with a particle of sense can see that he is exactly like a rope.'

Then the elephant moved on, and the six blind men sat by the roadside all day, and quarrelled about him. Each believed that he knew just how the animal looked; and each called the others hard names because they did not agree with him. *People who have eyes sometimes act as foolishly.* ❋

50

PRAHLADA, THE SON OF HIRANYAKASHIPU THE HORRIBLE

A STORY FROM THE BHAGAVATA PURANA; RETOLD BY SUDHA MADHAVAN

Do you know about the two doorkeepers of Lord Vishnu – Jaya and Vijaya? The story goes that they were cursed by the four young sages, known as the Sanath Kumaras, who came to pay their respects to Lord Vishnu and were stopped at the entrance by the doorkeepers.

He took pity on them and promised them only three births on earth. But *verrry* bad ones! That's what they were stuck with. Instead of a hundred good ones! So that they could return to their beloved master Vishnu, pronto!

And...umm...do you know their names in each of their births? Yes, that's right! – Hiranyakashipu and Hiranyaksha, Ravana and Kumbhakarna (who used to sleep for half the year at a stretch, but that is another story!), and Shishupala and Danthavakra! Both of them, in every birth they took on earth, picked up a roaring fight with Lord Vishnu, or with whatever avatar he took! And Lord Vishnu taught them a lesson in his own clever way each time! Each of these are wonderful stories! Let us now hear the first of those very interesting (and very bad births) that they took, shall we?

The demon King Hiranyakashipu lived in the first Yuga, the Krita Yuga. (The Hindu Cycle of Eras is divided into four different yugas: the Krita or Satya Yuga, considered the age of purity and goodness; the Treta Yuga, a time of less goodness, many wars and extreme weather; the Dwapara Yuga, full of anger, jealousy, fighting and greed; and the last Kali Yuga, which is supposed to be the worst of the lot!).

Hiranyakashipu troubled the people in his kingdom and was very cruel to them. But what was so special about this king was that he hated Vishnu with all his heart. There was not a moment in the day when he did not curse Narayana (which is another name for Vishnu) or call him names. Would such a man ever pray to God? Of course not! A...nd... if anyone in his kingdom so much as mentioned Vishnu's name, he went purple with rage. The unfortunate one was punished very severely indeed.

Hiranyakashipu was very angry with Vishnu because he had killed his brother Hiranyaksha. And he wanted to kill Vishnu and take revenge. So what could he do? Was he strong enough to kill Lord Vishnu?

Not at all!

So he decided that he would first get all the strength and magical powers possible. He prayed and prayed to Lord Brahma, who is the Creator of the whole world. He did penance for many years. In the olden days, whenever one wanted something very dearly they would follow a very difficult routine (or penance) of meditating quietly for lo-o-o-ong periods of time, like hundreds of years! That, too, often without food and water. And sometimes without breathing!

At last, pleased with his devotion, Brahma appeared before the demon king. Hiranyakashipu was very happy. 'My lord, thanks for coming to me!' he said and fell at Brahma's feet.

'That's all right!' said Lord Brahma 'Now go ahead and tell me what you want.'

'Well, I want to live forever and ever! I don't want to die!' said Hiranyakashipu rather greedily.

'I am sorry,' said Brahma, 'I can't grant you that. You are asking for a bit too much... Come on, give it another try! But don't ask for something I cannot grant.'

Hiranyakashipu thought for a while. Hmm...he had to be a little clever! He scratched his head. Aha! He had the perfect idea. He took a deep breath. 'My lord,' he said, 'grant me that I do not die at the hands of man or animal, nor by any weapon, neither in the day nor at night, neither on earth nor in space and...'

'Well, you are rather selfish, I must say,' interrupted Lord Brahma. 'Anyway, a promise is a promise – go on!'

'...nor by any living or non-living thing...'

'Finished?' said Brahma, a little worried.

'Just one more, just one more,' said Hiranyakashipu hurriedly. 'I should not die either inside a house nor outside!'

'Hmm...granted!' sighed Lord Brahma and vanished.

Hiranyakashipu was bursting with joy! No one could do anything to him any more. He was the greatest! He could do exactly what he wanted. He troubled everyone all the more. He bothered the devas – the gods in heaven – and the earthlings.

They all lived in great fear of him. No one in his kingdom could take Vishnu's name or pray to Him. They could only pray to Hiranyakashipu! They all bowed their heads in prayer and said 'Om Hiranyaya *namaha*!' If they said 'Om *namo* Narayanaya' he would cut off their heads!

Could things go on like this forever? No, of course not!

Lord Vishnu had other plans! He would save the devas and everyone else on earth from this horrible king. But he was in no hurry...

And so in time, to Hiranyakashipu was born a son, whom he named Prahlada. Hiranyakashipu was very happy. 'He shall be king after me – my son,' he thought. But Prahlada was very, very different from what he had imagined!

He was not at all like his father. He was very fond of Lord Vishnu. He prayed to Him every day. Everyone else in the kingdom chanted 'Om Hiranyaya *namaha*!' because they feared the king very much. But Prahlada said 'Om *namo* Narayanaya!'

At first, Hiranyakashipu chided Prahlada mildly and told him not to speak Vishnu's name! But Prahlada thought it very odd. He could not understand why he could not take Lord Vishnu's name. Wasn't it the right thing to do?

Hiranyakashipu scolded him. But Prahlada would not listen.

The king gave him a sound thrashing. But he could not make his little son bow to his wish.

As time went by Hiranyakashipu lost his patience:

'I was happy, so full of joy!
I finally had this wonderful boy,
But he's turning out to be a pest –
I'll get rid of him, I must.'

'The audacious little brat!' he said. 'I am sick and tired of telling him to mend his ways. I will have no more of his nonsense. Narayana, indeed!'

The demon king ordered that Prahlada be thrown into the ocean. 'Go!' roared Hiranyakashipu, ordering in soldiers. 'Tie him to a rock and toss him into the sea! I don't want to look at this stubborn son of mine any more!'

But God Vishnu saved him! Prahlada was back alive. Wonder of wonders!

'The ocean will not drown him?' thundered Hiranyakashipu. 'So what? Let me see how he gets away from under the elephant's foot, the upstart!'

But the elephant lifted the little boy happily and put him on his back!

'What is with this boy? How does he get away each time?' shouted Hiranyakashipu, in frustration. 'Not this time, though! Poison him!' ordered the merciless king.

But the poison turned to sweet nectar! What an absolute miracle! How did that happen? Well! Who do you think was working all this magic and saving Prahlada? Lord Vishnu, of course.

Hiranyakashipu was very puzzled and very angry indeed. Purple with rage, he called his son over to him. 'Who has taught you this?' raged Hiranyakashipu. 'Look at me, I am the greatest, can't you see! The whole world prays to me.'

'No,' said Prahlada, in his gentle voice, looking up at his mighty father, 'You are *not*! Lord Vishnu is the greatest! I will pray to him, not to you.'

'Ha, what rubbish!' roared Hiranyakashipu. 'Where is your Narayana, your Vishnu?'

'He is everywhere!' pat came the reply.

'HO, HO!' laughed Hiranyakashipu. 'Everywhere? What a joke. I can't see anyone!'

'But he is everywhere.' Prahlada was very sure!

'Show me then! Show me! Tell me, is he HERE, or HERE or HERE?' pointed Hiranyakashipu, flashing his sword all around.

'Yes, he is there, and there, and there,' said Prahlada.

'Is he in this pillar, then?' roared Hiranyakashipu and hit the column with his mace!

And, do you know what happened?

There was a huge flash of lightning and a crash of thunder!

The ground shook and trembled!

The pillar exploded!

And out of it came a figure that was huge and terrifying! It shone like the sun. It had the head of a lion and the body of a man. It had many arms. Its eyes were like live coals! Its mouth was like a huge cave with rows of sharp fangs like that of a beast! Its body was covered with hair. The hands had claws.

Its roar made the earth shake!

Do you know who that was?

It was none other than Lord Vishnu! But in a new and ferocious form of Narasimha – half man and half lion.

Why was that, do you think?

Yes, of course! It was to keep Brahma's promise to Hiranyakashipu! That neither man nor animal could kill him! SO HE TOOK THE FORM OF HALF MAN AND HALF ANIMAL!

HE CAME DURING THE EVENING, when it is neither day nor night! The second promise of Brahma to Hiranyakashipu!

THEN HE SAT AT THE THRESHOLD, so that he was neither outside the house nor inside!

And he picked up Hiranyakashipu as if he were a rag doll! HE PUT THE TERRIBLE DEMON KING ON HIS LAP, so that he was neither on earth nor in air!

Then tore him apart WITH HIS CLAWS, so that he did not use any weapon!

In this manner, all the promises that Brahma had made to Hiranyakashipu were kept by Lord Vishnu. He did not break any of the rules! But at the same time God Vishnu proved that he was cleverer than the demon king!

So that was the end of the terrible and evil Hiranyakashipu! That is how Lord Vishnu kept one of his promises to Jaya and Vijaya, in their first birth on earth!

Prahlada was very sad. But God made him understand that evil had to be punished. All those gathered fell at Lord Narasimha's feet and prayed to him to become calm. So he gave them a glimpse of what he actually was, the smiling Lord Vishnu.

This half-human, half-lion avatar of Lord Vishnu is the fiercest of his incarnations. But Hiranyakashipu had to be taught a lesson in his own special way. Lord Vishnu played by Hiranyakashipu's own rules. He had no choice, had he? ❋

51

THE SPIDER AND THE FLY

MARY HOWITT

'Will you walk into my parlour?' said the spider to the fly;
''Tis the prettiest little parlour that ever you did spy.
The way into my parlour is up a winding stair,
And I have many curious things to show when you are there.'
'Oh no, no,' said the little fly; 'to ask me is in vain,
For who goes up your winding stair can ne'er come down again.'

'I'm sure you must be weary, dear, with soaring up so high;
Will you rest upon my little bed?' said the spider to the fly.

'There are pretty curtains drawn around; the sheets are fine and thin,
And if you like to rest a while, I'll snugly tuck you in!'
'Oh no, no,' said the little fly, 'for I've often heard it said,
They never, never wake again who sleep upon your bed!'

Said the cunning spider to the fly: 'Dear friend, what can I do
To prove the warm affection I've always felt for you?
I have within my pantry good store of all that's nice;
I'm sure you're very welcome – will you please to take a slice?'
'Oh no, no,' said the little fly; 'kind sir, that cannot be:
I've heard what's in your pantry, and I do not wish to see!'

'Sweet creature!' said the spider, 'you're witty and you're wise;
How handsome are your gauzy wings; how brilliant are your eyes!
I have a little looking-glass upon my parlour shelf;
If you'll step in one moment, dear, you shall behold yourself.'

'I thank you, gentle sir,' she said, 'for what you're pleased to say,
And, bidding you good morning now, I'll call another day.'

The spider turned him round about, and went into his den,
For well he knew the silly fly would soon come back again:
So he wove a subtle web in a little corner sly,
And set his table ready to dine upon the fly;
Then came out to his door again, and merrily did sing:
'Come hither, hither, pretty fly, with pearl and silver wing;
Your robes are green and purple; there's a crest upon your head;
Your eyes are like the diamond bright, but mine are dull as lead!'

Alas, alas! How very soon this silly little fly,
Hearing his wily, flattering words, came slowly flitting by;
With buzzing wings she hung aloft, then near and nearer drew,
Thinking only of her brilliant eyes and green and purple hue,
Thinking only of her crested head. Poor, foolish thing! at last

Up jumped the cunning spider, and fiercely held her fast;
He dragged her up his winding stair, into the dismal den –
Within his little parlour – but she ne'er came out again!

And now, dear little children, who may this story read,
To idle, silly, flattering words I pray you ne'er give heed;
Unto an evil counsellor close heart and ear and eye,
And take a lesson from this tale of the spider and the fly. ❋

52

HOW THE CAMEL GOT HIS HUMP

RUDYARD KIPLING

In the beginning of years, when the world was so new and all, and the Animals were just beginning to work for Man, there was a Camel, and he lived in the middle of a Howling Desert because he did not want to work; and besides, he was a Howler himself. So he ate sticks and thorns and tamarisks and milkweed and prickles, most 'scruciating idle; and when anybody spoke to him he said 'Humph!' Just 'Humph!' and no more.

Presently the Horse came to him on Monday morning, with a saddle on his back and a bit in his mouth, and said, 'Camel, O Camel, come out and trot like the rest of us.'

'Humph!' said the Camel; and the Horse went away and told the Man.

Presently the Dog came to him, with a stick in his mouth, and said, 'Camel, O Camel, come and fetch and carry like the rest of us.'

'Humph!' said the Camel; and the Dog went away and told the Man.

Presently the Ox came to him, with the yoke on his neck and said, 'Camel, O Camel, come and plough like the rest of us.'

'Humph!' said the Camel; and the Ox went away and told the Man.

At the end of the day the Man called the Horse and the Dog and the Ox together, and said, 'Three, O Three, I'm very sorry for you (with the world so new-and-all); but that Humph-thing in the Desert can't work, or he would have been here by now, so I am going to leave him alone, and you must work double-time to make up for it.'

That made the Three very angry (with the world so new-and-all), and they held a palaver, and an *indaba*, and a *punchayet*, and a pow-wow on the edge of the Desert; and the Camel came chewing milkweed *most* 'scruciating idle and laughed at them. Then he said 'Humph!' and went away again.

Presently there came along the Djinn in charge of All Deserts, rolling in a cloud of dust (Djinns always travel that way because it is Magic), and he stopped to palaver and pow-pow with the Three.

'Djinn of All Deserts,' said the Horse, '*is* it right for anyone to be idle, with the world so new-and-all?'

'Certainly not,' said the Djinn.

'Well,' said the Horse, 'there's a thing in the middle of your Howling Desert (and he's a Howler himself) with a long neck and long legs, and he hasn't done a stroke of work since Monday morning. He won't trot.'

'Whew!' said the Djinn, whistling, 'that's my Camel, for all the gold in Arabia! What does he say about it?'

'He says "Humph!", said the Dog; 'and he won't fetch and carry.'

'Does he say anything else?'

'Only "Humph!"; and he won't plough,' said the Ox.

'Very good,' said the Djinn. 'I'll humph him if you will kindly wait a minute.'

The Djinn rolled himself up in his dust-cloak, and took a bearing across the desert, and found the Camel most 'scruciatingly idle, looking at his own reflection in a pool of water.

'My long and bubbling friend,' said the Djinn, 'what's this I hear of your doing no work, with the world so new-and-all?'

'Humph!' said the Camel.

The Djinn sat down, with his chin in his hand and began to think a Great Magic, while the Camel looked at his own reflection in the pool of water.

'You've given the Three extra work ever since Monday morning, all on account of your 'scruciating idleness,' said the Djinn; and he went on thinking Magics, with his chin in his hand.

'Humph!' said the Camel.

'I shouldn't say that again if I were you,' said the Djinn; 'you might say it once too often. Bubbles, I want you to work.'

And the Camel said 'Humph!' again; but no sooner had he said it than he saw his back, that he was so proud of, puffing up and puffing up into a great big lolloping humph.

'Do you see that?' said the Djinn. 'That's your very own humph that you've brought upon your very own self by not working. Today is Thursday, and you've done no work since Monday, when the work began. Now you are going to work.'

'How can I,' said the Camel, 'with this humph on my back?'

'That's made a-purpose,' said the Djinn, 'all because you missed those three days. You will be able to work now for three days without eating, because you can live on your humph; and don't you ever say I never did anything for you. Come out of the Desert and go to the Three, and behave. Humph yourself!'

And the Camel humphed himself, humph and all, and went away to join the Three. And from that day to this the Camel always wears a humph (we call it 'hump' now, not to hurt his feelings); but he has never yet caught up with the three days that he missed at the beginning of the world, and he has never yet learned how to behave.

The Camel's hump is an ugly lump
Which well you may see at the Zoo;
But uglier yet is the hump we get
From having too little to do.

Kiddies and grown-ups too-oo-oo,
If we haven't enough to do-oo-oo,
We get the hump –
Cameelious hump –
The hump that is black and blue!

We climb out of bed with a frouzly head
And a snarly-yarly voice.
We shiver and scowl and we grunt and we growl
At our bath and our boots and our toys;

And there ought to be a corner for me
(And I know there is one for you)
When we get the hump –
Cameelious hump –
The hump that is black and blue!

I get it as well as you-oo-oo –
If I haven't enough to do-oo-oo –
We all get hump –
Cameelious hump –
Kiddies and grown-ups, too! ❋

– Excerpted from the original story.

53

THE PENNY-WISE MONKEY

A JATAKA TALE; RETOLD BY
ELLEN C. BABBITT

Once upon a time the king of a large and rich country gathered together his army to take a faraway little country. The king and his soldiers marched all morning long and then went into camp in the forest.

When they fed the horses they gave them some peas to eat. One of the Monkeys living in the forest saw the peas and jumped down to get some of them. He filled his mouth and hands with them, and up into the tree he went again, and sat down to eat the peas.

As he sat there eating the peas, one pea fell from his hand to the ground. At once the greedy Monkey dropped all the peas he had in his hands, and ran down to hunt for the lost pea. But he could not find that one pea. He climbed up into his tree again, and sat still looking very glum. 'To get more, I threw away what I had,' he said to himself.

The king had watched the Monkey, and he said to himself, 'I will not be like this foolish Monkey, who lost much to gain a little. I will go back to my own country and enjoy what I now have.'

So he and his men marched back home. ❋

54

ICARUS AND DÆDALUS

A GREEK MYTH; RETOLD BY JOSEPHINE PRESTON PEABODY

Among all those mortals who grew so wise that they learned the secrets of the gods, none was more cunning than Dædalus.

He once built, for King Minos of Crete, a wonderful Labyrinth of winding ways so cunningly tangled up and twisted around that, once inside, you could never find your way out again without a magic clue. But the king's favour veered with the wind, and one day he had his master architect imprisoned in a tower. Dædalus managed to escape from his cell; but it seemed impossible to leave the island, since every ship that came or went was well guarded by order of the king.

At length, watching the seagulls in the air – the only creatures that were sure of liberty – he thought of a plan for himself and his young son Icarus, who was captive with him.

Little by little, he gathered a store of feathers great and small. He fastened these together with thread, moulded them in with wax, and so fashioned two great wings like those of a bird. When they were done, Dædalus fitted them to his own shoulders, and after one or two efforts, he found that by waving his arms he could winnow the air and cleave it, as a swimmer does the sea. He held himself aloft, wavered this way and that, with the wind, and at last, like a great fledgling, he learned to fly.

Without delay, he fell to work on a pair of wings for the boy Icarus, and taught him carefully how to use them. 'Remember,' said the father, 'never to fly very low or very high, for the fogs about the earth would weigh you down, but the blaze of the sun will surely melt your feathers apart if you go too near.'

For Icarus, these cautions went in at one ear and out by the other. Who could remember to be careful when he was to fly for the first time? Are birds careful? Not they! And not an idea remained in the boy's head but the one joy of escape.

The day came, and the fair wind that was to set them free. The father bird put on his wings, and, while the light urged them to be gone, he waited to see that all was well with Icarus, for the two could not fly hand in hand. Up they rose, the boy after his father. The hateful ground of Crete sank beneath them; and the country folk, who caught a glimpse of them when they were high above the treetops, took it for a vision of the gods – Apollo, perhaps, with Cupid after him.

At first there was a terror in the joy. The wide vacancy of the air dazed them – a glance downward made their brains reel. But when a great wind filled their wings, and Icarus felt himself sustained, like a halcyon-bird in the hollow of a wave, like a child uplifted by his mother, he forgot everything in the world but joy. He forgot Crete and the other islands that he had passed over: he saw but vaguely that winged thing in the distance before him that was his father Dædalus. He stretched out his arms to the sky and made towards the highest heavens.

Alas for him! Warmer and warmer grew the air. Those arms, that had seemed to uphold him, relaxed. His wings wavered, drooped. He fluttered his young hands vainly – he was falling. Wings; the feathers were falling, one by one, like snowflakes.

He fell like a leaf tossed down the wind, down, down, with one cry that overtook Dædalus far away. When he returned, and sought high and low for the poor boy, he saw nothing but the birdlike feathers afloat on the water, and he knew that Icarus was drowned.

The nearest island he named Icaria, in memory of the child; but he, in heavy grief, went to the temple of Apollo in Sicily, and there hung up his wings as an offering. Never again did he attempt to fly. ❃

55

THE COWHERD AND THE MOUND OF MYSTERY

A TALE FROM THE SINGHASAN BATTISI; RETOLD BY SUDHA MADHAVAN

In a far away village, on the outskirts of a kingdom, lived a cowherd.

Now, who do you think is a cowherd?

Well, a cowherd is one who looks after the cattle and takes them out grazing on juicy meadows of grass.

This young boy, too, along with his other cowherd friends, took his cattle out to graze every day.

While the cattle were grazing, swishing their tails happily to drive away the flies, the boys had their share of fun. They played hide-and-seek, told each other stories and opened their little bundles of lunch when they got hungry. They shared it with one another and joked and laughed as they ate.

But were they laughing all the time?

Hmm... well! Not all the time! Not when they got into a fight!

And when they did so, one of them would try and settle their fight. The boys would hold a small make-believe court and there would be a 'hearing'. The two boys who were fighting would each tell his side of the story. The one who settled the fight would have to think carefully before he spoke. But being a small boy himself, could he always be right?

No, of course not. And then the fight would start all over again!

One such day, the boys got into a row over their cows. The boy who was giving the verdict moved up the meadow and stood on a mound that was there. And wonder of wonders, he gave a very fair and intelligent verdict. He seemed to have become suddenly quite wise!

All the other cowherds were surprised and the two who were fighting were happy, too!

Now, another very strange thing happened! No sooner did the boy come down from the mound than his behaviour changed. He told a lie and misbehaved like any other boy.

So the boys got into the habit of climbing on to the mound after their fights to hear a verdict from one of the boys. And each time he spoke very wisely!

❋

This happened many times. Every time one of them climbed on to the mound, he would become a very different person! He would speak only the truth. His judgment would be very fair and correct!

The minute he climbed down, he would go back to his old ways!

Now, the king who ruled the neighbouring kingdom, was called Raja Bhoja. One day, his soldiers were passing by the village and saw the cowherds on their way. They also saw the cowherd give his very intelligent verdict once he climbed on to the mound!

That puzzled and fascinated them. The soldiers went and told their king about this!

'My lord,' said one of them. 'We saw a very strange thing today! We saw this bunch of cowherds. They had got into a fight. The one who solved their differences, climbed on to a mound and gave a very wise decision indeed!'

'Yes, my lord,' said the second, 'it was quite unbelievable! It was as if someone else spoke instead! Because once the boy stepped down from the mound, he was like any other.'

'Indeed, my lord,' said the third, 'It was as if they were two different boys!'

Raja Bhoja was himself a very wise king, and had many learned men and poets in his court. When he heard this he fell into deep thought. *What could be the reason for this strange thing?* he wondered. *Why should the boy speak differently when he climbed on to the mound?*

'Hmm...' The king sat tapping his chin, thoughtfully. At last he knew. *Aha, I know why!* said he to himself. *There must be something magical underneath it! I must find out!*

'Go!' he ordered his men. 'Go and dig up the mound! Let us find out what lies underneath!'

And so the king's men went and started to dig up the mound. The cowherds who came there every day stood around and looked in wonder. Why were the king's men digging up the mound?

The men dug for quite a few days...

At last their spade struck something hard!

The soldiers straightened up and wiped the sweat from their brows. They had found something! But what was it?

They came the next day and dug some more... And some more... And then some more!

Finally, all the eight men put their shoulders together and pulled out something that was covered with a lot of earth! *It looked like an ornamental throne!*

They carried it to their king. He ordered it to be cleaned.

And so they washed it and wiped it dry and polished it to a gleam!

And, children, what do you think it was?

It was a beautiful throne with sixteen steps up to the seat! And each step had a doll on either side!

So, how many dolls does that make? Yes, it makes thirty-two in all!

The king came and saw the throne. He was amazed.

He knew whose throne that was!

It was the throne of the very wise, very brave and the most wonderful king, Raja Vikramaditya! This king ruled over that very kingdom many, many years ago!

Raja Bhoja was very happy! He decided that he would keep the throne for himself and sit on it while in court: 'What a wonderful throne it must be to have such a magical effect while deep inside the earth! I must see how it feels to sit on it myself while in court!

And children, do you think he sat on it? And what do you think happened when he tried to do so?

Well, that is another story! ❋

– It's the next tale, in fact – read on!

56

RAJA BHOJA AND THE THRONE OF VIKRAMADITYA

A TALE FROM THE SINGHASAN BATTISI; RETOLD BY SUDHA MADHAVAN

You know the story of how the cowherds from a village stood on a mysterious mound and spoke very wisely indeed! And how, underneath that mound, the king's men found the throne of the mighty, wise and wonderful king, Vikramaditya the Great! Don't you?

Well! Let us see what happened after that, shall we?

Raja Bhoja was absolutely charmed by the throne! Being a very wise and brave king himself, he thought the throne was just right for him. So he got it placed in his court – he couldn't stop thinking about sitting on the wonderful throne, with its sixteen steps with dolls on either side.

Well, so one bright morning, the king had his royal bath with scented oils and perfumed scrubs, and dressed in his royal robes. He went straight to the palace temple and prayed to the gods. Then he went to the royal durbar.

He was as thrilled as a small child with a new toy! He was very anxious to sit on the wonderful throne but he was not yet sure if the time was right. He found it hard to wait!

So that night when all was quiet, he went secretly to where the beautiful throne was and put his foot respectfully on the first step.

A...nd...!

No sooner did he do that than an amazing thing happened!

There was a sound of tinkling laughter! The king stopped dead in his tracks. His foot midway in the air; he looked all around him in great surprise.

Whose voice was that?

There seemed to be no one around. He was there alone. How very strange indeed!

'Who's that?' he thundered in his commanding voice. His voice echoed in the silence. How eerie!

The king shook his head. *I must be hearing things!* he told himself.

He looked around once more.

And then, very cautiously, he put his foot up again on the first step!

To his great surprise, the tinkling laughter rang out again!

This time the king saw where it came from. He stood amazed!

He could not believe his eyes.

He could not trust his ears either!

The two dolls on either side of the first step were laughing at the king... And then one of them spoke!

'Dear Bhoja Raja, you are brave and wise! You are loved and respected by everyone! But do you know to whom this throne belongs? It belongs to the one and only – the great king – Vikramaditya!'

'Yes, of course, I know!' said the king.

The doll spoke again, 'O great king Bhoja! There has been no one like him before nor after! His glory was like the brilliant sun. In bravery he was like the lion. He spoke only the truth and was kind to his subjects. He had no equal as a warrior. While being such a great man, he was very humble!'

The king was silent.

The doll spoke again. 'To give you an example of his bravery and might, O King, I shall now tell you a story about him. Listen!'

The king sat down to hear the story.

The doll began...

> King Vikramaditya was fond of adventure. He was completely fearless! Once a learned man came to him and said, 'O King! You are a very brave man

and like to do the impossible! What I am about to tell you might interest you!'

'Indeed! Tell me!' said Vikramaditya.

'O King! Just outside of your kingdom, Ujjaini, there is a holy river, a 'Pushkarini'. Across it lies a beautiful 'Swarna Stambha' – a golden pillar. The wonder of it is that, as the sun moves up the sky, the Swarna Stambha rises too! At noon, my lord, as the sun touches the highest point in its path in the sky, the Stambha touches the 'Surya Mandala', the sun!'

'And then?' asked Bhoja Raja, very curious.

'Well, Raja Vikramaditya was very excited. No sooner did he get up in the morning, he went off in search of the holy river. What the learned man had said was true. There was a river exactly as he had said. And a Swarna Stambha (a pillar of gold) was lying right across it. The fearless king Vikramaditya got on to the Stambha! And do you know what happened? As the sun slowly glided up the sky, the Stambha rose too!'

'And?' asked Bhoja Raja, feeling a little breathless!

'Well, as it rose upwards, it grew in height as well!'

Bhoja Raja was struck with great wonder.

'As the sun rose higher in the sky the Stambha rose skywards! and as it moved higher and higher, the Stambha rose, growing ever taller, too! The king, sitting on it, began to get scorched by the heat! Exactly at noon the sun touched the zenith. And do you know what happened? *The golden pillar touched the Surya Mandala!*'

Bhoja Raja was amazed. He forgot to even breathe!

'The king was burnt almost black! He closed his eyes and folded his hands in prayer! He prayed to the Sun God to save him. But he did not lose heart!'

The king had not moved! 'And then?' he said. His voice was a whisper.

'Well,' went on the doll, 'The Sun God was very pleased with my lord King Vikramaditya's, fearlessness and courage! He blessed him and healed his burns.

'I am indeed, very pleased with you, O king! And with your outstanding courage and bravery!' said the Sun God. 'None other than you could have done that!'

Surya blessed him with a long life and told him that he would shine with a new brilliance henceforth!

Children, do you know what 'Vikramaditya' means? Vikram means courage and Adithya means the sun. And 'Vikram+aditya' means one who is like the sun in his courage!

> 'Surya then presented Vikramaditya with a pair of dazzling divine earrings or '*karna kundalas*'. He told the king that they would always protect him and give him a shower of gold coins that could fill the river many times over, every day!'

Raja Bhoja sat perfectly still, listening. He had never heard anything like this in his whole life!

> 'Once the sun started to go down again towards the west, the Swarna Stambha slowly came down again! At sunset the divine pillar came back to its place on the river! Raja Vikramaditya got off and started back to his palace.'

Bhoja Raja was dumbfounded!

'The story is not yet over!' continued the doll.

'Oh!' said the king.

> 'On his way back, a man in need came to him and said 'O King! O Vikramaditya! I have heard great praise of your kindness and large-heartedness. I am in the habit of feeding the poor every day, O King! But now I have no money. I request your highness to help me!'

> 'And do you know what Vikramaditya did? Without another thought, he handed the hard-won *karna kundala*s to the man in need.'

The doll finished telling the story.

It asked Bhoja Raja, 'O king! Now tell me this! Have you heard of anyone as brave as king Vikramaditya? Or as kind and charitable? Who received the blessings of the Sun God? and gave away the divine, hard-won gift to a man, without a second thought?'

Raja Bhoja fell deep into thought. He knew he was neither as brave nor as generous as Vikramaditya.

The doll saw that the king was silent. It said, 'Do you think, O King, that you are fit to sit on his throne? A throne on which such a great and fearless king sat? If you can become as courageous and kind as he was, only then do you deserve to sit on this wonderful throne!' Saying this, the doll became quiet.

The king could not fool himself! He went to the palace, but he could not sleep that night. He lay awake and wondered and wondered!

He made up his mind that he would become a stronger, kinder and just king. He started practising all the good qualities every day!

And each time he went back to climb up the next stair, the two dolls there told him two more stories about Vikramaditya and his amazing qualities and each time Bhoja Raja would step down and work hard on himself to become a better man and a greater king.

And imagine, this happened all of thirty-two times! And the dolls told him thirty-two stories in all!

Finally he felt that he was fit to sit on the throne of Vikramaditya.

By this time Raja Bhoja had become a much better person. He was now a braver, kinder, humbler and stronger king! He was not proud any more and was not selfish at all!

And by the time he could sit on the throne, he was a changed man and a wonderful king. But sadly for him, he never got to sit on the throne of the great king Vikramaditya!

And do you know why?

The time had come for the throne to go back to where it belonged! It belonged to Indra, the chief of the devas, who had given the throne to Vikramaditya as a gift. And no one else could use it.

Now, have we learnt something from this story? I'm sure we have.

We can all learn to be a little more brave, helpful, kind and unselfish, can we not? ❋

57

THE ELVES AND THE SHOEMAKER

THE BROTHERS GRIMM; TRANSLATED BY EDGAR TAYLOR AND MARIAN EDWARDES

There was once a shoemaker, who worked very hard and was very honest: but still he could not earn enough to live upon; and at last all he had in the world was gone, save just leather enough to make one pair of shoes.

Then he cut his leather out, all ready to make up the next day, meaning to rise early in the morning to his work. His conscience was clear and his heart light amidst all his troubles; so he went peaceably to bed, left all his cares to Heaven, and soon fell asleep.

In the morning after he had said his prayers, he sat himself down to his work; when, to his great wonder, there stood the shoes all readymade, upon the table. The good man knew not what to say or think at such an odd thing happening. He looked at the workmanship; there was not one false stitch in the whole job; all was so neat and true, that it was quite a masterpiece.

The same day a customer came in, and the shoes suited him so well that he willingly paid a price higher than usual for them; and the poor shoemaker, with the money, bought leather enough to make two pairs more. In the evening he cut out the work and went to bed early, that he might get up and begin betimes next day; but he was saved all the trouble, for when he got up in the morning the work was done and ready.

Soon in came buyers, who paid him handsomely for his goods, so that he bought leather enough for four pairs more. He cut out the work again overnight and found it done in the morning, as before; and so it went on for some time: what was got ready in the evening was always done by daybreak, and the good man soon became thriving and well off again.

❋

One evening, about Christmas-time, as he and his wife were sitting over the fire chatting together, he said to her, 'I should like to sit up and watch tonight, that we may see who it is that comes and does my work for me.' The wife liked the thought; so they left a light burning and hid themselves in a corner of the room, behind a curtain that was hung up there, and watched what would happen.

As soon as it was midnight, there came in two little naked dwarfs; and they sat themselves upon the shoemaker's bench, took up all the work that was cut out, and began to ply with their little fingers, stitching and rapping and tapping away at such a rate that the shoemaker was all wonder and could not take his eyes off them. And on they went, till the job was quite done, and the shoes stood ready for use upon the table. This was long before daybreak; and then they bustled away as quick as lightning.

The next day the wife said to the shoemaker. 'These little wights have made us rich, and we ought to be thankful to them and do them a good turn if we can. I am quite sorry to see them run about as they do; and indeed it is not very decent, for they have nothing upon their backs to keep off the cold. I'll tell you what, I will make each of them a shirt and a coat and waistcoat, and a pair of pantaloons into the bargain; and do you make each of them a little pair of shoes.'

The thought pleased the good cobbler very much; and one evening, when all the things were ready, they laid them on the table, instead of the work that they used to cut out, and then went and hid themselves, to watch what the little elves would do.

About midnight in they came, dancing and skipping, hopped round the room, and then went to sit down to their work as usual; but when they saw the clothes lying for them, they laughed and chuckled, and seemed mightily delighted.

Then they dressed themselves in the twinkling of an eye, and danced and capered and sprang about, as merry as could be; till at last they danced out at the door, and away over the green.

The good couple saw them no more; but everything went well with them from that time forward, as long as they lived. ❋

58

ADVENTURES OF TOM THUMB

A FAIRY TALE; RETOLD BY LOGAN MARSHALL

A long time ago, a woodcutter lived with his wife in a small cottage not far from a great forest. They had seven children – all boys; and the youngest was the smallest little fellow ever seen. He was called Tom Thumb. But though he was so small, he was far cleverer than any of his brothers, and he heard a great deal more than anybody ever imagined.

It happened that just at this time there was a famine in the land, and the woodcutter and his wife became so poor that they could no longer give their boys enough to eat.

One night – after the boys had gone to bed – the husband sighing deeply, said, 'We cannot feed our children any longer, and to see them starve before our eyes is more than I can bear. Tomorrow morning, therefore, we will take them into the forest and leave them in the thickest part of it, so that they will not be able to find their way back.'

His wife wept bitterly at the thought of leaving their children to perish in the forest; but she, too, thought it better than to see them die before her eyes. So she consented to her husband's plan.

But all this time Tom Thumb had been awake, and he had overheard all the conversation. He lay awake a long while thinking what to do. Then, slipping quietly out of bed, he ran down to the river and filled his pocket with small white pebbles from the river's brink.

In the morning the parents called the children, and, after giving them a crust of bread, they all set out for the wood. Tom Thumb did not say a word to his brothers of what he had overheard; but, lingering behind, he dropped the pebbles from his pocket one by one, as they walked, so that he should be able to find his way home. When they reached a very thick part of the forest, the father and mother told the children to wait while they went a little farther to cut wood, but as soon as they were out of sight they turned and went home by another way.

When darkness fell, the children began to realize that they were deserted, and they began to cry loudly. Tom Thumb, however, did not cry.

'Do not weep, my brothers,' he said encouragingly. 'Only wait until the moon rises, and we shall soon be able to find our way home.'

When at length the moon rose, it shone down upon the white pebbles which Tom Thumb had scattered; and, following this path, the children soon reached their father's house.

But at first they were afraid to go in and waited outside the door to hear what their parents were talking about.

Now, it happened that when the father and mother reached home, they found a rich gentleman had sent them ten crowns, in payment for work which had been done long before. The wife went out at once and bought bread and meat, and she and her husband sat down to make a hearty meal. But the mother could not forget her little ones; and at last she cried to her husband – 'Alas! where are our poor children? How they would have enjoyed this good feast!'

The children, listening at the door, heard this and cried out, 'Here we are, mother; here we are!' and, overjoyed, the mother flew to let them in and kissed them all round.

Their parents were delighted to have their little ones with them again; but soon the ten crowns were spent, and they found themselves as badly off as before.

Once more they agreed to leave the children in the forest, and once again Tom Thumb overheard them. This time he did not trouble himself very much; he thought it would be easy for him to do as he had done before. He got up very early the next morning to go and get the pebbles; but, to his dismay, he found the house door securely locked. Then, indeed, he did not know what to do, and for a little while he was in great distress. However, at breakfast the mother gave each of the children a slice of bread, and Tom Thumb thought he would manage to make his piece of bread do as well as the pebbles, by breaking it up and dropping the crumbs as he went.

This time the father and mother took the children still deeper and farther into the wood, and then, slipping away, left them alone.

Tom Thumb consoled his brothers as before; but when he came to look for the crumbs of bread, not one of them was left. The birds had eaten them all up, and the poor children were lost in the forest, with no possible means of finding their way home.

Tom Thumb did not lose courage. He climbed to the top of a high tree and looked round to see if there was any way of getting help. In the distance he saw a light burning, and, coming down from the tree, he led his brothers toward the house from which it came.

When they knocked at the door, it was opened by a pleasant-looking woman, and Tom Thumb told her they were poor children who had lost their road and begged her to give them a night's shelter.

'Alas, my poor children!' said the woman, 'you do not know where you have come to. This is the house of an ogre who eats up little boys and girls.'

'But, madam,' replied Tom Thumb, 'what shall we do? If we go back to the forest we are certain to be torn to pieces by the wolves. We had better, I think, stay and be eaten by the ogre.'

The ogre's wife had pity on the little things, and she thought she would be able to hide them from her husband for one night. She took them in, gave them food and let them warm themselves by the fire.

Very soon there came a loud knocking at the door. It was the ogre come home. His wife hid the children under the bed and then hurried to let her husband in.

No sooner had the ogre entered than he began to sniff this way and that. 'I smell flesh,' he said, looking round the room.

'It must be the calf which has just been killed,' said his wife.

'I smell child's flesh, I tell you!' cried the ogre, and he suddenly made a dive under the bed and drew out the children one by one.

'Oh, ho, madam!' said he; 'so you thought to cheat me, did you? But, really, this is very lucky! I have invited three ogres to dinner tomorrow; these brats will make a nice dish.'

He fetched a huge knife and began sharpening it, while the poor boys fell on their knees and begged for mercy. But their prayers and entreaties were useless. The ogre seized one of the children and was just about to kill him, when his wife said, 'What in the world makes you take the trouble of killing them tonight? Why don't you leave them till the morning? There will be plenty of time, and they will be much fresher.'

'That is very true,' said the ogre, throwing down the knife. 'Give them a good supper, so that they may not get lean, and send them to bed.'

Now, the ogre had seven young daughters, who were all about the same age as Tom Thumb and his brothers. These young ogresses all slept together in one large bed, and every one of them had a crown of gold on her head. There was another bed of the same size in the room, and in this the ogre's wife, having provided them all with nightcaps, put the seven little boys.

But Tom Thumb was afraid that the ogre might change his mind in the night, and kill him and his brothers while they were asleep. So he crept softly out of bed, took off his brothers' nightcaps and his own, and stole over to the bed where the young ogresses lay. He drew off their crowns very gently, and put the nightcaps on their heads instead. Then he put the crowns on his brothers' heads and his own, and got into bed again.

In the middle of the night the ogre woke up, and began to be sorry that he had put off killing the boys until the morning.

'Never put off till tomorrow what you can do today,' he said; and, jumping out of bed, he got his knife and walked stealthily to the room where the boys were. He walked up to the bed, and they were all asleep except Tom Thumb, who, however, kept his eyes fast shut, and did not show that he was awake. The ogre touched their heads, one after another, and feeling the crowns of gold, he said to himself, 'What a mistake I was going to make!' He then went to bed where his own daughters were sleeping, and, feeling the nightcaps, he said, 'Oh, ho, here you are, my lads!' and in a moment he had killed them all. He then went back to his own room to sleep till morning.

As soon as Tom Thumb heard him snoring, he roused his brothers, and told them to dress quickly and follow him. He led them downstairs and out of the house; and then, stealing on tiptoe through the garden, they jumped down from the wall into the road and ran swiftly away.

In the morning, when the ogre found what a dreadful thing he had done, he was terribly shocked.

'Fetch me my seven-league boots,' he cried to his wife. 'I will go and catch those young vipers. They shall pay for this piece of work!' And, drawing on the magic boots, the ogre set out.

He went striding over the country, stepping from mountain to mountain, and crossing rivers as if they had been streams. The poor children watched him coming in fear and trembling. They had found the way to their father's home and had very nearly reached it when they saw the ogre racing after them.

Tom Thumb thought for a moment what was to be done. Then he saw a hollow place under a large rock.

'Get in there,' he said to his brothers.

When they were all in he crept in himself, but kept his eyes fixed on the ogre, to see what he would do.

The ogre, seeing nothing of the children, sat down to rest himself on the very rock under which the poor boys were hiding. He was tired with his journey, and soon fell fast asleep, and began to snore so loudly that the little fellows were terrified. Tom Thumb told his brothers to creep out softly and run home; which they did. Then he crept up to the ogre, pulled off the seven-league boots very gently and put them on his own feet, for being fairy boots they could fit themselves to any foot, however small.

As soon as Tom Thumb had put on the ogre's seven-league boots, he took ten steps to the Palace, which was seventy miles off, and asked to see the King. He offered to carry news to the King's army, which was then a long way off; and so useful was he with his magic boots, that in a short time he had made money enough to keep himself, his father, his mother and his six brothers without the trouble of working for the rest of their lives.

And now let us see what has become of the wicked ogre, whom we left sleeping on the rock.

When he awoke he missed his seven-league boots, and set off for home very angry.

On his way he had to cross a bog; and, forgetting that he was no longer wearing his magic boots, he tried to cross it with one stride. But, instead, he put his foot down in the middle and began to sink. As fast as he tried to pull out one foot, the other sank deeper, until at last he was swallowed up in the black slime – and that was the end of him. ❋

59

WHY THE SEA IS SALT

A FAIRY TALE; RETOLD BY ANDREW LANG

Once upon a time, long, long ago, there were two brothers, the one rich and the other poor. When Christmas Eve came, the poor one had not a bite in the house, either of meat or bread; so he went to his brother, and begged him, in God's name, to give him something for Christmas Day. It was by no means the first time that the brother had been forced to give something to him, and he was not pleased at being asked.

'If you will do what I ask you, you shall have a whole ham,' said he. The poor one immediately thanked him, and promised this.

'Well, here is the ham, and now you must go straight to Dead Man's Hall,' said the rich brother, throwing the ham to him.

'Well, I will do what I have promised,' said the other, and he took the ham and set off. He went on and on for the livelong day, and at nightfall he came to a place where there was a bright light.

An old man with a long white beard was standing in the outhouse, chopping Yule logs.

'Good evening,' said the man with the ham.

'Good evening to you. Where are you going at this late hour?' said the man.

'I am going to Dead Man's Hall, if only I am on the right track,' answered the poor man.

'Oh! Yes, you are right enough, for it is here,' said the old man. 'When you get inside they will all want to buy your ham, for they don't get much meat to eat there; but you must not sell it unless you can get the hand-mill that stands behind the door for it. When you come out again I will teach you how to stop the hand-mill, which is useful for almost everything.'

So the man with the ham thanked the other for his good advice and rapped at the door.

When he got in, everything happened just as the old man had said it would: all the people, great and small, came round him like ants on an anthill, and each tried to outbid the other for the ham.

'By rights my old woman and I ought to have it for our Christmas dinner, but, since you have set your hearts upon it, I must just give it up to you,' said the man. 'But, if I sell it, I will have the hand-mill that is standing there behind the door.'

At first they would not hear of this, and haggled and bargained with the man, but he stuck to what he had said, and the people were forced to give him the hand-mill.

When the man came out again into the yard, he asked the old woodcutter how he was to stop the hand-mill, and when he had learned that, he thanked him and set off home with all the speed he could, but did not get there until after the clock had struck twelve on Christmas Eve.

'Where in the world have you been?' said the old woman. 'Here I have sat waiting hour after hour, and have not even two sticks to lay across each other under the Christmas porridge-pot.'

'Oh! I could not come before; I had something of importance to see about, and a long way to go, too; but now you shall just see!' said the man, and then he set the hand-mill on the table, and asked it to first grind light, then a tablecloth, and then meat, and beer, and everything else that was good for a Christmas Eve's supper; and the mill ground all that he ordered. 'Bless me!' said the old woman as one thing after another appeared; and she wanted to know where her husband had got the mill from.

'Never mind where I got it; you can see that it is a good one, and the water that turns it will never freeze,' said the man. So he ground meat and drink, and all kinds of good things, to last all Christmas-tide, and on the third day he invited all his friends to come to a feast.

Now when the rich brother saw all that there was at the banquet and in the house, he was both vexed and angry. 'On Christmas Eve he was so poor that he came to me and begged for a trifle, for God's sake, and now he gives a feast as if he were both a count and a king!' thought he.

'But, for heaven's sake, tell me where you got your riches from,' said he to his brother.

'From behind the door,' said he who owned the mill; but later in the evening, he could not stop himself from telling how he had come by the hand-mill. 'There you see what has brought me all my wealth!' said he, and brought out the mill, and made it grind first one thing and then another.

When the brother saw that, he insisted on having the mill, and after a great deal of persuasion got it; but he had to give three hundred dollars for it, and the poor brother was to keep it till the haymaking was over, for he thought: 'If I keep it as long as that, I can make it grind meat and drink that will last many a long year.'

When hay-harvest came the rich brother got it, but the other had taken good care not to teach him how to stop it. It was evening when the rich man got the mill home, and in the morning he asked the old woman go out and spread the hay after the mowers, and he would attend to the house himself that day, he said.

So, when dinner time drew near, he set the mill on the kitchen table, and said, 'Grind herrings and milk pottage, and do it both quickly and well.'

So the mill began to grind herrings and milk pottage, and first all the dishes and tubs were filled, and then it came out all over the kitchen floor. The man twisted and turned it, and did all he could to make the mill stop, but, howsoever he turned it and screwed it, the mill went on grinding, and in a short time the pottage rose so high that the man was likely to be drowned.

So he threw open the parlour door, but it was not long before the mill had ground the parlour full, too, and it was with difficulty and danger that the man could go through the stream of pottage and get hold of the door latch.

When he got the door open, he did not stay long in the room, but ran out, and the herrings and pottage came after him, and it streamed out over both farm and field.

Now the old woman, who was out spreading the hay, said to the women and the mowers, 'It may be that the master finds he is not good at making pottage and I should do well to help him.'

So they began to straggle homeward, but when they had got a little way up the hill they met the herrings and pottage and bread, all pouring forth and winding about one over the other, and the man himself in front of the flood.

'Take care that you are not drowned in the pottage!' he cried as he went by them as if Mischief were at his heels, down to where his brother dwelt. Then he begged him, for God's sake, to take the mill back again, and that in an instant, for, said he, 'If it grinds one hour longer the whole district will be destroyed by herrings and pottage.'

But the brother would not take it until the other paid him three hundred dollars. Now the poor brother had both the money and the mill again.

So it was not long before he had a farmhouse much finer than that in which his brother lived, but the mill ground him so much money that he covered it with plates of gold; and the farmhouse lay close by the seashore, so it shone and glittered far out to sea. Everyone who sailed by there now had to be put in to visit the rich man in the gold farmhouse, and everyone wanted to see the wonderful mill, for the report of it spread far and wide, and there was no one who had not heard of it.

After a long, long time came also a skipper* who wished to see the mill. He asked if it could make

* *Captain of a ship*

salt. 'Yes, it could make salt,' said he who owned it, and when the skipper heard that, he wished with all his might and main to have the mill, let it cost what it might, for, he thought, if he had it, he would get off having to sail far away over the perilous sea for freights of salt.

At first the man would not hear of parting with it, but the skipper begged and prayed, and at last the man sold it to him, and got many, many thousand dollars for it.

When the skipper had got the mill on his back he did not stay there long, for he was so afraid that the man would change his mind, and he had no time to ask how he was to stop it grinding, but got on board his ship as fast as he could.

When he had gone a little way out to sea he took the mill on deck. 'Grind salt, and grind both quickly and well,' said the skipper.

So the mill began to grind salt, till it spouted out like water, and when the skipper had got the ship filled he wanted to stop the mill, but whichsoever way he turned it, and how-much-so-ever he tried, it went on grinding, and the heap of salt grew higher and higher, until at last the ship sank. There lies the mill at the bottom of the sea, and still, day by day, it grinds on; and that is why the sea is salt. ❋

– *Abridged from the original story.*

60

RAPUNZEL

THE BROTHERS GRIMM

Once upon a time there lived a man and his wife who were very unhappy because they had no children. These good people had a little window at the back of their house, which looked into the most lovely garden, full of all manner of beautiful flowers and vegetables; but the garden was surrounded by a high wall, and no one dared to enter it, for it belonged to a witch of great power, who was feared by the whole world.

One day the woman stood at the window overlooking the garden and saw there a bed full of the finest rampion:* the leaves looked so fresh and green that she longed to eat them. The desire grew day by day, and she pined away and became quite pale and wretched. Then her husband grew alarmed and said, 'What ails you, dear wife?'

* *A plant whose root is used in salad in Europe*

'Oh,' she answered, 'if I don't get some rampion to eat out of the garden behind the house, I know I shall die.'

So at dusk the man climbed over the wall into the witch's garden, and, hastily gathering a handful of rampion leaves, he returned with them to his wife. She made them into a salad, which tasted so good that her longing for the forbidden food was greater than ever. There was nothing for it but that her husband should climb over the garden wall again and fetch her some more. So at dusk over he got, but when he reached the other side he drew back in terror, for there, standing before him, was the old Witch.

'How dare you,' she said, with a wrathful glance, 'climb into my garden and steal my rampion like a common thief? You shall suffer for your foolhardiness.'

'Oh!' he implored. 'Pardon my presumption; necessity alone drove me to the deed. My wife saw your rampion from her window and had such a desire for it that she would certainly have died if her wish had not been gratified.' Then the Witch's anger was a little appeased, and she said, 'If it's as you say, you may take as much rampion away with you as you like, but on one condition only – that you give me the child your wife will shortly bring into the world. I will look after it like a mother.'

The man in his terror agreed to everything she asked, and as soon as the child was born the Witch appeared, and having given it the name of Rapunzel, which is the same as rampion, she carried it off.

Rapunzel was the most beautiful child under the sun. When she was twelve years old the Witch shut her up in a tower, in the middle of a great wood, and the tower had neither stairs nor doors, only high up at the very top a small window. When the old Witch wanted to get in she stood underneath and called out:

'Rapunzel, Rapunzel,
Let down your golden hair,'

for Rapunzel had wonderful long hair, and it was as fine as spun gold. Whenever she heard the Witch's voice she unloosed her plaits, and let her hair fall down out of the window about twenty yards below, and the old Witch climbed up by it.

After they had lived like this for a few years, it happened one day that a Prince was riding through the wood and passed by the tower. As he drew near it he heard someone singing so sweetly that he stood still spellbound and listened. It was Rapunzel in her loneliness letting her sweet voice ring out into the wood. The Prince longed to see the owner of the voice, but he sought in vain for a door in the tower. He rode home, but he was so haunted by the song he had heard that he returned every day to the wood and listened. One day, while hiding behind a tree, he saw the old Witch approach and heard her call out:

'Rapunzel, Rapunzel,
Let down your golden hair.'

Then Rapunzel let down her plaits, and the Witch climbed up by them.

'So that's the staircase, is it?' said the Prince. 'Then I, too, will climb it and try my luck.'

So on the following day, at dusk, he went to the foot of the tower and cried:

'Rapunzel, Rapunzel,
Let down your golden hair,'

and as soon as she had let it down the Prince climbed up.

At first Rapunzel was terribly frightened when a man came in, for she had never seen one before, but the Prince spoke to her so kindly, and told her at once that his heart had been so touched by her singing, that he felt he should know no peace of mind till he had seen her.

Very soon Rapunzel forgot her fear, and when he asked her to marry him she consented at once. 'For,' she thought, 'I'll certainly be happier with him than with the old Witch.' So she put her hand in his and said, 'Yes, I will gladly go with you, only how am I to get down out of the tower? Every time you come to see me you must bring a skein of silk with you, and I will make a ladder of them, and when it is finished I will climb down by it, and you will take me away on your horse.'

They arranged that till the ladder was ready, he was to come to her every evening, because the old woman was with her during the day. The old Witch, of course, knew nothing of what was going on, till one day Rapunzel, not thinking of what she was about, turned to the Witch and said, 'How is it, good mother, that you are so much harder to pull up than the young Prince? He is always with me in a moment.'

'Oh! You wicked child,' cried the Witch. 'I thought I had hidden you safely from the whole world, and in spite of it you have managed to deceive me.'

In her wrath she seized Rapunzel's beautiful hair, wound it round and round her left hand, and then grasping a pair of scissors in her right, snip snap, off it came, and the beautiful plaits lay on the ground. And, worse than this, she was so hard-hearted that she took Rapunzel to a lonely desert place, and there left her to live in loneliness and misery.

But on the evening of the day in which she had driven poor Rapunzel away, the Witch fastened the plaits on to a hook in the window, and when the Prince came and called out:

'Rapunzel, Rapunzel,
Let down your golden hair,'

she let them down, and the Prince climbed up as usual, but instead of his beloved Rapunzel he found the old Witch, who fixed her evil, glittering eyes on him and cried mockingly, 'Ah, ah! The pretty bird has flown and its song is dumb; the cat caught it and will scratch out your eyes, too. Rapunzel is lost to you for ever.'

The Prince was beside himself with grief, and in his despair he jumped right down from the tower, and, though he escaped with his life, the thorns among which he fell pierced his eyes out. Then he wandered, blind and miserable, through the wood, eating nothing but roots and berries, and weeping and lamenting the loss of his lovely bride.

So he wandered about for some years, as wretched and unhappy as he could well be, and at last he came to the desert place where Rapunzel was living. Of a sudden he heard a voice which seemed strangely familiar to him. He walked eagerly in the direction of the sound, and when he was quite close, Rapunzel recognized him and fell on his neck and wept. But two of her tears touched his eyes, and in a moment he saw as well as he had ever done. Then he led her to his kingdom, where they lived happily ever after. ❋

– Abridged from the original story.

61

THUMBELINA

HANS CHRISTIAN ANDERSEN; RETOLD BY MABIE, HALE AND FORBUSH

She had a little house of her own, a little garden, too, this woman of whom I am going to tell you, but for all that she was not quite happy.

'If only I had a little child of my own,' she said, 'how the walls would ring with her laughter, and how the flowers would brighten at her coming. Then, indeed, I should be quite happy.'

And an old witch heard what the woman wished, and said, 'Oh, but that is easily managed. Here is a barleycorn. Plant it in a flowerpot and tend it carefully, and then you will see what will happen.'

The woman was in a great hurry to go home and plant the barleycorn, but she did not forget to say 'thank you' to the old witch. She not only thanked her, she even stayed to give her six silver pennies.

Then she hurried away to her home, took a flowerpot and planted her precious barleycorn.

And what do you think happened? Almost before the corn was planted, up shot a large and beautiful flower. It was still unopened. The petals were folded closely together, but it looked like a tulip. It really was a tulip, a red and yellow one, too.

The woman loved flowers. She stooped and kissed the beautiful bud. As her lips touched the petals, they burst open, and oh! wonder of wonders! there, in the very middle of the flower, there sat a little child. Such a tiny, pretty little maiden she was.

They called her Thumbelina. That was because she was no bigger than the woman's thumb.

And where do you think she slept? A little walnut shell, lined with blue, that was her cradle.

When she slept little Thumbelina lay in her cradle on a tiny heap of violets, with the petal of a pale pink rose to cover her.

And where do you think she played? A table was her playground. On the table the woman placed a plate of water. Little Thumbelina called that her lake.

Round the plate were scented flowers, the blossoms lying on the edge, while the pale green stalks reached thirstily down to the water.

In the lake floated a large tulip leaf. This was Thumbelina's little boat. Seated there she sailed from side to side of her little lake, rowing cleverly with two white horsehairs. As she rowed backwards and forwards she sang softly to herself. The woman listening heard, and thought she had never known so sweet a song.

And now such a sad thing happened.

In through the broken windowpane hopped a big toad, oh! such an ugly big toad. She hopped right on to the table, where Thumbelina lay dreaming in her tiny cradle, under the pale pink rose leaf.

She peeped at her, this ugly old toad.

'How beautiful the little maiden is,' she croaked. 'She will make a lovely bride for my handsome son.' And she lifted the little cradle, with Thumbelina in it, and hopped out through the broken windowpane, down into the garden.

At the foot of the garden was a broad stream. Here, under the muddy banks lived the old toad with her son.

How handsome she thought him! But he was really very ugly. Indeed, he was exactly like his mother.

When he saw little Thumbelina in her tiny cradle, he croaked with delight.

'Do not make so much noise,' said his mother, 'or you will wake the tiny creature. We may lose her if we are not careful. The slightest breeze would waft her far away. She is as light as gossamer.'

Then the old toad carried Thumbelina out into the middle of the stream. 'She will be safe here,' she said, as she laid her gently on one of the leaves of a large water lily, and paddled back to her son.

'We will make ready the best rooms under the mud,' she told him, 'and then you and the little maiden will be married.'

Poor little Thumbelina! She had not seen the ugly big toad yet, nor her ugly son.

When she woke up early in the morning, how she wept! Water all around her! How could she reach the shore? Poor little Thumbelina!

Down under the mud the old toad was very busy, decking the best room with buttercups and buds of water-lilies to make it gay for her little daughter-in-law, Thumbelina.

'Now we will go to bring her little bed and place it ready,' said the old toad, and together she and her son swam out to the leaf where little Thumbelina sat.

'Here is my handsome son,' she said, 'he is to be your husband,' and she bowed low in the water, for she wished to be very polite to the little maiden.

'Croak, croak,' was all the young toad could say, as he looked at his pretty little bride.

Then they took away the tiny little bed, and Thumbelina was left all alone.

How the tears stained her pretty little face! How fast they fell into the stream! Even the fish as they swam hither and thither thought, 'How it rains today,' as the tiny drops fell thick and fast.

They popped up their heads and saw the forlorn little maiden.

'She shall not marry the ugly toad,' they said, as they looked with eager eyes at the pretty child. 'No, she shall not marry the ugly toad.'

But what could the little fish do to help Thumbelina?

Oh! They were such clever little fish!

They found the green stem which held the leaf on which Thumbelina sat. They bit it with their little sharp teeth, and they never stopped biting, till at last they bit the green stem through; and away, down the stream, floated the leaf, carrying with it little Thumbelina.

'Free, free!' she sang, and her voice tinkled as a chime of fairy bells. 'Free, free!' she sang merrily as she floated down the stream, away, far away out of reach of the ugly old toad and her ugly son.

And as she floated on, the little wild birds sang round her, and on the banks the little wild harebells bowed to her.

Butterflies were flitting here and there in the sunshine. A pretty little white one fluttered on to the leaf on which sat Thumbelina. He loved the tiny maiden so well that he settled down beside her.

Now she was quite happy! Birds around her, flowers near her and the water gleaming like gold in the summer sunshine. What besides could little Thumbelina wish?

She took off her sash and threw one end of it round the butterfly. The other end she fastened firmly to the leaf. On and on floated the leaf, the little maiden and the butterfly.

Suddenly a great cockchafer buzzed along. Alas! He caught sight of little Thumbelina. He flew to her, put his claw round her tiny waist and carried her off, up on to a tree.

Poor little Thumbelina! How frightened she was! How grieved she was, too, for had she not lost her little friend the butterfly?

Would he fly away, she wondered, or would her sash hold him fast?

The cockchafer was charmed with the little maiden. He placed her tenderly on the largest leaf he could find. He gathered honey for her from the flowers, and as she sipped it, he sat near and told her how beautiful she looked.

But there were other chafers living in the tree, and when they came to see little Thumbelina, they said, 'She is not pretty at all.'

'She has only two legs,' said one.

'She has no feelers,' said another.

Some said she was too thin, others that she was too fat, and then they all buzzed and hummed together, 'How ugly she is, how ugly she is!' But all the time little Thumbelina was the prettiest, daintiest little maiden that ever lived.

And now the cockchafer who had flown off with little Thumbelina thought he had been rather foolish to admire her.

He looked at her again. 'Pretty? No, after all she was not very pretty.' He would have nothing to do with her, and away he and all the other chafers flew. Only first they carried little Thumbelina down from the tree and placed her on a daisy. She wept because she was so ugly – so ugly that the chafers could not live with her. But all the time, you know, she was the prettiest little maiden in the world.

She was living all alone in the wood now, but it was summer and she could not feel sad or lonely while the warm golden sunshine touched her so gently, while the birds sang to her, and the flowers bowed to her.

Yes, little Thumbelina was happy. She ate honey from the flowers, and drank dew out of the golden buttercups, and danced and sang the livelong day.

But summer passed away and autumn came. The birds began to whisper of flying to warmer countries, and the flowers began to fade and hang their heads, and as autumn passed away, winter came, cold, dreary winter.

Thumbelina shivered with cold. Her little frock was thin and old. She would certainly be frozen to death, she thought, as she wrapped herself up in a withered leaf.

Then the snow began to fall, and each snowflake seemed to smother her. She was so very tiny.

Close to the wood lay a cornfield. The beautiful golden grain had been carried away long ago, now there was only dry short stubble. But to little Thumbelina the stubble was like a great forest.

She walked through the hard field. She was shaking with cold. All at once she saw a little door just before her. She looked again – yes, it was a door.

The field-mouse had made a little house under the stubble and lived so cosily there. She had a big room full of corn, and she had a kitchen and pantry as well.

'Perhaps I shall get some food here,' thought the cold and hungry little maiden, as she stood knocking at the door, just like a tiny beggar child. She had had nothing to eat for two long days. Oh, she was very hungry!

'What a tiny thing you are!' said the field-mouse, as she opened the door and saw Thumbelina. 'Come in and dine with me.'

How glad Thumbelina was, and how she enjoyed dining with the field-mouse.

She behaved so prettily that the old field-mouse told her she might live with her while the cold weather lasted. 'And you shall keep my room clean and neat, and you shall tell me stories,' she added.

That is how Thumbelina came to live with the field-mouse and to meet Mr Mole. ❋

– This is an excerpt. Do read the rest of the story to find out what happened to Thumbelina!

62

THE OTTERS AND THE WOLF

A JATAKA TALE; RETOLD BY ELLEN C. BABBITT

One day a Wolf said to her mate, 'A longing has come upon me to eat fresh fish.'

'I will go and get some for you,' said he and he went down to the river.

There he saw two Otters standing on the bank looking for fish. Soon one of the Otters saw a great fish, and entering the water with a bound, he caught hold of the tail of the fish.

But the fish was strong and swam away, dragging the Otter after him. 'Come and help me,' the Otter called back to his friend. 'This great fish will be enough for both of us!'

So the other Otter went into the water. The two together were able to bring the fish to land. 'Let us divide the fish into two parts.'

'I want the half with the head on,' said one.

'You cannot have that half. That is mine,' said the other. 'You take the tail.'

The Wolf heard the Otters and he went up to them.

Seeing the Wolf, the Otters said, 'Lord of the grey-grass colour, this fish was caught by both of us together. We cannot agree about dividing him. Will you divide him for us?'

The Wolf cut off the tail and gave it to one, giving the head to the other. He took the large middle part for himself, saying to them, 'You can eat the head and the tail without quarrelling.' And away he ran with the body of the fish. The Otters stood and looked at each other. They had nothing to say, but each thought to himself that the Wolf had run off with the best of the fish.

The Wolf was pleased and said to himself, as he ran toward home, 'Now I have fresh fish for my mate.'

His mate, seeing him coming, came to meet him, saying, 'How did you get fish? You live on land, not in the water.'

Then he told her of the quarrel of the Otters. 'I took the fish as pay for settling their quarrel,' said he. ❋

63

CINDERELLA
OR
THE LITTLE GLASS SLIPPER

A FAIRY TALE; RETOLD BY ANONYMOUS

There was, many years ago, a gentleman who had a charming lady for his wife. They had one daughter only, who was very dutiful to her parents. But while she was still very young, her mamma died, to the grief of her husband and daughter. After a time, the little girl's papa married another lady. Now this lady was proud and haughty, and had two grown-up daughters as disagreeable as herself; so the poor girl found everything at home changed for the worse.

But she bore all her troubles with patience, not even complaining to her father, and, in spite of her hard toil, she grew more lovely every year.

Now the King's son gave a grand ball, and all persons of quality were invited to it. Our two young ladies were not overlooked. Nothing was now talked of but the rich dresses they were to wear.

At last the happy day arrived. The two proud sisters set off in high spirits. Cinderella followed them with her eyes until the coach was out of sight. She then began to cry bitterly. While she was sobbing, her godmother, who was a Fairy, appeared before her.

'Cinderella,' said the Fairy, 'I am your godmother, and for the sake of your dear mamma I have come to cheer you up, so dry your tears. You shall go to the grand ball tonight, but you must do just as I bid you. Go into the garden and bring me a pumpkin.'

Cinderella brought the finest that was there. Her godmother scooped it out very quickly, and then struck it with her wand, upon which it was changed into a beautiful coach.

Afterwards, the old lady peeped into the mousetrap, where she found six mice. She tapped them lightly with her wand, and each mouse became a fine horse. The rat-trap contained two large rats; one of these she turned into a coachman, and the other into a postilion.*

The old lady then told Cinderella to go into the garden and look for half-a-dozen lizards. These she changed into six footmen, dressed in the gayest livery.

When all these things had been done, the kind godmother, touching her with her wand, changed her worn-out clothes into a beautiful ball-dress embroidered with pearls and silver. She then gave her a pair of glass slippers, that is, they were woven of the most delicate spun-glass, fine as the web of a spider.

When Cinderella was thus attired, her godmother made her get into her splendid coach, giving her a warning to leave the ball before the clock struck twelve.

On her arrival, her beauty struck everybody with wonder. The gallant Prince gave her a courteous welcome, and led her into the ballroom; and the King and Queen were as much enchanted with her, as the Prince conducted her to the supper-table, and was too much occupied in waiting upon her to partake of anything himself. While seated, Cinderella heard the clock strike three-quarters past eleven. She rose to

* *A person who sits with the coachman to help guide the horses*

leave, the Prince pressing her to accept an invitation for the ball on the following evening.

On reaching home, her godmother praised her for being so punctual and agreed to let her go to the next night's ball.

Although she seemed to be tired, her sisters, instead of showing pity, teased her with glowing accounts of the splendid scene they had just left, and spoke particularly of the beautiful Princess. Cinderella was delighted to hear all this and asked them the name of the Princess, but they replied, nobody knew her. So much did they say in praise of the lady, that Cinderella expressed a desire to go to the next ball to see the Princess; but this only served to bring out their dislike of poor Cinderella still more, and they would not lend her the meanest of their dresses.

The next evening the two sisters went to the ball, and Cinderella also, who was still more splendidly dressed than before. Her enjoyment was even greater than at the first ball, and she was so occupied with the Prince's tender sayings that she was not so quick in marking the progress of time.

To her alarm she heard the clock strike twelve. She fled from the ballroom; but in a moment the coach changed again to a pumpkin, the horses to mice, the coachman and postilion to rats, the footmen to lizards, and Cinderella's beautiful dress to her old shabby clothes. In her haste she dropped one of her glass slippers, and reached home, out of breath, with none of her godmother's fairy gifts but one glass slipper.

When her sisters arrived after the ball, they spoke in terms of rapture of the unknown Princess, and told Cinderella about the little glass slipper she had dropped, and how the Prince picked it up. It was evident to all the Court that the Prince was determined if possible, to find out the owner of the slipper; and a few days afterwards a royal herald proclaimed that the King's son would marry her whose foot the glass slipper should be found exactly to fit.

This proclamation caused a great sensation. Ladies of all ranks were permitted to try on the slipper, but it was of no use. Cinderella now said, 'Let me try – perhaps it may fit me.' It slipped on in a moment. Great was the vexation of the two sisters at this; but what was their astonishment when Cinderella took the fellow slipper out of her pocket!

At that moment the godmother appeared and touched Cinderella's clothes with her wand. Her sisters then saw that she was the beautiful lady they had met at the ball, and, throwing themselves at her feet, craved her forgiveness.

A short time after, she was married to the Prince.

64

HOW THE RHINOCEROS GOT HIS SKIN

RUDYARD KIPLING

Once upon a time, on an uninhabited island on the shores of the Red Sea, there lived a Parsee from whose hat the rays of the sun were reflected in more-than-oriental splendour. And the Parsee lived by the Red Sea with nothing but his hat and his knife and a cooking-stove of the kind that you must particularly never touch. And one day he took flour and water and currants and plums and sugar and things, and made himself one cake which was two feet across and three feet thick. It was indeed a Superior Comestible (that's magic), and he put it on stove because he was allowed to cook on the stove, and he baked it and he baked it till it was all done brown and smelt most sentimental.

But just as he was going to eat it there came down to the beach from the Altogether Uninhabited Interior one Rhinoceros with a horn on his nose, two piggy eyes, and few manners. In those days the Rhinoceros's skin fitted him quite tight. There were no wrinkles in it anywhere. He looked exactly like a Noah's Ark Rhinoceros, but of course much bigger.

All the same, he had no manners then, and he has no manners now, and he never will have any manners. He said, 'How!' and the Parsee left that cake and climbed to the top of a palm tree with nothing on but his hat, from which the rays of the sun were always reflected in more-than-oriental splendour. And the Rhinoceros upset the oil-stove with his nose, and the cake rolled on the sand, and he spiked that cake on the horn of his nose, and he ate it, and he went away, waving his tail, to the desolate and Exclusively Uninhabited Interior which abuts on the islands of Mazanderan, Socotra, and Promontories of the Larger Equinox.

Then the Parsee came down from his palm tree and put the stove on its legs and recited the following *sloka*, which, as you have not heard, I will now proceed to relate:

Them that takes cakes
Which the Parsee-man bakes
Makes dreadful mistakes.

And there was a great deal more in that than you would think.

Because, five weeks later, there was a heatwave in the Red Sea, and everybody took off all the clothes they had. The Parsee took off his hat; but the Rhinoceros took off his skin and carried it over his shoulder as he came down to the beach to bathe. In those days it buttoned underneath with three buttons and looked like a waterproof. He said nothing whatever about the Parsee's cake, because he had eaten it all; and he never had any manners, then, since, or henceforward. He waddled straight into the water and blew bubbles through his nose, leaving his skin on the beach.

Presently the Parsee came by and found the skin, and he smiled one smile that ran all round his face two times. Then he danced three times round the skin and rubbed his hands. Then he went to his camp and filled his hat with cake-crumbs, for the Parsee never ate anything but cake, and never swept out his camp. He took that skin, and he shook that skin, and he scrubbed that skin, and he rubbed that skin just as full of old, dry, stale, tickly cake-crumbs and some burned currants as ever it could possibly hold. Then he climbed to the top of his palm tree and waited for the Rhinoceros to come out of the water and put it on.

And the Rhinoceros did. He buttoned it up with the three buttons, and it tickled like cake-crumbs in bed. Then he wanted to scratch, but that made it worse; and then he lay down on the sands and rolled and rolled and rolled, and every time he rolled the cake crumbs tickled him worse and worse and worse.

Then he ran to the palm tree and rubbed and rubbed and rubbed himself against it. He rubbed so much and so hard that he rubbed his skin into a great fold over his shoulders, and another fold underneath, where the buttons used to be (but he rubbed the buttons off), and he rubbed some more folds over his legs. And it spoiled his temper, but it didn't make the least difference to the cake-crumbs. They were inside his skin and they tickled.

So he went home, very angry indeed and horribly scratchy; and from that day to this every rhinoceros has great folds in his skin and a very bad temper, all on account of the cake-crumbs inside.

But the Parsee came down from his palm tree, wearing his hat, from which the rays of the sun were reflected in more-than-oriental splendour, packed up his cooking-stove, and went away in the direction of Orotavo, Amygdala, the Upland Meadows of Anantarivo and the Marshes of Sonaput.

THIS Uninhabited Island
Is off Cape Gardafui,
By the Beaches of Socotra
And the Pink Arabian Sea:
But it's hot—too hot from Suez
For the likes of you and me
Ever to go
In a P. and O.
And call on the Cake-Parsee! ❋

65

DAMON AND PYTHIAS

A GREEK LEGEND; RETOLD BY JAMES BALDWIN

A young man whose name was Pythias had done something which the tyrant Dionysius did not like. For this offence he was dragged to prison, and a day was set when he should be put to death. His home was far away, and he wanted very much to see his father and mother and friends before he died.

'Only give me leave to go home and say goodbye to those whom I love,' he said, 'and then I will come back and give up my life.'

The tyrant laughed at him. 'How can I know that you will keep your promise?' he said. 'You only want to cheat me, and save yourself.'

Then a young man whose name was Damon said, 'O king! Put me in prison in place of my friend Pythias, and let him go to put his affairs in order, and to bid his friends farewell. I know that he will come back as he promised, for he is a man who has never broken his word. But if he is not here on the day which you have set, then I will die in his stead.'

The tyrant was surprised that anybody should make such an offer. He at last agreed to let Pythias go, and gave orders that the young man Damon should be shut up in prison.

Time passed, and by and by the day drew near which had been set for Pythias to die; and he had not come back. The tyrant ordered the jailer to keep close watch upon Damon, and not let him escape. But Damon did not try to escape. He still had faith in the truth and honor of his friend. He said, 'If Pythias does not come back in time, it will not be his fault. It will be because he is hindered against his will.'

At last the day came, and then the very hour. Damon was ready to die. His trust in his friend was as firm as ever; and he said that he did not grieve at having to suffer for one whom he loved so much.

Then the jailer came to lead him to his death, but at the same moment Pythias came to the door. He had been delayed by storms and shipwreck, and he had feared that he was too late. He greeted Damon kindly, and then gave himself into the hands of the jailer.

The tyrant was not so bad but that he could see good in others. And so he set them both free.

'I would give all my wealth to have one such friend,' he said. ❋

66

BEAUTY AND THE BEAST

A FAIRY TALE; RETOLD BY LOGAN MARSHALL

There was once a Merchant who had three daughters, the youngest of whom was so beautiful that everybody called her Beauty. This made the two eldest very jealous; and, as they were spiteful and bad-tempered by nature, instead of loving their younger sister they felt nothing but envy and hatred towards her.

After some years there came a terrible storm at sea, and most of the Merchant's ships were sunk, and he became very poor. He and his family were obliged to live in a very small house and do without the servants and fine clothes to which they had been used. The two eldest sisters did nothing but weep and lament for their lost fortune, but Beauty did her best to keep the house bright and cheerful, so that her father might not miss too much all the comfort and luxury he was used to.

One day the Merchant told his daughters that he was going to take a journey into foreign lands in the hope of recovering some of his property. Then he asked them what they would like him to bring them home in case he should be successful. The eldest daughter asked for fine gowns and beautiful clothing; the second for jewels and gold and silver trinkets.

'And Beauty – what would Beauty like?' asked the father.

Beauty was so happy and contented always that there was scarcely anything for which she longed. She thought for a moment, then she said, 'I should like best of all a red rose!' The other sisters burst out laughing and scoffed at Beauty's simple request; but her father promised to bring her what she wanted.

He was away for nearly a year and was fortunate to win back a great part of his lost wealth. When the time came for his return, he was easily able to buy the things his eldest daughters wished for; but nowhere could he find a red rose to take home to Beauty.

When he was within a few miles journey of his home, he lost himself in a thick wood. Darkness came on, and he began to be afraid that he would have to pass the night under a tree, when suddenly he saw a bright light shining in the distance. He went towards it, and on his approach found it came from a great castle that was set right in the heart of the forest.

The Merchant made up his mind to ask if he might spend the night there; but to his surprise, when he reached the door he found it set wide open, and nobody about. After a while, finding that no one came in answer to his repeated knocking, he walked inside. There he found a table laid with every delicacy, and, being very hungry, he sat down and made a good repast. After he had finished his supper he laid himself down on a luxurious couch, and in a few minutes was fast asleep.

In the morning, after eating a hearty breakfast, which he found prepared for him, he left the mysterious castle, without having set eyes on a single person. As he was passing through the garden he found himself in an avenue of rose trees, all covered with beautiful red roses.

'Here are such thousands of flowers,' he said to himself, 'that, surely, one bud will not be missed;' and, thinking of Beauty, he broke off a rose from one of the bushes.

Scarcely had he done so when he heard a terrible noise, and, turning round, he saw coming towards him a hideous Beast, who exclaimed in an awful tone, 'Ungrateful wretch! You have partaken of my hospitality, have eaten of my food, have slept in my house, and in return you try to rob me of my roses. For this theft you shall die!'

The Merchant fell on his knees and begged for pardon, but the Beast would not listen to him.

'Either you must die now, or else you must swear to send me in your stead the first living thing that meets you on your return home,' he said; and the Merchant, overcome with terror, gave his promise.

But to his horror and dismay, it was his youngest daughter, Beauty, who first ran out to greet him on his return. She had seen him coming from afar and hastened to welcome him home.

She did not at first understand her father's grief at seeing her; but when he told her the story of the Beast and his promise she did her best to comfort him. 'Do not fear, dear father,' she said, 'perhaps the Beast will not prove so terrible as he looks. He spared your life; he may spare mine, since I have done him no harm.'

Her father shook his head mournfully but there was no help for it. He had promised to send the Beast the first living creature that met him on his return, so he was obliged to send Beauty herself in his place.

When he left Beauty at the palace of the Beast she found everything prepared for her comfort and convenience. A beautiful bedchamber was ready for her use; the rooms were filled with everything that she could possibly want, and in the great hall of the castle a table was set with every delicacy. And everywhere there were bowls full of red roses. No servants were visible; but there was no lack of service, for invisible hands waited upon her and attended to her every want. She had but to wish, and whatever she wanted was at once placed before her.

Beauty was filled with astonishment at all this luxury and magnificence. 'Surely the Beast does not wish to harm me,' she thought, 'or he would never have so ordered everything for my comfort.' And she waited with a good courage for the coming of the Lord of the Castle.

In the evening the Beast appeared. He was certainly very terrible to look at, and Beauty trembled at the sight of the hideous monster. But she forced herself to appear brave, and, indeed, there was no cause for her alarm. The Beast was kindness itself, and so gentle and respectful that Beauty soon lost all fear. She soon became very fond of him, and would have been quite happy had it not been for the thought of her father and sisters, and the grief which she knew her father would be suffering on her account. The thought of his sorrow made her sorrowful too; and one night, when the Beast came to visit her at his usual hour, she was so sad that he asked her what the matter was.

Then Beauty begged him to let her go and visit her father. The Beast was very unwilling to grant her request. 'If I let you go, I am afraid you will never come back to me,' he said, 'and then I shall die of grief.'

Beauty promised to come back to him if he would only allow her to spend a few days with her family; and at last the Beast yielded to her entreaties.

He gave her a ring, saying, 'Put this on your little finger when you go to bed tonight, and wish; and in the morning you will find yourself at home in your father's house. But if you do not return to me at the end of a week, I shall die of sorrow.'

Beauty's father was almost overcome with joy at seeing his daughter again, and he was delighted to hear of her happiness and good fortune. But her two sisters – who in the meantime had married – were more jealous than ever of their beautiful sister. They were not very happy with their husbands, who were poor and not over-lovable; and they were very envious of Beauty's clothes and of all the luxuries with which she told them she was surrounded. They tried to think of a plan by which they could prevent their sister from enjoying her good fortune.

'Let us keep her beyond the week that the Beast has allowed her,' they said; 'then, doubtless, he will be so angry that he will kill her.'

So they pretended to be very fond of Beauty, and when the time came for her return, they begged her not to leave them and to stay at least one more day with them. Beauty was distressed at their grief, and at last she agreed to stay just one more day; though her heart misgave her sorely when she thought of the poor Beast.

That night, as she lay in bed, she had a dream. She dreamt that she saw the Beast dying of sorrow at her forgetfulness; and so real did it seem that she woke up in an agony of dismay.

'How could I have been so cruel and ungrateful,' she cried. 'I promised faithfully that I would return at the end of the week. What will he think of me for breaking my promise!'

Hastily rising from bed, she searched for the ring the Beast had given her. Then putting it on her little finger she wished to be at the Palace of the Beast again. In a moment she found herself there; and quickly putting on her clothes she hurried out to look for the Beast. She searched through room after room; but nowhere could she find him. At last she ran out into the garden; and there, on a plot of grass, where he and she had often sat together, she found him lying as if dead upon the ground.

With a bitter cry she sank on her knees beside the poor Beast. 'Oh, Beast; my dear, dear Beast!' she cried. 'How could I have been so cruel and wicked and unkind? He has died of sorrow as he said he would!' And the tears fell down from her eyes as she spoke. Overcome with grief and remorse, she stooped down and tenderly kissed the ugly Beast.

In a moment there was a sudden noise, and Beauty was startled to find that the ugly Beast had vanished.

The Beast was a beast no longer, but a handsome Prince, who knelt at her feet, thanking her for having broken his enchantment.

'A wicked fairy,' he said, 'condemned me to keep the form of a beast until a beautiful maiden should forget my ugliness and kiss me. You, by your love and tenderness, have broken the spell and released me from my horrible disguise. Now, thanks to you, I can take my proper form again.' And then he begged Beauty to become his bride.

So Beauty married the Prince who had been a Beast, and they lived together in the castle and ruled over the Prince's country, and were happy ever after. ❋

67

ARJUNA AND THE TARGET

UPENDRAKISHORE RAY CHOWDHURY; TRANSLATED BY SWAPNA DUTTA

When Bheeshma requested Drona to take charge of the young hundred Kaurava and five Pandava princes he said to them, 'Dear boys, I shall make you experts at wielding weapons, but once you are trained you will have to do something for me.'

The other boys stood silent, but Arjuna immediately said, 'Of course, Gurudev. I shall definitely do whatever you ask.'

Drona was so moved by Arjuna's prompt response that he embraced him, his eyes filled with tears.

The training started in earnest. A few outsiders also came to take lessons from Drona, including a lad named Karna who was the son of Adhiratha, a charioteer. Karna hated Arjuna right from the beginning. But Duryodhana made friends with him and encouraged him to insult the Pandavas. No one picked up archery the way Arjuna did. Seeing his single-minded concentration, Drona told him, 'I shall teach you to how master every weapon so that you can be the best archer in the world.'

The others also learned to be competent fighters. Bhima and Duryodhana were especially adept at wielding the mace, Nakula and Sahadeva became experts in fighting with small swords (*khadga*) and Yudhishthira became an expert charioteer. But no one could beat Arjuna in archery. The Kaurava brothers grew extremely jealous of both Arjuna and Bhima.

One day Drona decided to test their ability. He got a craftsman to make a bird and had it fixed atop a tree. Then he sent for the princes and said, 'Stand ready with your bow and arrow. You must shoot down that bird on the treetop the moment I command you.'

Yudhishthira, being the eldest, was called first and stood ready with his bow and arrow. Drona asked him, 'What do you see?'

Yudhishthira replied, 'I see the tree, the bird and all of you.'

It was obvious to Drona that he was not concentrating. He made a wry face and said, 'Then you won't be able to shoot it. Please stand aside.'

There were many others after Yudhishthira, but Drona was not satisfied with anyone. Finally, it was Arjuna's turn. Drona asked him, 'What do you see?'

'The bird and nothing else' said Arjuna.

'The whole bird?' asked Drona.

'No, just the head.'

'Shoot,' said Drona.

The bird fell on the ground before his words were out.

Drona was exhilarated. He embraced Arjuna, feeling that teaching him had really been worthwhile! He felt sure that Arjuna would be able to do what he wanted.

Soon after, Drona was attacked by a crocodile while bathing in the river. He could have easily killed it, but he wanted to test his students, and cried for help, 'Please save me!'

The crocodile was so large and fierce that the princes were terrified and stood frozen to the spot. But brave Arjuna took up his bow and killed the crocodile immediately. Drona was so pleased with his prompt action that he gave him his *brahmashira*, an extremely potent and dangerous missile. He taught Arjuna how to use it and warned, 'Never use it on a human being as it will turn everything to ashes. You may use it only when you are fighting a deva.' ❋

– In other versions of the tale, Arjuna aims at the eye of the bird, or the eye of a fish. To know the whole story of the Kauravas and Pandavas, read the Mahabharata for Young Readers *by Upendrakishore Ray Chowdhury, translated by Swapna Dutta and published by Hachette India.*

68

THE WOODPECKER, TURTLE AND DEER

A JATAKA TALE; RETOLD BY ELLEN C. BABBITT

Once upon a time a Deer lived in a forest near a lake. Not far from the same lake, a Woodpecker had a nest in the top of a tree; and in the lake lived a Turtle. The three were friends and lived together happily.

A hunter, wandering about in the wood, saw the footprints of the Deer near the edge of the lake. 'I must trap the Deer, going down into the water,' he said, and setting a strong trap of leather, he went his way.

Early that night when the Deer went down to drink, he was caught in the trap, and he cried the cry of capture.

At once the Woodpecker flew down from her treetop, and the Turtle came out of the water to see what could be done.

Said the Woodpecker to the Turtle, 'Friend, you have teeth; you gnaw through the leather trap. I will go and see to it that the hunter keeps away. If we both do our best our friend will not lose his life.'

So the Turtle began to gnaw the leather, and the Woodpecker flew to the hunter's house.

At dawn the hunter came, knife in hand, to the front door of his house.

The Woodpecker, flapping her wings, flew at the hunter and struck him in the face.

The hunter turned back into the house and lay down for a little while. Then he rose up again, and took his knife. He said to himself, 'When I went out by the front door, a bird flew in my face; now I will go out by the back door.' So he did.

The Woodpecker thought: *The hunter went out by the front door before, so now he will leave by the back door.* So the Woodpecker sat in a tree near the back door.

When the hunter came out the bird flew at him again, flapping her wings in the hunter's face.

Then the hunter turned back and lay down again. When the sun arose, he took his knife and started out once more.

This time the Woodpecker flew back as fast as she could fly to her friends, crying, 'Here comes the hunter!'

By this time the Turtle had gnawed through all the pieces of the trap but one. The leather was so hard that it made his teeth feel as if they would fall out. His mouth was all covered with blood. The Deer heard the Woodpecker and saw the hunter, knife in hand, coming on. With a strong pull the Deer broke this last piece of the trap and ran into the woods.

The Woodpecker flew up to her nest in the treetop.

But the Turtle was so weak he could not get away. He lay where he was. The hunter picked him up and threw him into a bag, tying it to a tree.

The Deer saw that the Turtle was taken and made up his mind to save his friend's life. So the Deer let the hunter see him.

The hunter seized his knife and started after the Deer. The Deer, keeping just out of his reach, led the hunter into the forest.

When the Deer saw that they had gone far into the forest he slipped away from the hunter, and swift as the wind, he went by another way to where he had left the Turtle.

But the Turtle was not there. The Deer called, 'Turtle, Turtle!' and the Turtle called out, 'Here I am in a bag hanging on this tree.'

Then the Deer lifted the bag with his horns, and throwing it upon the ground, he tore the bag open, and let the Turtle out.

The Woodpecker flew down from her nest, and the Deer said to them, 'You two friends saved my life, but if we stay here talking, the hunter will find us, and we may not get away. So you, Friend Woodpecker, fly away. And you, Friend Turtle, dive into the water. I will hide in the forest.'

The hunter did come back, but neither the Deer, nor the Turtle, nor the Woodpecker was to be seen. He found his torn bag and, picking that up, he went back to his home.

The three friends lived together all the rest of their lives. ❋

69

SLEEPING BEAUTY

A FAIRY TALE; RETOLD BY LOGAN MARSHALL

Once upon a time there lived a King and Queen who had no children. They longed very much for a child; and when at last they had a little daughter they were both delighted, and great rejoicings took place.

When the time came for the little Princess to be christened, the King made a grand feast and invited all but one of the fairies in his kingdom to be godmothers. There happened to be thirteen fairies in the kingdom, but as the King had only twelve gold plates, he had to leave one of them out.

The twelve fairies that were invited came to the christening and presented the little Princess with the best gifts in their possession. One gave her beauty, one gave her wisdom, another grace, another goodness, until all but one had presented their offerings. Just as the last fairy was about to step forward and offer her gift, there came a tremendous knocking at the door, and before anybody could get there to open it, it was burst open, and in came the thirteenth fairy, in a furious rage at not having been invited to the feast.

When she saw all the gifts which the other fairies had presented the child, she laughed and exclaimed, 'A lot of good all this beauty and virtue and wealth will do to you, my pretty Princess! You shall pay for the slight your Royal Father has put upon me!' Then, turning to the terrified King and Queen, she said, in a loud voice, 'When the Princess is fifteen years old she shall prick her finger with a spindle and die!' Having said this she flew away as noisily as she came.

The King and Queen were in despair, and the courtiers stood aghast at the terrible disaster; while the little Princess began to cry piteously, as if she knew the fate in store for her. Then the twelfth fairy stepped forward.

'Do not be afraid,' she said, 'I have not yet given my gift. I cannot undo the wicked spell, but I can soften the evil. The Princess, on her fifteenth birthday, shall prick her finger with a spindle, but she shall not die. Instead, she shall fall asleep for a hundred years.'

'Alas!' cried the Queen, 'what comfort will that be to us? Long before the hundred years are past we shall be dead, and our darling child will be as lost to us as if she were indeed to die!'

'I can make that right,' said the fairy. 'When the Princess falls asleep, you shall sleep, too, and awaken with her when the hundred years have passed.'

But the King still hoped to save his daughter from such a terrible misfortune. So he ordered all the spinning wheels in his kingdom to be burnt or destroyed, and made a law that no one was to use one on pain of instant death. But all his care was useless. On her fifteenth birthday the Princess slipped away from her attendants and wandered all through the Palace. At last she came to a tower which she had never seen before, and, wondering what it contained, she climbed the stairs. From a room at the top came a curious humming noise, and the Princess, wondering what it could be, pushed open the door and stepped inside.

There sat an old woman, bent with age, working at a strangely shaped wheel. The Princess was full of curiosity. 'What is that funny-looking thing?' she asked.

'It is a spinning wheel, Princess,' answered the old woman, who was no other than the wicked fairy in disguise.

'A spinning wheel – what is that? I have never heard of such a thing,' said the Princess. She stood watching for a few minutes, then she added, 'It looks quite easy. May I try to do it?'

'Certainly, gracious lady,' said the wicked fairy, and the Princess sat down and tried to turn the wheel.

But no sooner did she lay her hand upon it than the spindle, which was enchanted, pricked her finger, and the Princess fell back against a silk-covered couch – fast asleep.

In a moment a deep silence fell upon all who were in the castle. The King fell asleep in the midst of his councillors, the Queen with her ladies-in-waiting. The horses in the stable, the pigeons on the roof, the flies upon the walls, even the very fire upon the hearth fell asleep, too. The meat which was cooking in the kitchen ceased to frizzle; and the cook, who was just about to box the kitchen boy's ears, fell asleep with her hand outstretched, and began to snore aloud.

A great hedge sprang up around the castle, which, as the years passed on, grew and grew until it formed an impenetrable barrier around the sleeping Palace. The old people of the country died, and their children grew up and died also, and their children, and their children, and the story of the sleeping Princess became a legend, handed down from one generation to another; and a cloud of mystery, as thick and impenetrable as the hedge of thorns, lay over the old castle. Many brave and gallant Princes tried to force their way through the magic hedge, in order to solve the mystery and to see for themselves the beautiful maiden who lay in an enchanted sleep behind that thorny barrier. But the thorns caught them and held them from going forward or back, and the gallant youths perished miserably in the thickets.

After many, many years there came a King's son into that country, who heard the story of the Princess and the hedge of briers; and he made up his mind to try and force his way to the castle to awake the sleeping Princess. People told him of the fate of the other Princes, who had also attempted this difficult task, but the Prince would not be warned.

'I have made up my mind to see this maiden of whose beauty I have heard so many wonderful tales,' he cried. 'I will force a way through the hedge of thorns and awake this Sleeping Beauty, or die in the attempt!'

Now, it happened that this day was the last day of the hundred years; and when the Prince came to the thicket that surrounded the castle and began to push his way through, he found that the briers yielded readily to his touch. The thorns had all blossomed into roses that scented the air with fragrance as he went by. Primroses sprang up before his feet and made a pathway to lead him straight to the castle gates; and the birds suddenly broke forth into singing, as if to tell the world that the hundred years of enchantment were over, and the Princess about to be awakened from her long sleep.

The Prince passed through the council chamber, where the King and his councillors were sleeping; through the room where the Queen and her ladies slept. He passed on from hall to hall, climbed from stair to stair, until at last he reached the tower chamber where the sleeping Princess lay. For a moment he stood and gazed in wonder at her lovely face; then he sank on his knees beside her, and kissed her as she lay asleep.

Instantly the spell was broken. The King and Queen awoke, and all the courtiers with them; the horses neighed in the stables, and shook their glossy manes; the pigeons cooed upon the roof; the flies on the wall moved again; the fire burnt up brightly; and the meat in the kitchen began to frizzle once more as the spit turned round. The cook gave the kitchen boy the tremendous box on the ear that she had started to give him a hundred years ago, and everything and everybody went on just as usual, as if nothing at all out of the common had occurred.

And up in the tower chamber the Princess opened her eyes to meet the gaze of the Prince, who had dared to risk his life for her sake. What they said to each other nobody quite knows, for nobody was there to hear or see. But whatever it was, it must have been something very satisfactory; for very soon after they were married, and lived happily ever afterwards. ❋

70

JACK AND THE BEANSTALK

A FAIRY TALE; RETOLD BY MABIE, HALE AND FORBUSH

There was once upon a time a poor widow who had an only son named Jack, and a cow named Milky-white. And all they had to live on was the milk the cow gave every morning which they carried to the market and sold. But one morning Milky-white gave no milk and they didn't know what to do.

'What shall we do, what shall we do?' said the woman, wringing her hands.

'Cheer up, mother, I'll go and get work somewhere,' said Jack.

'We've tried that before, and nobody would take you,' said his mother. 'We must sell Milky-white and with the money start a shop, or something.'

'All right, mother,' said Jack, 'it's market-day today, and I'll soon sell Milky-white, and then we'll see what we can do.'

So he took the cow's halter in his hand, and off he went. He hadn't gone far when he met a funny-looking old man who said to him, 'Good morning, Jack.'

'Good morning to you,' said Jack and wondered how he knew his name.

'Well, Jack, and where are you off to?' said the man.

'I'm going to market to sell our cow here.'

'Oh, you look the proper sort of chap to sell cows,' said the man. 'I wonder if you know how many beans make five.'

'Two in each hand and one in your mouth,' said Jack, as sharp as a needle.

'Right you are,' said the man, 'and here they are the very beans themselves,' he went on pulling out of his pocket a number of strange-looking beans. 'As you are so sharp,' said he, 'I don't mind doing a swop with you – your cow for these beans.'

'Walker!' said Jack. 'Wouldn't you like it?'

'Ah! you don't know what these beans are,' said the man. 'If you plant them overnight, by morning they grow right up to the sky.'

'Really?' said Jack. 'You don't say so.'

'Yes, that is so, and if it doesn't turn out to be true you can have your cow back.'

'Right,' said Jack and handed him over Milky-white's halter and pocketed the beans.

Back went Jack home, and as he hadn't gone very far it wasn't dusk by the time he got to his door.

'What – back, Jack?' said his mother; 'I see you haven't got Milky-white, so you've sold her. How much did you get for her?'

'You'll never guess, mother,' said Jack.

'No, you don't say so. Good boy! Five pounds, ten, fifteen, no, it can't be twenty.'

'I told you you couldn't guess – what do you say to these beans; they're magical, plant them overnight and –'

'What!' said Jack's mother. 'Have you been such a fool, such a dolt, such an idiot, as to give away my Milky-white, the best milker in the parish, for a set of paltry beans. Take that! Take that! Take that! And as for your precious beans here they go out of the window. And now off with you to bed. Not a sup shall you drink, and not a bit shall you swallow this very night.'

So Jack went upstairs to his little room in the attic, and sad and sorry he was, to be sure, as much for his mother's sake, as for the loss of his supper.

At last he dropped off to sleep.

When he woke up, the room looked so funny. The sun was shining into part of it, and yet all the rest was quite dark and shady. So Jack jumped up and dressed himself and went to the window. And what do you think he saw? Why, the beans his mother had thrown out of the window into the garden, had sprung up into a big beanstalk that went up and up and up till it reached the sky. So the man spoke the truth after all.

The beanstalk grew up quite close past Jack's window, so all he had to do was to open it and give a jump on to the beanstalk which was made like a big plaited ladder. So Jack climbed and he climbed and he climbed and he climbed and he climbed and he climbed and he climbed till at last he reached the sky. And when he got there he found a long broad road going as straight as a dart. So he walked along and he walked along and he walked along till he came to a great big tall house, and on the doorstep there was a great big tall woman.

'Good morning, mum*,' said Jack, quite polite-like. 'Could you be so kind as to give me some breakfast.' For he hadn't had anything to eat, you know, the night before and was as hungry as a hunter.

'It's breakfast you want, is it?' said the great big tall woman. 'It's breakfast you'll be if you don't move off from here. My man is an ogre and there's nothing he likes better than boys broiled on toast. You'd better be moving on or he'll soon be coming.'

'Oh! please, mum, do give me something to eat, mum. I've had nothing to eat since yesterday morning, really and truly, mum,' said Jack. 'I may as well be broiled, as die of hunger.'

* *Short for ma'am*

Well, the ogre's wife wasn't such a bad sort, after all. So she took Jack into the kitchen, and gave him a hunk of bread and cheese and a jug of milk. But Jack hadn't half finished these when thump! thump! thump! the whole house began to tremble with the noise of someone coming.

'Goodness gracious me! It's my old man,' said the ogre's wife, 'what on earth shall I do? Here, come quick and jump in here.' And she bundled Jack into the oven just as the ogre came in.

He was a big one, to be sure. At his belt he had three calves strung up by the heels, and he unhooked them and threw them down on the table and said, 'Here, wife, broil me a couple of these for breakfast. Ah what's this I smell?

Fee-fi-fo-fum,
I smell the blood of an Englishman,
Be he alive, or be he dead
I'll have his bones to grind my bread.'

'Nonsense, dear,' said his wife, 'you're dreaming. Or perhaps you smell the scraps of that little boy you liked so much for yesterday's dinner. Here, go you and have a wash and tidy up, and by the time you come back your breakfast will be ready for you.'

So the ogre went off, and Jack was just going to jump out of the oven and run off when the woman told him not to. 'Wait till he's asleep,' said she. 'He always has a snooze after breakfast.'

Well, the ogre had his breakfast, and after that he went to a big chest and took out of it a couple of bags of gold and sat down counting them till at last his head began to nod and he began to snore till the whole house shook again.

Then Jack crept out on tiptoe from his oven, and as he was passing the ogre he took one of the bags of gold under his arm, and off he pelted till he came to the beanstalk, and then he threw down the bag of gold which of course fell in to his mother's garden, and then he climbed down and climbed down till at last he got home and told his mother and showed her the gold and said, 'Well, mother, wasn't I right about the beans. They are really magical, you see.'

So they lived on the bag of gold for some time, but at last they came to the end of that so Jack made up his mind to try his luck once more up at the top of the beanstalk. So one fine morning he got up early, and got on to the beanstalk, and he climbed and he climbed and he climbed and he climbed and he climbed and he climbed till at last he got on the road again and came to the great big tall house he had been to before. There, sure enough, was the great big tall woman a-standing on the doorstep.

'Good morning, mum,' said Jack, as bold as brass, 'could you be so good as to give me something to eat?'

'Go away, my boy,' said the big, tall woman, 'or else my man will eat you up for breakfast. But aren't you the youngster who came here once before? Do you know, that very day, my man missed one of his bags of gold.'

'That's strange, mum,' said Jack, 'I dare say I could tell you something about that, but I'm so hungry I can't speak till I've had something to eat.'

Well, the big tall woman was so curious that she took him in and gave him something to eat. But he had scarcely begun munching it as slowly as he could when *thump! thump! thump!* they heard the giant's footstep, and his wife hid Jack away in the oven.

All happened as it did before. In came the ogre as he did before, said, 'Fee-fi-fo-fum,' and had his breakfast off three broiled oxen. Then he said, 'Wife, bring me the hen that lays the golden eggs.' So she brought it, and the ogre said, 'Lay,' and it laid an egg all of gold. And then the ogre began to nod his head, and to snore till the house shook.

Then Jack crept out of the oven on tiptoe and caught hold of the golden hen, and was off before you could say 'Jack Robinson.' But this time the hen gave a cackle which woke the ogre, and just as Jack got out of the house he heard him calling, 'Wife, wife, what have you done with my golden hen?'

And the wife said, 'Why, my dear?'

But that was all Jack heard, for he rushed off to the beanstalk and climbed down like a house on fire.

And when he got home he showed his mother the wonderful hen and said 'Lay,' to it; and it laid a golden egg every time he said 'Lay.'

Well, Jack was not content, and it wasn't very long before he determined to have another try at his luck up there at the top of the beanstalk. So one fine morning, he got up early, and went on to the beanstalk, and he climbed and he climbed and he climbed and he climbed till he got to the top. But this time he knew better than to go straight to the ogre's house. And when he got near it he waited behind a bush till he saw the ogre's wife come out with a pail to get some water, and then he crept into the house and got into the copper.* He hadn't been there long when he heard thump! thump! thump! as before, and in come the ogre and his wife.

'Fee-fi-fo-fum, I smell the blood of an Englishman,' cried out the ogre; 'I smell him, wife, I smell him.'

'Do you, my dearie?' said the ogre's wife. 'Then if it's that little rogue that stole your gold and the hen that laid the golden eggs, he's sure to have got into the oven.' And they both rushed to the oven. But Jack wasn't there, luckily, and the ogre's wife said, 'There you are again with your fee-fi-fo-fum. Why, of course it's the laddie you caught last night that I've broiled for your breakfast. How forgetful I am, and how

* *A container for boiling laundry in olden times*

careless you are not to tell the difference between a live 'un and a dead 'un.'

So the ogre sat down to the breakfast and ate it, but every now and then he would mutter, 'Well, I could have sworn –' and he'd get up and search the larder and the cupboards, and everything, only luckily he didn't think of the copper.

After breakfast was over, the ogre called out, 'Wife, wife, bring me my golden harp.' So she brought it and put it on the table before him. Then he said, 'Sing!' and the golden harp sang most beautifully. And it went on singing till the ogre fell asleep, and commenced to snore like thunder.

Then Jack lifted up the copper-lid very quietly and got down like a mouse and crept on hands and knees till he got to the table when he got up and caught hold of the golden harp and dashed with it towards the door. But the harp called out quite loud, 'Master! Master!' and the ogre woke up just in time to see Jack running off with his harp.

Jack ran as fast as he could and the ogre came rushing after, and would soon have caught him – only Jack had a start and dodged him a bit and knew where he was going. When he got to the beanstalk the ogre was not more than twenty yards away when suddenly he saw Jack disappear, and when he got up to the end of the road he saw Jack underneath climbing down for dear life. Well, the ogre didn't like trusting himself to such a ladder, and he stood and waited, so Jack got another start. But just then the harp cried out, 'Master! Master!' and the ogre swung himself down on to the beanstalk which shook with his weight. Down climbed Jack, and after him climbed the ogre. By this time Jack had climbed down and climbed down and climbed down till he was very nearly home. So he called out, 'Mother! Mother! Bring me an axe, bring me an axe.' And his mother came rushing out with the axe in her hand, but when she came to the beanstalk she stood stock-still with fright for there she saw the ogre just coming down below the clouds.

But Jack jumped down and got hold of the axe and gave a chop at the beanstalk which cut it half in two. The ogre felt the beanstalk shake and quiver so he stopped to see what was the matter. Then Jack gave another chop with the axe, and the beanstalk was cut in two and began to topple over. Then the ogre fell down and broke his crown, and the beanstalk came toppling after.

Then Jack showed his mother his golden harp, and what with showing that and selling the golden eggs, Jack and his mother became very rich, and he married a great princess, and they lived happy ever after. ❋

71

THE PIED PIPER OF HAMELIN

ROBERT BROWNING

Hamelin Town's in Brunswick,
By famous Hanover city;
The river Weser, deep and wide,
Washes its wall on the southern side;
A pleasanter spot you never spied;
But, when begins my ditty,
Almost five hundred years ago,
To see the townsfolk suffer so
From vermin, was a pity.

Rats!
They fought the dogs and killed the cats,
And bit the babies in the cradles,
And ate the cheeses out of the vats.

And licked the soup from the cook's own ladles,
Split open the kegs of salted sprats,
Made nests inside men's Sunday hats,
And even spoiled the women's chats,
By drowning their speaking
With shrieking and squeaking
In fifty different sharps and flats.

At last the people in a body
To the Town Hall came flocking:
'Tis clear,' cried they, 'our Mayor's a noddy;
And as for our Corporation – shocking
To think we buy gowns lined with ermine
For dolts that can't or won't determine
What's best to rid us of our vermin!
Rouse up, sirs! Give your brains a racking
To find the remedy we're lacking,
Or, sure as fate, we'll send you packing!'
At this the Mayor and Corporation
Quaked with a mighty consternation.

An hour they sate in council,
At length the Mayor broke silence:
'For a guilder I'd my ermine gown sell;
I wish I were a mile hence!
It's easy to bid one rack one's brain –
I'm sure my poor head aches again,
I've scratched it so, and all in vain.

Oh for a trap, a trap, a trap!'
Just as he said this, what should hap
At the chamber door but a gentle tap?
'Bless us,' cried the Mayor, 'what's that?'
'Only a scraping of shoes on the mat?
Anything like the sound of a rat
Makes my heart go pit-a-pat!'

'Come in!' – the Mayor cried, looking bigger:
And in did come the strangest figure!
His queer long coat from heel to head
Was half of yellow and half of red,
And he himself was tall and thin,
With sharp blue eyes, each like a pin,
And light loose hair, yet swarthy skin
No tuft on cheek nor beard on chin,
But lips where smiles went out and in;
There was no guessing his kith and kin:
And nobody could enough admire
The tall man and his quaint attire.

He advanced to the council-table:
And, 'Please your honours,' said he, 'I'm able,
By means of a secret charm, to draw
All creatures living beneath the sun,
That creep or swim or fly or run,
After me so as you never saw!
And I chiefly use my charm

On creatures that do people harm,
The mole and toad and newt and viper;
And people call me the Pied Piper.'
(And here they noticed round his neck
A scarf of red and yellow stripe,
To match with his coat of the self-same check;
And at the scarf's end hung a pipe;
And his fingers they noticed were ever straying
As if impatient to be playing
Upon his pipe, as low it dangled
Over his vesture so old-fangled.)
'Yet,' said he, 'poor Piper as I am,
In Tartary I freed the Cham,
Last June, from his huge swarms of gnats,
I eased in Asia the Nizam
Of a monstrous brood of vampire bats:
And as for what your brain bewilders,
If I can rid your town of rats
Will you give me a thousand guilders?'
'One? Fifty thousand!' – was the exclamation
Of the astonished Mayor and Corporation.

Into the street the Piper stept,
Smiling first a little smile,
As if he knew what magic slept
In his quiet pipe the while;
Then, like a musical adept,
To blow the pipe his lips he wrinkled,
And green and blue his sharp eyes twinkled,
Like a candle-flame where salt is sprinkled;

And ere three shrill notes the pipe uttered,
You heard as if an army muttered;
And the muttering grew to a grumbling;
And the grumbling grew to a mighty rumbling;
And out of the houses the rats came tumbling.
Great rats, small rats, lean rats, brawny rats,
Brown rats, black rats, grey rats, tawny rats,
Grave old plodders, gay young friskers,
Fathers, mothers, uncles, cousins,
Cocking tails and pricking whiskers,
Families by tens and dozens,
Brothers, sisters, husbands, wives –
Followed the Piper for their lives.
From street to street he piped advancing,
And step for step they followed dancing,
Until they came to the river Weser
Wherein all plunged and perished!

You should have heard the Hamelin people
Ringing the bells till they rocked the steeple
'Go,' cried the Mayor, 'and get long poles,
Poke out the nests and block up the holes!
Consult with carpenters and builders,
And leave in our town not even a trace
Of the rats!' – when suddenly up the face
Of the Piper perked in the marketplace,
With a, 'First, if you please, my thousand guilders!'

A thousand guilders! The Mayor looked blue;
So did the Corporation, too.
To pay this sum to a wandering fellow
With a gypsy coat of red and yellow!
'Beside,' quoth the Mayor with a knowing wink,
'Our business was done at the river's brink;
We saw with our eyes the vermin sink,
And what's dead can't come to life, I think.
So, friend, we're not the folks to shrink
From the duty of giving you something to drink,
And a matter of money to put in your poke;
But as for the guilders, what we spoke
Of them, as you very well know, was in joke.
Beside, our losses have made us thrifty.
A thousand guilders! Come, take fifty!'

The Piper's face fell, and he cried,
'No trifling! I can't wait, beside!
I've promised to visit by dinner time
Bagdad, and accept the prime
Of the Head-Cook's pottage, all he's rich in,
For having left, in the Caliph's kitchen,
Of a nest of scorpions no survivor:
With him I proved no bargain-driver,
With you, don't think I'll bate a stiver!
And folks who put me in a passion
May find me pipe after another fashion.'

'How,' cried the Mayor, 'd' ye think I brook
Being worse treated than a Cook?
Insulted by a lazy ribald
With idle pipe and vesture piebald?
You threaten us, fellow? Do your worst,
Blow your pipe there till you burst!'

Once more he stepped into the street,
And to his lips again
Laid his long pipe of smooth straight cane;

And ere he blew three notes

There was a rustling,
That seemed like a bustling
Of merry crowds justling at pitching and hustling,
Small feet were pattering, wooden shoes clattering,
Little hands clapping and little tongues chattering,
And, like fowls in a farmyard when barley is
scattering,
Out came the children running.
All the little boys and girls,
With rosy cheeks and flaxen curls,
And sparkling eyes and teeth like pearls.
Tripping and skipping,
Ran merrily after
The wonderful music with shouting and laughter.

The Mayor was dumb, and the Council stood
As if they were changed into blocks of wood,
Unable to move a step, or cry
To the children merrily skipping by.
– Could only follow with the eye
That joyous crowd at the Piper's back.
But how the Mayor was on the rack,
And the wretched Council's bosoms beat,
As the Piper turned from the High Street
To where the Weser rolled its waters
Right in the way of their sons and daughters!

However, he turned from South to West,
And to Koppelberg Hill his steps addressed,
And after him the children pressed;
Great was the joy in every breast.
'He never can cross that mighty top!
He's forced to let the piping drop,
And we shall see our children stop!'

When, lo, as they reached the mountainside,
A wondrous portal opened wide,
As if a cavern was suddenly hollowed;
And the Piper advanced and the children followed,
And when all were in to the very last,
The door in the mountainside shut fast. ❋

– Excerpted from the original poem.

72

HEIDI
'ON THE PASTURE'

JOHANNA SPYRI

Heidi was awakened early next morning by a loud whistle. Opening her eyes, she saw her little bed and the hay beside her bathed in golden sunlight. For a short while she did not know where she was, but when she heard her grandfather's deep voice outside, she recollected everything. She remembered how she had come up the mountain the day before and left old Ursula, who was always shivering with cold and sat near the stove all day.

While Heidi lived with Ursula, she had always been obliged to keep in the house, where the old woman could see her. Being deaf, Ursula was afraid to let Heidi go outdoors, and the child had often fretted in the narrow room and had longed to run outside. She was therefore delighted to find herself in her new home and hardly could wait to see the goats again. Jumping out of bed, she put on her few things and in a short time went down the ladder and ran outside. Peter was already there with his flock, waiting for Schwänli and Bärli, whom the grandfather was just bringing to join the other goats.

'Do you want to go with him to the pasture?' asked the grandfather.

'Yes,' cried Heidi, clapping her hands.

'Go now, and wash yourself first, for the sun will laugh at you if he sees how dirty you are. Everything is ready there for you,' he added, pointing to a large tub of water that stood in the sun. In the meanwhile the grandfather called to Peter to come into the hut and bring his bag along. The boy followed the old man, who commanded him to open the bag in which he carried his scanty dinner. The grandfather put into the bag a piece of bread and a slice of cheese, that were easily twice as large as those the boy had in the bag himself.

'The little bowl goes in, too,' said the Uncle. 'Milk two bowls full for her dinner. Look out that she does not fall over the rocks! Do you hear?'

Just then Heidi came running in. 'Grandfather, can the sun still laugh at me?' she asked. The child had rubbed herself so violently with the coarse towel which the grandfather had put beside the tub that her face, neck and arms were as red as a lobster. With a smile the grandfather said, 'No, he can't laugh any more now; but when you come home tonight you must go into the tub like a fish. When one goes about like the goats, one gets dirty feet. Be off!'

They started merrily up the Alp. A cloudless, deep-blue sky looked down on them, for the wind had driven away every little cloud in the night. The fresh green mountainside was bathed in brilliant sunlight, and many blue and yellow flowers had opened. Heidi was wild with joy and ran from side to side. In one place she saw big patches of fine red primroses, on another spot blue gentians sparkled in the grass, and everywhere the golden rock-roses were nodding to her. In her joy at finding such treasures, Heidi even forgot Peter and his goats. She ran far ahead of him and then strayed away off to one side, for the sparkling flowers tempted her here and there. Picking whole bunches of them to take home with her, she put them all into her little apron.

Peter, whose round eyes could only move about slowly, had a hard time looking out for her. The goats were even worse, and only by shouting and whistling, especially by swinging his rod, could he drive them together.

'Heidi, where are you now?' he called quite angrily.

'Here,' it sounded from somewhere. Peter could not see her, for she was sitting on the ground behind a little mound, which was covered with fragrant flowers. The whole air was filled with their perfume, and the child drew it in, in long breaths.

'Follow me now!' Peter called out. 'The grandfather has told me to look out for you, and you must not fall over the rocks.'

'Where are they?' asked Heidi without even stirring.

'Way up there, and we have still far to go. If you come quickly, we may see the eagle there and hear him shriek.'

That tempted Heidi, and she came running to Peter, with her apron full of flowers.

'You have enough now,' he declared. 'If you pick them all today, there won't be any left tomorrow.' Heidi admitted that, besides which she had her apron already full. From now on she stayed at Peter's side. The goats, scenting the pungent herbs, also hurried up without delay.

Peter generally took his quarters for the day at the foot of a high cliff, which seemed to reach far up into the sky. Overhanging rocks on one side made it dangerous, so that the grandfather was wise to warn Peter.

After they had reached their destination, the boy took off his bag, putting it in a little hollow in the ground. The wind often blew in violent gusts up there, and Peter did not want to lose his precious load. Then he lay down in the sunny grass, for he was very tired.

Heidi, taking off her apron, rolled it tightly together and put it beside Peter's bag. Then, sitting down beside the boy, she looked about her. Far down she saw the glistening valley; a large field of snow rose high in front of her. Heidi sat a long time without stirring, with Peter asleep by her side and the goats climbing about between the bushes. A light breeze fanned her cheek and those big mountains about her made her feel happy as never before. She looked up at the mountaintops till they all seemed to have faces, and soon they were familiar to her, like old friends. Suddenly she heard a loud, sharp scream, and looking up she beheld the largest bird she had ever seen, flying above her. With outspread wings he flew in large circles over Heidi's head. 'Wake up, Peter!' Heidi called. 'Look up, Peter, and see the eagle there!'

Peter got wide awake, and then they both watched the bird breathlessly. It rose higher and higher into the azure, till it disappeared at last behind the mountain peak.

'Where has it gone?' Heidi asked.

'Home to its nest,' was Peter's answer.

'Oh, does it really live way up there? How wonderful that must be! But tell me why it screams so loud?' Heidi inquired.

'Because it has to,' Peter replied.

'Oh, let's climb up there and see its nest!' implored Heidi, but Peter, expressing decided disapproval in his voice, answered, 'Oh dear, oh dear, not even goats could climb up there! Grandfather has told me not to let you fall down the rocks, so we can't go!'

Peter now began to call loudly and to whistle, and soon all the goats were assembled on the green field. Heidi ran into their midst, for she loved to see them leaping and playing about.

Peter in the meantime was preparing dinner for Heidi and himself, by putting her large pieces on one side and his own small ones on the other.

Then he milked Bärli and put the full bowl in the middle. When he was ready, he called to the little girl. But it took some time before she obeyed his call.

Heidi was watching the goats in the meantime, and asked Peter for their names.

The boy could tell them all to her, for their names were about the only thing he had to carry in his head. She soon knew them, too, for she had listened attentively. One of them was the Big Turk, who tried to stick his big horns into all the others. Most of the goats ran away from their rough comrade. The bold Thistlefinch alone was not afraid, and running his horns three or four times into the other, so astonished the Turk with his great daring that he stood still and gave up fighting, for the Thistlefinch had sharp horns and met him in the most warlike attitude. A small, white goat, called Snowhopper, kept up bleating in the most piteous way, which induced Heidi to console it several times. Heidi at last went to the little thing again, and throwing her arms around its head, she asked, 'What is the matter with you, Snowhopper?

Why do you always cry for help?' The little goat pressed close to Heidi's side and became perfectly quiet. Peter was still eating, but between the swallows he called to Heidi, 'She is so unhappy, because the old goat has left us. She was sold to somebody in Mayenfeld two days ago.'

'Who was the old goat?'

'Her mother, of course.'

'Where is her grandmother?'

'She hasn't any.'

'And her grandfather?'

'Hasn't any either.'

'Poor little Snowhopper!' said Heidi, drawing the little creature tenderly to her. 'Don't grieve any more; see, I am coming up with you every day now, and if there is anything the matter, you can come to me.'

Snowhopper rubbed her head against Heidi's shoulder and stopped bleating. When Peter had finally finished his dinner, he joined Heidi.

The little girl had just been observing that Schwänli and Bärli were by far the cleanest and prettiest of the goats. They evaded the obtrusive Turk with a sort of contempt and always managed to find the greenest bushes for themselves. She mentioned it to Peter, who replied, 'I know! Of course they are the prettiest, because the uncle washes them and gives them salt. He has the best stable by far.' ❋

– Excerpted from the original book.

73

THE GIRL MONKEY AND THE STRING OF PEARLS

A JATAKA TALE; RETOLD BY ELLEN C. BABBITT

One day the king went for a long walk in the woods. When he came back to his own garden, he sent for his family to come down to the lake for a swim.

When they were all ready to go into the water, the queen and her ladies left their jewels in charge of the servants, and then went down into the lake.

As the queen put her string of pearls away in a box, she was watched by a Girl Monkey who sat in the branches of a tree nearby. This Girl Monkey wanted to get the queen's string of pearls, so she sat still and watched, hoping that the servant in charge of the pearls would go to sleep.

At first the servant kept her eyes on the jewel box. But by and by she began to nod, and then she fell fast asleep.

As soon as the Monkey saw this, quick as the wind she jumped down, opened the box, picked up the string of pearls, and quick as the wind she was up in the tree again, holding the pearls very carefully. She put the string of pearls on, and then, for fear the guards in the garden would see the pearls, the Monkey hid them in a hole in the tree. Then she sat near by looking as if nothing had happened.

By and by the servant awoke. She looked in the box, and finding that the string of pearls was not there, she cried, 'A man has run off with the queen's string of pearls.'

Up ran the guards from every side.

The servant said, 'I sat right here beside the box where the queen put her string of pearls. I did not move from the place. But the day is hot, and I was tired. I must have fallen asleep. The pearls were gone when I awoke.'

The guards told the king that the pearls were gone.

'Find the man who stole the pearls,' said the king. Away went the guards looking high and low for the thief.

After the king had gone, the chief guard said to himself, 'There is something strange here. These pearls,' thought he, 'were lost in the garden. There was a strong guard at the gates, so that no one from the outside could get into the garden. On the other hand, there are hundreds of Monkeys here in the garden. Perhaps one of the Monkeys took the string of pearls.'

Then the chief guard thought of a trick that would tell whether a Girl Monkey had taken the pearls. So he bought a number of strings of bright-coloured glass beads.

After dark that night the guards hung the strings of glass beads here and there on the low bushes in the garden. When the Monkeys saw the strings of bright-coloured beads the next morning, each Monkey ran for a string.

But the Girl Monkey who had taken the queen's string of pearls did not come down. She sat near the hole where she had hidden the pearls.

The other Monkeys were greatly pleased with their strings of beads. They chattered to one another about them. 'It is too bad you did not get one,' they said to her as she sat quietly, saying nothing. At last she could stand it no longer. She put on the queen's string of pearls and came down, saying proudly, 'You have only strings of glass beads. See my string of pearls!'

Then the chief of the guards, who had been hiding nearby, caught the Girl Monkey. He took her at once to the king.

'It was this Girl Monkey, Your Majesty, who took the pearls.'

The king was glad enough to get the pearls, but he asked the chief guard how he had found out who took them.

The chief guard told the king that he knew no one could have come into the garden and so he thought they must have been taken by one of the Monkeys in the garden. Then he told the king about the trick he had played with the beads.

'You are the right man in the right place,' said the king, and he thanked the chief of the guards over and over again. ❋

74

SINGH RAJAH AND THE CUNNING JACKALS

AN INDIAN FOLKTALE; ADAPTED BY M. FRERE

Once upon a time, in a great jungle, there lived a great lion. He was rajah of all the country round, and every day he used to leave his den, in the deepest shadow of the rocks, and roar with a loud, angry voice. And when he roared, the other animals in the jungle, who were all his subjects, got very much frightened and ran here and there; and Singh Rajah would pounce upon them and kill them, and gobble them up for his dinner.

This went on for a long, long time until, at last, there were no living creatures left in the jungle but two little jackals – a Rajah Jackal and a Ranee Jackal – husband and wife.

A very hard time of it the poor little jackals had, running this way and that to escape the terrible Singh Rajah; and every day the little Ranee Jackal would say to her husband, 'I am afraid he will catch us today; do you hear how he is roaring? Oh, dear! Oh, dear!'

And he would answer her, 'Never fear; I will take care of you. Let us run on a mile or two. Come; come quick, quick, quick!' And they would both run away as fast as they could.

After some time spent in this way, they found, however, one fine day, that the lion was so close upon them that they could not escape.

Then the little Ranee Jackal said, 'Husband, husband, I feel much frightened. The Singh Rajah is so angry he will certainly kill us at once. What can we do?'

But he answered, 'Cheer up – we can save ourselves yet. Come, and I'll show you how we may manage it.'

So what did these cunning little jackals do but they went to the great lion's den; and, when he saw them coming, he began to roar and shake his mane, and he said, 'You little wretches, come and be eaten at once! I have had no dinner for three whole days, and all that time I have been running over hill and dale to find you. *Ro-a-ar! Ro-a-ar!* Come and be eaten, I say!' and he lashed his tail and gnashed his teeth, and looked very terrible indeed.

Then the Jackal Rajah, creeping quite close up to him, said, 'Oh, great Singh Rajah, we all know you are our master, and we would have come at your bidding long ago; but, indeed, sir, there is a much bigger rajah even than you in this jungle, and he tried to catch hold of us and eat us up, and frightened us so much that we were obliged to run away.'

'What do you mean?' growled Singh Rajah. 'There is no king in this jungle but me!'

'Ah, sire,' answered the jackal, 'in truth one would think so, for you are very dreadful. Your very voice is death. But it is as we say, for we, with our own eyes, have seen one with whom you could not compete – whose equal you can no more be than we are yours – whose face is as flaming fire, his step as thunder and his power supreme.'

'It is impossible!' interrupted the old lion. 'But show me this rajah of whom you speak so much, that I may destroy him instantly!'

Then the little jackals ran on before him until they reached a great well, and, pointing down to his own reflection in the water, they said, 'See, sire, there lives the terrible king of whom we spoke.'

When Singh Rajah looked down the well he became very angry, for he thought he saw another lion there. He roared and shook his great mane, and the shadow lion shook his and looked terribly defiant.

At last, beside himself with rage at the violence of his opponent, Singh Rajah sprang down to kill him at once, but no other lion was there – only the treacherous reflection – and the sides of the well were so steep that he could not get out again to punish the two jackals, who peeped over the top.

After struggling for some time in the deep water, he sank to rise no more. And the little jackals threw stones down upon him from above, and danced round and round the well, singing: '*Ao! Ao! Ao! Ao!* The king of the forest is dead, is dead! We have killed the great lion who would have killed us! *Ao! Ao! Ao! Ao!* Ring-a-ting – ding-a-ting! Ring-a-ting – ding-a-ting! *Ao! Ao! Ao!*' ❋

75

KRISHNA AND SUDAMA

A STORY FROM THE BHAGAVATA PURANA; RETOLD BY VKB

At the *gurukul* of Guru Sandipani in an ancient city called Ujjayini, two boys met for the first time. One was Krishna, the son of a royal family, and the other was Sudama, son of Matuka and Rochana Devi, a poor couple.

When Krishna first asked Sudama, 'Will you be my friend?' – Sudama was not sure what he should say. He felt that because there was so much of a difference in the way they had been brought up – one with everything, and the other with nothing much – the friendship would not last. But Krishna said he would never embarrass him by asking him for anything. 'But let's promise each other that we will always be friends,' he said.

The two boys lived in the *gurukul* for many years and their friendship became stronger. As was the duty of students those days, they carried out many errands for the guru and his wife. Once she asked them to bring firewood from the forest.

'Here are roasted gram for when you feel hungry,' she said, handing a small bundle to Sudama. 'I have packed enough for both of you.' The two friends spent the whole day collecting wood and did not notice that dark clouds, swollen with rain, had gathered in the sky. Just when they had as much wood as they could carry, it began to pour.

'Oh no!' said Sudama. 'All the wood will get wet if we wait here for the rain to stop.'

'Hmm,' Krishna looked around to find a place to keep the wood. 'Sudama, if we pile up the firewood on this flat stone, and cover it with these other boulders, it is likely to keep dry.'

They quickly set to work. Just as they were finishing, they heard a tiger roar nearby.

Sudama shivered with fear and looked at Krishna. It was already twilight.

'Hurry up and climb a tree,' said Krishna. 'I will follow you.'

They were forced to spend the night on the tree, for the tiger's roars showed that he was still hungry and had not gone away. Krishna dozed off on his thick, wide branch. Sudama was hungry, and lying on his branch, he quietly ate all the roasted gram he had.

When Krishna woke up, he asked Sudama for something to eat. Sudama did not want to tell him the truth and said that when he had frantically climbed up the tree, all the gram had fallen to the ground.

Krishna had heard Sudama chewing something, and asked him what that had been.

'Oh, I suddenly started to feel cold because of the rain,' said Sudama, 'and my teeth began chattering.'

Krishna, who was a good friend, decided to go hungry rather than make Sudama feel bad for not sharing the roasted gram, and for lying about it. Krishna ate only when they went back to the ashram at dawn.

Time went by. After their stay at the *gurukul* was over, Krishna went to Dwarka as king in his royal palace there, while Sudama went to his small, ramshackle hut in Porbandar.

Years passed.

One day, Susheela – Sudama's wife – beseeched him. 'We are so poor. Why don't you ask your friend for help?' But Sudama did not want to beg for anything.

His wife then said, 'Why don't you go to Dwarka to see your friend Krishna? You have told me about your deep friendship with him. I feel you will not need to *ask* him for anything, and he will by himself understand the reason for your visit.'

Sudama still looked reluctant.

'Think of our children, at least,' urged Susheela.

Finally, with the welfare of his children in mind, Sudama decided to go to Dwarka. All he could manage as a gift for his friend was some flattened rice, which his wife borrowed from a friend. With that tied in a worn-out old cloth, Sudama left for Dwarka.

He walked barefoot for several days and nights, and when he finally arrived at the city gates, he was awestruck. The town was gilded with gold. Its people led happy and prosperous lives. In contrast, Sudama had torn clothes and dirty feet.

When he reached the palace, the guards gave him a scornful look and waved him away.

Sudama was tired, but determined. 'Please,' he told the guards. 'Just tell the lord of Dwarka, Dwarkadheesh Krishna, my name once; tell him his old friend wants to see him. Just once.'

The guards laughed at him. 'How can the king have a friend like you?' they said.

Sudama waited and waited. In the end, one guard decided to take pity on him and informed the king.

No one could have imagined what happened next!

As soon as he heard Sudama's name, the great king, the revered Lord Krishna, ran out barefoot to receive him. Everyone in the palace, from the queen to the guards, could see happiness and sadness all together on his face as he embraced Sudama and welcomed him into the palace. As he seated his old friend on a silken throne and washed his feet himself, a gasp went through the room.

The two friends spent the next few days remembering their childhood at the *gurukul*, and its many shared stories. It seemed they would never stop talking.

Finally, the time came for Sudama to leave.

Of course he had not been able to bring up the reason for his visit and he had been too ashamed to give his royal friend the 'gift' he had brought. But he could not deceive Krishna's loving but sharp eyes.

As Sudama was ready to leave, his friend asked, 'What's that you are hiding? Was that something you brought for me in that little bag?'

Sudama could not lie this time round, and soon Krishna was eating the plain rice as if it was the tastiest dish on earth! Sudama was reminded of his starving family but could not bring himself to ask Krishna for any help. They bid each other goodbye.

The journey back was more painful for Sudama than the one to the golden city. He kept thinking about what he would tell his wife and what reason he would give for not having mentioned his problems to Krishna.

When he reached his village, with scratched, dirty feet and a layer of dust covering him, he could not find his little hut! He felt a little dizzy from exhaustion, and sat down with his head reeling, wondering if he had lost his way.

But how could he have?

Just then, a little distance away he saw a golden mansion that had never been there. He mustered up enough strength to go close. And who was standing in the doorway looking out but his wife, Susheela, in new, pretty clothes! As he stumbled in a daze toward the beautiful building, he saw his children running around happily in the garden, which was studded with fountains and teeming with flowers.

His wife was overjoyed to see him and exclaimed, 'See! Didn't I tell you?! This is all thanks to Shri Krishna.'

Sudama was moved to tears. After all, not a word had been spoken between the friends about this. Yet, as a true friend, Krishna had understood Sudama's silence more than any words. Sudama vowed to share his newfound riches and always help others, just as he had been helped by his old friend. ❋

76

THE SELFISH GIANT

OSCAR WILDE

Every afternoon, as they were coming from school, the children used to go and play in the Giant's garden.

It was a large, lovely garden, with soft green grass. Here and there over the grass stood beautiful flowers like stars, and there were twelve peach trees that in the springtime broke out into delicate blossoms of pink and pearl, and in the autumn bore rich fruit. The birds sat on the trees and sang so sweetly that the children used to stop their games in order to listen to them. 'How happy we are here!' they cried to each other.

One day the Giant came back. He had been to visit his friend the Cornish ogre and had stayed with him for seven years. After the seven years were over he had said all that he had to say, for his conversation was limited, and he determined to return to his own castle. When he arrived he saw the children playing in the garden.

'What are you doing here?' he cried in a very gruff voice, and the children ran away.

'My own garden is my own garden,' said the Giant; 'anyone can understand that, and I will allow nobody to play in it but myself.' So he built a high wall all round it, and put up a noticeboard.

TRESPASSERS
WILL BE
PROSECUTED

He was a very selfish Giant.

The poor children had now nowhere to play. They tried to play on the road, but the road was very dusty and full of hard stones, and they did not like it. They used to wander round the high wall when their lessons were over and talk about the beautiful garden inside. 'How happy we were there,' they said to each other.

Then the Spring came, and all over the country there were little blossoms and little birds. Only in the garden of the Selfish Giant it was still winter. The birds did not care to sing in it as there were no children, and the trees forgot to blossom. Once a beautiful flower put its head out from the grass, but when it saw the noticeboard it was so sorry for the children that it slipped back into the ground again and went off to sleep.

The only people who were pleased were the Snow and the Frost. 'Spring has forgotten this garden,' they cried, 'so we will live here all the year round.' The Snow covered up the grass with her great white cloak, and the Frost painted all the trees silver. Then they invited the North Wind to stay with them, and he came. He was wrapped in furs, and he roared all day about the garden and blew the chimney-pots down. 'This is a delightful spot,' he said, 'we must ask the Hail on a visit.' So the Hail came. Every day for three hours he rattled on the roof of the castle till he broke most of the slates, and then he ran round and round the garden as fast as he could go. He was dressed in grey, and his breath was like ice.

'I cannot understand why the Spring is so late in coming,' said the Selfish Giant, as he sat at the window and looked out at his cold white garden. 'I hope there will be a change in the weather.'

But the Spring never came, nor the Summer. The Autumn gave golden fruit to every garden, but to the Giant's garden she gave none. 'He is too selfish,' she said. So it was always Winter there, and the North Wind, and the Hail, and the Frost, and the Snow danced about through the trees.

One morning the Giant was lying awake in bed when he heard some lovely music. It sounded so sweet to his ears that he thought it must be the King's musicians passing by. It was really only a little linnet singing outside his window, but it was so long since he had heard a bird sing in his garden that it seemed to him to be the most beautiful music in the world. Then the Hail stopped dancing over his head, and the North Wind ceased roaring, and a delicious perfume came to him through the open casement. 'I believe the Spring has come at last,' said the Giant, and he jumped out of bed and looked out.

What did he see?

He saw a most wonderful sight. Through a little hole in the wall the children had crept in, and they were sitting in the branches of the trees. In every tree that he could see there was a little child. And the trees were so glad to have the children back again that they had covered themselves with blossoms, and were waving their arms gently above the children's heads. The birds were flying about and twittering with delight, and the flowers were looking up through the green grass and laughing. It was a lovely scene, only in one corner it was still winter.

It was the farthest corner of the garden, and in it was standing a little boy. He was so small that he could not reach up to the branches of the tree, and he was wandering all round it, crying bitterly. The poor tree was still quite covered with frost and snow, and the North Wind was blowing and roaring above it. 'Climb up, little boy,' said the Tree, and it bent its branches down as low as it could, but the boy was too tiny.

And the Giant's heart melted as he looked out. 'How selfish I have been!' he said. 'Now I know why the Spring would not come here. I will put that poor little boy on the top of the tree, and then I will knock down the wall, and my garden shall be the children's playground for ever and ever.' He was really very sorry for what he had done.

So he crept downstairs and opened the front door quite softly, and went out into the garden. But when the children saw him they were so frightened that they all ran away, and the garden became winter again. Only the little boy did not run, for his eyes were so full of tears that he did not see the Giant coming. And the Giant stole up behind him and took him gently in his hand and put him up into the tree. And the tree broke at once into blossom, and the birds came and sang on it, and the little boy stretched out his two arms and flung them round the Giant's neck, and kissed him. And the other children, when they saw that the Giant was not wicked any longer, came running back, and with them came the Spring.

'It is your garden now, little children,' said the Giant, and he took a great axe and knocked down the wall. And when the people were going to market at twelve o'clock they found the Giant playing with the children in the most beautiful garden they had ever seen.

All day long they played, and in the evening they came to the Giant to bid him goodbye.

'But where is your little companion?' he said. 'The boy I put into the tree.' The Giant loved him the best because he had kissed him.

'We don't know,' answered the children. 'He has gone away.'

'You must tell him to be sure and come here tomorrow,' said the Giant. But the children said that they did not know where he lived and had never seen him before; and the Giant felt very sad.

Every afternoon, when school was over, the children came and played with the Giant. But the little boy whom the Giant loved was never seen again. The Giant was very kind to all the children, yet he longed for his first little friend, and often spoke of him. 'How I would like to see him!' he used to say.

Years went over, and the Giant grew very old and feeble. He could not play about any more, so he sat in a huge armchair, and watched the children at their games, and admired his garden. 'I have many beautiful flowers,' he said, 'but the children are the most beautiful flowers of all.'

One winter morning he looked out of his window as he was dressing. He did not hate the Winter now, for he knew that it was merely the Spring asleep, and that the flowers were resting.

Suddenly he rubbed his eyes in wonder, and looked and looked. It certainly was a marvellous sight. In the farthest corner of the garden was a tree quite covered with lovely white blossoms. Its branches were all golden, and silver fruit hung down from them, and underneath it stood the little boy he had loved.

Downstairs ran the Giant in great joy, and out into the garden. He hastened across the grass and came near the child. And when he came quite close his face grew red with anger, and he said, 'Who has dared to wound you?' For on the palms of the child's hands were the prints of two nails, and the prints of two nails were on the little feet.

'Who has dared to wound you?' cried the Giant. 'Tell me, that I may take my big sword and slay him.'

'Nay,' answered the child, 'but these are the wounds of Love.'

'Who are you?' said the Giant, and a strange awe fell on him, and he knelt before the little child.

And the child smiled on the Giant, and said to him, 'You let me play once in your garden, today you shall come with me to my garden, which is Paradise.'

And when the children ran in that afternoon, they found the Giant lying dead under the tree, all covered with white blossoms. ❋

77

BHEESHMA AND DRONA

UPENDRAKISHORE RAY CHOWDHURY; TRANSLATED BY SWAPNA DUTTA

In the olden days, all princes learned archery along with other subjects right from their childhood. The Pandava princes had an excellent teacher named Kripacharya. One day the boys were playing with an iron ball and it fell into a dry well. They tried their best to get it out, but failed and felt really upset. They saw a slim middle-aged stranger, bow and arrow in hand, coming their way. He took in the situation at a glance and burst out laughing.

'Shame on you boys!' he said, 'You couldn't manage to pick up a simple ball? Disgraceful! I'll get it for you. But what will you give me in return?'

Yudhishthira said, 'Sir, if you succeed, you will never go without a meal in your life.'

The stranger laughed again and picked up a handful of arrows. He fitted the first to his bow and let go. The arrow gripped the ball in the well. Then he aimed another, which stuck to the first, and yet others, forming a long stick. Pulling up the ball was a simple matter after that. The boys stared amazed. After that the man threw his own ring into the well and retrieved it the same way. It was an incredible feat!

Yudhishthira saluted him and said, 'You must be some great personality, sir. Do tell us how we may serve you?'

He replied, 'Just go and tell your grandfather about me.'

The boys rushed to Bheeshma and told him about the incident.

Although Pandu and Dhritarashtra were Bheeshma's grandnephews, everyone addressed the great patriarch as 'grandfather'.

After listening to their story Bheeshma said, 'It must be Dronacharya. Such a feat is beyond anyone else.'

Bheeshma had long wanted Dronacharya to teach the strategies of warfare to his great-grandsons and was thrilled to know that he was here. He went to welcome him and requested him to take charge of the boys.

Bheeshma and Dronacharya were great men. It is not enough to just know their names. You should know more about their life. Let's begin with Bheeshma's story.

Ashtavasu or the eight Vasu brothers were inmates of heaven. One day they went to visit the ashram of sage Vasishtha with their wives. But the sage was away and the brothers saw Nandini, his cow, who could not only provide unlimited milk, but her milk was also said to make a person live for ten thousand years. The wife of Deu, the youngest of the Vasu brothers, wanted her badly and begged her husband to take her away. Deu persuaded his brothers to steal Nandini and take her with them. Vasishtha returned home soon after and could not find Nandini. Blessed with special powers, the sage knew at once what had happened.

Angry and incredulous, he cursed the Vasu brothers, saying, 'Since you stooped to stealing despite being devas, you shall be born as human beings.' He knew that Deu was the real culprit who had tempted the others so he said that while the other seven could become devas once again shortly, Deu would have to live the complete lifespan of a man.

The Vasu brothers were greatly upset and decided to seek Ganga's help. 'Mother, since there is no help for it, we must secure ourselves good parents at least,' they told her. 'King Pratip of Hastinapur is destined to have a wonderful son named Shantanu. We'd like him to be our father and you must be our mother. Please work it out somehow.'

Moved by their pleadings, Ganga agreed. She took the form of a baby girl, went to king Pratip who was meditating by the river, and sat on his lap. Pratip was amazed and said, 'You lovely child, who are you? I'd love to have you for my daughter-in-law.'

'Very well, father,' said Ganga, 'but I have a condition. Your son should never stop me from doing anything and never scold me even if he does not like it.'

'Very well, dear,' promised the king. Ganga disappeared soon after.

Prince Shantanu, the son of Pratip, grew up to be an excellent young man – brave, handsome, scholarly and competent in every way. Pratip crowned him king and went away to the forest to spend the rest of his days in prayers. Before going he told Shantanu, 'My son, a young angel had agreed to be your bride long ago and I had promised to have her for my daughter-in-law. If you ever come across her, do marry her and never stop her from doing anything she wants.'

Shantanu met her while hunting by the river and lost his heart to her instantly. When he asked her to be his queen, she agreed, but wanted him to promise that she would be free to act as she liked and that he would never try to stop her or question anything she chose to do. If he broke his promise, she would leave him instantly. Shantanu promised and returned home happily.

They were married and lived blissfully for a year. But soon after, a strange tragedy turned his life upside down. The queen had one angelic son after another and threw each of them into the river after they were born. It was heartbreaking for the king to witness it, but he remembered his promise and dared not say anything lest she should leave him.

Shantanu lost seven sons, his heart breaking every time. When the eighth one was born, the queen smiled for joy but Shantanu could not bear it any more. Forgetting his promise, he cried out, 'Dear queen, please don't kill this one! How can you be so heartless? Don't you know you are committing a great sin?'

The queen immediately placed the child in his arms and said, 'Here is your son. But do you remember your promise? I must leave you at once!'

When Ganga saw the depth of Shantanu's grief she told him gently who she really was, why she had married him and why she had to leave him now. The little prince was named Devabrata, and a heartbroken Shantanu went away to the forest to meditate and remained there for many years. In the meantime, prince Devabrata grew up to be a handsome and accomplished young man, scholarly, and adept at wielding all weapons.

One day, while Devabrata was chasing a deer in the forest, it jumped into the river to save itself. He shot an arrow that made the riverbed almost dry. Shantanu, praying by the river, was amazed and went to see who the fantastic archer was. He immediately recognized the young man as his son. He evoked Ganga, who appeared before him and said, 'Yes, this is indeed our son. I have looked after him all these years. He has studied the Vedas from sage Vasishtha and the Shastras from Brihaspati and Shukra. Parashurama himself has taught him to wield weapons. Do return home with him now.'

Shantanu happily returned to his kingdom and declared Devabrata the Prince Regent soon afterwards.

Some days later Shantanu saw a beautiful girl in the forest. She smelt like a lotus, her fragrance radiating for miles around. Shantanu asked her who she was.

'I am Satyavati, the daughter of a fisherman,' said the girl.

Shantanu sought her father and told him that he wanted to marry her.

The fisherman said, 'I can agree only if you promise that only the son born to my daughter, and no one else, will succeed you as king.'

Shantanu could not agree to such an absurd proposal when the entire kingdom knew that Devabrata was the heir apparent. He returned home dejected and his unhappiness told on him. Devabrata noticed his father's sadness and asked him what was troubling him.

Shantanu replied, 'I am fine, son. I feel worried lest anything should happen to you.'

Not satisfied with his father's reply, Devabrata went to his father's chief minister and asked him, 'Sir, what is wrong with my father? Is he ill?'

The old minister knew about the fisherman's daughter and told Devabrata about her. Devabrata immediately went with a group of his friends to the fisherman and said, 'Please let your daughter marry my father.'

'Nothing would make me happier, dear prince,' said the fisherman, 'but I am afraid the marriage would make my daughter unhappy. You are an invincible warrior. Who could stand up to you?'

Devabrata understood the implication of his words and said, 'There is no chance of my fighting with your grandson because I promise not to succeed my father's throne. Your grandson shall be the king.'

'I don't doubt your words,' said the fisherman, 'but what if your sons do not comply with your decision?'

'The question will arise only if I have sons,' said Devabrata. 'I vow here and now to remain unmarried all my life.'

As Devabrata took the vow, devas showered flowers on him from above. No one had taken such a tough vow before. He was renamed 'Bheeshma', meaning he who has taken a terrible vow — a name he was to be known by thereafter.

The fisherman was overjoyed and said, 'My daughter shall certainly marry the king.'

Bheeshma said to Satyavati, 'Mother, please let us go home in my chariot.'

Shantanu and Satyavati were married. Shantanu was so happy that he gave Devabrata a special boon, saying, 'You shall not die until you yourself wish it.'

Shantanu died after the birth of his two sons, Chitrangad and Vichitraveerya. When Chitrangad was old enough he was coronated as king, but he died in a battle soon after.

Vichitraveerya was still too young to be king, so Bheeshma looked after the kingdom on his behalf.

Now for Drona's story.

Drona, the son of sage Bharadwaj, was not just a scholar, but had learned to wield weapons from the great Parashurama himself. Parashurama gifted all his weapons to Drona and turned him into an invincible warrior.

As a young boy, Drona had been a close friend of Drupada, the prince of Panchala who had promised him, 'My friend, when I grow up, whatever I have will also be yours.'

Drona had not forgotten his words. He married the sister of Kripacharya and had a son named Ashwathama. But despite his qualifications, Drona was very poor and could not afford to buy milk for his son who cried whenever he saw his friends drinking it. The boys gave him rice powder mixed with water and said, 'Here is your milk, drink it.'

Ashwathama happily drank it, not realizing that it was not milk at all. The boys clapped their hands, teasing and shouting, 'Shame on you! Your father is so poor that he cannot even afford to buy you milk!'

Greatly upset by this incident, Drona remembered his friend Drupada's promise and decided to seek his help. He went to Panchala and told Drupada, 'My friend, do you remember that you had promised to look after me when you grew up? Well, I am here now.'

But Drupada, now the king of Panchala, refused to even recognize him!

'What an absurd story, my good man!' he said scornfully. 'How can a beggar like you possibly be the friend of a king? Who remembers what happened in your childhood! The maximum I can do for you is to provide you one meal.'

A dejected Drona went back to Hastinapur and vowed to make Drupada pay for this insult. ❋

– To know the whole story of the Kauravas and Pandavas, read the Mahabharata for Young Readers *by Upendrakishore Ray Chowdhury, translated by Swapna Dutta and published by Hachette India.*

78

SWAMI AND FRIENDS
'FATHER'S ROOM'

R.K. NARAYAN

It was Saturday and Rajam had promised to come in the afternoon. Swaminathan was greatly excited. Where was he to entertain him? Probably in his own 'room'; but his father often came in to dress and undress. No, he would be at Court, Swaminathan reminded himself with relief. He cleaned his table and arranged his books so neatly that his father was surprised and had a good word to say about it.

Swaminathan went to his grandmother. 'Granny,' he said, 'I have talked to you about Rajam, haven't I?

'Yes. That boy who is very strong but never passes his examination.'

'No. No. That is Mani.'

'Oh, now I remember, it is a boy who is called the Gram or something, that witty little boy.'

Swaminathan made a gesture of despair. 'Look here granny, you are again mistaking the Pea for him. I mean Rajam, who has killed tigers, whose father is the Police Superintendent, and who is great.'

'Oh,' granny cried, 'that boy, is he coming here? I am so glad.'

'H'm.... But I have got to tell you –'

'Will you bring him to me? I want to see him.'

'Let us see,' Swaminathan said vaguely, 'I can't promise. But I have got to tell you, when he is with me, you must not call me or come to my room.'

'Why so?' asked granny.

'The fact is – you are, well you are too old,' said Swaminathan with brutal candour. Granny accepted her lot cheerfully.

That he must give his friend something very nice to eat, haunted his mind. He went to his mother, who was squatting before a cutter with a bundle of plantain leaves beside her. He sat before her, nervously crushing a piece of leaf this way and that, and tearing it to minute bits.

'Don't throw all those bits on the floor. I simply can't sweep the floor any more,' she said.

'Mother, what are you preparing for the afternoon tiffin?'

'Time enough to think of it,' said mother.

'You had better prepare something very nice, something fine and sweet. Rajam is coming this afternoon. Don't make the sort of coffee that you usually give me. It must be very good and hot.' He remembered how in Rajam's house everything was brought to the room by the cook.

'Mother, would you mind if I don't come here for coffee and tiffin? Can you send it to my room?'

He turned to the cook and said: 'Look here, you can't come to my room in that dhoti. You will have to wear a clean white dhoti and shirt.'

After a while he said: 'Mother, can you ask father to lend me his room for just an hour or two?' She said that she could not as she was very busy. Why could he himself not go and ask?

'Oh, he will give more readily if you ask,' said Swaminathan.

He went to his father and said: 'Father, I want to ask you something.' Father looked up from the papers over which he was bent. 'Father, I want your room.'

'What for?'

'I have to receive a friend,' Swaminathan replied.

'You have your own room,' Father said.

'I can't show it to Rajam.'

'Who is this Rajam, such a big man?'

'He is the Police Superintendent's son. He is – he is not ordinary.'

'I see. Oh! Yes, you can have my room, but be sure not to mess up the things on the table.'

'Oh, I will be very careful. You are a nice father, Father.'

Father guffawed and said: 'Now run in, boy, and sit at your books.'

Rajam's visit went off much more smoothly that Swaminathan had anticipated. Father had left his room open; mother had prepared some marvel with wheat, plum and sugar. Coffee was really good. Granny had kept her promise and did not show her senile self to Rajam. Swaminathan was only sorry that the cook did not change his dhoti.

Swaminathan seated Rajam in his father's revolving chair. It was nearly three hours since he had come. They had talked out all subjects – Mani, Ebenezar, trains, tiger-hunting, police and ghosts.

'Which is your room?' Rajam asked.

Swaminathan replied with a grave face: 'This is my room, why?' Rajam took time to swallow this.

'Do you read such books?' he asked, eyeing the big gilt-edged law books on the table. Swaminathan was embarrassed. Rajam made matters worse with another question. 'But where are your books?' There was just a flicker of a smile on his lips.

'The fact is,' said Swaminathan, 'this table belongs to my father. When I am out, he meets his clients in this room.'

'But where do you keep your books?'

Swaminathan made desperate attempts to change the topic: 'You have seen my grandmother, Rajam?'

'No. Will you show her to me? I should love to see her,' replied Rajam.

'Wait a minute then,' said Swaminathan and ran out. He had one last hope that his granny might be asleep. It was infinitely safer to show one's friends a sleeping granny. He saw her sitting on her bed complacently. He was disappointed. He stood staring at her, lost in thought.

'What is it, boy?' granny asked. 'Do you want anything?'

'No. Aren't you asleep? Granny,' he said a few minutes later, 'I have brought Rajam to see you.'

'Have you?' cried granny, 'Come nearer, Rajam. I can't see your face well. You know I am old and blind.'

Swaminathan was furious and muttered under his breath that his granny had no business to talk all this drivel to Rajam. Rajam sat on her bed. Granny stroked his hair and said that he had fine soft hair, though it was really short and prickly. Granny asked what his mother's name was, and how many children she had. She then asked if she had many jewels. Rajam replied that his mother had a black trunk filled with jewels, and a green one containing gold and silver vessels. Rajam then described to her Madras, its lighthouse, its sea, its trams and buses, and its cinemas. Every item made granny gasp with wonder.

–To know everything about Swaminathan, his granny and his buddies, read Swami and Friends *by R.K. Narayan.* ❋

79

THE HAMMER OF THOR

A NORSE MYTH; RETOLD BY MABEL H. CUMMINGS & MARY H. FOSTER

Sif was the wife of mighty Thor, the thunder-god, and she was very proud of her beautiful golden hair, which she combed and braided with great care. One morning when she awoke she was filled with grief and dismay to find that her lovely hair had been cut off in the night, while she slept. Her husband happened to be away that day.

Thor, however, soon called for Sif, and when he saw what had been done to her, he was very angry. Now Thor had a quick temper; everyone feared his fierce anger. 'Who could have done this wicked deed?' thought he. 'There is only one among all the Æsir* who would think of doing such a thing!'

* *The main gods in Norse mythology*

Thor lost no time in finding Loki, and that mischief-god had to admit that he was the guilty one, but he begged Thor to give him just a few days, and he promised to get something for Sif that would make her look more beautiful than ever. So Thor decided to give him a chance to try, and commanded him to give back to Sif her golden hair.

Now Loki knew a place where some wonderful workmen lived, so he went off, as fast as he could go, to Niflheim, the home of the dwarfs, under the earth, and asked one of them to quickly make some golden hair for Sif. Besides this, he asked for two gifts to carry to the gods Odin and Frey, so that they might be on his side if Thor should bring his complaint before the Æsir.

Loki did not have to wait long before the dwarf brought him a quantity of beautiful hair, spun from the finest golden thread. It had the wonderful power of growing just like real hair, as soon as it touched anyone's head. Besides this, there was a spear for Odin, which never missed its aim, no matter how far it was thrown, and for Frey, a ship that could sail through the air as well as the sea. Although it was large enough to hold all the gods and their horses, yet it could be folded so that it was small enough to put in one's pocket.

Loki was greatly pleased with these wonderful presents and declared that this dwarf must be the most skilful workman of them all. Now it happened that another dwarf, named Brock, heard him say this, and he told Loki that he was sure he and his brother could make more wonderful things than these.

Loki did not believe that could be done, but he told Brock to try his skill; the Æsir should judge between them and the one who should fail in the trial must lose his head.

Then Brock called his brother, Sindri, and they set to work at once. They first built a great fire, and Sindri threw into it a lump of gold; then he told Brock to blow the bellows while he went out, and be sure not to stop blowing until he should come back.

Brock thought this an easy task, but his brother had not long been gone when a huge fly came in and buzzed about his face, and bothered him so that he could hardly keep on blowing; still he was able to finish his work, so that when Sindri came back, they took out of the fire an enormous wild boar, which gave out light, and could travel through the air with wonderful speed.

On the second day Sindri threw another lump of gold into the fire and left his brother to blow the bellows. Again the buzzing, stinging fly came, and was even more troublesome than before; but Brock tried very hard to be patient, and was able to bear it without stopping his work until Sindri returned. Then they took from the fire a magic ring of gold, from which eight new rings fell off every week.

The third day a lump of iron was put into the fire, and Brock was again left alone. In came the cruel fly –

have you guessed that it was really that mischief-maker Loki? He bit the poor little dwarf so hard on the forehead that the blood ran down into his eyes, and blinded him so that he could no longer see to do his work.

Poor Brock had to stop just before Sindri came home, but not before the hammer which they were making in the fire was nearly finished, only the handle came out rather too short. This magic hammer was named Miölnir. It had the power of never missing its mark and would always return to the hand which threw it.

When Loki appeared at last before the Æsir, with the two dwarf brothers and their gifts, it was declared that they had made the finest things, for the hammer, which was given to Thor, would surely be most useful in keeping the giants out of Asgard. When Loki found that the judgment was against him, he started to run away; but Thor soon made him turn back by threatening to throw his hammer after him.

Then Loki had to collect his wits, and think of some way to escape losing his head, instead of making the dwarfs pay the forfeit, as he had expected. At last he told Brock and Sindri that they could have his head, according to the agreement, but as nothing had been said about his neck, they could not, of course, touch that.

Thus the wily Loki, by his wit, saved his life. ❋

80

HOW THOR LOST HIS HAMMER

A NORSE MYTH; RETOLD BY MABEL H. CUMMINGS & MARY H. FOSTER

'Come, Loki, are you ready? My goats are eager to be off!' cried Thor, as he sprang into his chariot, and away they went, thundering over the hills. All day long they journeyed, and at night they lay down to rest by the side of a brook.

When Baldur, the bright Sun God, awoke them in the morning, the first thing Thor did was to reach out for Miölnir, his magic hammer, which he had carefully laid by his side the night before.

'Why, Loki!' cried he. 'Alas, my hammer is gone! Those evil frost giants must have stolen it from me while I slept. How shall we hold Asgard against them without my hammer? They will surely take our stronghold!'

'We must go quickly and find it!' replied Loki. 'Let us ask Freyja to lend us her falcon garment.'

Now the goddess, Freyja, had a wonderful garment made of falcon feathers, and whoever wore it looked just like a bird. As you may suppose, this was sometimes a very useful thing. So Thor and Loki went quickly back to Asgard, and drove with all speed to Freyja's palace, where they found her sitting among her maidens. 'Asgard is in great danger!' said Thor, 'and we have come to you, fair goddess, to ask if you will lend us your falcon garment, for my hammer has been carried off, and we must go in search of it.'

'Surely,' answered Freyja, 'I would lend you my falcon cloak, even if it were made of gold and silver!'

Then Loki quickly dressed himself in Freyja's garment and flew away to the land of the frost giants, where he found their king making collars of gold for his dogs and combing his horses. As Loki came near, he looked up and said, 'Ah, Loki, how fare the mighty gods in Asgard?'

'The Æsir are in great trouble,' replied Loki, 'and I am sent to fetch the hammer of Thor.'

'And do you think I am going to be foolish enough to give it back to you, after I have had all the trouble of getting it into my power?' said the king. 'I have buried it deep, deep, down in the earth, and there is only one way by which you can get it again. You must bring me the goddess Freyja to be my wife!'

Loki did not know what to say to this, for he felt sure that Freyja would never be willing to go away from Asgard to live among the fierce giants; but as he saw no chance of getting the hammer, he flew back to Asgard, to see what could be done.

Thor was anxiously looking out for him. 'What news do you bring, Loki?' cried he. 'Have you brought me my hammer again?'

'Alas, no!' said Loki. 'I bring only a message from the giant king. He will not give up your hammer until you persuade Freyja to marry him!'

Then Thor and Loki went together to Freyja's palace, and the fair goddess greeted them kindly, but when she heard their errand and found they wished her to marry the cruel giant, she was very angry and said to Thor, 'You should not have been so careless as to lose your hammer; it is all your own fault that it is gone, and I will never marry the giant to help you get it again.'

Thor then went to tell Father Odin, who called a meeting of all the Æsir, for it was a very serious matter they were to consider. If the king of the giants only knew the power of the mighty hammer, he might storm Asgard and carry off the fair Freyja to be his bride.

So the Æsir met together in their great judgment hall, in the palace of Gladsheim. Long and anxiously they talked over their peril, trying to find some plan for saving Asgard from these enemies. At last Heimdall, the faithful watchman of the rainbow bridge, proposed a plan.

'Let us dress Thor,' said he, 'in Freyja's robes, braid his hair and let him wear Freyja's wonderful necklace, and a bridal veil!'

'No, indeed!' cried Thor, angrily 'You would all laugh at me in a woman's dress; I will do no such thing! We must find some other way.' But when no other way could be found, at last Thor was persuaded to try Heimdall's plan, and the Æsir went to work to dress the mighty thunder-god like a bride. He was the tallest of them all, and, of course, he looked very queer to them in his woman's clothes, but he would be small enough beside a giant. Then they dressed Loki to look like the bride's waiting-maid, and the two set off for Utgard, the stronghold of the giants.

When the giant king saw them coming he asked his servants to prepare the wedding feast and invited all his giant subjects to come and celebrate his marriage with the lovely goddess Freyja.

So the wedding party sat down to the feast, and Thor, who was always a good eater, ate one ox and eight salmon, and drank three casks of mead. The king watched him, greatly surprised to see a woman eat so much, and said, "'Where have you seen such a hungry bride?'

But the watchful Loki, who stood nearby, as the bride's waiting-maid, whispered in the king's ear,

'Eight nights has Freyja fasted and would take no food, so anxious was she to be your bride!'

This pleased the giant, and he went toward Thor, saying he must kiss his fair bride. But when he lifted the bridal veil, such a gleam of light shot from Thor's eyes that the king started back and asked why Freyja's eyes were so sharp.

Again Loki replied, 'For eight nights the fair Freyja has not slept, so greatly did she long to reach here!' This again pleased the king, and he said, 'Now let the hammer be brought and given to the bride, for the hour has come for our marriage!'

All this time Thor was so eager to get his treasure back that he could hardly keep still, and if it had not been for what the wily Loki said, he might have been found out too soon. But at last the precious hammer was brought and handed to the bride, as was always the custom at weddings; as soon as Thor grasped it in his hand, he threw off his woman's robes and stood out before the astonished giants.

Then did the mighty Thunderer sweep down his foes, and many of the cruel frost giants were slain. Once more the sacred city of Asgard was saved from danger, for Thor was its defender, and he was careful never again to let his magic hammer be taken from him.

Besides the hammer, Thor had two other precious things, his belt of strength, which doubled his power when he tightened it, and his iron glove, which he put on when he was going to throw the hammer. ❋

81

LITTLE SNOW-WHITE

THE BROTHERS GRIMM; RETOLD BY LOGAN MARSHALL

Once upon a time in the middle of winter, when the flakes of snow were falling like feathers from the clouds, a Queen sat at her palace window, which had an ebony black frame, stitching her husband's shirts. While she was thus engaged and looking out at the snow she pricked her finger, and three drops of blood fell upon the snow. Now the red looked so well upon the white that she thought to herself, 'Oh, that I had a child as white as this snow, as red as this blood and as black as the wood of this frame!' Soon afterwards a little daughter came to her, who was as white as snow, and with cheeks as red as blood, and with hair as black as ebony, and from this she was named 'Snow-White'. And at the same time her mother died.

About a year afterwards the King married another wife, who was very beautiful, but so proud and haughty that she could not bear anyone to be better-looking than herself. She owned a wonderful mirror, and when she stepped before it and said:

'Mirror, mirror on the wall,
Who is the fairest of us all?'

it replied:

'The Queen is the fairest of the day.'

Then she was pleased, for she knew that the mirror spoke truly.

Little Snow-White, however, grew up, and became prettier and prettier, and when she was seven years old she was as fair as the noonday, and more beautiful than the Queen herself. When the Queen now asked her mirror:

'Mirror, mirror on the wall,
Who is the fairest of us all?'

it replied:

'The Queen was fairest yesterday;
Snow-White is the fairest, now, they say.'

This answer so angered the Queen that she became quite yellow with envy. From that hour, whenever she saw Snow-White, her heart was hardened against her, and she hated the little girl. Her envy and jealousy increased so that she had no rest day or night, and she said to a Huntsman, 'Take the child away into the forest. I will never look upon her again. You must kill her, and bring me her heart and tongue for a token.'

The Huntsman listened and took the maiden away, but when he drew out his knife to kill her, she began to cry, saying, 'Ah, dear Huntsman, give me my life! I will run into the wild forest and never come home again.'

This speech softened the Hunter's heart, and her beauty so touched him that he had pity on her and said, 'Well, run away then, poor child.' But he thought to himself, 'The wild beasts will soon devour you.' Still he felt as if a stone had been lifted from his heart, because her death was not by his hand.

Just at that moment a young boar came roaring along to the spot, and as soon as he clapped eyes upon it the Huntsman caught it, and, killing it, took its tongue and heart and carried them to the Queen as a token of his deed.

But now poor little Snow-White was left motherless and alone, and overcome with grief, she was bewildered at the sight of so many trees and knew not which way to turn. She ran till her feet refused to go farther, and as it was getting dark, and she saw a little house near, she entered in to rest. In this cottage everything was very small, but very neat and elegant. In the middle stood a little table with a white cloth over it and seven little plates upon it, each plate having a spoon and a knife and a fork, and there were also seven little mugs. Against the wall were seven little beds arranged in a row, each covered with snow-white sheets.

Little Snow-White, being both hungry and thirsty, ate a little morsel of porridge out of each plate, and drank a drop or two of wine out of each mug, for she did not wish to take away the whole share of anyone. After that, because she was so tired, she laid herself down on one bed, but it did not suit; she tried another, but that was too long; a fourth was too short, a fifth too hard. But the seventh was just the thing; and tucking herself up in it, she went to sleep, first saying her prayers as usual.

When it became quite dark the owners of the cottage came home, seven Dwarfs, who dug for gold and silver in the mountains. They first lighted seven little lamps, and saw at once – for they lit up the whole room – that somebody had been in, for everything was not in the order in which they had left it.

The first asked, 'Who has been sitting on my chair?' The second, 'Who has been eating off my plate?' The third said, 'Who has been nibbling at my bread?' The fourth, 'Who has been at my porridge?' The fifth, 'Who has been meddling with my fork?' The sixth grumbled out, 'Who has been cutting with my knife?' The seventh said, 'Who has been drinking out of my mug?'

Then the first, looking round, began again, 'Who has been lying on my bed?' he asked, for he saw that the sheets were tumbled. At these words the others came, and looking at their beds cried out too, 'Someone has been lying in our beds!' But the seventh little man, running up to his, saw Snow-White sleeping in it; so he called his companions, who shouted with wonder and held up their seven lamps, so that the light fell upon the little girl.

'Oh, heavens! Oh, heavens!' said they. 'What a beauty she is!' and they were so much delighted that they would not awaken her, but left her to sleep, and the seventh Dwarf, in whose bed she was, slept with each of his fellows one hour, and so passed the night.

As soon as morning dawned Snow-White awoke, and was quite frightened when she saw the seven little men; but they were very friendly, and asked her what she was called.

'My name is Snow-White,' was her reply.

'Why have you come into our cottage?' they asked.

When her tale was finished the Dwarfs said, 'Will you look after our household – be our cook, make the beds, wash, sew and knit for us, and keep everything in neat order? If so, we will keep you here, and you shall want for nothing.'

And Snow-White answered, 'Yes, with all my heart and will.' And so she remained with them, and kept their house in order.

In the morning the Dwarfs went into the mountains and searched for silver and gold, and in the evening they came home and found their meals ready for them. During the day the maiden was left alone, and therefore the good Dwarfs warned her and said, 'Be careful of your stepmother, who will soon know of your being here. So let nobody enter the cottage.'

The Queen meanwhile believed that she was now above all the most beautiful woman in the world. One day she stepped before her mirror, and said:

'Mirror, mirror on the wall,
Who is the fairest of us all?'

and it replied:

'The Queen was fairest yesterday;
Snow-White is fairest now, they say.
The Dwarfs protect her from your sway
Amid the forest, far away.'

This reply surprised her, but she knew that the mirror spoke the truth. She knew, therefore, that the

Huntsman had deceived her, and that Snow-White was still alive. So she dyed her face and clothed herself as a pedlar woman, so that no one could recognize her, and in this disguise she went over the seven hills to the house of the seven Dwarfs. She knocked at the door of the hut, and called out, 'Fine goods for sale! Beautiful goods for sale!'

Snow-White peeped out of the window and said, 'Good day, my good woman; what have you to sell?'

'Fine goods, beautiful goods!' she replied. 'Stay-laces of all colours.' And she held up a pair which were made of many-coloured silk threads.

'I may let in this honest woman,' thought Snow-White; and she unbolted the door and bargained for one pair of stay-laces.

'You can't think, my dear, how they become you!' exclaimed the old woman. 'Come, let me lace them up for you.'

Snow-White suspected nothing, and let her do as she wished, but the old woman laced her up so quickly and so tightly that all her breath went, and she fell down like one dead. 'Now,' thought the old woman to herself, hastening away, 'now am I once more the most beautiful of all!'

At eventide, not long after she had left, the seven Dwarfs came home, and were much frightened at seeing Snow-White lying on the ground, and neither moving nor breathing, as if she were dead. They raised her up. She began to breathe again, and little by little she revived. When the Dwarfs now heard what had taken place, they said, 'The old pedlar woman was no other than your wicked stepmother. Take more care of yourself and let no one enter when we are not with you.'

Meanwhile, the Queen had reached home, and, going before her mirror, she repeated her usual words:

'Mirror, mirror on the wall,
Who is the fairest of us all?'

and it replied as before:

'The Queen was fairest yesterday;
Snow-White is fairest now, they say.
The Dwarfs protect her from your sway
Amid the forest, far away.'

As soon as it had finished, all her blood rushed to her heart, for she was so angry to hear that Snow-White was yet living. 'But now,' thought she to herself, 'I will make something which shall destroy her completely.' Thus saying, she made a poisoned comb by arts which she understood, and then, disguising herself, she took the form of an old widow. She went over the seven hills to the house of the seven Dwarfs, and knocking at the door, called out, 'Good wares to sell today!'

Snow-White peeped out and said, 'You must go ahead for I dare not let you in.'

'But still you may look,' said the old woman, drawing out her poisoned comb and holding it up. The sight of this pleased the maiden so much that she opened the door. As soon as she had bought something the old woman said, 'Now let me for once comb your hair properly,' and Snow-White agreed. But scarcely was the comb drawn through the hair when the poison began to work, and the maiden fell down senseless.

Fortunately, evening soon came, and the seven Dwarfs returned, and as soon as they saw Snow-White lying, like dead, upon the ground, they suspected the Queen, and discovering the poisoned comb, they immediately drew it out. Then the maiden very soon revived and told them all that had happened. So again they warned her against the wicked stepmother and told her to open the door to nobody.

Meanwhile the Queen, on her arrival home, had again consulted her mirror and received the same answer as twice before. This made her tremble and foam with rage and jealousy, and she swore that Snow-White should die if it cost her her own life.

Thereupon she went into an inner secret chamber where no one could enter, and made an apple of the most deep and subtle poison. Outwardly it looked nice enough and had rosy cheeks which would make the mouth of everyone who looked at it water, but whoever ate the smallest piece of it would surely die. As soon as the apple was ready the Queen again dyed her face and clothed herself like a peasant's wife, and then over the seven mountains to the house of the seven Dwarfs she made her way.

She knocked at the door, and Snow-White stretched out her head and said, 'I dare not let anyone enter; the seven Dwarfs have forbidden me.'

'That is hard on me,' said the old woman, 'for I must take back my apples; but there is one which I will give you.'

'No,' answered Snow-White; 'no, I dare not take it.'

'What! Are you afraid of it?' cried the old woman. 'There, see – I will cut the apple in halves; you eat the red cheeks, and I will eat the core.' (The apple was so artfully made that the red cheeks alone were poisoned.) Snow-White very much wished for the beautiful apple, and when she saw the woman eating the core she could no longer resist, but, stretching out her hand, took the poisoned part. Scarcely had she placed a piece in her mouth when she fell down dead upon the ground. Then the Queen, looking at her with glittering eyes, and laughing bitterly, exclaimed, 'White as snow, red as blood, black as ebony! This time the Dwarfs cannot reawaken you.'

When she reached home and consulted her mirror –

'Mirror, mirror on the wall,
Who is the fairest of us all?'

it answered:

'The Queen is fairest of the day.'

Then her envious heart was at rest, as peacefully as an envious heart can rest.

When the little Dwarfs returned home in the evening they found Snow-White lying on the ground, and there appeared to be no life in her body; she seemed to be quite dead. They raised her up, and tried if they could find anything poisonous, but it was of no use.

Then they laid her upon a bier, and all seven placed themselves around it, and wept and wept for three days without ceasing. Then they prepared to bury her. But she looked still fresh and lifelike, and even her red cheeks had not deserted her, so they said to one another, 'We cannot bury her in the black ground.' Then they ordered a case to be made of glass. In this they could see the body on all sides, and the Dwarfs wrote her name with golden letters upon the glass, saying that she was a King's daughter. Now they placed the glass case upon the ledge on a rock, and one of them always remained by it watching. Even the birds bewailed the loss of Snow-White; first came an owl, then a raven, and last of all a dove.

For a long time Snow-White lay peacefully in her case, and changed not, but looked as if she were only asleep, for she was still white as snow, red as blood and black-haired as ebony. By and by it happened that a King's son was travelling in the forest and came to the Dwarfs' house to pass the night. He soon saw the glass case upon the rock and the beautiful maiden lying within, and he also read the golden inscription.

When he had examined it, he said to the Dwarfs, 'Let me have this case life-like and I will pay what you like for it.'

But the Dwarfs replied, 'We will not sell it for all the gold in the world.'

'Then give it to me,' said the Prince, 'for I cannot live without Snow-White. I will honour and protect her as long as I live.'

When the Dwarfs saw that he was so much in earnest, they pitied him, and at last gave him the case, and the Prince ordered it to be carried away on the shoulders of his attendants. Presently it happened that they stumbled over a rut, and with the shock the piece of poisoned apple which lay in Snow-White's mouth fell out. Very soon she opened her eyes, and raising the lid of the glass case, she rose up and asked, 'Where am I?'

Full of joy, the Prince answered, 'You are safe with me.' And he told to her what she had suffered, and how he would rather have her than any other for his wife, and he asked her to accompany him home to the castle of the King his father. Snow-White consented, and when they arrived there they were married with great splendour and magnificence.

Snow-White's stepmother was also invited to the wedding, and when she was dressed in all her finery to go, she first stepped in front of her mirror and asked:

'Mirror, mirror on the wall,
Who is the fairest of us all?'

and it replied:

'The Queen was fairest yesterday;
The Prince's bride is now, they say.'

At these words the Queen was in a fury and was so terribly mortified that she knew not what to do with herself. At first she resolved not to go to the wedding, but she could not resist the wish to see the Princess. So she went; but as soon as she saw the bride she recognized Snow-White, and was so terrified with rage and astonishment that she rushed out of the castle and was never heard of again. ❋

82

HANUMAN SETS LANKA ON FIRE

UPENDRAKISHORE RAY CHOWDHURY; TRANSLATED BY SWAPNA DUTTA

After climbing Mahendra Parvat, Hanuman selected a small flat area. Then he prayed to the gods with folded hands and got ready for the giant leap. His size had swelled so much at this point that Mahendra Parvat was unable to bear it. It crumbled up as water shot out from every direction and it looked just like a dishcloth that had been wrung! All the animals in the hill quite thought that it was the end of the world! Even the hermits fled the hill and looked at it curiously from a distance.

Hanuman poised his front legs on the ground, bloated up his tail, curled up his body and took such an enormous leap that was unlike any feat anyone had ever witnessed before. The impact of the leap was so startling that the trees of the hillside were uprooted and rushed along with him. The waves of the sea touched the sky. Hanuman looked just like an enormous mountain rushing across the sky.

By now Hanuman was quite close to Lanka and could see beautiful, lush green trees along the seashore. He did not wish to appear in his present huge form and made himself quite tiny once again. After crossing the ocean he alighted on top of a mountain. The city was located atop Lamba Parvat and was enclosed by walls made of gold. There were huge gates all along. The gates were made of gold too. Armed rakshasas stood all along the walls, guarding the city.

Hanuman entered the city of Lanka by scaling the wall. Then he looked through the rooms of every house but did not find Sita in any of them. Hanuman combed the entire kingdom, going from one room to another and one garden after another, leaving out not a single place.

Soon he came across the *ashokavana*, a grove of *ashoka* trees. As soon as he stepped inside the grove he had the feeling that perhaps he would discover something about Sita there. Hanuman hid himself among the leaves of a *sishu* tree nearby. After some time he saw a young woman, surrounded by rakshasis, come into the grove. Tears rolled down her cheeks as she sighed and seemed lost in thought. She had not combed or done up her hair; the yellow sari she wore looked crushed and crumpled. Hanuman immediately realized that she was none other than Sita.

Hanuman waited patiently for sundown. He crept down the tree and told Sita how he had met Rama and how he and the entire monkey tribe had been searching for her all these days. Finally, he gave her the ring Rama had given him for Sita. Hanuman ended up saying, 'Come with me, mother. I shall carry you on my back and take you to Rama.'

'I am sure you can do all that you say,' said Sita, 'but I dare not risk it. Why don't you bring Rama and Lakshmana here instead?'

After bidding farewell to Sita Hanuman thought it might be wise to find out also how adept the rakshasas were at fighting. Hanuman jumped and leaped about the grove and started breaking one tree after another. Very soon the entire place was in a shambles.

In the meantime, the rakshasas rushed to Ravana and said, 'Maharaj, a terrible monkey has appeared and ruined the *ashokavana*. Perhaps he has been sent by Rama.'

Ravana's eyes – ten pairs of them – turned bloodshot and flashed angry fire as he listened to the rakshasas. He gnashed his ten pairs of teeth and said, 'Go and capture him at once. Tie him up securely and bring him here.'

The rakshasas rushed to catch him with a stack of weapons. Hanuman broke off a rod from the main gate as soon as he saw them approaching and it hardly took him any time to pulverize their heads to dust. After that he climbed up the main gate once again and sat quietly. By then hundreds of watchmen and guards turned up, fully armed, to fight him.

I'm sure you can imagine what a furore Hanuman caused in Lanka! Big and hefty warriors arrived to fight him and Hanuman beat them all up one after the other. It was all over in the twinkling of an eye and he climbed up the gate once again.

After all this, Ravana's son Aksha came in his eight-horse-drawn chariot to fight Hanuman. He was quite a remarkable warrior and rained arrows on Hanuman at first. Hanuman felt bewildered but for an instant only! He slapped the horses so hard that along with the horses the chariot, too, was reduced to dust. Once more Hanuman took up his seat atop the gate.

When Ravana heard that his son Aksha was no more, he sent Indrajeet, his eldest son, to tackle Hanuman. Indrajeet was the bravest and the best warrior in Lanka. As soon as Hanuman saw his arrow approaching, he moved away and the arrow failed to touch him.

After trying in vain for a while, Indrajeet was so angry that he aimed the *Brahmastra* at Hanuman. Lord Brahma himself had gifted him the weapon. It was invincible and no one could stop it. But Brahma had given Hanuman a special boon because of which no weapon could kill him. So Indrajeet's *Brahmastra* did not kill Hanuman and merely tied him up, making him immobile.

Hanuman was only pleased to be tied up like this because he felt sure that they would now take him to Ravana and he would be able to speak to him. The rakshasas were overjoyed to find Hanuman tied up, and danced with glee. They brought stacks of jute rope and strapped him up within an inch of his life. But strangely enough, the knots of Indrajeet's *Brahmastra* got loose and came undone. This happened because they were bound to open if anyone tied any more ropes over it! But Hanuman did not let anyone suspect that the knots were now slack.

The rakshasas in the court were surprised to see Hanuman. Some of them said, 'Who is this monkey? How did it come here?' Some said, 'You'd better kill it.' Others said, 'He should be burnt to death.' Some suggested, 'Why not eat him?'

Hanuman did not speak. He merely looked at Ravana and his royal hall. Ravana was seated on his crystal throne studded with precious gems. Crowns of gold gleamed on his ten heads. His complexion was swarthy. He wore red sandalwood paste and a necklace of gleaming gold. His faces were wide and his teeth looked really sharp. Looking at him, it was quite obvious that he was a warrior of no mean order.

The rakshasas plied Hanuman with questions.

'From where did you come?'

'Why have you come here?'

'Why did you ruin our forest?'

'Who sent you here?'

'Better speak the truth or we shall kill you.'

Hanuman listened to the questions and addressed Ravana directly, 'Maharaj Ravana, I had come to Lanka to see you. I destroyed the trees in the forest because I could not find you. The rakshasas had come to fight with me, so I, too, fought back. I am Rama's messenger and the son of Pavan. My name is Hanuman. You are a great and wealthy ruler. Was it right on your part to have done something so wrong? I'm saying all this for your own good. Please listen to me and set Sita free. Or else you shall die.'

Ravana rolled his ten pairs of bloodshot eyes and said, 'Where have all my hangmen gone? Chop this fellow into pieces!' But Vibhishan stopped him. Vibhishan was Ravana's younger brother and a very wise man. He said, 'Have you lost all your senses, Maharaj? How can you order a messenger to be killed? It is a grave sin. Besides, if you have him killed, who will carry your message across to Rama? Unless Rama and Lakshmana know about your decision, why would they come here? And if they don't come, how are the rakshasas going to kill them and establish their supremacy?'

Ravana considered his words and said, 'You are quite right, Vibhishan. We'd better not kill him. Set his tail on fire instead. It will teach him a lesson...'

The rakshasas brought loads of rags and started wrapping them round Hanuman's tail. The more rags they wrapped, the thicker his tail became, and they kept on wrapping more and more cloth until virtually all the rags in Lanka had been used up. Then they poured buckets and buckets of oil over it until the rags were fairly dripping. Then they set his tail on fire.

Had they only foreseen what Hanuman would do they would never have done it! Hanuman turned his burning tail round and round and set the rakshasas on fire. The rakshasas raced all along the roads of Lanka with Hanuman dragging his burning tail and buffeting the rakshasas with it. The news soon reached Sita. Sita prayed earnestly to Agni, the god of fire, saying, 'Lord Agni, if I have done any good deed in my life, please don't let Hanuman get hurt.'

Hanuman was amazed to find that he felt no heat or pain although his tail was burning fiercely. In fact, the blazing fire felt like the touch of dew. Hanuman suddenly made his body very tiny so all the ropes that had been used to tie him up fell off him and he was free once again.

Hanuman now wondered what he should do next. He had crossed the sea, ruined the *ashokavana* and killed umpteen rakshasas. Now if only he could set Lanka on fire with his blazing tail, a large part of his work would be done. As soon as the thought occurred to him, he jumped up on the roof of a palace. From there he leaped from room to room, garden to garden, one house to another, setting them all ablaze with his tail, including the royal palace As the fire blazed, the wind blew hard and fanned it, making Hanuman roar in glee. Lanka appeared to have reached its doomsday. No matter which way one looked, there was just fire and more fire everywhere.

Hanuman put out the fire in his tail quite easily by dipping it into the sea, but no one succeeded in dousing the fire in Lanka.

Hanuman felt happy to think that he had avenged Sita's fate to some extent. But his joy was short-lived. All this time he had been so busy setting Lanka ablaze that he had not remembered Sita. Now he felt really scared and told himself, 'Oh God! Have I set Sita on fire along with the others?'

Then he heard a voice from the sky proclaim, 'It is a miracle that nothing has happened to Sita despite the blazing fire in Lanka.' When he heard these words Hanuman's heart filled with great joy. A few big leaps and he was before Sita herself. After bidding farewell to her, Hanuman climbed up the top of Arista Parvat close to Lanka and decided that it would be a good place to leap across the ocean. ❋

83

PINOCCHIO'S ADVENTURES

CARLO COLLODI; RETOLD BY J.H. STICKNEY

Master Cherry Finds a Queer Piece of Wood

There was once upon a time...

'A king!' my little readers will instantly exclaim. No, children, you are wrong. There was once upon a time a piece of wood.

This wood was not valuable; it was only a common log like those that are burnt in winter in the stoves and fireplaces to make a cheerful blaze and warm the rooms.

I cannot say how it came about, but the fact is, that one fine day this piece of wood was lying in the shop of an old carpenter of the name of Master Antonio. He was, however, called by everybody Master Cherry, on account of the end of his nose, which was always as red and polished as a ripe cherry.

No sooner had Master Cherry set his eyes on the piece of wood than his face beamed with delight and, rubbing his hands together with satisfaction, he said softly to himself, 'This wood has come at the right moment; it will just do to make the leg of a little table.'

Having said this he immediately took a sharp axe with which to remove the bark and the rough surface. Just, however, as he was going to give the first stroke he remained with his arm suspended in the air, for he heard a very small voice saying imploringly, 'Do not strike me so hard!'

Picture to yourselves the astonishment of good old Master Cherry!

He turned his terrified eyes all around the room to try and discover where the little voice could possibly have come from, but he saw nobody! He looked under the bench – nobody; he looked into a cupboard that was always shut – nobody; he looked into a basket of shavings and sawdust – nobody; he even opened the door of the shop and gave a glance into the street – and still nobody. Who, then, could it be?

'I see how it is,' he said, laughing and scratching his wig. 'Evidently that little voice was all my imagination. Let us set to work again.'

And taking up the axe he struck a tremendous blow on the piece of wood.

'Oh! Oh! You have hurt me!' cried the same little voice dolefully.

This time Master Cherry was petrified. His eyes started out of his head with fright, his mouth remained open and his tongue hung out almost to the end of his chin like a mask on a fountain. As soon as he had recovered the use of his speech, he began to say, stuttering and trembling with fear, 'But where on earth can that little voice have come from that said "Oh! Oh!?" ... Here there is certainly not a living soul. Is it possible that this piece of wood can have learnt to cry and to lament like a child? I cannot believe it. This piece of wood here it is; a log for fuel like all others, and thrown on the fire it would about suffice to boil a saucepan of beans.... How then? Can anyone be hidden inside it? If anyone is hidden inside, so much the worse for him. I will settle him at once.'

So saying he seized the poor piece of wood and commenced beating it without mercy against the walls of the room.

Then he stopped to listen if he could hear any little voice lamenting. He waited two minutes – nothing; five minutes – nothing; ten minutes – still nothing!

'I see how it is,' he then said, forcing himself to laugh and pushing up his wig, 'evidently, the little voice that said "Oh! Oh!" was all my imagination! Let us to work again.'

But all the same he was in a great fright; he tried to sing to give himself a little courage.

Putting the axe aside he took his plane to plane and polish the bit of wood; but whilst he was running it up and down he heard the same little voice say, laughing, 'Stop! You are tickling me all over!'

This time poor Master Cherry fell down as if he had been struck by lightning. When he at last opened his eyes he found himself seated on the floor.

His face was quite changed; even the end of his nose, instead of being crimson, as it was nearly always, had become blue from fright.

Geppetto Plans a Wonderful Puppet

At that moment someone knocked at the door.

'Come in,' said the carpenter, without having the strength to rise to his feet.

A lively little old man immediately walked into the shop. His name was Geppetto, but when the boys in the neighbourhood wished to put him in a passion they called him by the nickname of Polendina, because his yellow wig greatly resembled a pudding made of corn.

Geppetto was very fiery. Woe to him who called him Polendina! He became furious, and there was no holding him.

'Good day, Master Antonio,' said Geppetto; 'what are you doing there on the floor?'

'I am teaching the alphabet to the ants.'

'Much good may that do you.'

'What has brought you to me, neighbour Geppetto?'

'My legs. But to say the truth, Master Antonio, I have come to ask a favour of you.'

'Here I am ready to serve you,' replied the carpenter getting on his knees.

'This morning an idea came into my head.'

'Let us hear it.'

'I thought I would make a beautiful wooden puppet that should know how to dance, to fence, and to leap like an acrobat. With this puppet I would travel about the world to earn a piece of bread and a glass of wine. What do you think of it?'

'Bravo, Polendina!' exclaimed the same little voice, and it was impossible to say where it came from.

Hearing himself called Polendina, Geppetto became as red as a turkey-cock from rage, and turning to the carpenter he said in a fury, 'Why do you insult me?'

'Who insults you?'

'You called me Polendina!'

'It was not I!'

'Would you have it then, that it was I? It was you, I say!'

'No!'

'Yes!'

'No!'

'Yes!'

And becoming more and more angry, from words they came to blows, and flying at each other they bit, and fought, and scratched manfully.

When the fight was over Master Antonio was in possession of Geppetto's yellow wig, and Geppetto discovered that the grey wig belonging to the carpenter had remained between his teeth.

'Give me back my wig,' screamed Master Antonio.

'And you return me mine, and let us be friends.'

The two old men, having each recovered his own wig, shook hands and swore that they would remain friends to the end of their lives.

'Well then, neighbour Geppetto,' said the carpenter, to prove that peace was made, 'what is the favour that you wish of me?'

'I want a little wood to make my puppet; will you give me some?'

Master Antonio was delighted, and he immediately went to the bench and fetched the piece of wood that had caused him so much fear. Just as he was going to give it to his friend the piece of wood gave a shake and wriggling violently out of his hands struck with all its force against the dried-up shins of poor Geppetto.

'Ah! Is that the courteous way in which you make your presents, Master Antonio? You have almost lamed me!'

'I swear to you that it was not I!'

'Then you would have it that it was I?'

'The wood is entirely to blame!'

'I know that it was the wood, but it was you that hit my legs with it!'

'I did not hit you with it!'

'Liar!'

'Geppetto, don't insult me or I will call you Polendina!'

'Ass!'

'Polendina!'

'Donkey!'

'Polendina!'

'Baboon!'

'Polendina!'

On hearing himself called Polendina for the third time Geppetto, blind with rage, fell upon the carpenter and they fought desperately.

When the battle was over, Master Antonio had two more scratches on his nose, and his adversary had two buttons less on his waistcoat. Their accounts being thus squared they shook hands, and swore to remain good friends for the rest of their lives.

Geppetto carried off his fine piece of wood, and, thanking Master Antonio, returned limping to his house.

The Puppet Is Named Pinocchio

Geppetto lived in a small ground-floor room that was only lighted from the staircase. The furniture could not have been simpler – a bad chair, a poor bed and a broken-down table. At the end of the room there was a fireplace with a lighted fire; but the fire was painted, and by the fire was painted a saucepan that was boiling cheerfully and sending out a cloud of smoke that looked exactly like real smoke.

As soon as he reached home Geppetto took his tools and set to work to cut out and model his puppet.

'What name shall I give him?' he said to himself; 'I think I will call him Pinocchio. It is a name that will bring him luck. I once knew a whole family so called. There was Pinocchio the father, Pinocchia the mother and Pinocchi the children, and all of them did well.'

Having found a name for his puppet he began to work in good earnest, and he first made his hair, then his forehead and then his eyes.

The eyes being finished, imagine his astonishment when he perceived that they moved and looked fixedly at him.

Geppetto seeing himself stared at by those two wooden eyes, took it almost in bad part, and said in an angry voice, 'Wicked wooden eyes, why do you look at me?'

No one answered.

Then he proceeded to carve the nose; but no sooner had he made it than it began to grow. And it grew, and grew, and grew until in a few minutes it had become an immense nose that seemed as if it would never end.

Poor Geppetto tired himself out with cutting it off. But the more he cut and shortened it, the longer did that impertinent nose become!

The mouth was not even completed when it began to laugh and deride him.

'Stop laughing!' said Geppetto provoked; but he might as well have spoken to the wall.

'Stop laughing, I say!' he roared in a threatening tone.

The mouth then ceased laughing, but put out its tongue as far as it would go.

Geppetto, not to spoil his handiwork, pretended not to see, and continued his labours. After the mouth he fashioned the chin, then the throat, and then the shoulders, the stomach, the arms and the hands.

The hands were scarcely finished when Geppetto felt his wig snatched from his head. He turned round, and what did he see? He saw his yellow wig in the puppet's hand.

'Pinocchio!... Give me back my wig instantly!'

But Pinocchio instead of returning it, put it on his own head, and was as a result nearly smothered.

At this insolent and derisive behaviour, Geppetto felt sadder and more melancholy than he had ever been in his life before; and turning to Pinocchio he said to him, 'You young rascal! You are not yet completed, and you are already beginning to show want of respect to your father! That is bad, my boy, very bad.'

And he dried a tear.

The legs and feet remained to be done.

When Geppetto had finished the feet he received a kick on the point of the nose.

'I deserve it!' he said to himself. 'I should have thought of it sooner! Now it is too late!'

He then took the puppet under the arms and placed him on the floor to teach him to walk.

Pinocchio's legs were stiff and he could not move, but Geppetto led him by the hand and showed him how to put one foot before the other.

When his legs became flexible Pinocchio began to walk by himself and to run about the room – until, having gone out of the house door, he jumped into the street and escaped.

Poor Geppetto rushed after him but was not able to overtake him, for that rascal Pinocchio leapt in front of him like a hare, and knocking his wooden feet together against the pavement, made as much clatter as twenty pairs of peasant's clogs.

'Stop him! stop him!' shouted Geppetto; but the people in the street, seeing a wooden puppet running like a racehorse stood still in astonishment to look at it, and laughed, and laughed, and laughed, until it beats description... ❋

– Excerpted from the translated book.

84

ALADDIN AND THE WONDERFUL LAMP

A TALE FROM THE ARABIAN NIGHTS; RETOLD BY LOGAN MARSHALL

Aladdin was the only son of a poor widow who lived in China, but instead of helping his mother to earn their living, he let her do all the hard work, while he himself only thought of idling and amusement.

One day, as he was playing in the streets, a stranger came up to him, saying that he was his father's brother, and claiming him as his long-lost nephew. Aladdin had never heard that his father had had a brother; but as the stranger gave him money and promised to buy him fine clothes and set him up in business, he was quite ready to believe all that he told him. The man was a magician, who wanted to use Aladdin for his own purposes.

The next day the stranger came again, brought Aladdin a beautiful suit of clothes, gave him many good things to eat, and took him for a long walk, telling him stories all the while to amuse him. After they had walked a long way, they came to a narrow valley, bounded on either side by tall, gloomy-looking mountains.

Aladdin was beginning to feel tired, and he did not like the look of this place at all. He wanted to turn back; but the stranger would not let him. He made Aladdin follow him still farther, until at length they reached the place where he intended to carry out his evil design. Then he made Aladdin gather sticks to make a fire, and when they were in a blaze he threw into them some powder, at the same time saying some mystical words, which Aladdin could not understand.

Immediately they were surrounded with a thick cloud of smoke. The earth trembled, and burst open at their feet – disclosing a large flat stone with a brass ring fixed in it. Aladdin was so terribly frightened that he was about to run away, but the Magician gave him such a blow on the ear that he fell to the ground.

Poor Aladdin rose to his feet with eyes full of tears, and said, reproachfully, 'Uncle, what have I done that you should treat me so?'

'You should not have tried to run away from me,' said the Magician, 'when I have brought you here only for your own advantage. Under this stone there is hidden a treasure which will make you richer than the richest monarch in the world. You alone may touch it. If I assist you in any way, the spell will be broken, but if you obey me faithfully, we shall both be rich for the rest of our lives. Come, take hold of the brass ring and lift the stone.'

Aladdin forgot his fears in the hope of gaining this wonderful treasure and took hold of the brass ring. It yielded at once to his touch, and he was able to lift the great stone quite easily and move it away, which disclosed a flight of steps, leading down into the ground.

'Go down these steps,' commanded the Magician, 'and at the bottom you will find a great cavern, divided into three halls, full of vessels of gold and silver; but take care you do not meddle with these. If you touch anything in the halls you will meet with instant death. The third hall will bring you into a garden, planted with fine fruit trees. When you have crossed the garden, you will come to a terrace, where you will find a niche, and in the niche a lighted lamp. Take the lamp down, and when you have put out the light and poured away the oil, bring it to me. If you would like to gather any of the fruit of the garden you may do so, provided you do not linger.'

Then the Magician put a ring on Aladdin's finger, which he told him was to preserve him from evil, and sent him down into the cavern.

Aladdin found everything just as the Magician had said. He passed through the three halls, crossed the garden, took down the lamp from the niche, poured out the oil, put the lamp into his bosom and turned to go back.

As he came down from the terrace, he stopped to look at the trees of the garden, which were laden with wonderful fruits. To Aladdin's eyes it appeared as if these fruits were only bits of coloured glass, but in reality they were jewels of the rarest quality. Aladdin filled his pockets full of the dazzling things, for though he had no idea of their real value, he was attracted by their dazzling brilliance. He had so loaded himself with these treasures that when at last he came to the steps he was unable to climb them without assistance.

'Pray, Uncle,' he said, 'give me your hand to help me out.'

'Give me the lamp first,' replied the Magician.

'Really, Uncle, I cannot do so until I am out of this place,' answered Aladdin, whose hands were, indeed, so full that he could not get at the lamp.

But the Magician refused to help Aladdin up the steps until he had handed over the lamp. Aladdin was equally determined not to give it up until he was out of the cavern, and, at last, the Magician fell into a furious rage. Throwing some more of the powder into the fire, he again said the magic words. No sooner had he done so than there was a tremendous thunderclap, the stone rolled back into its place, and Aladdin was a prisoner in the cavern. The poor boy cried aloud to his supposed uncle to help him, but it was all in vain – his cries could not be heard. The doors in the garden were closed by the same enchantment, and Aladdin sat down on the steps in despair, knowing that there was little hope of his ever seeing his mother again.

For two terrible days he lay in the cavern waiting for death. On the third day, realizing that it could not now be far off, he clasped his hands in anguish, thinking of his mother's sorrow; and in so doing he accidently rubbed the ring which the Magician had put upon his finger.

Immediately a genie of enormous size rose out of the earth, and, as Aladdin started back in fright and horror, said to him, 'What do you wish me to do?'

'Who are you?' gasped Aladdin.

'I am the slave of the ring. I am ready to obey thy commands,' came the answer.

Aladdin was still trembling; but the danger he was in already made him answer without hesitation, 'Then, if you are able to, free me, I beg you, from this place.'

Scarcely had he spoken, when he found himself lying on the ground at the place to which the Magician had first brought him.

He hastened home to his Mother, who had mourned him as dead. As soon as he had told her all his adventures, he begged her to get him some food, for he had now been three days without eating.

'Alas, child!' replied his Mother, 'I have not a bit of bread to give you.'

'Never mind, Mother,' said Aladdin, 'I will go and sell the old lamp which I brought home with me. Doubtless I shall get a little money for it.'

His Mother reached down the lamp; but seeing how dirty it was, she thought it would sell better if she cleaned it. But no sooner had she begun to rub it than a hideous genie appeared before her and said in a voice like thunder, 'What do you wish me to do? I am ready to obey your commands, I and all the other slaves of the lamp.'

Aladdin's Mother fainted away at the sight of this creature; but Aladdin, having seen the genie of the ring, was not so frightened, and said boldly, 'I am hungry, bring me something to eat.'

The genie disappeared, but returned in an instant with twelve silver dishes, filled with different kinds of savoury meats, six large white loaves, two bottles of wine and two silver drinking cups. He placed these things on the table and then vanished.

Aladdin fetched water, and sprinkling some on his mother's face soon brought her back to life again.

When she opened her eyes and saw all the good things the genie had provided, she was overcome with astonishment.

'To whom are we indebted for this feast?' she cried. 'Has the Sultan heard of our poverty and sent us these fine things from his own table?'

'Never mind now how they came here,' said Aladdin. 'Let us first eat, then I will tell you.'

Mother and son made a hearty meal, and then Aladdin told his mother that it was the genie of the lamp who had brought them the food. His mother was greatly alarmed, and begged him to have nothing further to do with genies, advising him to sell the lamp at once. But Aladdin would not part with such a wonderful possession, and resolved to keep both the ring and the lamp safely, in case he should ever need them again. He showed his mother the fruits which he had gathered in the garden, and his mother admired their bright colours and dazzling radiance, though she had no idea of their real value. ❋

– *Want to know what happened next? Read the whole story of 'Aladdin and the Wonderful Lamp'.*

85

PUSS IN BOOTS

GIOVANNI FRANCESCO STRAPAROLA; RETOLD BY J.H. STICKNEY

Once upon a time there was a miller, who was so poor that at his death he had nothing to leave to his three children but his mill, his donkey and his cat. The eldest son took the mill, and the second the donkey, so there was nothing left for poor Jack but to take Puss.

Jack could not help thinking that he had been treated shabbily. 'My brothers will be able to earn an honest livelihood,' he sighed, 'but as for me, though Puss may feed himself by catching mice, I shall certainly die of hunger.'

The cat, who had overheard his young master, jumped upon his shoulder, and, rubbing himself gently against his cheek, began to speak. 'Dear master,' said he, 'do not grieve. I am not as useless as you think me, and will undertake to make your fortune for you, if only you will buy me a pair of boots and give me that old bag.'

Now, Jack had very little money to spare, but, knowing Puss to be a faithful old friend, he made up his mind to trust him, and so spent all he possessed upon a smart pair of boots made of buff-coloured leather. They fitted perfectly, so Puss put them on, took the old bag which his master gave him, and trotted off to a neighbouring warren in which he knew there was a great number of rabbits.

Having put some bran and fresh parsley into the bag, he laid it upon the ground, hid himself and waited. Presently two foolish little rabbits, sniffing the food, ran straight into the bag, when the clever cat drew the strings and caught them. Then, slinging the bag over his shoulder, he hastened off to the palace, where he asked to speak to the King. Having been shown into the royal presence, he bowed and said, 'Sire, my Lord the Marquis of Carabas has commanded me to present these rabbits to Your Majesty, with his respects.'

The monarch having desired his thanks to be given to the Marquis (who, as you will guess, was really our poor Jack), then ordered his head cook to dress the rabbits for dinner, and he and his daughter dined on them with great enjoyment.

Day by day Puss brought home stores of good food, so that he and his master lived in plenty, and besides that, he did not fail to keep the King and his courtiers well supplied with game.

Sometimes he would lay a brace of partridges at the royal feet, sometimes a fine large hare, but whatever it was, it always came with the same message: 'From my Lord the Marquis of Carabas'; so that everyone at Court was talking of this strange nobleman, whom no one had ever seen, but who sent such generous presents to His Majesty.

At length Puss decided that it was time for his master to be introduced at Court. So one day he persuaded him to go and bathe in a river near, having heard that the King would soon pass that way.

Jack stood shivering up to his neck in water, wondering what was to happen next, when suddenly the King's carriage appeared in sight. At once Puss began to call out as loudly as he could, 'Help, help! My Lord the Marquis of Carabas is drowning!'

The King put his head out of the carriage window and, recognizing the cat, ordered his attendants to go to the assistance of the Marquis. While Jack was being taken out of the water, Puss ran to the King and told him that some robbers had run off with his master's clothes whilst he was bathing, the truth of the matter being that the cunning cat had hidden them under a stone.

On hearing this story the King instantly despatched one of his grooms to fetch a handsome suit of purple and gold from the royal wardrobe, and dressed in this, Jack, who was a fine, handsome fellow, looked so well that no one for a moment supposed but that he was some noble foreign lord.

The King and his daughter were so pleased with his appearance that they invited him into their carriage. At first Jack hesitated, for he felt a little shy about sitting next to a Princess, but she smiled at him so sweetly, and was so kind and gentle, that he soon forgot his fears and fell in love with her there and then.

As soon as Puss had seen his master seated in the royal carriage, he whispered directions to the coachman, and then ran on ahead as fast as he could trot, until he came to a field of corn, where the reapers were busy.

'Reapers,' said he fiercely, 'the King will shortly pass this way. If he should ask you to whom this field belongs, remember that you say, 'To the Marquis of Carabas.' If you dare to disobey me, I will have you all chopped up as fine as mincemeat.' The reapers were so afraid the cat would keep his word that they promised to obey. Puss then ran on and told all the other labourers whom he met to give the same answer, threatening them with terrible punishments if they disobeyed.

Now, the King was in a very good humour, for the day was fine, and he found the Marquis a very pleasant companion, so he told the coachman to drive slowly, in order that he might admire the beautiful country. 'What a fine field of wheat!' he said presently. 'To whom does it belong?' Then the men answered as they had been told: 'To our Lord the Marquis of Carabas.' Next they met a herd of cattle, and again to the King's question, 'To whom do they belong?' they were told, 'To the Marquis of Carabas.' And it was the same with everything they passed.

The Marquis listened with the greatest astonishment and thought what a very wonderful cat his dear Puss was; and the King was delighted to find that his new friend was as wealthy as he was charming.

Meanwhile, Puss, who was well in advance of the royal party, had arrived at a stately castle, which belonged to a cruel Ogre, the richest ever known, for all the lands the King had admired so much belonged to him. Puss knocked at the door and asked to see the Ogre, who received him quite civilly, for he had never seen a cat in boots before and the sight amused him.

So he and Puss were soon chatting away together.

The Ogre, who was very conceited, began to boast of what clever tricks he could play, and Puss sat and listened, with a smile on his face.

'I once heard, great Ogre,' he said at last, 'that you possessed the power of changing yourself into any kind of animal you chose – a lion or an elephant, for instance.'

'Well, so I can,' replied the Ogre.

'Dear me! How much I should like to see you do it now,' said Puss sweetly.

The Ogre was only too pleased to find a chance of showing How very clever he was, so he promised to transform himself into any animal Puss might mention.

'Oh! I will leave the choice to you,' said the cat politely.

Immediately there appeared where the Ogre had been seated, an enormous lion, roaring, and lashing with its tail, and looking as though it meant to gobble the cat up in a trice.

Puss was really very much frightened, and, jumping out of the window, managed to scramble on to the roof, though he could scarcely hold on to the tiles on account of his high-heeled boots.

There he sat, refusing to come down, until the Ogre changed himself into his natural form and laughingly called to him that he would not hurt him.

Then Puss ventured back into the room and began to compliment the Ogre on his cleverness. 'Of course, it was all very wonderful,' he said, 'but it would be more wonderful still if you, who are so great and fierce, could transform yourself into some timid little creature, such as a mouse. That, I suppose, would be quite impossible?'

'Not at all,' said the vain Ogre; 'one is quite as easy to me as the other, as I will show you.' And in a moment a little brown mouse was frisking about all over the floor, whilst the Ogre had vanished.

'Now or never,' said Puss, and with a spring he seized the mouse and gobbled it up as fast as he could.

At the same moment all the gentlemen and ladies whom the wicked Ogre had held in his castle under a spell, became disenchanted. They were so grateful to their deliverer that they would have done anything to please him, and readily agreed to enter into the service of the Marquis of Carabas when Puss asked them to do so.

So now the cat had a splendid castle, which he knew to be full of heaped-up treasures, at his command, and ordering a magnificent feast to be prepared, he took up his station at the castle gates to welcome his master and the royal party.

As soon as the castle appeared in sight, the King enquired whose it was, 'For,' said he, 'I have never seen a finer one.'

Then Puss, bowing low, threw open the castle gates, and cried, 'May it please Your Majesty to alight and enter the home of the most noble the Marquis of Carabas.'

Full of surprise, the King turned to the Marquis. 'Is this splendid castle indeed yours?' he asked. 'Not even our own palace is more beautiful, and doubtless it is as splendid within as without.'

Puss then helped His Majesty to alight and conducted him into the castle, where a group of gentlemen and ladies were waiting to receive them. Jack, or the Marquis as he was now called, gave his hand to the young Princess and led her to the banquet. Long and merrily they feasted, and when at length the guests rose to depart, the King embraced the Marquis, and called him his dear son.

And so the miller's son married the King's daughter, and there were great rejoicings throughout the land.

On the evening of the wedding day a great ball was given, to which princes and noblemen from far and near were invited. Puss opened the ball, wearing for the occasion a pair of boots made of the finest leather, with gold tassels and scarlet heels. I only wish you could have seen him.

When the old King died, the Princess and her husband reigned in his stead, and their most honoured and faithful friend at Court was Puss himself, for his master never forgot to whom he owed all his good fortune. He lived upon the daintiest meat and most delicious cream, and was petted and made much of all the days of his life, and never again ran after mice and rats, except for exercise and amusement. ❋

86

THE GREEN HORSE

AN AKBAR-BIRBAL STORY; RETOLD BY VKB

Have you heard of Akbar and Birbal?

Well, just in case you haven't, Akbar was a Mughal emperor who ruled in India and Raja Birbal was a minister in his court. Birbal was a very clever and wise man, and was known for his witty solutions to tricky problems. Often, in his own roundabout way he was able to tell the emperor many things others would have been too scared to tell him.

In turn, Akbar liked to keep twisty puzzles that no one could solve before Birbal to challenge him. And Birbal would always end up solving them.

There are many stories about Akbar and Birbal. Here's one of them:

Akbar loved to spend time in his palace garden when he could get away from his duties as king.

The garden was very big. It had many trees, a carpet of grass bordered by beautiful flowers, and many winding paths. One day the emperor went there riding on his horse. As always, Birbal was with him, riding another horse.

While enjoying his ride in the royal gardens, surrounded by greenery as far as he could see, the emperor thought, 'How wonderful it would be if my horse, too. matched the garden, and was green!'

He immediately ordered his minister: 'Birbal, I order you to find me a horse that is as green as the grass of the royal gardens. If you can't, well, that day will be your last one at my court.'

Birbal was used to his emperor's strange demands, but even he was puzzled this time. Brown and white horses he had seen, and brown-and-white ones. Fawn and black horses he had surely seen, and fawn-and-black ones. But a green horse was unheard of!

Grasshoppers were green, caterpillars and frogs could be green, chameleons could *turn* green, but horses! Everyone knew that horses were *never* EVER green.

He realized that the emperor wanted to test him.

Birbal asked for a week to find the green horse. Then he did not attend the court for a week. When Emperor Akbar asked the other ministers where Birbal was, they looked at each other, and muttered, 'Sire...uh...horse...um...green.'

*

A week flew by.

On the eighth day, the emperor noticed that Birbal was still absent from the court and said, 'I see that Raja Birbal has not brought a green horse to me. And so, this must be his last day at my court.'

The other ministers and courtiers stared at each other, aghast. This was indeed a harsh punishment for something that seemed impossible to do.

Suddenly, they saw Birbal entering the pillared hallway of the palace. He greeted the emperor and said, 'Your Majesty, I have found a green horse!'

Akbar wondered what clever solution Birbal had found this time! 'Where is it?' he said, walking down from the throne. 'Show it to me immediately!'

Birbal replied, 'Your Highness, I surely will, but the owner of the horse was willing to give it to me only on two conditions...'

'What conditions?' Akbar asked eagerly. He was so keen to see how Birbal had found a green horse that he forgot that he could actually order the horse owner to just bring the horse to him.

'The first condition is that you will have to go and bring the horse yourself,' said Birbal.

'That's not a problem,' said Akbar. Who wouldn't go to find a green horse! 'And what about the second condition?'

'Well, Your Majesty,' said Birbal slowly, 'you are the emperor, most mighty and powerful. I'm sure this will be really easy for you. As the colour of the horse is very unusual, you have to go to fetch it on an unusual day. The owner insists that you may go and pick up the horse on any day except the seven days of the week...'

What a strange condition. Akbar was speechless.

Then Birbal smiled and said, 'Your Majesty, if one *really* wants a green horse, then one has to fulfil its owner's demands...'

Akbar understood that once again Birbal had shown just how clever he was! He was happy at having such a quick-witted minister and burst out laughing. ❋

87

THE SLOW-COOKING KHICHRI

AN AKBAR-BIRBAL STORY; RETOLD BY VKB

One winter night, Emperor Akbar, the Mughal king who ruled in India, went for a stroll with his courtiers along the banks of the River Yamuna.

It was very, very cold, when suddenly the emperor dipped a finger into the river. *Brrr*! The water was like ice. He quickly drew back his finger and said, 'Really, this water is freezing. If someone is forced to stand in it, it would be impossible! What do you think, Birbal?'

Raja Birbal, who was Akbar's cleverest minister, said, 'Your Majesty, human beings can do anything if they are determined to. Or if, for some reason, they *have* to do it.'

The emperor was taken aback. 'So you think that someone can stand in this chilly water overnight in the river?'

'Surely,' Birbal replied.

Akbar did not like Birbal disagreeing with him. As was Akbar's habit, he decided to put Birbal in a spot. He declared, 'If you think so Raja Birbal, then please have an announcement carried to every corner of the city tomorrow – if anyone can spend a whole night standing in the Yamuna waters, they will be awarded a thousand gold coins.'

The next day, the whole city was abuzz with the news. But no one had the courage to accept the emperor's challenge. Except a poor washerman.

❋

Now you may wonder why anyone, *anyone* at all, would want to stand in ice-cold water for a whole night. This man's wife was sick and he needed money.

Again, you might be curious why the emperor would not just give him money to help him! Well, rulers could often be like that – stubborn and wilful, asking for things that didn't make any sense.

Anyhow, Akbar's soldiers took the washerman to the riverbank. He dipped his toe into the water... he shivered.

Then he mustered up courage and all the strength in his body, and walked into the river up to his waist.

And that's how he stood there, while the guards kept a watchful eye on him.

❋

The next day the soldiers took him to the court and presented him before the emperor.

Akbar was surprised and suspicious. 'Did you really stand in the river the whole night? The *entire* night? *All* hours of the night? How did you manage to do that?' he asked.

The poor man replied, 'Sire, I looked up and I saw the royal palace. And in one of the arches of the building, a lamp was lit up the whole night. I kept watching it...and the night passed.'

The emperor lost his cool as soon as he heard this. 'You cheat!' he shouted in anger. 'You do not deserve the reward, because you lied. You did not stand in the cold water. In fact, you were kept warm by the light of that palace lamp through the night – so actually, *really*, you deserve punishment, *not* gold coins. Soldiers, throw him in prison!'

Birbal was present at the court. He was very upset to see an innocent man being punished, but he did not say anything at that time.

The next day, there was an important discussion to be held at court. But Birbal was missing!

'Where is Birbal?' the king demanded. 'Why has he not sent a message about his absence?'

No one knew.

The emperor sent soldiers to Birbal's house to bring him. They came back without Birbal, but with a message: 'Your Majesty, Minister Birbal is cooking khichri. he will come as soon as he has eaten it.'

Day fell, but Birbal still did not come.

The emperor was not used to waiting for anyone, so he grew angry. But as more hours passed, he began to suspect that something was wrong.

He decided to go to Birbal's house and find out what was going on!

When Emperor Akbar reached Birbal's house, he had to cross the garden to reach the house.

The first thing he saw was that there was a pot hanging from a tree. Under it a *tiny, teeny-weeny* fire was burning. Close by, Birbal was lying on a charpoy.

Akbar was puzzled, and upset, too. 'What exactly do you think you are doing, Birbal?' he roared.

Birbal got up slowly from the cot and bowed. 'Your Majesty, I'm cooking khichri,' he said.

'Do you think I am a fool?' the emperor demanded. 'How will the khichri *ever* cook with that small fire so far away?'

'Sire...' Birbal said, 'if a lamp in the palace can keep a man warm so far off in a freezing river, then this fire is at least closer to the pot – why will it not cook the khichri...?'

Akbar quickly understood what Birbal was trying to say. He felt ashamed of the challenge he had put before his people, and of how he had treated the poor washerman. He had the man released immediately – and gave him *two* thousand gold coins! ❋

88

THE UGLY DUCKLING

HANS CHRISTIAN ANDERSEN; RETOLD BY HAMILTON WRIGHT MABIE

The country was lovely just then; it was summer! The wheat was golden and the oats still green; the hay was stacked in the rich, low-lying meadows, where the stork was marching about on his long red legs, chattering in Egyptian, the language his mother had taught him.

Round about field and meadow lay great woods, in the midst of which were deep lakes. Yes, the country certainly was delicious. In the sunniest spot stood an old mansion surrounded by a deep moat, and great dock leaves grew from the walls of the house right down to the water's edge, some of them were so tall that a small child could stand upright under them. In among the leaves it was as secluded as in the depths of a forest, and there a duck was sitting on her nest.

Her little ducklings were just about to be hatched, but she was nearly tired of sitting, for it had lasted such a long time. Moreover, she had very few visitors, as the other ducks liked swimming about in the moat better than waddling up to sit under the dock leaves and gossip with her.

At last one egg after another began to crack. 'Cheep, cheep!' they said. All the chicks had come to life, and were poking their heads out.

'Quack! Quack!' said the duck; and then they all quacked their hardest, and looked about them on all sides among the green leaves; their mother allowed them to look as much as they liked, for green is good for the eyes.

'How big the world is to be sure!' said all the young ones, for they certainly had ever so much more room to move about than when they were inside the eggshell.

'Do you imagine this is the whole world?' said the mother. 'It stretches a long way on the other side of the garden, right into the parson's field; but I have never been as far as that! I suppose you are all here now?' and she got up. 'No! I declare I have not got you all yet! The biggest egg is still there; how long is it going to last?' and then she settled herself on the nest again.

'Well, how are you getting on?' said an old duck who had come to pay her a visit.

'This one egg is taking such a long time,' answered the sitting duck, 'the shell will not crack; but now you must look at the others; they are the finest ducklings I have ever seen! They are all exactly like their father, the rascal! He never comes to see me.'

'Let me look at the egg which won't crack,' said the old duck. 'You may be sure that it is a turkey's egg! I have been cheated like that once, and I had no end of trouble and worry with the creatures, for I may tell you that they are afraid of the water. I could not get them into it; I quacked and snapped at them, but it was no good. Let me see the egg! Yes, it is a turkey's egg! You just leave it alone and teach the other children to swim.'

'I will sit on it a little longer; I have sat so long already that I may as well go on till the Midsummer Fair comes round.'

'Please yourself,' said the old duck, and she went away.

At last the big egg cracked. 'Cheep, cheep!' said the young one and tumbled out; how big and ugly he was! The duck looked at him.

'That is a monstrous big duckling,' she said; 'none of the others looked like that; can he be a turkey chick? Well, we shall soon find that out; into the water he shall go, if I have to kick him in myself.'

Next day was gloriously fine, and the sun shone on all the green dock leaves. The mother duck with her whole family went down to the moat.

Splash, into the water she sprang. 'Quack, quack!' she said, and one duckling plumped in after the other. The water dashed over their heads, but they came up again and floated beautifully; their legs went of themselves, and they were all there, even the big ugly gray one swam about with them.

'No, that is no turkey,' she said; 'see how beautifully he uses his legs and how erect he holds himself; he is my own chick! After all, he is not so bad when you come to look at him properly. Quack, quack! Now come with me and I will take you into the world, and introduce you to the duck-yard, but keep close to me all the time, so that no one may tread upon you, and beware of the cat!'

Then they went into the duck-yard. There was a fearful uproar going on, for two broods were fighting for the head of an eel, and in the end the cat captured it.

'That's how things go in this world,' said the mother duck; and she licked her bill, for she wanted the eel's head for herself.

'Use your legs,' said she; 'mind you quack properly, and bend your necks to the old duck over there! She is the grandest of them all; she has Spanish blood in her veins and that accounts for her size, and, do you see? she has a red rag round her leg; that is a wonderfully fine thing, and the most extraordinary mark of distinction any duck can have. It shows clearly that she is not to be parted with, and that she is worthy of recognition both by beasts and men! Quack now! don't turn your toes in, a well brought up duckling keeps his legs wide apart just like father and mother; that's it, now bend your necks, and say quack!'

They did as they were told, but the other ducks round about looked at them and said, quite loud, 'Just look there! now we are to have that tribe! just as if there were not enough of us already, and, oh dear! how ugly that duckling is, we won't stand him!' and a duck flew at him at once and bit him in the neck.

'Let him be,' said the mother; 'he is doing no harm.'

'Very likely not, but he is so ungainly and queer,' said the biter, 'he must be whacked.'

'They are handsome children,' said the old duck with the rag round her leg, 'all good-looking except this one, and he is not a good specimen. It's a pity you can't make him over again.'

'That can't be done, your grace,' said the mother duck. 'He is not handsome, but he is a thorough good creature, and he swims as beautifully as any of the others; nay, I think I might venture even to add that I think he will improve as he goes on, or perhaps in time he may grow smaller! He was too long in the egg, and so he has not come out with a very good figure.' And then she patted his neck and stroked him down. 'Besides, he is a drake,' said she, 'so it does not matter so much. I believe he will be very strong, and I don't doubt but he will make his way in the world.'

'The other ducklings are very pretty,' said the old duck. 'Now make yourselves quite at home, and if you find the head of an eel you may bring it to me!'

After that they felt quite at home. But the poor duckling which had been the last to come out of the shell, and who was so ugly, was bitten, pushed about and made fun of both by the ducks and the hens.

'He is too big,' they all said; and the turkey-cock, who was born with his spurs on, and therefore thought himself quite an emperor, puffed himself up like a vessel in full sail, made for him, and gobbled and gobbled till he became quite red in the face. The poor duckling was at his wit's end, and did not know which way to turn; he was in despair because he was so ugly and the butt of the whole duck-yard.

So the first day passed, and afterwards matters grew worse and worse. The poor duckling was chased and hustled by all of them; even his brothers and sisters ill-used him, and they were always saying, 'If only the cat would get hold of you, you hideous object!' Even his mother said, 'I wish to goodness you were miles away.' The ducks bit him, the hens pecked him and the girl who fed them kicked him aside.

Then he ran off and flew right over the hedge, where the little birds flew up into the air in a fright.

'That is because I am so ugly,' thought the poor duckling, shutting his eyes, but he ran on all the same. Then he came to a great marsh where the wild ducks lived; he was so tired and miserable that he stayed there the whole night.

In the morning the wild ducks flew up to inspect their new comrade.

'What sort of a creature are you?' they inquired, as the duckling turned from side to side and greeted them as well as he could. 'You are frightfully ugly,' said the wild ducks, 'but that does not matter to us, so long as you do not marry into our family!' Poor fellow! He had no thought of marriage; all he wanted was permission to lie among the rushes, and to drink a little of the marsh water.

He stayed there two whole days. Then two wild geese came, or, rather, two wild ganders; they were not long out of the shell, and therefore rather pert.

'I say, comrade,' they said, 'you are so ugly that we have taken quite a fancy to you; will you join us and be a bird of passage? There is another marsh close by, and there are some charming wild geese there; all sweet young ladies, who can say quack! You are ugly enough to make your fortune among them.' Just at that moment, *bang! bang!* was heard up above, and both the wild geese fell dead among the reeds, and the water turned blood red. *Bang! bang!* went the guns, and whole flocks of wild geese flew up from the rushes and the shot peppered among them again.

There was a grand shooting party, and the sportsmen lay hidden round the marsh; some even sat on the branches of the trees which overhung the water. The blue smoke rose like clouds among the dark trees and swept over the pool.

The water-dogs wandered about in the swamp – splash! splash! The rushes and reeds bent beneath their tread on all sides. It was terribly alarming to the poor duckling. He twisted his head round to get it under his wing, and just at that moment a frightful big dog appeared close beside him; his tongue hung right out of his mouth and his eyes glared wickedly. He opened his great chasm of a mouth close to the duckling, showed his sharp teeth, and – *splash!* – went on without touching him.

'Oh, thank Heaven!' sighed the duckling, 'I am so ugly that even the dog won't bite me!'

Then he lay quite still while the shots whistled among the bushes, and bang after bang rent the air. It only became quiet late in the day, but even then the poor duckling did not dare to get up; he waited several hours more before he looked about, and then he hurried away from the marsh as fast as he could. He ran across fields and meadows, and there was such a wind that he had to work hard to make his way.

Towards night he reached a poor little cottage. It was such a miserable hovel that it could not make up its mind which way to fall even, and so it remained standing. The wind whistled so fiercely round the duckling that he had to sit on his tail to resist it, and it blew harder and harder; then he saw that the door had fallen off one hinge and hung so crookedly that he could creep into the house through the crack, and by this means he made his way into the room.

An old woman lived there with her cat and her hen. The cat, which she called 'Sonnie,' could arch his back, purr and give off electric sparks – that is to say, if you stroked his fur the wrong way. The hen had quite tiny short legs, and so she was called 'Chuckie-low-legs.' She laid good eggs, and the old woman was as fond of her as if she had been her own child.

In the morning the strange duckling was discovered immediately, and the cat began to purr and the hen to cluck.

'What on earth is that!' said the old woman, looking round; but her sight was not good, and she thought the duckling was a fat duck which had escaped. 'This is a capital find,' said she; 'now I shall have duck's eggs if only it is not a drake. We must find out about that!'

So she took the duckling on trial for three weeks, but no eggs made their appearance. The cat was the master of the house and the hen the mistress, and they always spoke of 'we and the world,' for they thought that they represented the half of the world, and that quite the better half.

The duckling thought there might be two opinions on the subject, but the cat would not hear of it.

'Can you lay eggs?' she asked.

'No!'

'Will you have the goodness to hold your tongue, then!'

And the cat said, 'Can you arch your back, purr, or give off sparks?'

'No.'

'Then you had better keep your opinions to yourself when people of sense are speaking!'

The duckling sat in the corner nursing his ill-humour. Then he began to think of the fresh air and the sunshine, an uncontrollable longing seized him to float on the water, and at last he could not help telling the hen about it.

'What on earth possesses you?' she asked. 'You have nothing to do; that is why you get these freaks into your head. Lay some eggs or take to purring, and you will get over it.'

'But it is so delicious to float on the water,' said the duckling; 'so delicious to feel it rushing over your head when you dive to the bottom.'

'That would be a fine amusement,' said the hen. 'I think you have gone mad. Ask the cat about it, he is the wisest creature I know; ask him if he is fond of floating on the water or diving under it. I say nothing about myself. Ask our mistress yourself, the old woman; there is no one in the world cleverer than she is. Do you suppose she has any desire to float on the water or to duck underneath it?'

'You do not understand me,' said the duckling.

'Well, if we don't understand you, who should? I suppose you don't consider yourself cleverer than the cat or the old woman, not to mention me. Don't make a fool of yourself, child, and thank your stars for all the good we have done you! Have you not lived in this warm room, and in such society that you might have learned something? But you are an idiot, and there is no pleasure in associating with you. You may believe me – I mean well, I tell you home truths, and there is no surer way than that of knowing who one's friends are. You just see about laying some eggs, or learn to purr, or to emit sparks.'

'I think I will go out into the wide world,' said the duckling.

'Oh, do so by all means!' said the hen.

So away went the duckling. He floated on the water and ducked underneath it, but he was looked askance at by every living creature for his ugliness. Now the autumn came on, the leaves in the woods turned yellow and brown; the wind took hold of them and they danced about. The sky looked very cold, and the clouds hung heavy with snow and hail. A raven stood on the fence and croaked *Caw! Caw!* from sheer cold; it made one shiver only to think of it.

One evening the sun was just setting in wintry splendour when a flock of beautiful large birds appeared out of the bushes. The duckling had never seen anything so beautiful. They were dazzlingly white with long waving necks; they were swans; and, uttering a peculiar cry, they spread out their magnificent broad wings, and flew away from the cold regions to warmer lands and open seas.

They mounted so high, so very high, and the ugly little duckling became strangely uneasy; he circled round and round in the water like a wheel, craning his neck up into the air after them. Then he uttered a shriek so piercing and so strange that he was quite frightened by it himself.

Oh, he could not forget those beautiful birds, those happy birds! And as soon as they were out of sight he ducked right down to the bottom, and when he came up again he was quite beside himself. He did not know what the birds were or to where they flew, but all the same he was more drawn towards them than he had ever been by any creatures before. He did not even envy them in the least. How could it occur to him even to wish to be such a marvel of beauty; he would have been thankful if only the ducks would have tolerated him among them.

The winter was so bitterly cold that the duckling had to swim about in the water to keep it from freezing, but every night the hole in which he swam got smaller and smaller. Then it froze so hard that the surface ice cracked, and the duckling had to use his legs all the time, so that the ice should not close in round him; at last he was so weary that he could move no more, and he was frozen fast into the ice.

Early in the morning a peasant came along and saw him. He went out on to the ice and hammered a hole in it with his heavy wooden shoe, and carried the duckling home to his wife. There it soon revived. The children wanted to play with it, but the duckling thought they were going to ill-treat him and rushed in his fright into the milk pan, and the milk spurted out all over the room. The woman shrieked and threw up her hands; then it flew into the butter cask, and down into the meal tub and out again. Just imagine what it looked like by this time! The woman screamed and tried to hit it with the tongs, and the children tumbled over one another in trying to catch it, and they screamed with laughter. By good luck the door stood open, and the duckling flew out among the bushes and the new fallen snow, and it lay there thoroughly exhausted.

It would be too sad to mention all the misery it had to go through during that hard winter. When the sun began to shine warmly again the duckling was in the marsh, lying among the rushes. The larks were singing and the beautiful spring had come.

Then all at once it raised its wings, and they flapped with much greater strength than before and bore him off vigorously. Before he knew where he was he found himself in a large garden where the apple trees were in a full blossom, and the air was scented with lilacs, the long branches of which overhung the indented shores of the lake. Oh! The spring freshness was so delicious!

Just in front of him he saw three beautiful white swans advancing towards him from a thicket; with rustling feathers they swam lightly over the water. The duckling recognized the majestic birds, and he was overcome by a strange melancholy.

I will fly to them, the royal birds, and they will hack me to pieces, because I, who am so ugly, venture to approach them! But it won't matter; better be killed by them than be snapped at by the ducks, pecked by the hens, or spurned by the henwife, or suffer so much misery in the winter.'

So he flew into the water and swam towards the stately swans. They saw him and darted towards him with ruffled feathers. 'Kill me, oh, kill me!' said the poor creature, and bowing his head towards the water he awaited his death. But what did he see reflected in the transparent water?

He saw below him his own image; but he was no longer a clumsy, dark, grey bird, ugly and ungainly. He was himself a swan! It does not matter in the least having been born in a duck-yard if only you come out of a swan's egg!

He felt quite glad of all the misery and tribulation he had gone through; he was the better able to appreciate his good fortune now, and all the beauty which greeted him. The big swans swam round and round him, and stroked him with their bills.

Some little children came into the garden with corn and pieces of bread, which they threw into the water; and the smallest one cried out, 'There is a new one!' The other children shouted with joy, 'Yes, a new one has come!' And they clapped their hands and danced about, running after their father and mother. They threw the bread into the water, and one and all said that 'the new one was the prettiest; he was so young and handsome.' And the old swans bent their heads and did homage before him.

He felt quite shy and hid his head under his wing. He did not know what to think; he was so very happy, but not at all proud – a good heart never becomes proud. He thought of how he had been pursued and scorned, and now he heard them all say that he was the most beautiful of all beautiful birds. The lilacs bent their boughs right down into the water before him, and the bright sun was warm and cheering, and he rustled his feathers and raised his slender neck aloft, saying, with exultation in his heart, 'I never dreamed of so much happiness when I was the Ugly Duckling!' ❋

89

THE RAILWAY CHILDREN 'THE BEGINNING OF THINGS'

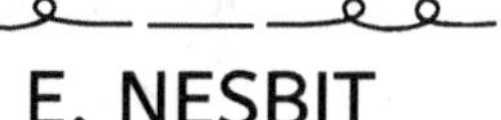

E. NESBIT

They were not railway children to begin with. I don't suppose they had ever thought about railways except as a means of getting to Maskelyne and Cook's, the Pantomime, Zoological Gardens and Madame Tussaud's. They were just ordinary suburban children, and they lived with their Father and Mother in an ordinary red-brick-fronted villa, with coloured glass in the front door, a tiled passage that was called a hall, a bathroom with hot and cold water, electric bells, French windows, and a good deal of white paint, and 'every modern convenience', as the house-agents say.

There were three of them. Roberta was the eldest. Of course, mothers never have favourites, but if their Mother HAD had a favourite, it might have been Roberta. Next came Peter, who wished to be an engineer when he grew up; and the youngest was Phyllis, who meant extremely well.

Mother did not spend all her time in paying dull calls to dull ladies and sitting dully at home waiting for dull ladies to pay calls to her. She was almost always there, ready to play with the children, and read to them, and help them to do their home-lessons. Besides this she used to write stories for them while they were at school and read them aloud after tea, and she always made up funny pieces of poetry for their birthdays and for other great occasions, such as the christening of the new kittens, or the refurnishing of the doll's house, or the time when they were getting over the mumps.

These three lucky children always had everything they needed: pretty clothes, good fires, a lovely nursery with heaps of toys and a Mother Goose wallpaper. They had a kind and merry nursemaid, and a dog who was called James, and who was their very own. They also had a Father who was just perfect – never cross, never unjust, and always ready for a game – at least, if at any time he was NOT ready, he always had an excellent reason for it, and explained the reason to the children so interestingly and funnily that they felt sure he couldn't help himself.

You will think that they ought to have been very happy. And so they were, but they did not know HOW happy till the pretty life in the Red Villa was over and done with, and they had to live a very different life indeed.

The dreadful change came quite suddenly.

Peter had a birthday – his tenth. Among his other presents was a model engine more perfect than you could ever have dreamed of. The other presents were full of charm, but the Engine was fuller of charm than any of the others were.

Its charm lasted in its full perfection for exactly three days. Then, owing either to Peter's inexperience or Phyllis's good intentions, which had been rather pressing, or to some other cause, the Engine suddenly went off with a bang. James was so frightened that he went out and did not come back all day. All the Noah's Ark people who were in the tender were broken to bits, but nothing else was hurt except the poor little engine and the feelings of Peter. The others said he cried over it – but of course boys of ten do not cry, however terrible the tragedies may be which darken their lot. He said that his eyes were red because he had a cold. This turned out to be true, though Peter did not know it was when he said it, the next day he had to go to bed and stay there. Mother began to be afraid that he might be sickening for measles, when suddenly he sat up in bed and said, 'I hate gruel – I hate barley water – I hate bread and milk. I want to get up and have something REAL to eat.'

'What would you like?' Mother asked.

'A pigeon-pie,' said Peter, eagerly, 'a large pigeon-pie. A very large one.'

So Mother asked the Cook to make a large pigeon-pie. The pie was made. And when the pie was made, it was cooked. And when it was cooked, Peter ate some of it. After that his cold was better. Mother made a piece of poetry to amuse him while the pie was being made. It began by saying what an unfortunate but worthy boy Peter was, then it went on:

He had an engine that he loved
With all his heart and soul,
And if he had a wish on earth
It was to keep it whole.

One day – my friends, prepare your minds;
I'm coming to the worst –
Quite suddenly a screw went mad,
And then the boiler burst!

With gloomy face he picked it up
And took it to his mother,
Though even he could not suppose
That she could make another;

For those who perished on the line
He did not seem to care,
His engine being more to him
Than all the people there.

And now you see the reason why
Our Peter has been ill:
He soothes his soul with pigeon-pie
His gnawing grief to kill.

He wraps himself in blankets warm
And sleeps in bed till late,
Determined thus to overcome
His miserable fate.

And if his eyes are rather red,
His cold must just excuse it:
Offer him pie; you may be sure
He never will refuse it.

Father had been away in the country for three or four days. All Peter's hopes for the curing of his afflicted Engine were now fixed on his Father, for Father was most wonderfully clever with his fingers. He could mend all sorts of things. He had often acted as veterinary surgeon to the wooden rocking-horse; once he had saved its life when all human aid was despaired of, and the poor creature was given up for lost, and even the carpenter said he didn't see his way to do anything. And it was Father who mended the doll's cradle when no one else could; and with a little glue and some bits of wood and a pen-knife made all the Noah's Ark beasts as strong on their pins as ever they were, if not stronger.

Peter, with heroic unselfishness, did not say anything about his Engine till after Father had had his dinner and his after-dinner cigar. The unselfishness was Mother's idea – but it was Peter who carried it out. And needed a good deal of patience, too.

At last Mother said to Father, 'Now, dear, if you're quite rested, and quite comfy, we want to tell you about the great railway accident and ask your advice.'

'All right,' said Father, 'fire away!'

So then Peter told the sad tale and fetched what was left of the Engine.

'Hum,' said Father, when he had looked the Engine over very carefully.

The children held their breaths.

'Is there NO hope?' said Peter, in a low, unsteady voice.

'Hope? Rather! Tonnes of it,' said Father, cheerfully; 'but it'll want something besides hope – a bit of brazing say, or some solder, and a new valve. I think we'd better keep it for a rainy day. In other words, I'll give up Saturday afternoon to it, and you shall all help me.'

'CAN girls help to mend engines?' Peter asked doubtfully.

'Of course they can. Girls are just as clever as boys, and don't you forget it! How would you like to be an engine-driver, Phil?'

'My face would be always dirty, wouldn't it?' said Phyllis, in unenthusiastic tones, 'and I expect I should break something.'

'I should just love it,' said Roberta – 'do you think I could when I'm grown up, Daddy? Or even a stoker?'

'You mean a fireman,' said Daddy, pulling and twisting at the engine. 'Well, if you still wish it, when you're grown up, we'll see about making you a fire-woman. I remember when I was a boy –'

Just then there was a knock at the front door.

'Who on earth!' said Father. 'An Englishman's house is his castle, of course, but I do wish they built semi-detached villas with moats and drawbridges.'

Ruth – she was the parlour-maid and had red hair – came in and said that two gentlemen wanted to see the master.

'I've shown them into the Library, Sir,' said she.

'I expect it's the subscription to the Vicar's testimonial,' said Mother, 'or else it's the choir holiday fund. Get rid of them quickly, dear. It does break up an evening so, and it's nearly the children's bedtime.'

But Father did not seem to be able to get rid of the gentlemen at all quickly.

'I wish we HAD got a moat and drawbridge,' said Roberta, 'then, when we didn't want people, we could just pull up the drawbridge and no one else could get in. I expect Father will have forgotten about when he was a boy if they stay much longer.'

Mother tried to make the time pass by telling them a new fairy story about a Princess with green eyes, but it was difficult because they could hear the voices of Father and the gentlemen in the Library, and Father's voice sounded louder and different to the voice he generally used to people who came about testimonials and holiday funds.

Then the Library bell rang and everyone heaved a breath of relief.

'They're going now,' said Phyllis. 'He's rung to have them shown out.'

But instead of showing anybody out, Ruth showed herself in, and she looked queer, the children thought.

'Please'm,' she said, 'the Master wants you to just step into the study. He looks like the dead, mum; I think he's had bad news. You'd best prepare yourself for the worst, 'm – p'raps it's a death in the family or a bank busted or –'

'That'll do, Ruth,' said Mother gently, 'you can go.'

Then Mother went into the Library. There was more talking. Then the bell rang again, and Ruth fetched a cab. The children heard boots go out and down the steps. The cab drove away, and the front door shut. Then Mother came in. Her dear face was as white as her lace collar, and her eyes looked very big and shining. Her mouth looked like just a line of pale red – her lips were thin and not their proper shape at all.

'It's bedtime,' she said. 'Ruth will put you to bed.'

'But you promised we should sit up late tonight because Father's come home,' said Phyllis.

'Father's been called away – on business,' said Mother. 'Come, darlings, go at once.'

They kissed her and went. Roberta lingered to give Mother an extra hug and to whisper, 'It wasn't bad news, Mammy, was it? Is anyone dead – or –'

'Nobody's dead – no,' said Mother, and she almost seemed to push Roberta away. 'I can't tell you anything tonight, my pet. Go, dear, go NOW.'

So Roberta went.

Ruth brushed the girls' hair and helped them to undress. (Mother almost always did this herself.) When she had turned down the gas and left them she found Peter, still dressed, waiting on the stairs.

'I say, Ruth, what's up?' he asked.

'Don't ask me no questions and I won't tell you no lies,' the red-headed Ruth replied. 'You'll know soon enough.'

Late that night Mother came up and kissed all three children as they lay asleep. But Roberta was the only one whom the kiss woke, and she lay mousey-still and said nothing.

'If Mother doesn't want us to know she's been crying,' she said to herself as she heard through the dark the catching of her Mother's breath, 'we WON'T know it. That's all.'

When they came down to breakfast the next morning, Mother had already gone out.

'To London,' Ruth said, and left them to their breakfast.

'There's something awful the matter,' said Peter, breaking his egg. 'Ruth told me last night we should know soon enough.'

'Did you ASK her?' said Roberta, with scorn.

'Yes, I did!' said Peter, angrily. 'If you could go to bed without caring whether Mother was worried or not, I couldn't. So there.'

'I don't think we ought to ask her things Mother doesn't tell us,' said Roberta.

'That's right, Miss Goody-goody,' said Peter, 'preach away.'

'I'm not goody,' said Phyllis, 'but I think Bobbie's right this time.'

'Of course. She always is. In her own opinion,' said Peter.

'Oh, DON'T!' cried Roberta, putting down her egg-spoon. 'Don't let's be horrid to each other. I'm sure some dire calamity is happening. Don't let's make it worse!'

'Who began, I should like to know?' said Peter.

Roberta made an effort and answered, 'I did, I suppose, but –'

'Well, then,' said Peter, triumphantly. But before he went to school he thumped his sister between the shoulders and told her to cheer up.

❋

The children came home to one o'clock dinner, but Mother was not there. And she was not there at tea-time.

It was nearly seven before she came in, looking so ill and tired that the children felt they could not ask her any questions. She sank into an armchair. Phyllis took the long pins out of her hat, while Roberta took off her gloves, and Peter unfastened her walking shoes and fetched her soft velvety slippers for her.

When she had had a cup of tea, and Roberta had put eau-de-cologne on her poor head that ached, Mother said, 'Now, my darlings, I want to tell you something. Those men last night did bring very bad news, and Father will be away for some time. I am very worried about it, and I want you all to help me, and not to make things harder for me.'

'As if we would!' said Roberta, holding Mother's hand against her face.

'You can help me very much,' said Mother, 'by being good and happy and not quarrelling when I'm away' – Roberta and Peter exchanged guilty glances – 'for I shall have to be away a good deal.'

'We won't quarrel. Indeed we won't,' said everybody. And meant it, too.

'Then,' Mother went on, 'I want you not to ask me any questions about this trouble; and not to ask anybody else any questions.'

Peter cringed and shuffled his boots on the carpet.

'You'll promise this, too, won't you?' said Mother.

'I did ask Ruth,' said Peter, suddenly. 'I'm very sorry, but I did.'

'And what did she say?'

'She said I should know soon enough.'

'It isn't necessary for you to know anything about it,' said Mother. 'It's about business, and you never do understand business, do you?'

'No,' said Roberta; 'is it something to do with Government?' For Father was in a Government Office.

'Yes,' said Mother. 'Now it's bedtime, my darlings. And don't YOU worry. It'll all come right in the end.'

'Then don't YOU worry either, Mother,' said Phyllis, 'and we'll all be as good as gold.'

Mother sighed and kissed them.

'We'll begin being good the first thing tomorrow morning,' said Peter, as they went upstairs.

'Why not NOW?' said Roberta.

'There's nothing to be good ABOUT now, silly,' said Peter.

'We might begin to try to FEEL good,' said Phyllis, 'and not call names.'

'Who's calling names?' said Peter. 'Bobbie knows right enough that when I say "silly", it's just the same as if I said Bobbie.'

'WELL,' said Roberta.

'No, I don't mean what you mean. I mean it's just a – what is it Father calls it? – a germ of endearment! Good night.'

The girls folded up their clothes with more than usual neatness – which was the only way of being good that they could think of.

'I say,' said Phyllis, smoothing out her pinafore, 'you used to say it was so dull – nothing happening, like in books. Now something HAS happened.'

'I never wanted things to happen to make Mother unhappy,' said Roberta. 'Everything's perfectly horrid.'

Everything continued to be perfectly horrid for some weeks.

Mother was nearly always out. Meals were dull and dirty. The between-maid was sent away, and Aunt Emma came on a visit. Aunt Emma was much older than Mother. She was going abroad to be a governess. She was very busy getting her clothes ready, and they were very ugly, dingy clothes, and she had them always littering about, and the sewing-machine seemed to whir – on and on all day and most of the night. Aunt Emma believed in keeping children in their proper places. And they more than returned the compliment. Their idea of Aunt Emma's proper place was anywhere where they were not. So they saw very little of her. They preferred the company of the servants, who were more amusing. Cook, if in a good temper, could sing comic songs, and the housemaid, if she happened not to be offended with you, could imitate a hen that has laid an egg, a bottle of champagne being opened, and could mew like two cats fighting.

The servants never told the children what the bad news was that the gentlemen had brought to Father. But they kept hinting that they could tell a great deal if they chose – and this was not comfortable.

One day when Peter had made a booby trap over the bathroom door, and it had acted beautifully as Ruth passed through, that red-haired parlour-maid caught him and boxed his ears.

'You'll come to a bad end,' she said furiously, 'you nasty little limb, you! If you don't mend your ways, you'll go where your precious Father's gone, so I tell you straight!'

Roberta repeated this to her Mother, and next day Ruth was sent away.

Then came the time when Mother came home and went to bed and stayed there two days and the Doctor came, and the children crept wretchedly about the house and wondered if the world was coming to an end.

Mother came down one morning to breakfast, very pale and with lines on her face that used not to be there. And she smiled, as well as she could, and said, 'Now, my pets, everything is settled. We're going to leave this house, and go and live in the country. Such a ducky dear little white house. I know you'll love it.'

A whirling week of packing followed – not just packing clothes, like when you go to the seaside, but packing chairs and tables, covering their tops with sacking and their legs with straw.

All sorts of things were packed that you don't pack when you go to the seaside. Crockery, blankets, candlesticks, carpets, bedsteads, saucepans, and even fenders and fire-irons.

The house was like a furniture warehouse. I think the children enjoyed it very much. Mother was very busy, but not too busy now to talk to them, and read to them, and even to make a bit of poetry for Phyllis to cheer her up when she fell down with a screwdriver and ran it into her hand.

'Aren't you going to pack this, Mother?' Roberta asked, pointing to the beautiful cabinet inlaid with red turtleshell and brass.

'We can't take everything,' said Mother.

'But we seem to be taking all the ugly things,' said Roberta.

'We're taking the useful ones,' said Mother; 'we've got to play at being Poor for a bit, my chickabiddy.'

When all the ugly useful things had been packed up and taken away in a van by men in green-baize aprons, the two girls and Mother and Aunt Emma slept in the two spare rooms where the furniture was all pretty. All their beds had gone. A bed was made up for Peter on the drawing-room sofa.

'I say, this is larks,' he said, wriggling joyously, as Mother tucked him up. 'I do like moving! I wish we moved once a month.'

Mother laughed.

'I don't!' she said. 'Good night, Peterkin.'

As she turned away Roberta saw her face. She never forgot it.

'Oh, Mother,' she whispered all to herself as she got into bed, 'how brave you are! How I love you! Fancy being brave enough to laugh when you're feeling like THAT!'

Next day boxes were filled, and boxes and more boxes; and then late in the afternoon a cab came to take them to the station.

Aunt Emma saw them off. They felt that THEY were seeing HER off, and they were glad of it.

'But, oh, those poor little foreign children that she's going to governess!' whispered Phyllis. 'I wouldn't be them for anything!'

At first they enjoyed looking out of the window, but when it grew dusk they grew sleepier and sleepier, and no one knew how long they had been in the train when they were roused by Mother's shaking them gently and saying, 'Wake up, dears. We're there.'

They woke up, cold and melancholy, and stood shivering on the draughty platform while the baggage was taken out of the train. Then the engine, puffing and blowing, set to work again, and dragged the train away. The children watched the tail lights of the guard's van disappear into the darkness.

This was the first train the children saw on that railway which was in time to become so very dear to them. They did not guess then how they would grow to love the railway, and how soon it would become the centre of their new life, nor what wonders and changes it would bring to them. They only shivered and sneezed and hoped the walk to the new house would not be long. Peter's nose was colder than he ever remembered it to have been before. Roberta's hat was crooked, and the elastic seemed tighter than usual. Phyllis's shoelaces had come undone. ❋

– *Want to know why these children are called the 'Railway Children'. You don't have to guess! Just read the book, from which this excerpt has been taken.*

90

ALICE'S ADVENTURES IN WONDERLAND

'DOWN THE RABBIT-HOLE'

LEWIS CARROLL

Alice was beginning to get very tired of sitting by her sister on the bank, and of having nothing to do: once or twice she had peeped into the book her sister was reading, but it had no pictures or conversations in it, 'and what is the use of a book,' thought Alice 'without pictures or conversations?'

So she was considering in her own mind (as well as she could, for the hot day made her feel very sleepy and stupid), whether the pleasure of making a daisy-chain would be worth the trouble of getting up and picking the daisies, when suddenly a White Rabbit with pink eyes ran close by her.

There was nothing so *very* remarkable in that; nor did Alice think it so *very* much out of the way to hear the Rabbit say to itself, 'Oh dear! Oh dear! I shall be late!' (when she thought it over afterwards, it occurred to her that she ought to have wondered at this, but at the time it all seemed quite natural); but when the Rabbit actually *took a watch out of its waistcoat-pocket*, and looked at it, and then hurried on, Alice started to her feet, for it flashed across her mind that she had never before seen a rabbit with either a waistcoat-pocket, or a watch to take out of it, and burning with curiosity, she ran across the field after it, and fortunately was just in time to see it pop down a large rabbit-hole under the hedge.

In another moment down went Alice after it, never once considering how in the world she was to get out again.

The rabbit-hole went straight on like a tunnel for some way, and then dipped suddenly down, so suddenly that Alice had not a moment to think about stopping herself before she found herself falling down a very deep well.

Either the well was very deep, or she fell very slowly, for she had plenty of time as she went down to look about her and to wonder what was going to happen next. First, she tried to look down and make out what she was coming to, but it was too dark to see anything; then she looked at the sides of the well, and noticed that they were filled with cupboards and bookshelves; here and there she saw maps and pictures hung upon pegs. She took down a jar from one of the shelves as she passed; it was labelled 'ORANGE MARMALADE', but to her great disappointment it was empty: she did not like to drop the jar for fear of killing somebody underneath, so managed to put it into one of the cupboards as she fell past it.

'Well!' thought Alice to herself. 'After such a fall as this, I shall think nothing of tumbling down stairs! How brave they'll all think me at home! Why, I wouldn't say anything about it, even if I fell off the top of the house!' (Which was very likely true.)

Down, down, down. Would the fall *never* come to an end? 'I wonder how many miles I've fallen by this time?' she said aloud. 'I must be getting somewhere near the centre of the earth. Let me see: that would be four thousand miles down, I think –' (for, you see, Alice had learnt several things of this sort in her lessons in the schoolroom, and though this was not a *very* good opportunity for showing off her knowledge, as there was no one to listen to her, still it was good practice to say it over) '– yes, that's about the right distance – but then I wonder what Latitude or Longitude I've got to?' (Alice had no idea what

Latitude was, or Longitude either, but thought they were nice grand words to say.)

Presently she began again. 'I wonder if I shall fall right *through* the earth! How funny it'll seem to come out among the people that walk with their heads downward! The Antipathies, I think –' (she was rather glad there *was* no one listening, this time, as it didn't sound at all the right word) '– but I shall have to ask them what the name of the country is, you know. Please, Ma'am, is this New Zealand or Australia?' (and she tried to curtsey as she spoke – fancy *curtseying* as you're falling through the air! Do you think you could manage it?) 'And what an ignorant little girl she'll think me for asking! No, it'll never do to ask: perhaps I shall see it written up somewhere.'

Down, down, down. There was nothing else to do, so Alice soon began talking again. 'Dinah'll miss me very much tonight, I should think!' (Dinah was the cat.) 'I hope they'll remember her saucer of milk at teatime. Dinah, my dear! I wish you were down here with me! There are no mice in the air, I'm afraid, but you might catch a bat, and that's very like a mouse, you know. But do cats eat bats, I wonder?' And here Alice began to get rather sleepy, and went on saying to herself, in a dreamy sort of way, 'Do cats eat bats? Do cats eat bats?' and sometimes, 'Do bats eat cats?' for, you see, as she couldn't answer either question, it didn't much matter which way she put it. She felt that she was dozing off, and had just begun to dream that she was walking hand in hand with Dinah, and saying to her very earnestly, 'Now, Dinah, tell me the truth: did you ever eat a bat?' when suddenly, *thump! thump!* down she came upon a heap of sticks and dry leaves, and the fall was over.

Alice was not a bit hurt, and she jumped up on to her feet in a moment: she looked up, but it was all dark overhead; before her was another long passage, and the White Rabbit was still in sight, hurrying down it. There was not a moment to be lost: away went Alice like the wind, and was just in time to hear it say, as it turned a corner, 'Oh my ears and whiskers, how late it's getting!' She was close behind it when she turned the corner, but the Rabbit was no longer to be seen: she found herself in a long, low hall, which was lit up by a row of lamps hanging from the roof.

There were doors all round the hall, but they were all locked; and when Alice had been all the way down one side and up the other, trying every door, she walked sadly down the middle, wondering how she was ever to get out again.

Suddenly she came upon a little three-legged table, all made of solid glass; there was nothing on it except a tiny golden key, and Alice's first thought was that it might belong to one of the doors of the hall; but, alas! either the locks were too large, or the key was too small, but at any rate it would not open any of them. However, on the second time round, she came upon a low curtain she had not noticed before, and behind it was a little door about fifteen inches high: she tried the little golden key in the lock, and to her great delight it fitted!

Alice opened the door and found that it led into a small passage, not much larger than a rat-hole: she knelt down and looked along the passage into the loveliest garden you ever saw. How she longed to get out of that dark hall, and wander about among those beds of bright flowers and those cool fountains, but she could not even get her head through the doorway; 'and even if my head would go through,' thought poor Alice, 'it would be of very little use without my shoulders. Oh, how I wish I could shut up like a telescope! I think I could, if I only knew how to begin.' For, you see, so many out-of-the-way things had happened lately, that Alice had begun to think that very few things indeed were really impossible.

There seemed to be no use in waiting by the little door, so she went back to the table, half hoping she might find another key on it, or at any rate a book of rules for shutting people up like telescopes: this time she found a little bottle on it, ('which certainly was not here before,' said Alice,) and round the neck of the bottle was a paper label, with the words 'DRINK ME,' beautifully printed on it in large letters.

It was all very well to say 'Drink me,' but the wise little Alice was not going to do *that* in a hurry. 'No, I'll look first,' she said, 'and see whether it's marked '*poison*' or not'; for she had read several nice little histories about children who had got burnt, and eaten up by wild beasts and other unpleasant things, all because they *would* not remember the simple rules their friends had taught them: such as, that a red-hot poker will burn you if you hold it too long; and that if you cut your finger *very* deeply with a knife, it usually bleeds; and she had never forgotten that, if you drink much from a bottle marked 'poison,' it is almost certain to disagree with you, sooner or later.

However, this bottle was *not* marked 'poison,' so Alice ventured to taste it, and finding it very nice, (it had, in fact, a sort of mixed flavour of cherry-tart, custard, pineapple, roast turkey, toffee and hot buttered toast,) she very soon finished it off.

'What a curious feeling!' said Alice; 'I must be shutting up like a telescope.'

And so it was indeed: she was now only ten inches high, and her face brightened up at the thought that she was now the right size for going through the little door into that lovely garden. First, however, she waited for a few minutes to see if she was going to shrink any further: she felt a little nervous about this; 'for it might end, you know,' said Alice to herself, 'in my going out altogether, like a candle. I wonder what I should be like then?'

After a while, finding that nothing more happened, she decided on going into the garden at once; but, alas for poor Alice! when she got to the door, she found she had forgotten the little golden key, and when she went back to the table for it, she found she could not possibly reach it: she could see it quite plainly through the glass, and she tried her best to climb up one of the legs of the table, but it was too slippery; and when she had tired herself out with trying, the poor little thing sat down and cried.

Soon her eye fell on a little glass box that was lying under the table: she opened it, and found in it a very small cake, on which the words 'EAT ME' were beautifully marked in currants. 'Well, I'll eat it,' said Alice, 'and if it makes me grow larger, I can reach the key; and if it makes me grow smaller, I can creep under the door; so either way I'll get into the garden, and I don't care which happens!' ❋

– *Want to know what happened to Alice? Read* Alice's Adventures in Wonderland, *from which this excerpt has been taken.*

91

THE ADVENTURES OF TOM SAWYER 'WHITEWASHING'

MARK TWAIN

Saturday morning was come, and all the summer world was bright and fresh, and brimming with life. There was a song in every heart; and if the heart was young the music issued at the lips. There was cheer in every face and a spring in every step. The locust-trees were in bloom and the fragrance of the blossoms filled the air. Cardiff Hill, beyond the village and above it, was green with vegetation and it lay just far enough away to seem a Delectable Land, dreamy, reposeful and inviting.

Tom appeared on the sidewalk with a bucket of whitewash and a long-handled brush. He surveyed the fence, and all gladness left him and a deep melancholy settled down upon his spirit. Thirty yards of board fence nine feet high. Life to him seemed hollow, and existence but a burden. Sighing, he dipped his brush and passed it along the topmost plank; repeated the operation; did it again; compared the insignificant whitewashed streak with the far-reaching continent of unwhitewashed fence, and sat down on a tree-box discouraged.

Jim came skipping out at the gate with a tin pail, and singing 'Buffalo Gals'. Bringing water from the town pump had always been hateful work in Tom's eyes, before, but now it did not strike him so. He remembered that there was company at the pump. Boys and girls were always there waiting their turns, resting, trading playthings, quarrelling, fighting, skylarking. And he remembered that although the pump was only a hundred and fifty yards off, Jim never got back with a bucket of water under an hour – and even then somebody generally had to go after him. Tom said, 'Say, Jim, I'll fetch the water if you'll whitewash some.'

Jim shook his head and said, 'Can't, Mars Tom. Ole missis, she tole me I got to go an' git dis water an' not stop foolin' roun' wid anybody. She say she spec' Mars Tom gwine to ax me to whitewash, an' so she tole me go 'long an' 'tend to my own business – she 'lowed *she'd* 'tend to de whitewashin'.'

'Oh, never you mind what she said, Jim. That's the way she always talks. Gimme the bucket – I won't be gone only a a minute. *She* won't ever know.'

'Oh, I dasn't, Mars Tom. Ole missis she'd take an' tar de head off'n me. 'Deed she would.'

'*She*! She never licks anybody – whacks 'em over the head with her thimble – and who cares for that, I'd like to know. She talks awful, but talk don't hurt – anyways it don't if she don't cry. Jim, I'll give you a marvel. I'll give you a white alley*!'

Jim began to waver.

'White alley, Jim! And it's a bully taw**.'

'My! Dat's a mighty gay marvel, I tell you! But Mars Tom I's powerful 'fraid ole missis –'

'And besides, if you will I'll show you my sore toe.'

Jim was only human – this attraction was too much for him. He put down his pail, took the white alley, and bent over the toe with absorbing interest while the bandage was being unwound. In another moment he was flying down the street with his pail and a tingling rear, Tom was whitewashing with vigour, and Aunt Polly was retiring from the field with a slipper in her hand and triumph in her eye.

But Tom's energy did not last. He began to think of the fun he had planned for this day, and his sorrows multiplied. Soon the free boys would come tripping along on all sorts of delicious expeditions, and they

** and **: Kinds of marbles*

would make a world of fun of him for having to work – the very thought of it burnt him like fire. He got out his worldly wealth and examined it – bits of toys, marbles and trash; enough to buy an exchange of *work*, maybe, but not half enough to buy so much as half an hour of pure freedom. So he returned his straitened means to his pocket, and gave up the idea of trying to buy the boys. At this dark and hopeless moment an inspiration burst upon him! Nothing less than a great, magnificent inspiration.

He took up his brush and went tranquilly to work. Ben Rogers hove in sight presently – the very boy, of all boys, whose ridicule he had been dreading. Ben's gait was the hop-skip-and-jump – proof enough that his heart was light and his anticipations high. He was eating an apple, and giving a long, melodious whoop, at intervals, followed by a deep-toned ding-dong-dong, ding-dong-dong, for he was personating a steamboat. As he drew near, he slackened speed, took the middle of the street, leaned far over to starboard and rounded to ponderously and with laborious pomp and circumstance – for he was personating the Big Missouri, and considered himself to be drawing nine feet of water. He was boat and captain and engine-bells combined, so he had to imagine himself standing on his own hurricane-deck giving the orders and executing them: 'Stop her, sir! Ting-a-ling-ling!' The headway ran almost out, and he drew up slowly toward the sidewalk.

'Ship up to back! Ting-a-ling-ling!' His arms straightened and stiffened down his sides.

'Set her back on the stabboard! Ting-a-ling-ling! Chow! ch-chow-wow! Chow!' His right hand, meantime, describing stately circles – for it was representing a forty-foot wheel.

'Let her go back on the labboard! Ting-a-ling-ling! Chow-ch-chow-chow!' The left hand began to describe circles.

'Stop the stabboard! Ting-a-ling-ling! Stop the labboard! Come ahead on the stabboard! Stop her! Let your outside turn over slow! Ting-a-ling-ling! Chow-ow-ow! Get out that head-line! *lively* now! Come – out with your spring-line – what're you about there! Take a turn round that stump with the bight of it! Stand by that stage, now – let her go! Done with the engines, sir! Ting-a-ling-ling! SH'T! S'H'T! SH'T!' (trying the gauge-cocks).

Tom went on whitewashing – paid no attention to the steamboat. Ben stared a moment and then said, '*Hi-Yi! You're* up a stump, ain't you!'

No answer. Tom surveyed his last touch with the eye of an artist, then he gave his brush another gentle sweep and surveyed the result, as before. Ben ranged up alongside of him. Tom's mouth watered for the apple, but he stuck to his work. Ben said, 'Hello, old chap, you got to work, hey?'

Tom wheeled suddenly and said, 'Why, it's you, Ben! I warn't noticing.'

'Say – I'm going in a-swimming, I am. Don't you wish you could? But of course you'd druther *work* – wouldn't you? Course you would!'

Tom contemplated the boy a bit and said, 'What do you call work?'

'Why, ain't *that* work?'

Tom resumed his whitewashing and answered carelessly, 'Well, maybe it is, and maybe it ain't. All I know, is, it suits Tom Sawyer.'

'Oh come, now, you don't mean to let on that you *like* it?'

The brush continued to move.

'Like it? Well, I don't see why I oughtn't to like it. Does a boy get a chance to whitewash a fence every day?'

That put the thing in a new light. Ben stopped nibbling his apple. Tom swept his brush daintily back and forth – stepped back to note the effect – added a touch here and there – criticized the effect again – Ben watching every move and getting more and more interested, more and more absorbed. Presently he said, 'Say, Tom, let *me* whitewash a little.'

Tom considered, was about to consent, but he changed his mind: 'No – no – I reckon it wouldn't hardly do, Ben. You see, Aunt Polly's awful particular about this fence – right here on the street, you know – but if it was the back fence I wouldn't mind and *she* wouldn't. Yes, she's awful particular about this fence; it's got to be done very careful; I reckon there ain't one boy in a thousand, maybe two thousand, that can do it the way it's got to be done.'

'No – is that so? Oh come, now – lemme just try. Only just a little – I'd let *you*, if you was me, Tom.'

'Ben, I'd like to, honest injun; but Aunt Polly – well, Jim wanted to do it, but she wouldn't let him; Sid wanted to do it, and she wouldn't let Sid. Now don't you see how I'm fixed? If you was to tackle this fence and anything was to happen to it – '

'Oh, shucks, I'll be just as careful. Now lemme try. Say – I'll give you the core of my apple.'

'Well, here – No, Ben, now don't. I'm afeard –'

'I'll give you *all* of it!'

Tom gave up the brush with reluctance in his face, but alacrity in his heart. And while the late steamer Big Missouri worked and sweated in the sun, the retired artist sat on a barrel in the shade close by, dangled his legs, munched his apple and planned the slaughter of more innocents. There was no lack of material; boys happened along every little while; they came to jeer, but remained to whitewash. By the time Ben was fagged out, Tom had traded the next chance to Billy Fisher for a kite, in good repair; and when he played out, Johnny Miller bought in for a dead rat and a string to swing it with – and so on, and so on, hour after hour.

And when the middle of the afternoon came, from being a poor poverty-stricken boy in the morning,

Tom was literally rolling in wealth. He had besides the things before mentioned, twelve marbles, part of a Jew's-harp, a piece of blue bottle-glass to look through, a spool cannon, a key that wouldn't unlock anything, a fragment of chalk, a glass stopper of a decanter, a tin soldier, a couple of tadpoles, six fire-crackers, a kitten with only one eye, a brass door-knob, a dog collar – but no dog – the handle of a knife, four pieces of orange peel and a dilapidated old window sash.

He had had a nice, good, idle time all the while – plenty of company – and the fence had three coats of whitewash on it! If he hadn't run out of whitewash he would have bankrupted every boy in the village. ❋

– *This is an excerpt from* The Adventures of Tom Sawyer. *Read the book to get to know all about his escapades!*

92

THE GOLDEN TOUCH

NATHANIEL HAWTHORNE

Once upon a time, there lived a very rich man, and a king besides, whose name was Midas, and he had a little daughter, Marygold.

This King Midas was fonder of gold than of anything else in the world. He valued his royal crown chiefly because it was composed of that precious metal. If he loved anything better, or half so well, it was the one little maiden who played so merrily around her father's footstool. But the more Midas loved his daughter, the more did he desire and seek for wealth. He thought, foolish man! that the best thing he could possibly do for this dear child would be to bequeath her the immensest pile of yellow, glistening coin, that had ever been heaped together since the world was made.

Thus, he gave all his thoughts and all his time to this one purpose. If ever he happened to gaze for an instant at the gold-tinted clouds of sunset, he wished that they were real gold and that they could be squeezed safely into his strong box. When little Marygold ran to meet him with a bunch of buttercups and dandelions, he used to say, 'Poh, poh, child! If these flowers were as golden as they look, they would be worth the plucking!'

And yet, in his earlier days, before he was so entirely possessed of this insane desire for riches, King Midas had shown a great taste for flowers. He had planted a garden, in which grew the biggest and beautifulest and sweetest roses that any mortal ever saw or smelt. But now, if he looked at them at all, it was only to calculate how much the garden would be worth if each of the innumerable rose petals were a thin plate of gold.

At length (as people always grow more and more foolish, unless they take care to grow wiser and wiser), Midas had got to be so exceedingly unreasonable, that he could scarcely bear to see or touch any object that was not gold. He made it his custom, therefore, to pass a large portion of every day in a dark and dreary apartment, underground, at the basement of his palace. It was here that he kept his wealth. To this dismal hole – for it was little better than a dungeon – Midas betook himself, whenever he wanted to be particularly happy.

Here, after carefully locking the door, he would take a bag of gold coin, or a gold cup as big as a washbowl, or a heavy golden bar, or a peck-measure of gold-dust, and bring them from the obscure corners of the room into the one bright and narrow sunbeam that fell from the dungeon-like window. And then would he reckon over the coins in the bag; toss up the bar, and catch it as it came down; sift the gold-dust through his fingers; look at the funny image of his own face, as reflected in the burnished circumference of the cup; and whisper to himself, 'O Midas, rich King Midas, what a happy man are you!'

Midas called himself a happy man, but felt that he was not yet quite so happy as he might be. The very tip-top of enjoyment would never be reached, unless the whole world were to become his treasure-room and be filled with yellow metal which should be all his own.

Now, I need hardly remind such wise little people as you are, that in the old, old times, when King Midas was alive, a great many things came to pass, which we should consider wonderful if they were to happen in our own day and country. And, on the other hand, a great many things take place nowadays, which seem not only wonderful to us, but at which the people of old times would have stared their eyes out.

Midas was enjoying himself in his treasure-room, one day, as usual, when he perceived a shadow fall over the heaps of gold; and, looking suddenly up, what should he behold but the figure of a stranger, standing in the bright and narrow sunbeam! Certainly, although his figure intercepted the sunshine, there was now a brighter gleam upon all the piled-up treasures than before. Even the remotest corners had their share of it, and were lighted up, when the stranger smiled, as with tips of flame and sparkles of fire.

As Midas knew that he had carefully turned the key in the lock, and that no mortal strength could possibly break into his treasure-room, he, of course, concluded that his visitor must be something more than mortal.

The stranger gazed about the room; and when his lustrous smile had glistened upon all the golden objects that were there, he turned again to Midas.

'You are a wealthy man, friend Midas!' he observed. 'I doubt whether any other four walls, on earth, contain so much gold as you have contrived to pile up in this room.'

'I have done pretty well – pretty well,' answered Midas, in a discontented tone. 'But, after all, it is but a trifle, when you consider that it has taken me my whole life to get it together. If one could live a thousand years, he might have time to grow rich!'

'What!' exclaimed the stranger. 'Then you are not satisfied?'

Midas shook his head.

'And pray what would satisfy you?' asked the stranger. 'Merely for the curiosity of the thing, I should be glad to know.'

So Midas thought, and thought, and thought, and heaped up one golden mountain upon another, in his imagination, without being able to imagine them big enough. At last, a bright idea occurred to King Midas. It seemed really as bright as the glistening metal which he loved so much.

'It is only this,' replied Midas. 'I am weary of collecting my treasures with so much trouble, and beholding the heap so diminutive, after I have done my best. I wish everything that I touch to be changed to gold!'

The stranger's smile grew so very broad, that it seemed to fill the room like an outburst of the sun.

'The Golden Touch!' exclaimed he. 'You certainly deserve credit, friend Midas, for striking out so brilliant a conception. But are you quite sure that this will satisfy you?'

'How could it fail?' said Midas.

'And will you never regret the possession of it?'

'What could induce me?' asked Midas. 'I ask nothing else, to render me perfectly happy.'

'Be it as you wish, then,' replied the stranger, waving his hand in token of farewell. 'Tomorrow, at sunrise, you will find yourself gifted with the Golden Touch.'

The figure of the stranger then became exceedingly bright, and Midas involuntarily closed his eyes. On opening them again, he beheld only one yellow sunbeam in the room, and, all around him, the glistening of the precious metal which he had spent his life in hoarding up.

Day had hardly peeped over the hills, when King Midas was broad awake, and, stretching his arms out of bed, began to touch the objects that were within reach. He was anxious to prove whether the Golden Touch had really come, according to the stranger's promise.

So he laid his finger on a chair by the bedside, and on various other things, but was grievously disappointed to perceive that they remained of exactly the same substance as before. Indeed, he felt very much afraid that he had only dreamed about the lustrous stranger, or else that the latter had been making game of him.

All this while it was only the grey of the morning, with but a streak of brightness along the edge of the sky, where Midas could not see it. He lay in a very disconsolate mood, and kept growing sadder and sadder, until the earliest sunbeam shone through the window, and gilded the ceiling over his head. It seemed to Midas that this bright yellow sunbeam was reflected in rather a singular way on the white covering of the bed. Looking more closely, what was his astonishment and delight, when he found that this linen fabric had been transmuted to what seemed a woven texture of the purest and brightest gold! The Golden Touch had come to him with the first sunbeam!

Midas started up, in a kind of joyful frenzy, and ran about the room, grasping at everything that happened to be in his way. He seized one of the bedposts, and it became immediately a fluted golden pillar. He pulled aside a window-curtain, in order to admit a clear spectacle of the wonders which he was performing; and the tassel grew heavy in his hand – a mass of gold. He took up a book from the table. At his first touch, it assumed the appearance of a splendidly bound and gilt-edged volume, but, on running his fingers through the leaves, behold! it was a bundle of thin golden plates, in which all the wisdom of the book had grown illegible. He hurriedly put on his clothes and was enraptured to see himself in a magnificent suit of gold cloth, which retained its flexibility and softness, although it burdened him a little with its weight. He drew out his handkerchief, which little Marygold had hemmed for him. That was likewise gold, with the dear child's neat and pretty stitches running all along the border, in gold thread!

Somehow or other, this last transformation did not quite please King Midas. He would rather that his little daughter's handiwork should have remained just the same as when she climbed his knee and put it into his hand.

But it was not worthwhile to vex himself about a trifle. Midas now took his spectacles from his pocket, and put them on his nose, in order that he might see more distinctly what he was about. In those days, spectacles for common people had not been invented, but were already worn by kings; else, how could Midas have had any? To his great perplexity, however, excellent as the glasses were, he discovered that he could not possibly see through them. But this was the most natural thing in the world; for on taking them off, the transparent crystals turned out to be plates of yellow metal, and, of course, were worthless as spectacles, though valuable as gold. It struck Midas as rather inconvenient that, with all his wealth, he could never again be rich enough to own a pair of serviceable spectacles.

'It is no great matter, nevertheless,' said he to himself, very philosophically. 'We cannot expect any great good, without its being accompanied with some small inconvenience. The Golden Touch is worth the sacrifice of a pair of spectacles, at least, if not of one's very eyesight. My own eyes will serve for ordinary purposes, and little Marygold will soon be old enough to read to me.'

Wise King Midas was so exalted by his good fortune that the palace seemed not sufficiently spacious to contain him. He therefore went downstairs, and smiled, on observing that the balustrade of the staircase became a bar of burnished gold, as his hand passed over it in his descent. He lifted the door-latch (it was brass only a moment ago, but golden when his fingers quitted it) and emerged into the garden. Here, as it happened, he found a great number of beautiful roses in full bloom, and others in all the stages of lovely bud and blossom. Very delicious was their fragrance in the morning breeze. Their delicate blush was one of the fairest sights in the world; so gentle, so modest, and so full of sweet tranquillity did these roses seem to be.

But Midas knew a way to make them far more precious, according to his way of thinking, than roses had ever been before. So he took great pains in going from bush to bush, and exercised his magic touch most indefatigably; until every individual flower and bud, and even the worms at the heart of some of them, were changed to gold. By the time this good work was completed, King Midas was summoned to breakfast; and as the morning air had given him an excellent appetite, he made haste back to the palace.

What was usually a king's breakfast in the days of Midas, I really do not know, and cannot stop now to investigate. To the best of my belief, however, on this particular morning, the breakfast consisted of hot cakes, some nice little brook trout, roasted potatoes, fresh boiled eggs, and coffee, for King Midas himself, and a bowl of bread and milk for his daughter Marygold.

Little Marygold had not yet made her appearance. Her father ordered her to be called, and, seating himself at table, awaited the child's coming, in order to begin his own breakfast. To do Midas justice, he really loved his daughter, and loved her so much the more this morning, on account of the good fortune which had befallen him. It was not a great while before he heard her coming along the passageway, crying bitterly.

This circumstance surprised him, because Marygold was one of the cheerfullest little people whom you would see in a summer's day, and hardly shed a thimbleful of tears in a twelvemonth. When Midas heard her sobs, he determined to put little Marygold into better spirits, by an agreeable surprise; so, leaning across the table, he touched his daughter's bowl (which was a China one, with pretty figures all around it), and transmuted it to gleaming gold.

Meanwhile, Marygold slowly and disconsolately opened the door, and showed herself with her apron at her eyes, still sobbing as if her heart would break.

'How now, my little lady!' cried Midas. 'Pray what is the matter with you, this bright morning?'

Marygold, without taking the apron from her eyes, held out her hand, in which was one of the roses which Midas had so recently transmuted.

'Beautiful!' exclaimed her father. 'And what is there in this magnificent golden rose to make you cry?'

'Ah, dear father!' answered the child, as well as her sobs would let her, 'it is not beautiful, but the ugliest flower that ever grew! As soon as I was dressed I ran into the garden to gather some roses for you; because I know you like them, and like them the better when gathered by your little daughter. But, oh dear, dear me! What do you think has happened? Such a misfortune! All the beautiful roses, that smelled so sweet and had so many lovely blushes, are blighted and spoilt! They are grown quite yellow, as you see this one, and have no longer any fragrance! What can have been the matter with them?'

'Poh, my dear little girl – pray don't cry about it!' said Midas, who was ashamed to confess that he himself had wrought the change which so greatly afflicted her. 'Sit down and eat your bread and milk! You will find it easy enough to exchange a golden rose like that (which will last hundreds of years) for an ordinary one which would wither in a day.'

'I don't care for such roses as this!' cried Marygold, tossing it contemptuously away. 'It has no smell, and the hard petals prick my nose!'

The child now sat down to table, but was so occupied with her grief for the blighted roses that she did not even notice the wonderful transmutation of her China bowl. Perhaps this was all the better; for Marygold was accustomed to take pleasure in looking at the queer figures, and strange trees and houses, that were painted on the circumference of the bowl; and these ornaments were now entirely lost in the yellow hue of the metal.

Midas, meanwhile, had poured out a cup of coffee, and, as a matter of course, the coffee pot, whatever metal it may have been when he took it up, was gold when he set it down. He thought to himself, that it was rather an extravagant style of splendour, in a king of his simple habits, to breakfast off a service of gold, and began to be puzzled with the difficulty of keeping his treasures safe. The cupboard and the kitchen would no longer be a secure place of deposit for articles so valuable as golden bowls and coffee pots.

Amid these thoughts, he lifted a spoonful of coffee to his lips, and, sipping it, was astonished to perceive that the instant his lips touched the liquid, it became molten gold, and the next moment, hardened into a lump!

'Ha!' exclaimed Midas, rather aghast.

'What is the matter, father?' asked little Marygold, gazing at him, with the tears still standing in her eyes.

'Nothing, child, nothing!' said Midas. 'Eat your milk, before it gets quite cold.'

He took one of the nice little trouts on his plate, and, by way of experiment, touched its tail with his finger. To his horror, it was immediately transmuted from an admirably fried brook trout into a gold-fish, though not one of those goldfishes which people often keep in glass globes, as ornaments for the parlour. No; but it was really a metallic fish, and looked as if it had been very cunningly made by the nicest goldsmith in the world. A very pretty piece of work, as you may suppose; only King Midas, just at that moment, would much rather have had a real trout in his dish than this elaborate and valuable imitation of one.

'I don't quite see,' thought he to himself, 'how I am to get any breakfast!'

He took one of the smoking-hot cakes, and had scarcely broken it, when, to his cruel mortification, though, a moment before, it had been of the whitest wheat, it assumed the yellow hue of Indian meal.*

Almost in despair, he helped himself to a boiled egg, which immediately underwent a change similar to those of the trout and the cake. The egg, indeed, might have been mistaken for one of those which the famous goose, in the storybook, was in the habit of laying; but King Midas was the only goose that had had anything to do with the matter.

'Well, this is a quandary!' thought he, leaning back in his chair, and looking quite enviously at little Marygold, who was now eating her bread and milk with great satisfaction. 'Such a costly breakfast before me, and nothing that can be eaten!'

Hoping that he might avoid what he now felt to be a considerable inconvenience, King Midas next snatched a hot potato, and attempted to cram it into his mouth, and swallow it in a hurry. But the Golden Touch was too nimble for him. He found his mouth full, not of mealy potato, but of solid metal, which so burnt his tongue that he roared aloud, and, jumping

* *Maize flour*

up from the table, began to dance and stamp about the room, both with pain and fright.

'Father, dear father!' cried little Marygold, who was a very affectionate child, 'pray what is the matter? Have you burnt your mouth?'

'Ah, dear child,' groaned Midas dolefully, 'I don't know what is to become of your poor father!'

And, truly, my dear little folks, did you ever hear of such a pitiable case in all your lives? Here was literally the richest breakfast that could be set before a king, and its very richness made it absolutely good for nothing. The poorest labourer, sitting down to his crust of bread and cup of water, was far better off than King Midas, whose delicate food was really worth its weight in gold. And what was to be done?

Already, at breakfast, Midas was excessively hungry. Would he be less so by dinner time? And how ravenous would be his appetite for supper, which must undoubtedly consist of the same sort of indigestible dishes as those now before him!

These reflections so troubled wise King Midas, that he began to doubt whether, after all, riches are the one desirable thing in the world, or even the most desirable. But this was only a passing thought.

Nevertheless, so great was his hunger, and the perplexity of his situation, that he again groaned aloud, and very grievously too. Our pretty Marygold could endure it no longer. She sat, a moment, gazing at her father, and trying with all the might of her little wits to find out what was the matter with him. Then, with a sweet and sorrowful impulse to comfort him, she started from her chair, and, running to Midas, threw her arms affectionately about his knees. He bent down and kissed her. He felt that his little daughter's love was worth a thousand times more than he had gained by the Golden Touch.

'My precious, precious Marygold!' cried he.

But Marygold made no answer.

Alas, what had he done? How fatal was the gift which the stranger bestowed! The moment the lips of Midas touched Marygold's forehead, a change had taken place. Her sweet, rosy face, so full of affection as it had been, assumed a glittering yellow color, with yellow teardrops congealing on her cheeks. Her beautiful brown ringlets took the same tint. Her soft and tender little form grew hard and inflexible within her father's encircling arms. Little Marygold was a human child no longer, but a golden statue!

It had been a favourite phrase of Midas, whenever he felt particularly fond of the child, to say that she was worth her weight in gold. And now the phrase had become literally true.

It would be too sad a story, if I were to tell you how Midas began to wring his hands and bemoan himself; and how he could neither bear to look at Marygold, nor yet to look away from her.

While he was in this tumult of despair, he suddenly beheld a stranger standing near the door. Midas bent down his head, without speaking; for he recognized the same figure which had appeared to him, the day before, in the treasure-room, and had bestowed on him this disastrous faculty of the Golden Touch. The stranger's countenance still wore a smile, which seemed to shed a yellow lustre all about the room, and gleamed on little Marygold's image, and on the other objects that had been transmuted by the touch of Midas.

'Well, friend Midas,' said the stranger, 'pray how do you succeed with the Golden Touch?'

Midas shook his head.

'I am very miserable,' said he.

'Very miserable, indeed!' exclaimed the stranger. 'And how happens that? Have I not faithfully kept my promise with you? Have you not everything that your heart desired?'

'Gold is not everything,' answered Midas. 'And I have lost all that my heart really cared for.'

'Ah! So you have made a discovery, since yesterday?' observed the stranger. 'Let us see, then. Which of these two things do you think is really worth the most – the gift of the Golden Touch, or one cup of clear cold water?'

'O blessed water!' exclaimed Midas. 'It will never moisten my parched throat again!'

'The Golden Touch,' continued the stranger, 'or a crust of bread?'

'A piece of bread,' answered Midas, 'is worth all the gold on earth!'

'The Golden Touch,' asked the stranger, 'or your own little Marygold, warm, soft and loving as she was an hour ago?'

'Oh, my child, my dear child!' cried poor Midas, wringing his hands. 'I would not have given that one small dimple in her chin for the power of changing this whole big earth into a solid lump of gold!'

'You are wiser than you were, King Midas!' said the stranger, looking seriously at him. 'Your own heart, I perceive, has not been entirely changed from flesh to gold. Were it so, your case would indeed be desperate. But you appear to be still capable of understanding that the commonest things, such as lie within everybody's grasp, are more valuable than the riches which so many mortals sigh and struggle after. Tell me, now, do you sincerely desire to rid yourself of this Golden Touch?'

'It is hateful to me!' replied Midas.

A fly settled on his nose, but immediately fell to the floor; for it, too, had become gold. Midas shuddered.

'Go, then,' said the stranger, 'and plunge into the river that glides past the bottom of your garden. Take a vase of the same water and sprinkle it over any object that you may desire to change back again from gold into its former substance. If you do this in earnestness and sincerity, it may possibly repair the mischief which your avarice has occasioned.'

King Midas bowed low – and when he lifted his head, the lustrous stranger had vanished.

You will easily believe that Midas lost no time in snatching up a great earthen pitcher (but, alas me! it was no longer earthen after he touched it), and hastening to the riverside. As he scampered along, and forced his way through the shrubbery, it was positively marvellous to see how the foliage turned yellow behind him, as if the autumn had been there, and nowhere else. On reaching the river's brink, he plunged headlong in, without waiting so much as to pull off his shoes.

'Poof! poof! poof!' snorted King Midas, as his head emerged out of the water. 'Well, this is really a refreshing bath, and I think it must have quite washed away the Golden Touch. And now for filling my pitcher!' As he dipped the pitcher into the water, it gladdened his very heart to see it change from gold into the same good, honest earthen vessel which it had been before he touched it. He was conscious, also, of a change within himself. A cold, hard and heavy weight seemed to have gone out of his bosom.

Perceiving a violet that grew on the bank of the river, Midas touched it with his finger, and was overjoyed to find that the delicate flower retained its purple hue, instead of undergoing a yellow blight. The curse of the Golden Touch had therefore really been removed from him.

King Midas hastened back to the palace and the first thing he did, as you need hardly be told, was to sprinkle it by handfuls over the golden figure of little Marygold. No sooner did it fall on her than you would have laughed to see how the rosy colour came back to the dear child's cheek! and how she began to sneeze and sputter! – and how astonished she was to find herself dripping wet, and her father still throwing more water over her!

Her father did not think it necessary to tell his beloved child how very foolish he had been, but contented himself with showing how much wiser he had now grown. For this purpose he led little Marygold into the garden, where he sprinkled all the remainder of the water over the rose bushes, and with such good effect that above five thousand roses recovered their beautiful bloom. ❋

– Exerpted from the original story.

93

THE VELVETEEN RABBIT
OR HOW TOYS BECOME REAL

MARGERY WILLIAMS

There was once a velveteen rabbit, and in the beginning he was really splendid. He was fat and bunchy, as a rabbit should be; his coat was spotted brown and white, he had real thread whiskers, and his ears were lined with pink sateen. On Christmas morning, when he sat wedged in the top of the Boy's stocking, with a sprig of holly between his paws, the effect was charming.

There were other things in the stocking – nuts and oranges and a toy engine, and chocolate almonds and a clockwork mouse – but the Rabbit was quite the best of all. For at least two hours the Boy loved him, and then Aunts and Uncles came to dinner, and there was a great rustling of tissue paper and unwrapping of parcels, and in the excitement of looking at all the new presents the Velveteen Rabbit was forgotten.

For a long time he lived in the toy cupboard or on the nursery floor, and no one thought very much about him. He was naturally shy, and being only made of velveteen, some of the more expensive toys quite snubbed him.

The mechanical toys were very superior and looked down upon everyone else; they were full of modern ideas, and pretended they were real. The model boat, who had lived through two seasons and lost most of his paint, caught the tone from them and never missed an opportunity of referring to his rigging in technical terms.

The Rabbit could not claim to be a model of anything, for he didn't know that real rabbits existed. He thought they were all stuffed with sawdust like himself, and he understood that sawdust was quite out-of-date and should never be mentioned in modern circles.

Even Timothy, the jointed wooden lion, who was made by the disabled soldiers, and should have had broader views, put on airs and pretended he was connected with Government. Between them all the poor little Rabbit was made to feel himself very insignificant and commonplace, and the only person who was kind to him at all was the Skin Horse.

The Skin Horse had lived longer in the nursery than any of the others. He was so old that his brown coat was bald in patches and showed the seams underneath, and most of the hairs in his tail had been pulled out to string bead necklaces. He was wise, for he had seen a long succession of mechanical toys arrive to boast and swagger, and by and by break their mainsprings and pass away, and he knew that they were only toys, and would never turn into anything else. For nursery magic is very strange and wonderful, and only those playthings that are old and wise and experienced like the Skin Horse understand all about it.

'What is REAL?' asked the Rabbit one day, when they were lying side by side near the nursery fender, before Nana came to tidy the room. 'Does it mean having things that buzz inside you and a stick-out handle?'

'Real isn't how you are made,' said the Skin Horse. 'It's a thing that happens to you. When a child loves you for a long, long time, not just to play with, but REALLY loves you, then you become Real.'

'Does it hurt?' asked the Rabbit.

'Sometimes,' said the Skin Horse, for he was always truthful. 'When you are Real you don't mind being hurt.'

'Does it happen all at once, like being wound up,' he asked, 'or bit by bit?'

'It doesn't happen all at once,' said the Skin Horse. 'You become. It takes a long time. That's why it doesn't happen often to people who break easily, or have sharp edges, or who have to be carefully kept. Generally, by the time you are Real, most of your hair has been loved off, and your eyes drop out and you get loose in the joints and very shabby. But these things don't matter at all, because once you are Real you can't be ugly, except to people who don't understand.'

'I suppose *you* are Real?' said the Rabbit. And then he wished he had not said it, for he thought the Skin Horse might be sensitive. But the Skin Horse only smiled.

'The Boy's Uncle made me Real,' he said. 'That was a great many years ago; but once you are Real you can't become unreal again. It lasts for always.'

The Rabbit sighed. He thought it would be a long time before this magic called Real happened to him. He longed to become Real, to know what it felt like; and yet the idea of growing shabby and losing his eyes and whiskers was rather sad. He wished that he could become it without these uncomfortable things happening to him.

There was a person called Nana who ruled the nursery. Sometimes she took no notice of the playthings lying about, and sometimes, for no reason whatever, she went swooping about like a great wind and hustled them away in cupboards. She called this 'tidying up,' and the playthings all hated it, especially the tin ones. The Rabbit didn't mind it so much, for wherever he was thrown he came down soft.

One evening, when the Boy was going to bed, he couldn't find the china dog that always slept with him. Nana was in a hurry, and it was too much trouble to hunt for china dogs at bedtime, so she simply looked about her, and seeing that the toy cupboard door stood open, she made a swoop.

'Here,' she said, 'take your old Bunny! He'll do to sleep with you!' And she dragged the Rabbit out by one ear, and put him into the Boy's arms.

That night, and for many nights after, the Velveteen Rabbit slept in the Boy's bed. At first he found it rather uncomfortable, for the Boy hugged him very tight, and sometimes he rolled over on him, and sometimes he pushed him so far under the pillow that the Rabbit could scarcely breathe.

And he missed, too, those long moonlight hours in the nursery, when all the house was silent, and his talks with the Skin Horse. But very soon he grew to like it, for the Boy used to talk to him, and made nice tunnels for him under the bedclothes that he said were like the burrows the real rabbits lived in. And they had splendid games together, in whispers, when Nana had gone away to her supper and left the night-light burning on the mantelpiece.

And when the Boy dropped off to sleep, the Rabbit would snuggle down close under his little warm chin and dream, with the Boy's hands clasped close round him all night long.

And so time went on, and the little Rabbit was very happy – so happy that he never noticed how his beautiful velveteen fur was getting shabbier and shabbier, and his tail becoming unsewn, and all the pink rubbed off his nose where the Boy had kissed him.

Spring came, and they had long days in the garden, for wherever the Boy went the Rabbit went too. He had rides in the wheelbarrow, and picnics on the grass, and lovely fairy huts built for him under the raspberry canes behind the flower border.

And once, when the Boy was called away suddenly to go out to tea, the Rabbit was left out on the lawn until long after dusk, and Nana had to come and look for him with the candle because the Boy couldn't go to sleep unless he was there. He was wet through with the dew and quite earthy from diving into the burrows the Boy had made for him in the flower bed, and Nana grumbled as she rubbed him off with a corner of her apron.

'You must have your old Bunny!' she said. 'Fancy all that fuss for a toy!'

The Boy sat up in bed and stretched out his hands.

'Give me my Bunny!' he said. 'You mustn't say that. He isn't a toy. He's REAL!'

When the little Rabbit heard that he was happy, for he knew that what the Skin Horse had said was true at last. The nursery magic had happened to him, and he was a toy no longer. He was Real. The Boy himself had said it. ❋

– Excerpted from the original story.

94

SEVEN AT ONE BLOW

THE BROTHERS GRIMM; RETOLD BY MABIE, HALE AND FORBUSH

A tailor sat in his workroom one morning, stitching away busily at a coat for the Lord Mayor. He whistled and sang so gaily that all the little boys who passed the shop on their way to school thought what a fine thing it was to be a tailor, and told one another that when they grew to be men they'd be tailors, too.

'How hungry I feel, to be sure!' cried the little man, at last; 'but I'm far too busy to trouble about eating. I must finish his lordship's coat before I touch a morsel of food,' and he broke once more into a merry song.

'Fine new jam for sale,' sang out an old woman, as she walked along the street.

'Jam! I can't resist such a treat,' said the tailor; and, running to the door, he shouted, 'This way for jam, dame; show me a pot of your very finest.'

The woman handed him jar after jar, but he found fault with all. At last he hit upon some to his liking.

'And how many pounds will you take, sir?'

'I'll take four ounces,' he replied, in a solemn tone, 'and mind you give me good weight.'

The old woman was very angry, for she had expected to sell several pounds, at least; and she went off grumbling, after she had weighed out the four ounces.

'Now for a feed!' cried the little man, taking a loaf from the cupboard as he spoke. He cut off a huge slice and spread the jam on quite half an inch thick; then he suddenly remembered his work.

'It will never do to get jam on the Lord Mayor's coat, so I'll finish it off before I take even one bite,' said he. So he picked up his work once more, and his needle flew in and out like lightning.

The tailor glanced longingly at his slice of bread and jam once or twice, but when he looked the third time it was quite covered with flies, and a fine feast they were having off it.

This was too much for the little fellow. Up he jumped, crying: 'So you think I provide bread and jam for you, indeed! Well, we'll very soon see! Take that!' and he struck the flies such a heavy blow with a duster that no fewer than seven lay dead upon the table, while the others flew up to the ceiling in great haste.

'Seven at one blow!' said the little man with great pride. 'Such a brave deed ought to be known all over the town, and it won't be my fault if folks fail to hear of it.'

So he cut out a wide belt, and stitched on it in big golden letters the words 'Seven at one blow.' When this was done he fastened it round him, crying, 'I'm cut out for something better than a tailor, it's quite clear. I'm one of the world's great heroes, and I'll be off at once to seek my fortune.'

He glanced round the cottage, but there was nothing of value to take with him. The only thing he possessed in the world was a small cheese.

'You may as well come, too,' said he, stowing away the cheese in his pocket, 'and now I'm off.'

When he got into the street the neighbours all crowded round him to read the words on his belt.

'Seven at one blow!' said they to one another. 'What a blessing he's going; for it wouldn't be safe to have a man about us who could kill seven of us at one stroke.'

You see, they didn't know that the tailor had only killed flies; they took it to mean men.

He jogged along for some miles until he came to a hedge, where a little bird was caught in the branches.

'Come along,' said the tailor, 'I'll have you to keep my cheese company.' So he caught the bird and put it carefully into his pocket with the cheese.

Soon he reached a lofty mountain, and he made up his mind to climb it and see what was going on at the other side. When he reached the top, there stood a huge giant, gazing down into the valley below.

'Good day,' said the tailor.

The giant turned round, and seeing nobody but the little tailor there, he cried with scorn, 'And what might you be doing here, might I ask? You'd best be off at once.'

'Not so fast, my friend,' said the little man, 'read this.'

'Seven at one blow,' read the giant, and he began to wish he'd been more civil. 'Well, I'm sure nobody would think it to look at you,' he said, 'but since you are so clever, do this,' and he picked up a stone and squeezed it until water ran out.

'Do that! Why, it's mere child's play to me,' and the man took out his cheese and squeezed it until the whey ran from it. 'Now who is cleverer?' asked the tailor. 'You see, I can squeeze milk out, while you only get water.'

The giant was too surprised to utter a word for a few minutes; then, taking up another stone, he threw it so high into the air that for a moment they couldn't see where it went; then down it fell to the ground again.

'Good!' said the tailor; 'but I'll throw a stone that won't come back again at all.'

Taking the little bird from his pocket, he threw it into the air, and the bird, glad to get away, flew right off and never returned.

This sort of thing didn't suit the giant at all, for he wasn't used to being beaten by any one.

'Here's something that you'll never manage,' said he to the little man. 'Just come and help me to carry this fallen oak tree for a few miles.'

'Delighted!' said the tailor, 'and I'll take the end with the branches, for it's sure to be heavier.'

'Agreed,' replied the giant, and he lifted the heavy trunk on to his shoulder, while the tailor climbed up among the branches at the other end, and sang with all his might, as though carrying a tree was nothing to him.

The poor giant, who was holding the tree trunk and the little tailor as well, soon grew tired.

'I'm going to let it fall!' he shouted, and the tailor jumped down from the branches, and pretended he had been helping all the time.

'The idea of a man your size finding a tree too heavy to carry!' laughed the little tailor.

'You are a clever little fellow, and no mistake,' replied the giant, 'and if you'll only come and spend the night in our cave, we shall be delighted to have you.'

'I shall have great pleasure in coming, my friend,' answered the little tailor, and together they set off for the giant's home.

There were seven more giants in the cave, and each one of them was eating a roasted pig for his supper. They gave the little man some food, and then showed him a bed in which he might pass the night. It was so big that, after tossing about for half an hour in it, the tailor thought he would be more comfortable if he slept in the corner, so he crept out without being noticed.

In the middle of the night the giant stole out of bed and went up to the one where he thought the little man was fast asleep. Taking a big bar of iron, he struck such a heavy blow at it that he woke up all the other giants.

'Keep quiet, friends,' said he. 'I've just killed the little scamp.'

The tailor made his escape as soon as possible, and he journeyed on for many miles, until he began to feel very tired, so he lay down under a tree, and was soon fast asleep. When he awoke, he found a big crowd of people standing round him. Up walked one very wise-looking old man, who was really the King's prime minister.

'Is it true that you have killed seven at one blow?' he asked.

'It is a fact,' answered the little tailor.

'Then come with me to the King, my friend, for he's been searching for a brave man like you for some time past. You are to be made captain of his army, and the King will give you a fine house to live in.'

'That I will,' replied the little man. 'It is just the sort of thing that will suit me, and I'll come at once.'

He hadn't been in the King's service long before everyone grew jealous of him. The soldiers were afraid that, if they offended him, he would make short work of them all, while the members of the King's household didn't fancy the idea of making such a fuss over a stranger.

So the soldiers went in a body to the King and asked that another captain should be put over them, for they were afraid of this one.

The King didn't like to refuse, for fear they should all desert, and yet he didn't dare get rid of the captain, in case such a strong and brave man should try to have his revenge.

At last the King hit upon a plan. In some woods close by there lived two giants, who were the terror of the countryside; they robbed all the travellers, and if any resistance was offered they killed the men on the spot.

Sending for the little tailor, he said, 'Knowing you to be the bravest man in my kingdom, I want to ask a favour of you. If you will kill these two giants, and bring me back proof that they are dead, you shall marry the Princess, my daughter, and have half my kingdom. You shall also take one hundred men to help you, and you are to set off at once.'

'A hundred men, Your Majesty! Pray, what do I want with a hundred men? If I can kill seven at one blow, I needn't be afraid of two. I'll kill them fast enough, never fear.'

The tailor chose ten strong men and told them to await him on the border of the wood, while he went on quite alone. He could hear the giants snoring for quite half an hour before he reached them, so he knew in which direction to go.

He found the pair fast asleep under a tree, so he filled his pockets with stones and climbed up into the branches over their heads. Then he began to pelt one of the giants with the missiles, until after a few minutes one of the men awoke. Giving the other a rough push, he cried, 'If you strike me like that again, I'll know the reason why.'

'I didn't touch you,' said the other giant crossly, and they were soon fast asleep once more.

Then the tailor threw stones at the other man, and soon he awoke as the first had done.

'What did you throw that at me for?' said he.

'You are dreaming,' answered the other. 'I didn't throw anything.'

No sooner were they fast asleep again, than the little man began to pelt them afresh.

Up they both sprang, and seizing each other, they began to fight in real earnest. Not content with using their fists, they tore up huge trees by the roots and beat each other until very soon the pair lay dead on the ground.

Down climbed the little tailor, and taking his sword in his hand he plunged it into each giant, and then went back to the edge of the forest where the ten men were waiting for him.

'They are as dead as two doornails,' shouted the little man. 'I don't say that I had an easy task, for they tore up trees by their roots to try to protect themselves with, but, of course, it was no good. What were two giants to a man who has slain seven at one blow?'

Back they went to the King, but instead of handing over half his kingdom, as he had promised, His Majesty told the little tailor that there was still another brave deed for him to do before he got the Princess for his bride.

'Just name it, then; I'm more than ready,' was the man's reply.

'You are to kill the famous unicorn that is running wild in the forest and doing so much damage. When this is done you shall have your reward at once.'

'No trouble at all, Your Majesty. I'll get rid of him in a twinkling.'

He made the ten men wait for him at the entrance to the wood as they had done the first time, and taking a stout rope and a saw he entered the forest alone.

Up came the unicorn, but just as it was about to rush at the man he darted behind a big tree.

The unicorn dashed with such force against the tree that its horn was caught quite fast and it was kept a prisoner.

Taking his rope, the man tied it tightly round the animal, and, after sawing off the horn, back he went to the palace, leading the unicorn by his side.

But even then the King was not satisfied, and he made the little tailor catch a wild boar that had been seen wandering in the woods.

He took a party of huntsmen with him, but again he made them wait on the outskirts of the forest while he went on by himself.

The wild boar made a dash at the little tailor; but the man was too quick for it. He slipped into a little building close by, with the animal at his heels. Then, catching sight of a small window, he forced his way out into the forest again, and while the boar, who was too big and clumsy to follow, stood gazing at the spot where he had disappeared, the tailor ran round and closed the door, keeping the animal quite secure inside. Then he called the hunters, who shot the boar and carried the body back to the palace.

This time the King was obliged to keep his promise; so the little tailor became a Prince, and a grand wedding they had, too.❋

– *Excerpted from the original story.*

95

THE DIVINE PARROT

A TENALI RAMAN STORY; RETOLD BY VKB

In the olden days, kings had very wise people in their court, to advise them. They often told the king the right things in clever ways when others dared not.

This is a story (there are many!) about Tenali Raman, a famous poet and very knowledgeable person in the court of King Krishna Deva Raya, who ruled the powerful Vijayanagara Empire in south India.

So it happened that the king got a parrot as a gift. It was a parrot like any other – green feathers, curved red beak and bright naughty eyes. But the king could not stop admiring and singing its praises. That was because could chant mantras. People believed that the parrot had divine powers.

The king told Tenali Raman about the unique bird. 'We must make this bird our teacher,' he said. 'We, too, will be blessed with good fortune if we chant mantras like this parrot.' Saying this, the king took Raman to the golden cage and offered a delicious fruit to the parrot. As soon as it received its favourite fruit, the parrot began to chant prayers. Then it quickly gobbled up the fruit.

Raman was sure that the parrot didn't have any magical powers or intelligence. 'Your Majesty,' he said, 'the bird is just an ordinary one, but it has been trained to chant mantras when given food.'

The king was annoyed and asked Tenali Raman to prove what he was saying. He offered a hundred gold coins to Raman if he succeeded in his mission.

The next day, Raman brought a cat and tied near the parrot's cage.

Meow!

Qwack!

Meeeeoooow!

SQUAWCK!

Seeing the cat, the parrot started to squawk loudly. It thought that the cat would kill him. When the king offered the parrot fruit, it quickly lunged at it and swallowed it down quickly, but did not chant any prayers. It was worried for its life after all!

Raman smiled.

The king realized that the parrot had no special powers and he gave Raman the promised reward. ❋

96

A ROYAL PROBLEM

A TENALI RAMAN STORY; RETOLD BY VKB

You have heard of the great king Krishna Deva Raya, who ruled over the Vijayanagara kingdom in south India, and of the clever poet Tenali Raman at his court. Here's another story about the two.

The king once had a quarrel with his queen Thirumalambal. (Yes, believe it or not, kings, too, quarrelled with their wives!) And he did what most people do when they have a fight. Yes, you guessed it right – he stopped speaking to her. Days passed. Then weeks. Then a whole month!

That was too much.

The queen called Tenali Raman and asked him to help. She knew that Tenali Raman could solve problems that nobody could and in ways no one else could think of.

Tenali Raman said, 'O Queen, let's start from the reason for the quarrel...'

The queen replied, 'Well, it started with the king's poem...'

'What sort of poem?' asked Tenali.

'Oh, ummm, I can't remember the whole of it,' the queen said. 'It went something like this:

'A sun in the day,
A moon in the night,
And a sprinkling of stars,
A few cloudy towers,
The beautiful sky is like a
Plate of flowers –
It is different during summer showers...

'It was not at all a pretty poem. In fact, it made no sense.'

It turned out that the king had requested and cajoled each of his courtiers and ministers to listen to him reciting the poem. He tried all day and evening, but they had all slipped away with one excuse or another.

Finally, the king went to the palace at night. As soon as he reached he began to recite the poem to the sleepy queen. It made Thirumalambal even more drowsy and she could not help yawning.

The king though this was disrespectful – to yawn while he, the great king, was reciting his own poem! Unforgivable!

The king was upset and angry with the queen. 'How dare you yawn, O Queen!' he said and left the room in a huff.

The queen was upset because the king was so angry with her.

Raman assured her that he would find a solution to the problem.

He waited for the right time.

One day, soon after this happened, the king's court was discussing a serious problem. It was about rice farming. The king said growing more grain would make sure that no one would go hungry for a long time. Several ministers suggested different and better ways of using the water of the river Tungabhadra for farming.

Then came the turn of Tenali Raman. He came before the king with a plate of rice seeds. Holding them up, he said, 'These are a new type of special rice seeds! They can solve food shortages in Vijayanagara forever. If sowed by *the right person*, they will give three times more rice than normal seeds.'

The king asked, 'All the farmers are the *right* people. They know the most about soil, sowing, manure and harvesting.'

But Raman pretended as if he had not heard the king at all. 'Your Majesty, these seeds have to be sown by THE RIGHT PERSON.'

The king did not understand what Raman was trying to say. 'What do you mean by the Right Person? A woman or man?'

'That does not matter, Your Majesty,' said Raman, 'it has to be THE RIGHT PERSON.'

'Out with it, Raman,' ordered the king.

'Sire,' said Raman, 'these seeds should be sown only by a person who has never yawned, never does and never will.'

The ministers began to murmur among themselves – what a strange condition, they thought! The king was flummoxed and tired. He himself felt like yawning. Putting his hand in front of his mouth, he asked, 'What does this MEAN? How is it POSSIBLE? Is this a JOKE? Is there anybody in the world who does not YAWN?'

As soon as he had said this, he realized the mistake he had made earlier with his queen by scolding her for yawning. He realized that it was quite natural for people to yawn, especially when they felt sleepy!

He went to meet the queen and said he was sorry for being unfair to her.

The king and queen together rewarded Raman for his clever solution. ❋

97

THE REMARKABLE ROCKET

OSCAR WILDE

The king's son was going to be married, so there were general rejoicings. He had waited a whole year for his bride, and at last she had arrived. She was a Russian Princess and had driven all the way from Finland in a sledge drawn by six reindeer. The sledge was shaped like a great golden swan, and between the swan's wings lay the little Princess herself. Her long ermine-cloak reached right down to her feet, on her head was a tiny cap of silver tissue, and she was as pale as the Snow Palace in which she had always lived. So pale was she that as she drove through the streets all the people wondered. 'She is like a white rose!' they cried, and they threw down flowers on her from the balconies.

At the gate of the Castle the Prince was waiting to receive her. He had dreamy violet eyes, and his hair was like fine gold. When he saw her he sank upon one knee and kissed her hand.

'Your picture was beautiful,' he murmured, 'but you are more beautiful than your picture'; and the little Princess blushed.

'She was like a white rose before,' said a young Page to his neighbour, 'but she is like a red rose now'; and the whole Court was delighted.

For the next three days everybody went about saying, 'White rose, Red rose, Red rose, White rose'; and the King gave orders that the Page's salary was to be doubled. As he received no salary at all this was not of much use to him, but it was considered a great honour and was duly published in the Court Gazette.

When the three days were over the marriage was celebrated. It was a magnificent ceremony, and the bride and bridegroom walked hand in hand under a canopy of purple velvet embroidered with little pearls. Then there was a State Banquet, which lasted for five hours. The Prince and Princess sat at the top of the Great Hall and drank out of a cup of clear crystal. Only true lovers could drink out of this cup, for if false lips touched it, it grew grey and dull and cloudy.

'It's quite clear that they love each other,' said the little Page, 'as clear as crystal!' and the King doubled his salary a second time. 'What an honour!' cried all the courtiers.

After the banquet there was to be a Ball. The bride and bridegroom were to dance the Rose-dance together, and the King had promised to play the flute. He played very badly, but no one had ever dared to tell him so, because he was the King. Indeed, he knew only two airs, and was never quite certain which one he was playing; but it made no matter, for, whatever he did, everybody cried out, 'Charming! Charming!'

The last item on the programme was a grand display of fireworks, to be let off exactly at midnight. The little Princess had never seen a firework in her life, so the King had given orders that the Royal Pyrotechnist should be in attendance on the day of her marriage.

'What are fireworks like?' she had asked the Prince, one morning, as she was walking on the terrace.

'They are like the Aurora Borealis,' said the King, who always answered questions that were addressed to other people, 'only much more natural. I prefer them to stars myself, as you always know when they are going to appear, and they are as delightful as my own flute-playing. You must certainly see them.'

So at the end of the King's garden a great stand had been set up, and as soon as the Royal Pyrotechnist had put everything in its proper place, the fireworks began to talk to each other.

'The world is certainly very beautiful,' cried a little Squib. 'Just look at those yellow tulips. Why! if they were real crackers they could not be lovelier. I am very glad I have travelled. Travel improves the mind wonderfully and does away with all one's prejudices.'

'The King's garden is not the world, you foolish squib,' said a big Roman Candle. 'The world is an enormous place, and it would take you three days to see it thoroughly.'

'Any place you love is the world to you,' exclaimed a pensive Catherine Wheel, who had been attached to an old deal* box in early life, and prided herself on her broken heart; 'but love is not fashionable any more, the poets have killed it. They wrote so much about it that nobody believed them, and I am not surprised. True love suffers, and is silent. I remember myself once – but it is no matter now. Romance is a thing of the past.'

'Nonsense!' said the Roman Candle, 'Romance never dies. It is like the moon, and lives for ever. The bride and bridegroom, for instance, love each other very dearly. I heard all about them this morning from a brown-paper cartridge, who happened to be staying in the same drawer as myself, and knew the latest Court news.'

But the Catherine Wheel shook her head. 'Romance is dead, Romance is dead, Romance is dead,' she murmured. She was one of those people who think that, if you say the same thing over and over a great many times, it becomes true in the end.

* *Wooden*

Suddenly, a sharp, dry cough was heard, and they all looked round.

It came from a tall, supercilious-looking Rocket, who was tied to the end of a long stick. He always coughed before he made any observation, so as to attract attention.

'Ahem! Ahem!' he said, and everybody listened except the poor Catherine Wheel, who was still shaking her head, and murmuring, 'Romance is dead.'

'Order! Order!' cried out a Cracker. He was something of a politician and had always taken a prominent part in the local elections, so he knew the proper Parliamentary expressions to use.

'Quite dead,' whispered the Catherine Wheel, and she went off to sleep.

As soon as there was perfect silence, the Rocket coughed a third time and began. He spoke with a very slow, distinct voice, as if he was dictating his memoirs, and always looked over the shoulder of the person to whom he was talking. In fact, he had a most distinguished manner.

'How fortunate it is for the King's son,' he remarked, 'that he is to be married on the very day on which I am to be let off. Really, if it had been arranged beforehand, it could not have turned out better for him, but Princes are always lucky.'

'Dear me!' said the little Squib, 'I thought it was quite the other way, and that we were to be let off in the Prince's honour.'

'It may be so with you,' he answered. 'Indeed, I have no doubt that it is, but with me it is different. I am a very remarkable Rocket and come of remarkable parents. My mother was the most celebrated Catherine Wheel of her day and was renowned for her graceful dancing. When she made her great public appearance she spun round nineteen times before she went out, and each time that she did so she threw into the air seven pink stars. She was three feet and a half in diameter, and made of the very best gunpowder. My father was a Rocket like myself, and of French extraction. He flew so high that the people were afraid that he would never come down again. He did, though, for he was of a kindly disposition, and he made a most brilliant descent in a shower of golden rain. The newspapers wrote about his performance in very flattering terms. Indeed, the Court Gazette called him a triumph of Pylotechnic art.'

'Pyrotechnic, Pyrotechnic, you mean,' said a Bengal Light; 'I know it is Pyrotechnic, for I saw it written on my own canister.'

'Well, I said Pylotechnic,' answered the Rocket, in a severe tone of voice, and the Bengal Light felt so crushed that he began at once to bully the little squibs, in order to show that he was still a person of some importance.

'I was saying,' continued the Rocket, 'I was saying – what was I saying?'

'You were talking about yourself,' replied the Roman Candle.

'Of course; I knew I was discussing some interesting subject when I was so rudely interrupted. I hate rudeness and bad manners of every kind, for I am extremely sensitive. No one in the whole world is so sensitive as I am, I am quite sure of that.'

'What is a sensitive person?' said the Cracker to the Roman Candle.

'A person who, because he has corns himself, always treads on other people's toes,' answered the Roman Candle in a low whisper, and the Cracker nearly exploded with laughter.

'Pray, what are you laughing at?' inquired the Rocket; 'I am not laughing.'

'I am laughing because I am happy,' replied the Cracker.

'That is a very selfish reason,' said the Rocket angrily. 'What right have you to be happy? You should be thinking about others. In fact, you should be thinking about me. I am always thinking about myself, and I expect everybody else to do the same. That is what is called sympathy. It is a beautiful virtue, and I possess it in a high degree. Suppose, for instance, anything happened to me tonight, what a misfortune that would be for everyone! The Prince and Princess would never be happy again, their whole married life would be spoiled; and as for the King, I know he would not get over it. Really, when I begin to reflect on the importance of my position, I am almost moved to tears.'

'If you want to give pleasure to others,' cried the Roman Candle, 'you had better keep yourself dry.'

'Certainly,' exclaimed the Bengal Light, who was now in better spirits; 'that is only common sense.'

'Common sense, indeed!' said the Rocket indignantly; 'You forget that I am very uncommon, and very remarkable. Why, anybody can have common sense, provided that they have no imagination. But I have imagination, for I never think of things as they really are; I always think of them as being quite different. As for keeping myself dry, there is evidently no one here who can at all appreciate an emotional nature. Fortunately for myself, I don't care. The only thing that sustains one through life is the consciousness of the immense inferiority of everybody else, and this is a feeling that I have always cultivated. But none of you have any hearts. Here you are laughing and making merry just as if the Prince and Princess had not just been married.'

'Well, really,' exclaimed a small Fire-balloon, 'Why not? It is a most joyful occasion, and when I soar up into the air I intend to tell the stars all about it. You will see them twinkle when I talk to them about the pretty bride.'

'Ah! What a trivial view of life!' said the Rocket, 'but it is only what I expected. There is nothing in you; you are hollow and empty. Why, perhaps the Prince and Princess may go to live in a country where there is a deep river, and perhaps they may have one only son, a little fair-haired boy with violet eyes like the Prince himself; and perhaps some day he may go out to walk with his nurse; and perhaps the nurse may go to sleep under a great elder tree; and perhaps the little boy may fall into the deep river and be drowned. What a terrible misfortune! Poor people, to lose their only son! It is really too dreadful! I shall never get over it.'

'But they have not lost their only son,' said the Roman Candle. 'No misfortune has happened to them at all.'

'I never said that they had,' replied the Rocket; 'I said that they might. If they had lost their only son there would be no use in saying anything more about the matter. I hate people who cry over spilt milk. But when I think that they might lose their only son, I certainly am very much affected.'

'You certainly are!' cried the Bengal Light. 'In fact, you are the most affected person I ever met.'

'You are the rudest person I ever met,' said the Rocket, 'and you cannot understand my friendship for the Prince.'

'Why, you don't even know him,' growled the Roman Candle.

'I never said I knew him,' answered the Rocket. 'I dare say that if I knew him I should not be his friend at all. It is a very dangerous thing to know one's friends.'

'You had really better keep yourself dry,' said the Fire-balloon. 'That is the important thing.'

'Very important for you, I have no doubt,' answered the Rocket, 'but I shall weep if I choose'; and he actually burst into real tears, which flowed down his stick like raindrops and nearly drowned two little beetles, who were just thinking of setting up house together, and were looking for a nice dry spot to live in.

'He must have a truly romantic nature,' said the Catherine Wheel, 'for he weeps when there is nothing at all to weep about.' And she heaved a deep sigh and thought about the deal box.

But the Roman Candle and the Bengal Light were quite indignant, and kept saying, 'Humbug! Humbug!' at the top of their voices. They were extremely practical and whenever they objected to anything they called it humbug.

Then the moon rose like a wonderful silver shield; and the stars began to shine, and a sound of music came from the palace.

The Prince and Princess were leading the dance. They danced so beautifully that the tall white lilies peeped in at the window and watched them, and the great red poppies nodded their heads and beat time.

Then ten o'clock struck, and then eleven, and then twelve, and at the last stroke of midnight everyone came out on the terrace, and the King sent for the Royal Pyrotechnist.

'Let the fireworks begin,' said the King; and the Royal Pyrotechnist made a low bow and marched down to the end of the garden. He had six attendants with him, each of whom carried a lighted torch at the end of a long pole.

It was certainly a magnificent display.

Whizz! Whizz! went the Catherine Wheel, as she spun round and round. *Boom! Boom!* went the Roman Candle. Then the Squibs danced all over the place, and the Bengal Lights made everything look scarlet. 'Goodbye,' cried the Fire-balloon, as he soared away, dropping tiny blue sparks. *Bang! Bang!* answered the Crackers, who were enjoying themselves immensely. Everyone was a great success except the Remarkable Rocket. He was so damp with crying that he could not go off at all. The best thing in him was the gunpowder, and that was so wet with tears that it was of no use. All his poor relations, to whom he would never speak, except with a sneer, shot up into the sky like wonderful golden flowers with blossoms of fire. *Huzza! Huzza!* cried the Court; and the little Princess laughed with pleasure.

'I suppose they are reserving me for some grand occasion,' said the Rocket; 'no doubt that is what it means,' and he looked more supercilious than ever.

The next day the workmen came to put everything tidy. 'This is evidently a deputation,' said the Rocket; 'I will receive them with becoming dignity' so he put his nose in the air and began to frown severely as if he were thinking about some very important subject. But they took no notice of him at all till they were just going away. Then one of them caught sight of him. 'Hallo!' he cried, 'What a bad rocket!' and he threw him over the wall into the ditch.

'Bad Rocket? Bad Rocket?' he said, as he whirled through the air. 'Impossible! Grand Rocket, that is what the man said. Bad and Grand sound very much the same, indeed they often are the same.' And he fell into the mud.

'It is not comfortable here,' he remarked, 'but no doubt it is some fashionable watering-place, and they have sent me away to recruit my health. My nerves are certainly very much shattered, and I require rest.'

Then a little Frog, with bright jewelled eyes and a green mottled coat, swam up to him.

'A new arrival, I see!' said the Frog. 'Well, after all there is nothing like mud. Give me rainy weather and a ditch, and I am quite happy. Do you think it will be a wet afternoon? I am sure I hope so, but the sky is quite blue and cloudless. What a pity!'

'Ahem! Ahem!' said the Rocket, and he began to cough.

'What a delightful voice you have!' cried the Frog. 'Really it is quite like a croak, and croaking is of course the most musical sound in the world. You will hear our glee-club this evening. We sit in the old duck pond close by the farmer's house, and as soon as the moon rises we begin. It is so entrancing that everybody lies awake to listen to us. In fact, it was only yesterday that I heard the farmer's wife say to her mother that she could not get a wink of sleep at night on account of us. It is most gratifying to find oneself so popular.'

'Ahem! Ahem!' said the Rocket angrily. He was very much annoyed that he could not get a word in.

'A delightful voice, certainly,' continued the Frog. 'I hope you will come over to the duck-pond. I am off to look for my daughters. I have six beautiful daughters, and I am so afraid the Pike may meet them. He is a perfect monster and would have no hesitation in breakfasting off them. Well, goodbye: I have enjoyed our conversation very much, I assure you.'

'Conversation, indeed!' said the Rocket. 'You have talked the whole time yourself. That is not conversation.'

'Somebody must listen,' answered the Frog, 'And I like to do all the talking myself. It saves time, and prevents arguments.'

'But I like arguments,' said the Rocket.

'I hope not,' said the Frog complacently. 'Arguments are extremely vulgar, for everybody in good society holds exactly the same opinions. Goodbye a second time; I see my daughters in the distance.' And the little Frog swam away.

'You are a very irritating person,' said the Rocket, 'and very ill-bred. I hate people who talk about themselves, as you do, when one wants to talk about oneself, as I do. It is what I call selfishness, and selfishness is a most detestable thing, especially to any one of my temperament, for I am well known for my sympathetic nature. In fact, you should take example by me; you could not possibly have a better model. Now that you have the chance you had better avail yourself of it, for I am going back to Court almost immediately. I am a great favourite at Court; in fact, the Prince and Princess were married yesterday in my honour. Of course you know nothing of these matters, for you are a provincial.'

'There is no good talking to him,' said a Dragonfly, who was sitting on the top of a large brown bulrush, 'no good at all, for he has gone away.'

'Well, that is his loss, not mine,' answered the Rocket. 'I am not going to stop talking to him merely because he pays no attention. I like hearing myself talk. It is one of my greatest pleasures. I often have long conversations all by myself, and I am so clever that sometimes I don't understand a single word of what I am saying.'

'Then you should certainly lecture on Philosophy,' said the Dragonfly; and he spread a pair of lovely gauze wings and soared away into the sky.

'How very silly of him not to stay here!' said the Rocket. 'I am sure that he has not often got such a chance of improving his mind. However, I don't care a bit. Genius like mine is sure to be appreciated some day.' And he sank down a little deeper into the mud.

After some time a large White Duck swam up to him. She had yellow legs and webbed feet, and was considered a great beauty on account of her waddle.

'Quack, quack, quack,' she said. 'What a curious shape you are! May I ask were you born like that, or is it the result of an accident?'

'It is quite evident that you have always lived in the country,' answered the Rocket, 'otherwise you would know who I am. However, I excuse your ignorance. It would be unfair to expect other people to be as remarkable as oneself. You will no doubt be surprised to hear that I can fly up into the sky and come down in a shower of golden rain.'

'I don't think much of that,' said the Duck, 'as I cannot see what use it is to anyone. Now, if you could plough the fields like the ox, or draw a cart like the horse, or look after the sheep like the collie-dog, that would be something.'

'My good creature,' cried the Rocket in a very haughty tone of voice, 'I see that you belong to the lower orders. A person of my position is never useful. We have certain accomplishments, and that is more than sufficient. I have no sympathy myself with industry of any kind, least of all with such industries as you seem to recommend. Indeed, I have always been of opinion that hard work is simply the refuge of people who have nothing whatever to do.'

'Well, well,' said the Duck, who was of a very peaceable disposition and never quarrelled with anyone, 'everybody has different tastes. I hope, at any rate, that you are going to take up your residence here.'

'Oh! Dear no,' cried the Rocket. 'I am merely a visitor, a distinguished visitor. The fact is that I find this place rather tedious. There is neither society here, nor solitude. In fact, it is essentially suburban. I shall probably go back to Court, for I know that I am destined to make a sensation in the world.'

'I had thoughts of entering public life once myself,' remarked the Duck. 'There are so many things that need reforming. Indeed, I took the chair at a meeting some time ago, and we passed resolutions condemning everything that we did not like. However, they did not seem to have much effect. Now I go in for domesticity and look after my family.'

'I am made for public life,' said the Rocket, 'and so are all my relations, even the humblest of them. Whenever we appear we excite great attention. I have not actually appeared myself, but when I do so it will be a magnificent sight. As for domesticity, it ages one rapidly, and distracts one's mind from higher things.'

'Ah! The higher things of life, how fine they are!' said the Duck. 'And that reminds me how hungry I feel.' And she swam away down the stream, saying, 'Quack, quack, quack.'

'Come back! Come back!' screamed the Rocket, 'I have a great deal to say to you.' But the Duck paid no attention to him. 'I am glad that she has gone,' he said to himself, 'she has a decidedly middle-class mind.' And he sank a little deeper still into the mud, and began to think about the loneliness of genius, when suddenly two little boys in white smocks came running down the bank, with a kettle and a bundle of firewood.

'This must be the deputation,' said the Rocket, and he tried to look very dignified.

'Hallo!' cried one of the boys, 'look at this old stick! I wonder how it came here'; and he picked the rocket out of the ditch.

'Old Stick!' said the Rocket. 'Impossible! Gold Stick, that is what he said. Gold Stick is very complimentary. In fact, he mistakes me for one of the Court dignitaries!'

'Let us put it into the fire!' said the other boy. 'It will help to boil the kettle.'

So they piled the firewood together, and put the Rocket on top, and lit the fire.

'This is magnificent,' cried the Rocket. 'They are going to let me off in broad daylight, so that everyone can see me.'

'We will go to sleep now,' they said, 'and when we wake up the kettle will be boiled.' And they lay down on the grass and shut their eyes.

The Rocket was very damp, so he took a long time to burn. At last, however, the fire caught him.

'Now I am going off!' he cried, and he made himself very stiff and straight. 'I know I shall go much higher than the stars, much higher than the moon, much higher than the sun. In fact, I shall go so high that – '

Fizz! Fizz! Fizz! and he went straight up into the air.

'Delightful!' he cried, 'I shall go on like this for ever. What a success I am!'

But nobody saw him.

Then he began to feel a curious tingling sensation all over him.

'Now I am going to explode,' he cried. 'I shall set the whole world on fire and make such a noise that nobody will talk about anything else for a whole year.' And he certainly did explode. *Bang! Bang! Bang!* went the gunpowder. There was no doubt about it.

But nobody heard him, not even the two little boys, for they were sound asleep.

Then all that was left of him was the stick, and this fell down on the back of a Goose who was taking a walk by the side of the ditch.

'Good heavens!' cried the Goose. 'It is going to rain sticks'; and she rushed into the water.

'I knew I should create a great sensation,' gasped the Rocket, and he went out. ❋

98

THE STORY OF PRAJAPATI

A STORY FROM THE UPANISHADS; RETOLD BY ROOPA PAI

Prajapati, Supreme Father, had children of two kinds – demons and gods. The demons, who were older, were misguided, selfish, grasping and always willing to trample over others; in short, they were not the best role models for their younger siblings. Fortunately, younger siblings are often smarter, so the gods did not look to their brothers, but to their own sweet natures, for guidance, and tried their best to be kind, virtuous and unselfish.

Unfortunately, younger siblings are also often bullied, and so it was with the gods. Their older brothers were always snatching things from them – Heaven, for instance. Fed up, the gods decided to perform a big yagna, and overcome their exasperating brothers by means of the power of the High Chant, the Udgitha or Aum.

So the gods went to Speech, and said, 'O Speech, we beg you, chant the Udgitha for us at the yagna.' Speech chanted the Udgitha, thus gaining for the gods the great joy that comes from being able to say things. As for itself, Speech asked for the ability to say only what was pleasant, and received it. This threw the demons into a tizzy. 'With this pleasant Udgatri*, the gods' yagna is sure to be a success,' they said, wringing their hands. 'We can't let that happen!' So they rushed at Speech and pitted it with unpleasantness. And that is why we often say awful things.

With their first Udgatri gone, the gods went to Smell, and said. 'O Smell, we beg you, chant the Udgitha for us at the yagna.' Smell chanted the Udgitha, thus gaining for the gods the great joy that comes from being able to smell. As for itself, Smell asked for the ability to smell only what was agreeable, and received it. This threw the demons into a tizzy. 'With this agreeable Udgatri, the gods' yagna is sure to be a success,' they said, wringing their hands. 'We can't let that happen!' So they rushed at Smell and pitted it with disagreeable things. And that's why we often smell things that make us screw up our noses.

With their second Udgatri gone, the gods went to Sight, and said. 'O Sight, we beg you, chant the Udgitha for us at the yagna.' Sight chanted the Udgitha, thus

**A priest*

gaining for the gods the great joy that comes from being able to see. As for itself, Sight asked for the ability to see only what was beautiful, and received it. This threw the demons into a tizzy. 'With this beauty-filled Udgatri, the gods' yagna is sure to be a success,' they said, wringing their hands. 'We can't let that happen!' So they rushed at Sight and pitted it with ugliness. And that's why we often see things that make us weep.

With their third Udgatri gone, the gods went to Hearing, and said. 'O Hearing, we beg you, chant the Udgitha for us at the yagna.' Hearing chanted the Udgitha, thus gaining for the gods the great joy that comes from being able to hear. As for itself, Hearing asked for the ability to hear only what was harmonious, and received it. This threw the demons into a tizzy. 'With this calm Udgatri, the gods' yagna is sure to be a success,' they said, wringing their hands. 'We can't let that happen!' So they rushed at Hearing and pitted it with disharmony. And that's why we often hear things that make us anxious.

With their fourth Udgatri gone, the gods went to the Mind, and said. 'O Mind, we beg you, chant the Udgitha for us at the yagna.' Mind chanted the Udgitha, thus gaining for the gods the great joy that comes from being able to think. As for itself, Mind asked for the ability to think only good thoughts, and received it. This threw the demons into a tizzy. 'With this righteous Udgatri, the gods' yagna is sure to be a success,' they said, wringing their hands. So they rushed at Mind and pitted it with evil. And that's why we often have terrible thoughts.

The gods, now desperate, went to Prana, the lifebreath, and said. 'O Breath, we beg you, chant the Udgitha for us at the yagna.' Breath, without which there would be neither gods nor demons, chanted the Udgitha, and asked for nothing for itself. This threw the demons into a tizzy. 'With this noble Udgatri, the gods' yagna is sure to be a success,' they said, wringing their hands. So they rushed at Breath and tried to pit it with all manner of vice. But just as a clod of earth hurled against a rock smashes into bits and flies off in all directions, the demons who rushed at Breath were smashed to bits and destroyed. And that is how the gods won, and the demons were defeated. ❋

99

THE TEMPEST

WILLIAM SHAKESPEARE; RETOLD BY E. NESBIT

Prospero, the Duke of Milan, was a learned and studious man, who lived among his books, leaving the management of his dukedom to his brother Antonio, in whom indeed he had complete trust. But that trust was ill-rewarded, for Antonio wanted to wear the duke's crown himself, and, to gain his ends, would have killed his brother but for the love the people had for him.

However, with the help of Prospero's great enemy, Alonso, King of Naples, he managed to get into his hands the dukedom with all its honour, power and riches. For they took Prospero to sea, and when they were far away from land, forced him into a little boat with no tackle, mast or sail. In their cruelty and hatred they put his little daughter, Miranda (not yet three years old), into the boat with him, and sailed away, leaving them to their fate.

But one among the courtiers with Antonio was true to his rightful master, Prospero. To save the duke from his enemies was impossible, but much could be done to remind him of a subject's love. So this worthy lord, whose name was Gonzalo, secretly placed in the boat some fresh water, provisions and clothes, and what Prospero valued most of all – some of his precious books.

The boat was cast on an island, and Prospero and his little one landed in safety. Now this island was enchanted, and for years had lain under the spell of a witch, Sycorax, who had imprisoned in the trunks of trees all the good spirits she found there. She died shortly before Prospero was cast on those shores, but the spirits, of whom Ariel was the chief, still remained in their prisons.

Prospero was a great magician, for he had devoted himself almost entirely to the study of magic during the years in which he allowed his brother to manage the affairs of Milan. By his art he set free the imprisoned spirits, yet kept them obedient to his will, and they were more truly his subjects than his people in Milan had been. For he treated them kindly as long as they did his bidding, and he exercised his power over them wisely and well.

One creature alone he found it necessary to treat with harshness: this was Caliban, the son of the wicked old witch, a hideous, deformed monster, horrible to look on, and vicious and brutal in all his habits.

When Miranda had grown up into a maiden, sweet and fair, it chanced that Antonio and Alonso, with Sebastian, his brother, and Ferdinand, his son, were at sea together with old Gonzalo, and their ship came near Prospero's island. Prospero, knowing they were there, raised by his art a great storm, so that even the sailors on board gave themselves up for lost. First among them all, Prince Ferdinand leaped into the sea, and, as his father thought in his grief, was drowned. But Ariel brought him safely ashore. And all the rest of the crew, although they were washed overboard, landed unhurt in different parts of the island, and the good ship herself, which they all thought had been wrecked, lay at anchor in the harbour where Ariel had brought her. Such wonders could Prospero and his spirits perform.

While the tempest was raging, Prospero showed his daughter the brave ship labouring in the trough of the sea and told her that it was filled with living human beings like themselves. She, in pity of their lives, pleaded with him, who had raised this storm, to quell it. Then her father asked her to have no fear, for he intended to save every one of them.

Then, for the first time, he told her the story of his life and hers, and that he had caused this storm to rise so that his enemies, Antonio and Alonso, who were on board, might be delivered into his hands.

When he had reached the end of his story he charmed her into sleep, for Ariel was at hand, and he had work for him to do. Ariel, who longed for his complete freedom, grumbled to be kept in drudgery, but on being threateningly reminded of all the sufferings he had undergone when Sycorax ruled in the land, and of the debt of gratitude he owed to the master who had made those sufferings end, he ceased to complain, and promised faithfully to do whatever Prospero might command.

'Do so,' said Prospero, 'and in two days I will free you.'

Then he bade Ariel take the form of a water nymph and sent him in search of the young prince. And Ariel, invisible to Ferdinand, hovered near him, singing. And Ferdinand followed the magic singing, as the song changed to a solemn air, and the words brought grief to his heart, and tears to his eyes, for thus they ran –

'Full fathom five your father lies;
Of his bones are coral made.
Those are pearls that were his eyes,
Nothing of him that does fade,
But does suffer a sea change
Into something rich and strange.
Sea nymphs hourly ring his knell.
Hark! now I hear them – ding dong bell!'

And so singing, Ariel led the spellbound prince into the presence of Prospero and Miranda. Then, behold! all happened as Prospero desired. For Miranda, who had never, since she could first remember, seen any human being save her father, looked on the youthful prince with reverence in her eyes and love in her secret heart.

And Ferdinand, beholding her beauty with wonder and delight, exclaimed, 'Most sure the goddess on whom these airs attend!' Scarcely had they exchanged half a dozen sentences before he vowed to make her his queen if she were willing. But Prospero, though secretly delighted, pretended wrath.

'You come here as a spy,' he said to Ferdinand. 'I will manacle your neck and feet together, and you shall feed on freshwater mussels, withered roots and husk, and have seawater to drink. Follow me.'

'No,' said Ferdinand, and drew his sword. But on the instant Prospero charmed him so that he stood there like a statue, still as stone; and Miranda in terror prayed her father to have mercy on him. But he harshly refused her and made Ferdinand follow him to his cell. There he set the Prince to work, making him remove thousands of heavy logs of timber and pile them up; and Ferdinand obeyed patiently, and thought his toil all too well repaid by the sympathy of the sweet Miranda.

She in very pity would have helped him in his hard work, but he would not let her, yet he could not keep from her the secret of his love, and she, hearing it, rejoiced and promised to be his wife.

Then Prospero released him from his servitude, and glad at heart, he gave his consent to their marriage.

In the meantime, Antonio and Sebastian in another part of the island were plotting the murder of Alonso, the King of Naples, for Ferdinand being dead, as they thought, Sebastian would succeed to the throne on Alonso's death. And they would have carried out their wicked purpose while their victim was asleep, but Ariel woke him in good time.

Many tricks did Ariel play on them. Once he set a banquet before them, and just as they were going to fall to it, he appeared to them amid thunder and lightning in the form of a harpy, and immediately the banquet disappeared. Then Ariel vanished, too.

Prospero by his enchantments drew them all to the grove outside his cell, where they waited, trembling and afraid, and now at last bitterly repenting their sins.

Prospero decided to make one last use of his magic power, 'And then,' said he, 'I'll break my staff, and deeper than did ever plummet sound I'll drown my book.'

So he made heavenly music to sound in the air, and appeared to them in his proper shape as the Duke of Milan. Because they repented, he forgave them and told them the story of his life since they had cruelly committed him and his baby daughter to the mercy of wind and waves. Alonso, who seemed sorriest of them all for his past crimes, lamented the loss of his heir. But Prospero drew back a curtain and showed them Ferdinand and Miranda playing at chess. Great was Alonso's joy to greet his loved son again, and when he heard that the fair maid with whom Ferdinand was playing was Prospero's daughter, and that the young folks had decided to get married, he said, 'Give me your hands, let grief and sorrow embrace his heart that does not wish you joy.'

So all ended happily. The ship was safe in the harbour, and the next day they all set sail for Naples, where Ferdinand and Miranda were to be married. Ariel gave them calm seas and auspicious gales; and many were the rejoicings at the wedding.

Then Prospero, after many years of absence, went back to his own dukedom, where he was welcomed with great joy by his faithful subjects. He practised the arts of magic no more, but his life was happy, and not only because he had found his own again, but chiefly because, when his bitterest foes who had done him deadly wrong lay at his mercy, he took no vengeance on them, but nobly forgave them.

As for Ariel, Prospero made him free as air, so that he could wander where he would, and sing with a light heart his sweet song –

Where the bee sucks, there suck I:
In a cowslip's bell I lie;
There I couch when owls do cry.
On the bat's back I do fly
After summer, merrily:
Merrily, merrily, shall I live now,
Under the blossom that hangs on the bough.' ❋

100

HARD TIMES
'THE ONE THING NEEDFUL'

CHARLES DICKENS

'NOW, what I want is, Facts. Teach these boys and girls nothing but Facts. Facts alone are wanted in life. Plant nothing else, and root out everything else. You can only form the minds of reasoning animals upon Facts: nothing else will ever be of any service to them. This is the principle on which I bring up my own children, and this is the principle on which I bring up these children. Stick to Facts, sir!'

The scene was a plain, bare, monotonous vault of a schoolroom, and the speaker's square forefinger emphasized his observations by underscoring every sentence with a line on the schoolmaster's sleeve. The emphasis was helped by the speaker's square wall of a forehead, which had his eyebrows for its base, while his eyes found commodious cellarage in two dark caves, overshadowed by the wall. The emphasis was helped by the speaker's mouth, which was wide, thin, and hard set. The emphasis was helped by the speaker's voice, which was inflexible, dry, and dictatorial. The emphasis was helped by the speaker's hair, which bristled on the skirts of his bald head, a plantation of firs to keep the wind from its shining surface, all covered with knobs, like the crust of a plum pie, as if the head had scarcely warehouse-room for the hard facts stored inside. The speaker's obstinate carriage, square coat, square legs, square shoulders – nay, his very neckcloth, trained to take him by the throat with an unaccommodating grasp, like a stubborn fact, as it was – all helped the emphasis.

'In this life, we want nothing but Facts, sir; nothing but Facts!'

The speaker, and the schoolmaster, and the third grown person present, all backed a little, and swept with their eyes the inclined plane of little vessels then and there arranged in order, ready to have imperial gallons of facts poured into them until they were full to the brim.

...'Girl number twenty,' said Mr Gradgrind, squarely pointing with his square forefinger, 'I don't know that girl. Who is that girl?'

'Sissy Jupe, sir,' explained number twenty, blushing, standing up and curtseying.

'Sissy is not a name,' said Mr Gradgrind. 'Don't call yourself Sissy. Call yourself Cecilia.'

'It's father as calls me Sissy, sir,' returned the young girl in a trembling voice, and with another curtsey.

'Then he has no business to do it,' said Mr Gradgrind. 'Tell him he mustn't. Cecilia Jupe. Let me see. What is your father?'

'He belongs to the horse riding, if you please, sir.'

Mr Gradgrind frowned, and waved off the objectionable calling with his hand.

'We don't want to know anything about that, here. You mustn't tell us about that, here. Your father breaks horses, don't he?'

'If you please, sir, when they can get any to break, they do break horses in the ring, sir.'

'You mustn't tell us about the ring, here. Very well, then. Describe your father as a horsebreaker. He doctors sick horses, I dare say?'

'Oh yes, sir.'

'Very well, then. He is a veterinary surgeon, a farrier and horsebreaker. Give me your definition of a horse.'

(Sissy Jupe thrown into the greatest alarm by this demand.)

'Girl number twenty unable to define a horse!' said Mr. Gradgrind, for the general behoof of all the little pitchers. 'Girl number twenty possessed of no facts, in reference to one of the commonest of animals! Some boy's definition of a horse. Bitzer, yours.'

The square finger, moving here and there, lighted suddenly on Bitzer…

'Bitzer,' said Thomas Gradgrind. 'Your definition of a horse.'

'Quadruped. Graminivorous. Forty teeth, namely twenty-four grinders, four eye-teeth, and twelve incisive. Sheds coat in the spring; in marshy countries, sheds hoofs, too. Hoofs hard, but requiring to be shod with iron. Age known by marks in mouth.' …'Now girl number twenty,' said Mr. Gradgrind. 'You know what a horse is.'

…The third gentleman now stepped forth. 'Very well,' said this gentleman, briskly smiling, and folding his arms. 'That's a horse. Now, let me ask you girls and boys, Would you paper a room with representations of horses?'

After a pause, one half of the children cried in chorus, 'Yes, sir!' Upon which the other half, seeing in the gentleman's face that Yes was wrong, cried out in chorus, 'No, sir!' 'Very well, then. He is a veterinary surgeon, a farrier and horsebreaker. Give me your definition of a horse.'

(Sissy Jupe thrown into the greatest alarm by this demand.)

As the custom is, in these examinations.

'Of course, No. Why wouldn't you?'

A pause. One corpulent slow boy, with a wheezy manner of breathing, ventured the answer, Because he wouldn't paper a room at all, but would paint it.

'You *must* paper it,' said the gentleman, rather warmly.

'You must paper it,' said Thomas Gradgrind, 'whether you like it or not. Don't tell *us* you wouldn't paper it. What do you mean, boy?'

'I'll explain to you, then,' said the gentleman, after another and a dismal pause, 'why you wouldn't paper a room with representations of horses. Do you ever see horses walking up and down the sides of rooms in reality 'Very well, then. He is a veterinary surgeon, a farrier and horsebreaker. Give me your definition of a horse.'

(Sissy Jupe thrown into the greatest alarm by this demand.)

In fact? Do you?'

'Yes, sir!' from one half. 'No, sir!' from the other.

'Of course no,' said the gentleman, with an indignant look at the wrong half. 'Why, then, you are not to see anywhere, what you don't see in fact; you are not to have anywhere, what you don't have in fact. What is called Taste, is only another name for Fact.'

'This is a new principle, a discovery, a great discovery,' said the gentleman. 'Now, I'll try you again. Suppose you were going to carpet a room. Would you use a carpet having a representation of flowers upon it?'

There being a general conviction by this time that 'No, sir!' was always the right answer to this gentleman, the chorus of NO was very strong. Only a few feeble stragglers said Yes: among them Sissy Jupe.

'Girl number twenty,' said the gentleman, smiling in the calm strength of knowledge.

Sissy blushed and stood up.

'So you would carpet your room – or your husband's room, if you were a grown woman, and had a husband – with representations of flowers, would you?' said the gentleman. 'Why would you?'

'If you please, sir, I am very fond of flowers,' returned the girl.

'And is that why you would put tables and chairs upon them, and have people walking over them with heavy boots?'

'It wouldn't hurt them, sir. They wouldn't crush and wither, if you please, sir. They would be the pictures of what was very pretty and pleasant, and I would fancy—'

'Ay, ay, ay! But you mustn't fancy,' cried the gentleman, quite elated by coming so happily to his point. 'That's it! You are never to fancy.'

'You are not, Cecilia Jupe,' Thomas Gradgrind solemnly repeated, 'to do anything of that kind.'

'Fact, fact, fact!' said the gentleman. And 'Fact, fact, fact!' repeated Thomas Gradgrind.

'You are to be in all things regulated and governed,' said the gentleman, 'by fact. We hope to have, before long, a board of fact, composed of commissioners of fact, who will force the people to be a people of fact, and of nothing but fact. You must discard the word Fancy altogether. You have nothing to do with it. You are not to have, in any object of use or ornament, what would be a contradiction in fact. You don't walk upon flowers in fact; you cannot be allowed to walk upon flowers in carpets. You don't find that foreign birds and butterflies come and perch upon your crockery; you cannot be permitted to paint foreign birds and butterflies upon your crockery. You never meet with quadrupeds going up and down walls; you must not have quadrupeds represented upon walls. You must use,' said the gentleman, 'for all these purposes, combinations and modifications (in primary colours) of mathematical figures which are susceptible of proof and demonstration. This is the new discovery. This is fact. This is taste.'

The girl curtseyed and sat down. She was very young, and she looked as if she were frightened by the matter-of-fact prospect the world afforded. ❋

– *Excerpted from* Hard Times *by Charles Dickens.*

COPYRIGHT ACKNOWLEDGEMENTS

- 'The Big Juicy Carrot': Excerpted from *Springtime Stories* by Enid Blyton © Hodder & Stoughton Limited
- 'Mr Pink-Whistle Comes Along': Excerpted from *Winter Stories* by Enid Blyton © Hodder & Stoughton Limited
- 'Mr Twiddle's Cold': Excerpted from *Mr Twiddle Fetches Polly and Other Stories* (Star Reads Series 3) by Enid Blyton © Hodder & Stoughton Limited
- 'The Cold Snowman': Excerpted from *Christmas Wishes* by Enid Blyton © Hodder & Stoughton Limited
- 'The Doll's Feast' and 'Gopal's Books' by Sukumar Ray, excerpted from *The Mad and Magical World of Sukumar Ray,* published by Hachette India 2019; translation © Sreejata Guha
- 'The Moon's Messenger', 'The Wishing Tree', 'The Mice That Ate Iron' and 'The Jackal and the Drum' by Somadeva, excerpted from *A Treasury of Tales from the Kathasaritasagara,* published by Hachette India 2019; retelling © Jayashree Bhat
- 'Hanuman Sets Lanka on Fire': Excerpted from *Ramayana for Young Readers* by Upendrakishore Ray Chowdhury, published by Hachette India 2013; translation © Swapna Dutta
- 'How Bheema Got Strong – and Stronger', 'Arjuna and the Target' and 'Bheeshma and Drona': Excerpted

50 GREATEST STORIES FOR OLDER CHILDREN

The most remembered tales, by the best storytellers ever!

Oh, the writers you will read – from the full-of-surprises O. Henry to the ever-popular Enid Blyton, from the super-imaginative H.G. Wells to the adventurous Rudyard Kipling, from heart-tugging Munshi Premchand to tongue-in-cheek Sukumar Ray, and a whole lot of other unforgettable authors…

Ah, the places they will take you – from a densely thicketed cantonment in eastern India to a battlefield in ancient Greece, from mysterious islands in unknown locations to the depths of the ocean, and from thundering rivers to chilly pine forests, and a host of thrilling landscapes…

Ooh, the characters you will meet – adventurous heroes and brave royals, monkey-kings and fairies, dragons and snarks, mongooses and many-headed hydras, and several others who will fascinate you...

This treasury of fifty timeless stories is a must-have, to read and revisit again and again.

Look in the book for stories by:
Andrew Lang, Angela Brazil, Anton P. Chekhov, Arthur Conan Doyle, Charles Dickens, Dhan Gopal Mukerji, D.H. Lawrence, Edgar Allan Poe, E. Nesbit, Enid Blyton, Frank R. Stockton, Guy de Maupassant, H.G. Wells, Jack London, Jules Verne, Katherine Mansfield, Kenneth Grahame, Kottarathil Sankunni, Lal Behari Day, Leo Tolstoy, Lewis Carroll, Luigi Pirandello, Mark Twain, Munshi Premchand, Nathaniel Hawthorne, O. Henry, Oscar Wilde, Rabindranath Tagore, Richard Connell, Rudyard Kipling, Saki, Somadeva, Stephen Leacock, Sukumar Ray, Upendrakishore Ray Chowdhury, Washington Irving, William Shakespeare, Zane Grey, and more…

A TREASURY OF TALES FROM THE KATHASARITASAGARA

Jayashree Bhat

Fantastic Fables and Where to Read Them...

Pssst...come here. A little closer. Yes, yes, right here. Now, what sort of story are you looking for? One with action and adventure, wily villains and valiant warriors? Or something that will make you laugh till your stomach hurts? Or perhaps you'd prefer a tale with some good old-fashioned magic?

Well, whatever it is, you'll find it all here – in this delightful trove of stories picked from one of India's oldest classics, Somadeva's *Kathasaritasagara* (The Ocean of the Streams of Story), dusted and polished for a new generation of readers.

Go on, step in, but be careful – the shape-shifters aren't quite what they seem (obviously), the tricksters are always looking for someone to fool, and don't be shocked if you meet a talking animal. Oh, and one last thing – make sure you ace the vetala's quiz. Or else...

OOP & LILA: LOST IN THE SCARABEAN SEA

Olivier Lafont

The Scarabean Sea. Ruled by gigantic sea scarabs that hunt whales and ships. Claimed by the mighty Brutish Empire. Home to a hundred proud kingdoms fighting for freedom, and haunt of fierce pirates.

For Oop, nothing could be worse than babysitting his little sister, Lila, at the Mega Mela. And where does she take him? To some fake fakir so she can have her fortune told. Things take a frightening turn, however, when Lila discovers the fakir's bag of 99 wish-fulfilling candies.

Accidentally transported by the candy to the Scarabean Sea, right in the middle of a midnight raid on the Brutish Empire's treasures, the two end up being hunted by the devious fakir. But Oop and Lila have allies: the fearsome Captain Angry and his crew of cut-throat pirates…

Grab your eyepatch and cutlass and climb aboard this rollicking adventure on the high seas!

www.ingramcontent.com/pod-product-compliance
Lightning Source LLC
LaVergne TN
LVHW010553100826
845148LV00014B/2695

* 9 7 8 9 3 5 7 3 1 5 2 4 1 *